SAFETY

A DEVIL'S PRIDE NOVEL

JENNIFER TURNER

Copyright © 2020 Jennifer Turner
All rights reserved.

CONTENTS

Copyright	2
Dedication	7
Prologue	9
Grace	33
Noah	40
Grace	52
Noah	58
Grace	64
Noah	72
Grace	80
Grace	83
Noah	90
Grace	102
Noah	108
Grace	117
Noah	121
Grace	127
Noah	134
Grace	138
Noah	142
Grace	145

Noah	148
Grace	153
Noah	159
Grace	166
Noah	172
Grace	178
Noah	183
Grace	192
Noah	196
Grace	206
Noah	215
Grace	219
Noah	227
Grace	233
Noah	239
Grace	245
Noah	252
Grace	259
Noah	268
Grace	273
Noah	275
Grace	279
Noah	283
Grace	286
Noah	290
Grace	294
Noah	299
Grace	301

Noah	302
Grace	304
Noah	306
Grace	307
Noah	309
Grace	310
Noah	311
Grace	313
Noah	317
Grace	319
Noah	321
Grace	324
Noah	328
Grace	332
Noah	334
Grace	336
Noah	339
Grace	343

Dedicated to the many people who helped me make this dream come true. To my parents for always pushing me and asking me when I was going to finish and when I was going to release. To my wonderful friends who helped me edit and read over details and urged me on. And to my wonderful boyfriend who gave me the time to complete this adventure.

I love you all.

PROLOGUE

Crisp, cool autumn air assaulted my cheeks as I stepped off the bus in the early morning. The air was enough to chill someone to the bone, but me...I welcomed it. I've been living in hell for the past three years. It was a life different from one I would have chosen for myself and I wanted my old life back. My old life was hidden in Duluth, Minnesota. And that was right where I was putting my feet. The life I was leaving behind was a good one in ways, but it wasn't for me. And it would have been better if I didn't endure what I did.

What I had done was met Maxwell Beckett. A corporate lawyer who transformed my old life into this new extravagant non-adventure. He showered me in gifts to lure me in. It was a life I wasn't used to and all he wanted in return was that I'd give up my old life. At first, I resisted but soon I was cut off from everything. No contact from anyone that wasn't immediate family. I was living his rules. It had become official, he had taken over my life. It became so much that I even cut my family out. I don't know if it was out of shame or embarrassment, but I didn't want my family to see what I had become.

Looking around me, my old ways began seeping back into my bones. The life I've always wanted to hold .onto was coming back and I couldn't have been more grateful. Fear was still a constant nagging feeling that no matter how hard I tried, I couldn't get rid of. I had left that life behind as of a six hours ago.

Scanning the lot before me, I watched as people met up with loved ones. Hugs and kisses being given and received. A feeling of emptiness set over my heart. Knowing that I had to start over was hard, but it was exactly what I needed to do. I needed to find myself again after letting chaos and abuse take over my life. Setting my bag on the ground and my ass on a bench, I let happy thoughts come to me. I was about to see my family after not even a phone call for three years. Everything was so surreal. My memories faded as my eyes spotted the one man I had been waiting for. The one man I've had contact with throughout the last three years.

His leather cut showed the best and most familiar thing I've ever known. The Devil's Pride MC logo was staring right at me. I watched as Beast, or Cody as I knew him, bent his head over a lighter to light his cigarette. Memories of myself telling him smoking was a horrible habit to indulge in raked through my mind. His eyes were low, focused on the task at hand. Another man was with him speaking intently. A smile tugging on my lips making me pick up my bag and make my way across the asphalt to Cody and the mystery man. Cody focused on the other man, his mouth moving as he spoke words I couldn't yet hear. His gaze left the other man's before falling to meet mine. A grin slowly spread across his lips as he took a long drag off his cigarette before flicking it on the ground. His footsteps thundered across the pavement as he began walking towards me. Smoke falling from his nose and lips from his last drag. Opening his arms wide, I ran into them leaving my bag on the pavement behind a parked car. Tears were spilling as the familiar smell and feel of Cody overwhelmed me. "It's so good to see you." His voice was raw from his own emotions as he held onto me. My arms tightened around him as words stopped in my throat. A sob wracked my body as memories flooded my eye lids of our childhood together. The last memory I saw was the one of a single hug Cody and I shared before I left with Maxwell.

Cody's hand slid gently across my side as he pulled away. The slight pressure made me wince in pain as the muscles around my ribs spasmed and I was pulled back to reality. Dropping my eyes to the asphalt, I wiped the tears from my cheeks. Turning to grab my bag, Cody's hand put pressure on my wrist. "Grace." The rawness turned to a soft almost cooing version of Cody's voice. Releasing a breath on a sigh, I looked up not fully meeting his gaze. "Did...Did he hurt you again?" he asked. The pain that showed in the depths of his eyes clawed my heart out. The infliction of pain I felt when looking into his eyes was worse than anything Max could have done to me. Nodding my head just once I leaned my forehead against his chest. The leather creaked as his arms wrapped round me once more. "I got you." He whispered as his hand began stroking my hair. "Twinkle, grab her bag and strap it to your bike. We need to get her home. Jack doesn't even know she's coming home yet." He demanded making Twinkle, according to the man's cut, jump into action and rush towards my bag.

Placing my hands on his chest I pushed back to look up at him. His hand cupped my neck as his eyes met mine. The anger flashed across his expression before softening. The intent on murder stayed behind in his eyes. Fear was beginning to rise in my chest, constricting my breathing. No matter how hard I tried to block them, the nightmares assaulted my thoughts. My life had never been like this. Growing up I was the fearless child that was always around motorcycles and rowdy men. I smart mouthed my way through situations in life and school. I shouldn't have ever been this afraid of anyone. I loved Cody like a brother, but it had gotten hard to even be around anyone with a penis. I wasn't going to be able to stay at the club or at my parents with how many men come around to both places. I was just hoping that at this point my best friend Beth would be forgiving about the scarcity I've thrust on everyone. I still needed the courage to call her, but right now I had to focus on not blacking out. Looking up at Cody again spots began dancing before my eyes. Stress and fear made my body do this. The spots grew bigger as the seconds passed. Before I knew it I was blanketed in darkness.

Soft leather pressed against my neck, cushioning my head from the hard concrete beneath the rest of my body. Swinging my head to the side while using my hand to shield my eyes from the sun, I looked around as best I could. "Grace?" His voice was soft against the ringing in my ears. My eyes found his. The worry was prominent in his expression. It took a moment for my brain to register what had even happened. My cheeks flushed with embarrassment as a sigh escaped my lips.

"I'm okay." I croaked after a quick mental check over my body. Cody had another cigarette hanging between his lips. It was amazing how his voice didn't get muffled whenever he spoke with that cancer stick hanging from his mouth. My arms felt like jelly as I slowly sat up. His hand supported my neck and back taking over my efforts.

"You told me it was bad but nothing like this." He whispered. The attacks had been getting worse and worse day by day, month by month, year by year, hit after hit. The next one was always worse than the last. Closing my eyes for a moment I inhaled a breath releasing it slowly before opening my eyes again. Shaking my head, I got to my feet.

"Cody...I'll tell you everything eventually, but right now I just can't. I'm not ready to share everything." His arms came around me pulling my body into his. He had only gotten a partial story of everything that had happened. I should have let him come and get me when he offered.

"I'll always be here for you. I'll wait until you're ready." He pressed his lips to my temple. Knowing that I could take my time with him was the greatest gift he could have given me at this very moment. Nodding my approval, I went towards his bike, stepping out of his grasp.

"Shall we?" I asked gesturing towards the bike. Nerves were causing acid to ride its own hellish path up my throat. It burned as I tried to keep the vomit down. My mouth was watering telling me there was quite a possibility of throwing chunks. I hadn't been on a bike in years. Between blacking out and now having to face a fear that Max had instilled in me? What was I going to do? The fear of motorcycles was something I tried to resist but every time they came up it was a lecture on how dangerous they were followed by stories about a guy Max knew that almost got themselves killed. I never found out if he just told me those stories to get me to fear motorcycles or if he had a friend who went through those traumatic experiences. For all I knew the stories came out of his ass, he was a corporate lawyer after all. Shit poured out of his ass all the time, literal and figuratively.

I watched as Cody swung his leg over the bike and turned towards me. The way he looked at me told me everything. He was in love with me. It was moments like this one where you could see the lust and emotion in his eyes, the cigarette hanging out his mouth, the five o'clock shadow starting in already, and the masculinity of the man that made me wish I could love him the way he loves me. Smiling slightly, I got on the back pulling the helmet Cody offered me onto my head.

Feeling the cold air against my face, my body relaxed and took in the old feelings of being home that were rushing forward, making my insides feel like the wind against my cheeks was colder than it was. The Minnesota autumn was already nearing an end, winter was close, closer than I would have liked. Getting over the shit that was forced into my brain would have to wait until spring. That was, if I was able to stay here and if I could get more rides in. I wanted more than anything to jump on my own bike and saddle up with the open road.

The clubhouse didn't look any different from what I remembered. It looked like a warehouse on the outside with no colors or identifying properties of the club. None of it could be found anywhere on the outside. To the right of the clubhouse there is a normal looking home that was used as guest housing and a security house. Across the parking lot from the clubhouse there is another warehouse but smaller that was used as the legal work, a mechanics shop. Cars and bikes a like came in to get work done. The parking lot was lined with bikes with a few sprinkled cars.

Cody parked his bike holding his hand out over his

shoulder to help me off. The engine cut as soon as I was on my feet. "Beast, it's not even ten in the morning and you picked up a chick already?!" a familiar voice hollered from the clubhouse door. Looking over my shoulder, I saw my father. Unclipping the helmet, I shook my hair out fulling turning around to face him. My father took a drag off a cigarette. Slowly, I watched the realization dawn on him. In a matter of seconds, the cigarette was on the ground and he was coming towards me. Handing Cody the helmet I ran into my father's outstretched arms. He folded them around me and held on tight to me. "Oh darling, your mother and sister are going to be so happy to see you." It was just like my father to think of his family before himself. "We've missed you so much Gracie." I wrapped my arms around him tighter and held on like my life depended on it.

"I missed you too daddy." I whispered as a single tear slipped down my cheek. I reigned in a sniffle making my father pull away. His smile glistened at me as his eyes crinkled at the corners. He had aged more than I expected. His thumb swiped my tear away as he cupped my face in his hands. The joy in his eyes was everything I needed, everything that let me know that I was finally home. "I'm home, finally." I exhaled with relief. Emotions were still swimming inside of me but being here with my dad, I knew I was going to be just fine. My father put his arm around my waist and began leading me towards the clubhouse. Leaning into him, we walked inside side by side.

It was like walking into the past. Everywhere I looked images danced around the room. Memories of being little and being with my father. Looking to the left at the stage, I saw and heard the soft music playing as my father and I danced around the room. To the right of me, I watched as my past self lay across the bar coloring while my father was in the kitchen cooking pancakes. The pool table was dancing with memories also. Multiple playing out in front of me. A little girl playing pool with her father and her mother coming in to tell them they were having a baby girl. Two little girls running around their father's feet one blonde, one brown. A teenage girl playing against members of the club hustling them for money for a concert ticket, even though they let her win. A small smile played on my lips as the last memory played. I was seventeen. My memory self laid on her back, panties hanging off a heel, skirt hiked up around her chest. The man between her legs had the Devil's Pride cut hanging off his shoulders, pants around his knees. I could feel a blush creeping up my neck and cheeks.

Hot breath skidded across my neck. "What are you thinking about?" the voice that saved me from so many things over time pulled me from my memories. Turning around I was face to face with the man who had taken my innocence that night. My eyes fluttered as a smile quirked his lips. Shaking my head, I took a step back and looked around.

"Nothing, Cody." I whispered, my eyes landing on the prospect coming through the door with my bag. "Thank you." I said stepping forward to take it. He hesitated to let me take the bag from him but finally let go, letting the weight transfer to my hand. He nodded without saying a word. I smiled and looked at Cody knowing exactly what was going on in the prospects mind. He thought I was just some club whore who needed help and I was attached to the president behind the queen's back. But dad wouldn't do that to my mother. Cody rolled his eyes and turned to him.

"You need to show some god damn respect boy. She thanked you." Cody said grabbing onto the collar of the prospects cut and pulling him towards Cody. "She's not some whore that's here for help from the club. She's one of the motherfucking princesses." The prospect, Twinkle, looked shell shocked as he looked over at me again. "That's right this is Grace Sinner, M.C. Princess." Hearing the title, I was given since I was born was weird. After not having it hanging onto my name for quite some time, I wasn't used to it anymore. Cody let go of the prospect and draped his arm around my shoulders. "She's not just some whore. Whore's have no where to go. She on the other hand is going to change the world. And I can guarantee you try to go after her fine ass, your chances of patching in will be with you on the outside of that door right behind you. We won't hesitate to let it hit you in the ass on the way out either." Cody scolded and praised. I rolled my eyes. The feeling that I was falling back into the easy back and forth bickering with him was…Amazing.

"Cody, you're going to make the guy scared of everything this club is about." I chided as I pushed my shoulder into his ribs. He pulled his arm off my shoulders and rubbed his ribcage. Taking my bag, I went towards the hallway where I had seen my father disappear before everything between Cody and the prospect.

"The club doesn't have to worry about her too much. She's a mean bitch when she needs to be. Packs a powerful punch too that woman does." I heard Cody say as I walked down the hall. A small smile played at my lips as I recounted the time I had hit him. We had something going after the time I lost my innocence to him and I caught him with a whore hanging on him. Opening the door to the President's bedroom, I had every intention of getting changed quickly. As I looked through my bag I realized I wasn't too prepared for Duluth's fall season. At least I could always go shopping. My mind wandered to shopping and leaving a paper trail around the city. I didn't want Max to be able to pinpoint where I was. It was bad enough that he knew I was coming here. Of course, it was by my own damn admission at my last job. I should have known he would probably ask questions there first. Maybe my boss would have the grace to say I was somewhere else, or that I didn't give details. I needed to tell my father about that. Sighing, I pulled out the warmest clothes I could find in my bag and pulled them on. The clothes I traveled in were not motorcycle material against the cool wind and high speeds Cody liked. I sat on the bed and ran my fingers through a mess of a hair do I was currently sporting. A knock sounded on the door making my hands stop mid-run. "Come in."

My father poked his head inside the door. "There you are. I had been looking for you. Your mother and sister are on their way, I didn't tell them why they needed to be here. So, you should stay hidden until they get here. Preferably in here, that way I can find ya." His request was cute. I could tell he was happy and giddy with excitement. I missed the man so much I don't know how I kept him out of my life for so long. Getting up from the bed, I walked over to the door and opened it more wrapping my arms around him.

"I'm so glad I came here, daddy." I whispered feeling my father's arms wrap around me. "I have to tell you something though." I said after holding onto him for a few moments. "He's going to figure out I'm here. My old boss knows where I went. I'm hoping they don't say anything to Max." My father smiled. It wasn't a pleasant smile however. Oh no, it was a devil may care kind of smile. The smile that drew my mother into his arms so many years ago. My father was a handsome man, stood six foot five with the start of salt and pepper hair. He was the protector of the family and club. He was the best person I could have run to and he knew it. Max had no idea who he was messing with if he decided to come for me.

"We will deal with that when the times come darling." He said. My father closed the door as he left. I sat on the bed and decided to text Elizabeth. I read the text over and over again before sending it. I felt lame asking for so much but if it didn't work out then I guess I'd stay with my parents. I'd have to, especially if I didn't want to go back. There was a knock on the door. Walking the short distance, I opened it up.

"Hello..." my voice trailed off. Before me stood someone, I hadn't seen in a long time.

"Hi. Is Jack back here?" His voice had grown rougher over the years and it rumbled through my body. I stared at him a little longer than I should have. He had bright intelligent blue eyes and some of the blackest hair I had ever seen. Blinking a few times, I looked away from him. I knew what he was thinking just by looking at his awkward stance. He was thinking the exact same thing Twinkle had. I was just a whore used for my father's games. Had he been doing that behind my mother's back? I could always find out but I didn't know if I wanted to know the truth. If it was true, it would tear me apart.

"Jack...I don't know where he is right now. He said he'd be back here in a few minutes with my mother and sister." I whispered bringing my eyes back to his. I could get lost in those eyes for a long time. I had a feeling I'd never want to leave them either.

"Ah, well if you see him an you tell him his Road Captain is looking for him." I almost wished he would stay and keep talking. His voice was doing things to me, things I hadn't felt in a long time. Letting out a breath, I looked back up at him.

"Well if you would like you could wait here with me until he gets back. I'm not allowed to leave the room and I don't really know how long he's going to be." Speaking the unthinkable. I just invited this man into my father's bedroom. He stared down at me for a little while. "You don't have to. I just figured that you were waiting for him and I'm all alone, so we could keep each other company until he showed up. Then I could find out what's been going on around here for the past few years. Haven't talked to any family for a while, so I know nothing about anything around here." I was word vomiting. A smile toyed with the corner of his lips and he stepped inside closing the door.

"All right. What do you want to know sweetheart?" He asked while walking towards the bed. I stood there dumbfounded. I didn't expect him to stay. I didn't expect that shit to come spewing out of my mouth either. Plastering a small smile on my face, I went and sat on the bed a little ways away from him. If I sat too close, I might not be able to keep my hands off him. What did I want to know though?

"What's been going on over the last three years? When did you become a member? How did you come to know of the club? Has Jack gotten into any trouble lately? I don't need to know details just how bad it was and if there was any." I was now shooting him with questions…More word vomiting. He chuckled.

"Slow your roll, sweetheart. Jack has gotten into trouble but nothing to worry about. I was picked off the streets, actually. Someone that knows Jack and myself asked Jack for a favor to get me out of some trouble. The club has a reputation like that." My dad pretty much forced Cody into the club so he wouldn't end up on the streets. Taught him everything he knows. "I became a member about two years ago. Jack saw potential in me I guess. Took me a year to prospect. The last three years haven't been too eventful. Mostly just parties and working in the shop." He went silent for a moment. "A lot of that was questions about myself though." He had caught me. I was mentally slapping myself for it.

"Well I think we've only really met once. I like to know the guys around here." He raised an eyebrow at me. I looked around the room for a moment, folding my hands in my lap.

"So, are you a whore or something? What are you doing here?" I don't think my head has ever spun so fast in my life. Eyes wide I stared at him. Did he really think I was some club whore?

"No. I'm here to visit family and hopefully move back into town." I said. He nodded.

"Sorry. Jack usually hides girls back here when Delilah is coming around." As he said it, I felt my heart break. My father was cheating on my mother. My hand covered my mouth and I could feel my eyes well up with tears.

"They are as young as me? Does Delilah know about all of this?" I whispered. He shrugged his answer at me. God this was going to kill her.

"I…it doesn't feel like my place to meddle. So, I haven't said anything." My shoulders slumped while my head hung forward. If he knew the whole club knew about it.

"You really have no idea who I am do you?" I asked, my voice barely a whisper. His finger slipped under my chin and he pulled m head up to meet his eyes.

"No." It was almost a relief but after that bomb...I didn't want him to know.

"My name is Grace. Grace Sinner." I saw the realization dawn on him.

"Oh shit." He pulled his hand away and wiped them on his jeans as if they were sweaty. "Fuck, I'm sorry I dropped that on you. If I would have known..." I nodded.

"You wouldn't have told me."

"It's not common that he has a woman back here. It's rare. I haven't seen him hide anyone in almost a year. I believe the whole splurging thing is over. I also don't know what was going on between your parents." A knock sounded on the door. I wasn't prepared for seeing anyone anymore. I was crushed. I hope they were separated or something to justify my father's actions. They always seemed perfect to me. They were the couple that all my fantasies streamed from. The man got up and opened the door.

"Noah, what the hell are you doing in here?" My father's voice sounded from behind the door.

"Uh...well I was looking for you and she told me that you'd be coming back here soon so I figured I'd hang out until then. I have to talk to you about the run. There's an issue in the plan."

"Noah, give me some time then I'll find you. First I'd like to spend time with my family." Dad wasn't giving anything away to my mother and sister. A smile started to toy with me, even though I was feeling like crap.

"Daddy! What is going on? What is this surprise?" Mackenzie was hollering from behind him. Noah slipped passed them all and I stood up.

"Jack. What's going on?" My mother's voice was like heaven to me. Tears started to form and before anything else could happen I pulled the door open wider.

"Hi momma." My mother's eyes widened to saucers. Mackenzie stared at me and then flew at me. A blood curdling scream echoing off the walls as her arms fling around me.

"What in the world are you doing here?!" Mac yelled in my ear. I smiled and hugged her.

"I'm moving home." I said. Looking at my mother, I could see tears rolling off her cheeks.

"Oh Gracie!" My mother was next to come forward and wrap me into a hug. "I can't believe you are actually here. Are you really moving back here?"

"Yes momma. I'm moving back. I'm going to see if Elizabeth will let me crash with her for a bit."

"Oh nonsense. You can stay with us." I stiffened. As much as I liked the sound of that, I knew it was a bad idea.

"I...I can't do that Mom. There's too many men around." I was shaking by the time my mother let go of me.

"Too many men?" The confusion was clearly written on her fact. Nodding, I wiped my tears.

"I can't be around too many men once. There're too many bad memories connected to men right now." I whispered.

"Oh, my baby girl." My mother was crying this time. I mean full on sobs. Looking at the floor, I watched my toes wiggle. "It was that bad?" She sobbed.

"I made myself faint when Cody picked me up today. It's what I did when Max...when he would do things to me. I was unconscious for most of the horror. But after I woke up every time, it was worse. I would replay everything for me. Broke my ribs a few times. Raped me. Even got some of his friends to join in. He was a monster momma. I'm glad I got out of there alive." As I said everything I was feeling and tears rolled down my cheeks, I could see black spots dancing in front of my eyes. "Like right now..." I heard a thunk and had only blackness to watch.

I expected the cool hardwood floor to be beneath me when the blackness faded. Reliving the scenes of what Max did to me, it was a horrific experience the first time, the second time almost made everything worse. I didn't know if I'd ever get past this. Thoughts swirled in my mind. I needed to get back to reality, but would I really be able to get out of this hell known as my life? Groaning, I felt my world shift, the memories fading, the blackness turning to light once again. I was on the bed in the room and comfortably taken care of.

"Gracie?" My mother's voice was stricken with emotions. Letting out a sigh, I lifted my hand to my face covering my eyes. "She's awake. Mac go tell your father." I heard rustling as my sister got off the bed and hurried out the door. Sitting up slowly, I looked over at my mother. Worry was etched all over her face. "Sweetheart, are you alright?"

"It's horrible mom. I can't make it stop. I only started forcing the black outs, so I didn't have to deal with anything Max did..." I choked on my words. Tears began flowing freely, my hands covering my face trying to keep the sobs at bay. My body was aching, my heart broken, not to mention my trust. I wanted to go back to life when Max wasn't a part of it and where everything was like it use to be. I could be around the club and around the people I loved without having a break down, without blacking out. "I need to get out of here." I said standing up. I looked up to see Mac and my father in the doorway. "I'm sorry I can't be here right now." I whispered walking out the door. The front door felt like it was miles away from me. It was like the hallway was expanding with every step I took. My legs felt like jelly and moved as far as I could before stopping and dropping to my knees. Leaning forward, I dropped onto my hands. It was work to take a breath deep enough to feel like I was able to breathe. Colored lights were dancing before my eyes this time. I crawled my way into the bathroom and made it to the toilet before the actual vomit burned its way out.

Hands swept my hair back from my face and held as I dry heaved. One hand went to my back and rubbed trying to calm me down. Grabbing some toilet paper, I wiped my mouth before I flushed. "You going to be okay?" Cody's voice was relaxing to me. I nodded letting him know that I was done. He stopped what he was doing and helped me get off the floor. I turned to see him holding out a wash cloth and some mouth wash. "It's the best I can do right now. I don't want to dig through your things to find a toothbrush." I smiled slightly taking them from him, rinsing my mouth out and pressing the cool cloth to my forehead.

"It's much appreciated. Thank you." I croaked. I could see his smile in his reflection in the mirror and the look in his eyes. Lust was swirling around in them. It had been long since I had pleasure of my own. Staring into his eyes, my mind went back to the one and only time we had been together. His hand settled on my waist, pulling me closer to him.

"Are you feeling better?" His breath grazed my ear, making mine catch. My face flushed, and I turned to him.

"Much better." I whispered. He smiled as his lips caressed my neck. "Cody..." It was more moan than anything. His hands caressed their way up my body cupping my breaths. My nipples ached pressing against my bra. "I need to brush my teeth." I said instantly killing the mood. He pulled away from me.

"Do what you need to babe." He said and kissed my forehead before heading out of the bathroom. I felt as if a bucket of ice-cold water had been dumped over my head. I ran my fingers through my hair to straighten it out and pinched my cheeks to bring color back to them.

As I stepped into the deserted hallway, relief washed over me, and I hurried to the bedroom to my things. Dumping my thing out I searched for my toothbrush. Cody has seen me at my absolute worst and he still wanted me, even after all these years apart. Scurrying into the bathroom I cleaned my mouth out as much as I could while the details of our first night kept playing in my mind. It had been the celebration night of Cody receiving his patch and becoming a brother.

Most of the members were drunk, stoned, or getting fucked in a bedroom for most of the night. Four in the morning rolled around and it was just Cody and me in the main room playing pool. The club members were hidden away or at home by then. He had come behind me to show me the right way to take a certain shot. His hand slid over my back and down to my ass cupping it, making my jump completely missing the shot. His lips came down on the back of my neck. I dropped the pool stick just then before pressing my ass into the palm of his hand. I looked over my shoulder at him, biting my lip. We hadn't dated, and I didn't think we ever would, but I knew he wanted to. He wanted to make me his.

His hands gripped my waist pulling off the table and spinning me around. We both had been drinking and it probably was a bad idea but being seventeen and without a date was weighing on me. No one wants to date the daughter of a motorcycle club president. No one except Cody. His lips pressed to mine before he lifted me to sit on the table. He positioned himself between my legs, making sure I felt the length of him. I nibbled on his lip and received a groan in return. A knife came out of his picket and before I had time to be afraid it disappeared. Across the room. I scooted myself closer and realized what he had done with the knife. The string on my panties was severed. He smiled at me and wrapped his arm around my back lifting me off the table and smoothly baring my ass to him and the rest of the empty room.

I fluttered my lashes at him flirtatiously and his mouth found mine again. The kiss was becoming urgent and feverish, setting a fire in my belly. Before I knew what he was doing, I was on my back and his hand was between my legs. His expert touch almost took me over the edge immediately. "Hold on baby. Just wait it out it'll get better. I promise." His voice was rough and oh so masculine. I pulled my lip in and tried to relax. My mouth went lax as he inserted a finger inside me. My toes already starting to curl. "Fuck, baby you're almost ready for me." I heard his knees hit the floor and then there was nothing but his hot breath between my legs. "I've waited so long for this." He whispered before lapping at my core. I let out a moan and grabbed the only thing nearest me to hold on to. With solid balls in both hands, I gripped them and let Cody have his way with his mouth on me. Tingles were shooting down into my legs as I started to shake from pleasure. My breathing started to get shallow. Cody moved one of my legs and hung it over his shoulder. My back raised into an arch as I tried to stay quiet. His hand reached up under my shirt moving my bra and he flicked my nipple with the pad of his thumb. Pleasure ripped through my body. The orgasm had me flying higher than a kite.

Once back on earth and aware of things, I saw Cody with his pants around his knees. Having not seen the opposite sex naked before only mad me that much more excited when I saw his cock. It was standing proud and at attention. I liked my lips and watched as he stroked it. My eyes met his hooded ones. "Take your shirt and bra off Grace. I want to watch everything." He growled. Without hesitation, I pulled my clothes off and laid back down. My eyes watched his lips as his tongue came out and stroked his lip. "Ready for me?" He was hungry and just by the look he was giving me I could have come again. He slid the head of his penis against me and I groaned. "Relax babe. It only hurts for a moment. Then it's all pleasure." He whispered leaning down and kissing me. My hands came up and cupped his cheeks. He eased the head inside before slamming forward. His mouth stayed on mine muffling my scream. It hurt like a bitch.

A knock came on the bathroom door pulling me out of the memory. I shook my head and opened the door. Noah was standing there. "Hey, they wanted to make sure you were okay. Beast and Jack had to take off for something. I pretty much have to babysit you." Great, just what I needed. I was now stuck with a man who had me burning up and yet I was thinking about my first time and what Cody did to me. Not to mention all the shit that had me blacking out. Now let's add dad thinking I need to be watched at all times, by a man. My father was probably going to be the death of me.

"Uh...well okay. I wasn't really planning on going anywhere. Probably just going to stay in the bedroom and relax after traveling here. I can let you know if plans change." I said. He nodded. He pulled out a piece of paper and wrote his number down.

"Call me then. I'll probably be out in the garage." He said handing the paper to me. I nodded and watched him walk away. Going back to the room, I grabbed my phone and saw a message from Elizabeth.

You have some explaining to do! -E
I know I do. Come see me? I'm under surveillance. -G
Where are you? -E
The club. -G
On my way! -E

I hoped I could get through explaining all of this to her without passing out. It was getting old.

Less than twenty minutes later Beth had her arms around me and was practically crying on my shoulder. "What the hell did you think you were doing?! Cutting everyone off for three fucking years! Grace, this was so not you! Just disappearing and not calling anyone! I can't believe this! You fucking chose a guy over me and your family!" She kept going on, mostly repeating herself. I hauled myself away from her and pulled her into the bedroom.

"Beth, I can't even begin to tell you everything. Every time I tell anyone, I faint." I sighed and looked at her. Her eyes became sad and pitiful. "Look, I was forced into dropping everyone. I'll try and explain as much as I can, but as soon as it gets too bad, I'm going to have to stop and switch to something else." She gave me a nod and took my hand. Lord get me through this just once. She deserved to know everything. I recounted the nightmare I had been living for three years to Beth. The raping by Max and his gang, the abuse, and the abandonment. I took a deep relaxing breath after explaining and felt relief when I didn't faint. Beth stared at me with wide eyes.

"You went through all of that and weren't able to tell

anyone? That's just horrible. Why didn't you go to the police or something?" Easier said than done.

"I wouldn't be here telling you all of this if I had." At the time death seemed like the only option I was going to have in order to get out of the mess. But now, I had walked out of there with my scars and determination to be a better person. Beth reached out and pulled me into another hug.

"So, now what?" It was a simple question with a not so simple answer. What was I going to do?

"I'm staying here but there're too many men at the club and they come around my parent's house a lot. I'm not comfortable being around so many right now. So, I don't know what I'm going to do." She pulled away from me and grinned.

"I have an extra room. We could have a margarita night. There's this amazing bar that makes margaritas the size of fish bowls. They are huge and so delicious!" She exclaimed, extending her pronunciation of so. I laughed.

"Thank you. I'm taking you up on that offer." I said and stood up. "I'm going to find out if my dad still has my car here or if he got rid of it."

"You didn't' drive here?" She asked. I shook my head.

"Max had a tracking device installed on the car I was using, and I could never find it to disengage it. I had to take a bus here and Cody picked me up." Beth was the only person to know about my past with Cody. She smiled and got up.

"Thinking of repeating the past?" She asked wiggling her eyebrows at me. I let out a laugh.

"No, no past performances. Although I'm pretty sure he wants that to happen." My lips stayed in a smile. "I'm going to go find my father or my babysitter." I said leaving the room. She followed me out.

"It's been so long since I've been around this place. I have to come with. I mean it's not every day your best friend is around extremely good-looking men twenty-four seven." I swear she was in it for the men and not for me at all. I rolled my eyes and went toward the garage.

My babysitter was bent over a car when I entered the garage and he was shirtless. I looked towards Beth and mouthed babysitter to her. Her eyes went wide, and she covered her mouth in a giggle. It was just like high school all over again. Giddy teenage girls and shirtless men, except the shirtless men were usually on posters, usually. I smiled and leaned against the car he was working on. "Hey Noah." He glanced my way then back at the engine. "This is my friend Beth. I'm going to move into her place. Any idea when my father is coming back here?" Another sideways glance and back to what her was doing. "Not going to talk to me anymore?" I asked turning to lean over the engine.

"I'm working at the moment. I don't know when your father is coming back princess." He said still looking at the engine. I took the time to inspect him. He was magnificent. He moved the wrench around and I watched his muscles ripple beneath his skin. Beth moved to the other side of the hood and leaned over to watch. A smile spread on my lips.

"What are you fixing?" Noah looked at me and rolled his eyes standing up straight.

"I'm fixing this piece of shit car. It's got an oil leak, antifreeze leak and the head gasket is going." He said wiping his hands on a towel.

"Head gasket, you have to drop the engine out for that. Do you have a flashlight?" He raised his eyebrow and pulled one out of his back pocket. I took it and moved to the front of the car to get a better look. There was a small tear in the radiator hose. "Radiator hose is the antifreeze leak and oil leak..." I laid on the ground and crawled my way under the car. "The oil leak looks like a loose oil pan plug." A socket wrench appeared before me and I took it securing the oil pan plug. Sliding out, I came face to face with Noah. I held the socket wrench up to him and then pushed myself up to sit.

"I'm impressed princess." He whispered before holding his hand out to me and helping met to my feet. He handed the rag to me and I looked at it confused. "You have oil on your face." I smiled and took it going over to a mirror and getting it off the best I could.

The sound of motorcycles roared as my father and Cody pulled into the lot. I smiled and went back to Noah sticking the rag in the back pocket of his jeans before heading over to my father. He cut the engine when I reached him and smiled. "Already showing the boys how it's done?" He asked nodding towards the garage. I broke out into a grin and kissed his cheek.

"No, just helping out. Beth came over though and I'm going to move in with her. The only thing is, I don't have anything with me besides what's in my backpack. Would you mind helping me out until I could get a job to pay you back. I kind of need new clothes and a bed." He smiled and pulled out his wallet.

"Don't go too overboard. Thousand max." He said. I saw Cody smile behind my dad.

"Still wrapped around your finger, huh Grace?" Cody said with a chuckle. I smiled.

"Wouldn't have it any other way." My father answered and hugged me.

"I have a bed you could use." Cody said. "Literally being used as decoration right now." I looked over at him."

"Are you sure?" I asked. He nodded.

"Of course. I can bring it over to you later if you'd like. Just have to finish some things here." He smiled. I smiled and went over to him hugging him.

"Thank you, that would be wonderful." I said. He patted my back then got off his bike. I looked over at Beth, who was still over by Noah. "I think she likes my babysitter." Cody's eyes went over to Noah.

"There are worse people she cold be flirting with." He said bumping his shoulder into mine. I smiled and pushed him away.

"You're horrible. She's probably just looking for some fun anyways. Not sure she's had any in a while. Besides, if she went after you I'd be ok with it." I said and looked back over at them. Beth was laughing, and Noah leaned against the grill of the car. His eyes swept over meeting mine and I smiled at him.

"Looks like Beth isn't the only one who wants Noah." I hadn't even felt him so close until his breath hit my ear. I looked over at Cody.

"I'm only being polite. I don't want anyone right now Cody. I need to heal and focus on myself." I looked away and walked toward the clubhouse. Beth could have her fun for now. I needed to rally my things together and find out if dad still had my car.

I poked my head inside my dad's office and smiled. Seeing him behind the desk brought back childhood memories, happy memories. Maybe this had been the right place to come after all. I knocked on the door. His head lifted from some papers on his desk and his lips split into a grin. "Hi Gracie."

"Hi Daddy. I was just wondering, do you still have my car sitting around her somewhere?" I asked leaning against the doorframe. He got up and walked over to the wall on the left of him and picked up a set of keys.

"I'd never get rid of it. It was the only thing I had left of you baby girl." He said and handed me the keys. "Your bike is still here too. Noah knows where it is, just ask him. He is to go shopping with you too. I want someone to keep an eye on you for a while until we know Max isn't a threat." He said cupping my cheek. I nodded and threw my arms around him.

"I'm so sorry for everything Daddy. I thought it was going to be different when I moved in with him. I didn't expect anything like that to happen." His arms came around me as one hand stroked my hair. He placed a kiss on top of my head.

"No one expects to go through that shit baby girl. I'm just glad you're back and okay." I nodded and pulled away.

"Thank you for everything you do for me Daddy." I said and wiped a stray tear away. He had a soft smile on his face.

"Go have fun. Just make sure you bring Noah. I mean it

Grace. Don't try and take off on him." He was stern, but he had to be with two daughters and a whole club full of horny men.

"Bye Daddy. I'll stop by later." I said before leaving his office and going back out into the main area. Forgetting about my things, I saw Cody, Noah and Beth all sitting around the bar. "Hey Noah. I'm supposed to ask you where my car is." He turned to look at me with a confused look on his face. "The black '68 Chevelle SS." I said. A look of surprise crossed his face and he stood up.

"Follow me." He was stoic as he led me to my car. He opened a shed behind the garage and there she was. It was still the most beautiful thing I had laid eyes on. I pressed my hand to the hood and smiled. I moved to the driver's side door and opened it up. It even smelled as I remembered. Oil and peppermint. "I didn't realize this beauty belonged to you. I figured it was a side project your dad was doing or something." I smiled and looked over at him.

"Yeah...My dad and I built her when I turned sixteen. I was so angry at my ex for making me leave her behind. It should have been red flags back then, but I thought I was in love. I guess Disney was right, people do crazy things when they are in love. Well, think they are in love." I looked down and saw a chain on the floor. I picked it up and inspected it. It was my locket that I had dropped in the car the first fight I had ever had with my father. The one that sent me right into Max's arms and abuse.

I had just gotten back from a date with Max. The date where he asked me to move in with him. At the time I wasn't all for it. I wanted to talk to my father about it, see if he would keep his cool about me moving in with a boyfriend. My father hated Max with more passion than I had ever seen him show my mother. At first, I was thinking he was upset that it wasn't someone in the club, like Cody. Being nineteen and feeling like an adult but not being treated like one, that was the feeling that put me over the edge. The one that had sent me flying into Max's arms and sent me hours away near Max's law firm.

"That's pretty. Guessing it's yours since you found it in your car." His voice pulled me out of my thoughts. He was close to me, closer than I cared to acknowledge. My eyes met his and I stared at him.

"Thank you." I whispered putting the necklace in my pocket. "Do you have a lot to do around the club today?" I asked him. I was still deciding if I was going to ditch him or obey orders.

"Nothing that can't wait princess." I hated that label, but with it coming off his lips it felt almost endearing and made my toes want to curl. I nodded and got in the car rolling the window down. "We should probably just put her in neutral and push her out. Wouldn't want to shoot exhaust on that bike back there. I pulled myself out the window and stared at the bike behind my car. It was still as beautiful as ever. The burnt orange color glared back at me angrily. I had to remember to apologize to her. She's too beautiful to have had to sit in the back of a storage unit for so long. I looked over at Noah and sank back into the seat. I had missed this life so much I was glad I was back.

GRACE

It had been exactly two weeks since I had moved in with Beth. It had been great, we were able to catch up with each other and I even landed myself an interview for a job. I was hoping that it was going to be the finance department as that's where my degree had been focused. It was about the only thing Max had let me do on my own. I had been scared that he was going to follow me to classes or something, but I got lucky and he didn't. The time I spent in school was the time I didn't have bruises that could show. It had been a nice change for a while.

This job would allow me to do everything I needed to. I could help Beth with rent and help her with groceries. I did all the cleaning for now since I wasn't able to pay rent and wouldn't be able to until about a month down the road. She was understanding, and it was everything I needed at this time in my life. She supported me in everything I did and made me feel at home. I wouldn't have made it around all the men my father was associated with. I did notice that wherever I went I had a tail. They weren't hard to spot since they always had a Harley instead of something subtle, like a car. Every time I saw them, I smiled and rolled my eyes. My dad was being protective of me and it was a great feeling of relief after the shit show I had been through.

The morning of the interview I wore a pinstriped pencil skirt, a blue blouse with three buttons undone at the top, and black strap back heels. It was a killer power outfit and brought out my eyes without needing too much make up. Beth sat on my bed and whistled low. "I think your new boss is going to love you." I glanced at her.

"Not what I was going for Beth. I don't want him to love me on looks, I want him to hire me because I can do the job." I said and looked back at the mirror. My hair flowed down over my shoulders and I hoped it wouldn't frizz or fly to the point of no return. I was nervous there was no doubt of that. I hadn't had a job interview in a little over two years. Max made me stay home after my boss asked about a bruise. I kept going anyways and that's when the beatings came in heavy. I shook my head and shivered. I couldn't go back to that, and I knew it was going to come back to bite me in the ass later. I grabbed my purse and made sure I had everything I needed, such as documentation of my existence and identification. I wanted this job bad. No, I needed this job, badly. My dad wasn't going to be able to fuel my car forever or cover my portion of the rent. I needed to be an adult. I needed to control my life and keep it in my control.

My car roared to life as soon as I turned the key. The sound of the engine made me giddy every time I heard it. I roared out of the parking lot and down the road towards downtown Duluth. The building was easy to find but parking was harder to find. It was like every spot available was taken by every person in Duluth. Okay, maybe that was an exaggeration. There're over eighty thousand people in Duluth and probably twenty parking spaces. I turned the car around and found a spot two blocks down from the building. I was going to be late for sure, with bloody feet.

The walk had been long but not as painful as I thought. The elevators opened as soon as my finger made contact with the button lighting it up. The elevator was a smooth ride up and gave me enough time to check the length o f my skirt. I just hoped everything would go well for me during this interview. I didn't have any qualities that would put me to the top of the list but I sure as hell had determination.

Stepping into the lobby, the front desk of the office was empty. My eyes peeled around the room looking for someone that would be able to help me. A man appeared out a doorway not far down the hallway behind the desk. He had brown hair that was slicked back and shaved on the sides. He was about the height of my father maybe a little taller. His eyebrows were drawn together and when he finally looked up, he looked a little startled. I bit my lower lip and watched him unsure of what to do. "Hello." His voice was rich and deep, the hello rolled off his tongue that made a woman want to fan herself. "Can I help you?" I smiled and hitched my purse higher on my shoulder.

"Hello. I'm here for a job interview. I'm looking for Mr. Steel. Is he available?" I asked straightening myself out. The man before me smiled and came toward me.

"You've found him. Please call me Tanner." He held his hand out and I took it giving it a firm shake. "You must be Grace Sinner?" I nodded.

"Yes, that would be me." He turned away and walked down the hallway. Defeat settled in the pit of my stomach. I hadn't even gotten to talk to him about qualifications before he walked away. I shook my head knowing this had been too good to be true. I ran my fingers through my hair.

"Grace?" He called down the call. I looked up and saw him looking back at me holding the office door open. "Please come in. Unfortunately, I don't have a lot of time since my last assistant walked out."

"Oh, sorry to hear that." I said and hurried down the hall and into the office. "Thank you for holding the door for me."

"My mother would have rolled in her grave had I not done it." He said with a simple smile. "Please have a seat." He said as he rounded the desk and sat down behind it. I took the seat in a chair across from him. "So, I didn't have much time to look over your resume. But I did notice that you were last employed a little over two years ago. Do you mind me asking why that is?" It should have been a simple answer like, I was continuing school, or I decided to work on myself and was supported by my boyfriend, but that wasn't it. I let out a sigh.

"To be honest...that's a hard question. I'll tell you, but I'm just letting you know I might struggle with it." I was almost whispering. Fear was taking over my body and I casted my eyes downward to keep tears at bay. "I had an amazing job in the finance department. My boyfriend at the time, he forced me to quit." I was starting to feel my throat swell making me choke on my words. I was telling my life to a complete stranger, and I didn't know how to put it without out right saying it. "My boss pulled me into his office one day and asked me if my home relationship...if I felt safe in my relationships at home. I was in denial because everything was just starting. We had just moved in together. I went home and told my boyfriend. He told me I had to quit without notice. But I ended up explaining everything to my boss and he allowed me to do some side work from home." I was beginning to whisper and feel light headed. I leaned back in the chair taking deep breaths. In the nose and out the mouth, in the nose and out the mouth. I fanned my face to keep up with the breathing.

"I'm sorry." Ah the final moment. I didn't even make it though the interview. "Are you still with him?" He asked. I shook my head.

"I came back home to Duluth about two weeks ago and left him behind. I needed out, badly." He nodded and looked at papers on his desk.

"I know you have a finance degree and I wish I had something open for that, but unfortunately I'm looking for a personal assistant. Would you be interested in that position?" I looked up at him meeting his eyes. They were gorgeous hazel eyes.

"I'm interested in anything you can give me. I'm living with a friend and feel terrible that I can't contribute to her rent. Not to mention I've been eating all her food." I was spewing words now. He chuckled.

"I think we've all been there. When can you start?" That was it? When can I start? My heart was hammering in my chest.

"When would you like me to start?" His smile remained.

"Right now. But I can manage today on my own. How about tomorrow morning at nine am?" I nodded and got up holding my hand out.

"I'll be here and not a minute later."

"That's what I like to here. I'll see you tomorrow." He said getting up, shaking my hand. "I'll walk you out." He said grabbing his coat. "Where did you park? I know the parking ramp has to be hell at this time." I smiled at him.

"You don't have to walk me to my car. It's two blocks away." I informed him.

"Nonsense. I'm on my way out to get lunch anyways. And there's a perfect spot about two blocks away." I didn't know what else to say. No one had been this nice to me in a long time. He led the way out of the office and through the lobby to the elevators. "I'm sorry your ex was a dick to you. No one deserves to be treated that way." I didn't want pity but knowing a complete stranger could see my worth was an overwhelming feeling.

"Thank you." I looked at the floor, sighing. "It was horrific, and I hope no one goes through that but I know that he wasn't the first or the last man to do something like that to a woman. It's about control for them. He knew he had complete control over me since day one and that I wanted out of the empire my father had built even though it was all I had known. I'm just glad it's my safety net right now." He stayed silent.

The elevator doors opened on the first floor and he held his arm out indicating for me to go first. Stepping out of the elevator, I walked towards the door leading to the street. Tanner caught up to me and held the door open. I smiled up at him and stepped through the door. "I'm sorry the past has been rough for you. I hope everything stays calm for you and you will consider talking to me if something gets too rough for you during the time you are with my company." He said. I nodded and headed towards my car.

"I'll definitely do that." I replied.

"Even if it's something as simple as needing the day off to take care of something. I'd rather have you able to focus than not be able to. It's a demanding job at times, and I don't want you to be overwhelmed."

"Thank you so much. You don't even know how much that would help me." He gave me a smile and walked me to my car.

"Thank you for walking me to my car." I said turning to him.

"It's no problem at all. I'll see you tomorrow at nine?" I smiled and nodded.

"I will be there at nine." He opened my car door for me and I slid into it. He shut me inside and I watched the mirror as he walked back about half a block and turned into a building. I pulled away from the curb and drove back to Beth's. My body sagged against the door as soon as it was closed. Beth came out of her room and smiled at me.

"How did it go?" She asked. I looked over at her as a grin plastered itself to my face.

"I'm not in finance but I have a job." I said. She hollered and ran over to me hugging me.

"Step two complete!" She yelled, and I laughed.

"I'm going to my father's. I just figured you wanted to know about the job." I said. She smiled.

"Cody or Noah?" I rolled my eyes.

"Neither. They are club property. I don't want to be like my mother." I said and opened the door again.

"Have fun. Take pictures of the men for me!" She yelled as I went out the door and back to my car. The drive is short from the apartment to the clubhouse.

Pulling in the lot, I saw more men than I ever thought I would see in a long time and that's when I looked down at my clothes. I should have changed. Sighing, I got out and began making my way to the door of the club.

"Hey baby, wanna have a good time?" Someone said

smacking my ass. I turned my head and looked at the man who had said it. He had long brown hair and a clean-shaven face. He reminded me of Jesus. If looks could kill he would have been dead. I was used to men grabbing me before I left. However, now was a different story. The bitch alarm was about to go off. "Just asking. A pretty lady like yourself isn't normally seen around here unless they are looking for a good time." I rolled my eyes.

"I'm not looking for anything or anyone except for my father." I said over the other men talking. A few of them grew quiet and looked over at us.

"Oh yeah, and who's your father. Maybe I know him." A slick smile that gave me all the wrong feelings came onto his face. It hit me that this man wasn't a new member or anything for the club my father ran, he was from a different charter. I smiled knowing that once I said my father's name he'd be on the ground practically begging for forgiveness.

"Jack." I said. The look of shock on the man's face was priceless. He looked as if I had punched him in the balls.

"Fuck. I'm sorry, Princess. I didn't know who you were." He was mumbling. I turned on my heel and went over to the club. Cody stepped in front of me.

"You okay? What happened?" He asked. I shook my head.

"The usual. He grabbed my ass." Cody's nostrils flared as he put his hands on my shoulder and had me step to the side. I turned and watched him walk over to the man. My heart was thundering as I watched a path sweep clear to the man who had grabbed me. Cody had looked so angry. Something bad was about to go down.

NOAH

I stepped out of the clubhouse, running almost directly into Grace. "What's up, Princess?" She spun around and looked at me. Her big blue eyes looked like they were looking through me and looking desperate for help. She sighed and looked over at where Beast was. "I take it you had something to do with this?" She glanced over at me as she rubbed her forehead.

"I might have." A small smile graced my lips and I watched the fight unfold. You didn't get to touch a woman without her permission, especially one of Jack's princesses. Club whores were a completely different breed of woman though. Those bitches you could drag around the block and they'd come back begging for more. They were the women who were hanging around hoping that someone would pick them up to make them an ol'lady.

"So, what happened?" She turned fully toward me. Her eyes meeting mine.

"The guy Cody is beating the fuck out of grabbed my ass. I wasn't going to tell anyone, but he saw the whole thing and well..." She lifted her arm indicating toward the fight. We watched as Beast threw a punch knocking the guy on his ass. Beast said something to him as he crouched down to his level.

"Well that lasted long." Grace looked over at me again and I smiled walking back into the clubhouse. The whole club knew that Cody wanted to claim Grace as his own. But he hadn't said anything to her about it. I knocked on the office door to the president.

"What?!" He hollered from inside. I pushed open the door and leaned against the doorframe. I was still sporting a smile. "What's that look for?"

"Your daughter is starting fights between your men and other members." I said. He rolled his eyes.

"What the fuck is Mac doing now?" That got a bigger smile out of me.

"It wasn't Mac." He stared at me stunned.

"Are you fucking kidding me right now?" I shook my head.

"Jesus grabbed Grace's ass. Beast took care of it though." I watched my president as he leaned his head back against the chair and sighed.

"She was never a problem. What has gotten into her?" He asked and got up. I moved out of the doorway and allowed him to pass through. He walked down the hall like a freight train, obviously unhappy with his daughter. I followed him and sat on a barstool watching him walk out the door.

My eyes strayed to the ol'ladies prepping for the party tonight. It was sure to be a wild one with how many chapters were going to be showing up. It was going to be chaos, but that's how we did it around here in October. With the cold coming and bikes being put away, we partied the winter away and made the most of everything around here. It was the time when members took time to be with their families and go on vacation. Activity with the club was slow, but car problems were never slow. Our garage was currently filled with car problems. The winter months were hard though too. You had to go to a fucking bar to get any kind of action. When the ol'ladies are around no whores can come out and play. It keeps the ol'ladies from finding out if someone is cheating. The club didn't need those problems.

Jack had been one of the members that use to cheat. I hadn't seen it in a long time, but that shit is hard to watch when his wife acts like your own mother since you never had one. He always had the same whore around too, easier to keep it quiet I guess. The shit bothered me.

The door slammed open and Grace came stomping inside. I looked over at her. "Princess has her panties in a twist." She glared over at me and I smiled. "Looks don't kill princess." I said standing up. She huffed and sat on a stool. "Need a stress relief?" I asked knowing it was going to bite me in the ass. She looked up at me and I raised an eyebrow at her.

"What kind of stress relief?" She asked looking so innocent.

"What kind of stress relief would you like? There's alcohol, sex, motorcycles?"

"You're hitting on me too now?" I smiled and shook my head.

"Just offering services." It was simple where I stood. She was stressed from being around the club and I could help, I wanted to help. For some god damned reason, I was drawn to her. She was like kryptonite to Superman. I needed to stay away but I always ended up back here, back next to her. Jack walked in and other members followed him.

"Church now." He looked right at me and pointed to the double wooden doors across from the bar. I nodded and looked back at Grace.

"Duty calls." I said and walked to the doors opening them up for everyone to file in. Closing the doors behind the last person in, I took my seat and looked around the room. Jack was rubbing his hands against his graying hair. When he finally looked up, he looked fucking tired.

"I'm going to make this statement once and only once. If explanation is needed you come to me. No one, and I mean no one, is to touch Grace or Mac. They don't need the shit you guys can give. I just got Grace back. I don't need one of you fuck faces driving her away. If anyone fucking touches Grace, I will personally put a bullet in them. So, keep your dicks in your pants when it comes to my daughters." He finished his point then looked around at everyone. No one said a god damn word. Something like this you didn't go against the president. He wouldn't hesitate to blow your head off.

"Anything else need to be covered?" Texan asked from

across the room. Jack looked over and shook his head.

"No, it was just easier to call church to say this than to try and tell you fuckers individually." Jack said slamming the gavel down. Every man rose from the table and filed out of the room. I stayed back and stroked my beard. There went my offers to her. I leaned my head back against the chair and sighed. A hand clapped my shoulder and I looked up to see Bullet, Sargent at Arms. He was a big guy about the same height as me but well build almost like a body builder. He was the military type of guy who had the buzz cut to match and steel eyes that you could tell saw some shit in the past.

"You all right brother?" He asked. I nodded and stood up.

"I'll be just fine." I said making my way out of the room spotting Grace in the same spot I left her. Her eyes met mine and I looked away quickly before making my way to the bar. "All right princess. What's your poison?"

"Sex." My eyes shot up to hers and I smiled.

"No can do on that promise, princess You'll have to have alcohol or motorcycles."

"Let me guess. My father told everyone they can't touch me?" I cracked my neck smiling.

"You and your sister. Yes, that's exactly what he said."

"Be a rule breaker then. We could go somewhere on a bike ride." It was tempting. Good lord was it tempting. Lord help me.

"Got pants? It's getting pretty cold out." I commented.

"Just would have to run home. Take over protective duty so I don't have some fucking prospect following me." I licked my lips and nodded.

"Twinkle! I'm taking over protection tonight. You can have her back tomorrow." The prospect looked scared but nodded his head. She smiled and got up leaving the club. I grabbed my jacket and helmet on my way over to my bike.

The drive was short to her new apartment. I watched as she ran inside, and god damn the waiting part was took longer than driving over here did. She just needed to put fucking pants and a jacket on. I turned the bike off, lighting a cigarette keeping my eyes trained on the door. This woman was going to kill me keeping me waiting like this. It's just fucking pants for a bike ride.

Her friend Beth, or at least I think that's what her name is, came out of the building and smiled before coming over to me. I groaned inwardly taking a drag off the cigarette, trying to keep my feelings about this woman in check. She was fine at first, but damn she annoyed the hell out of me trying to flirt. I needed to just get Grace out of my system and then I could avoid both of them…I hoped. "Hey Noah." Beth said waving to me.

"Hey." She smiled stopping in front of me.

"You know smoking is bad for you." She said. I raised my eyebrow. Smoking kept me calm and I needed to be calm especially right now.

"Yeah and motorcycles are dangerous." I said leaning forward a bit crossing my legs at the ankles and planting my ass against my bike. Her smile broadened. I had to force myself not to roll my eyes at her.

"Good thing you have a helmet then." Okay the eye roll thing was getting harder to control. "Are you the guard dog right now?" she asked. I looked up at her nodding. I could have told her that I was planning on fucking Grace into the next dimension, that would get her to stop attempting to flirt with me. If she was trying to flirt with me anyways. I better play it safe for now.

"Yup, guard dog for now." She smiled.

"Well, have fun. She's a handful." She walked away after that and I smiled as relief flooded through me. I didn't like being social especially when forced into it. It felt like the woman was trying to get into my pants. I've had that happen plenty of times but when it's the friend of the woman who's pants I'm trying to get into…Never works out how they want it. It's a vicious cycle. I finished the cigarette and flicked it to the ground stomping the heel of my boot over the cherry and continued to wait for Grace.

A moment later the door to the building opened and Grace walked out. It was about damn time too. I was getting restless. My eyes raked up her body and I felt the smug smile fall into place on my lips. Her makeup was fixed, her clothes tighter. I watched her move towards me. Her pants were skin tight and her boots went up past her knees. And shit her heels were so spiked she could kill a man with them. My dick was already throbbing against my zipper. Her leather jacket hung open and a low-cut shirt exposed the top of her breasts. "I thought you were getting on warmer clothes not tighter." I said. A smile graced her lips as I took her waist and pulled her towards me. "Not that I don't like these clothes." I whispered in her ear before running my nose along the crook of her neck. Her hands went to my cut gripping the edges.

"We could go up to the apartment. Beth is gone." Her voice was barely a whisper in my ear. My hands cascaded down to her ass and pulled her closer.

"Or I could do you right here and let everyone who drives by see you on full display as you reach climax, curling your toes, and screaming my name." her hands cupped my cheeks as her lips grazed mine. I smiled and pressed against her deepening the kiss. Pulling away from her I leaned my forehead against hers. "All right, we are going to have to make this quick. Ride or Fuck?" I asked staring into her eyes. She stared back at me, the lust obvious in her eyes.

"Fuck me like a porn star." The line caught me off guard and I couldn't help but laugh.

"Darling, I won't be fucking you like a porn star. They don't enjoy it. I'll make sure that you enjoy every minute with me." I said taking her hand going to the building. She rummaged through her bag for her keys and the look of horror that crossed her face had me losing my hard on. We weren't getting in that building. "Left your key inside?" I leaned against the side of the building and looked down at my dick.

"I'm sorry, Noah. I must have forgotten to grab it." I nodded.

"It's probably for the best anyways. Your father would have my balls on a silver platter if I slept with you. Actually, he made that clear he'd put a bullet in anyone who tried. I should really know better." I said walking towards my bike. "Come on I'll give you a ride to where ever your roommate is, you can get her key. The prospect will meet us here when we get back though. I can't risk getting shot over you." I didn't need to get laid by her. I could have any chick that roamed that club, that wasn't taken anyways. I shouldn't have even followed her over here. The shit men do for sex, the risks we take. How fucking stupid are we?

"I can just wait here until she gets back…She was only going to the store." I looked over at her. Fuck me.

"Sweetheart I can't leave you here alone. You either come with me or we are both waiting. And if we do the second option I'll have you up against the side of the building half naked and balls deep inside of you before you can say fuck." Her eyes got big and round as she watched me. I wonder if she looked like that while taking cock in her mouth. I picked up the helmet and leaned against the bike trying to keep my head clear. "So, what will it be, Darling?"

"I can't say I don't want that to happen. I do…I'm just at a loss right now. I want it but I was thinking about it all. I've been…so many times I can't count the times on all my fingers and toes. I shouldn't just be having sex. But at the same time, they have made me realize that it's just sex. I don't have to get attached to someone to have sex." Her eyes met mine and I held her stare waiting for more. "But I don't think you should get shot for having sex with me."

"Your father made the threat because he feels that you've been through enough with Maxwell Beckett." Hearing his name, she shrunk back and looked around. "He can't hurt you while I'm with you Grace." Grace nodded and covered her mouth with one of her hands. Tears were glistening around the edge of her eyes.

"I know he can't...it's just hard to hear his name. I feel like I'm finally moving on from him but he still scares the hell out of me." I nodded and stood up putting the helmet back down.

"Come on. You need a distraction. But no one, and I mean no one, can find out about this." I pulled her around the building and into a corner where we would be hidden from wandering eyes. It was perfect with a couple trees that would hide us. I looked around quickly and pushed her behind the trees. "You have to be quiet no matter what. I'm going to go hard and fast so that we aren't out here exposed for too long." She nodded and my lips met hers in a fever. Her pants went down without a fight only to remember that she had fucking knee high boots on. Guess I'm going from behind. I smiled and ran my finger along her core. She shivered against me and her mouth went lax against my ear. A rush of air left her lips when my finger made contact with her clit. The bundle of nerves twitched under my touch. My lips caressed her neck before I flipped her to face the wall. "Bend over." I gritted the words out as my hands worked to get my cock free from my jeans.

It was the quickest and tightest fuck I had ever had. I couldn't have just kept my dick in my motherfucking pants. I wanted to keep going but I'd already busted a nut, all over her panties. I leaned against her. Her breaths were coming in quick short bursts. "That." Breath. "Was." Breath. "Amazing." Breath. I smiled and took a step back from her, palming my cock. She turned around and leaned against the building looking at me. "Are you... You're still hard." I nodded. Fucking rock hard was more like it. A smile crossed her lips and I watched as she sunk to her knees in front of me. My dick was pulsing by the time she got close enough to put her lips on the tip. My eyes had to have been saucers. I wasn't expecting shit from her except for the fuck. Yet, here she was on her knees in front of me and wrapping those blood red lips around my cock. It happened quickly. The moment she put those sweet lips around my dick, I lost it. My hand clenched her hair and my hips surged forward making her choke. She took it all like a champ. My hips pounding her mouth making sure my dick hit the back of her throat each time. I wasn't going to lie I wanted her pussy again but her lips would have to do for now, until I got her in a bed. I felt my balls tighten and I tried to pull back. Her nails dug into my ass and put my dick to the back of her throat again. It was the hottest fucking thing I had seen in my life. I held on until her tongue slid along the underside and I was coming. It felt like it was going on forever.

When I finally finished I looked up at the sky. She was gorgeous and took semen like a fucking porn star. My head whipped forward the instant I felt her swallow. Well, fuck me. She's a swallower. My dick swelled again, and I smiled. The surprise on her face couldn't be hidden. That's right baby I'm a fucking horse. Her eyes met mine and I bent over pulling her to her feet.

One zipper on a boot slid down and I pulled off half her pants and the boot. I wanted to hold her as I fucked her against the wall again. I should have known this shit was going to happen. I was never satisfied with just once unless I did some fucked up shit. Lifting her leg, I kissed her and slid my dick inside her cunt. She moaned into my mouth as my hips began slamming into her. I needed to get this shit over with. I couldn't sit here and fuck her black and blue. Quick thinking, or rather no thinking on my part, I put my hand around her throat squeezing. She groaned and I moved quickening my pace with her. My lips covered hers and my other hand pinched her nipple. She shuddered against me and I felt her tighten around my cock. Within seconds we were both on the ride with ecstasy. I sagged against her pulling out slowly. "Shit." She looked down.

"It's okay Noah. I'm on the pill. I'm not too worried about it." She smiled at me and I raised my eyebrow.

"Let me know if you do end up…Ya know. Cause then there will be questions. Questions from your father that we both will have to answer to. Hopefully, I won't be dead though." I whispered and tucked myself away. She looked at me hesitantly. "Grace...Everything will be fine. I doubt your father will find out about this," I said waving between us. "But we have to make sure to keep our distance with each other. I can't keep relieving the prospect to come see you. I, maybe, can do it two more times without something going wrong. Maybe." I pulled a knife from my pocket and bent down cutting her panties in half. There wasn't much cloth there, but I could clean her up a little. I balled the scrap up and used it to wipe between her legs. Her hands gripped my shoulders as I cleaned her. Stuffing the thong in my pocket I held her pants out to help her get back in them. She quickly got the job done and pulled her boot on as soon as she could.

"Do you have anything else planned for tonight?" She whispered keeping her hands on my shoulders as I stood up. I smiled and wrapped my arms around her.

"Club party is starting soon." She smiled up at me and pressed her lips to mine. I kept it light and pulled away after a short time. "We should get going. Find out when your roommate is going to be home, so you can get inside and...change." I said walking out from behind the trees. I pulled a cigarette out and lit it taking a nice, long drag off it. My feet continued to the corner of the building where I looked at my bike. It was still there and nothing around it. Good. I didn't need something happening to my baby when I was fucking someone. I'd kill whoever did it and I'd do it with my pants around my ankles if necessary.

A member's bike was his pride and joy. Most of them were made from scratch or purchased from the members hard earned money doing odd jobs. Not one member is rich enough to walk in and buy a bike off a show room floor, but we are rich in other ways. Materialistic ways. Motorcycles and babes. It was the one thing we always had supply of. If one was taken out it could be replaced with blood and sweat for motorcycles and babes...well they flocked the club. Any member had their choosing for a bitch to fuck.

Grace came out from behind the trees a moment later with her clothing back in place. "Beth said she's on her way back now. So, we might as well wait here." I nodded at her and smoked my cigarette while keeping my eye on Grace. This woman was going to be the reason of death on my death certificate. I shook my head to clear my thoughts. Grace stayed close to me and it made me look around the parking lot for anything that could be a threat. Grace was looking around too and froze. Something caught her eye. I stepped behind her and my eyes followed the direction she was looking. All I saw was vehicles that were empty.

"Grace?" I asked putting my hands on her shoulders. She backed up into me and I turned her away from whatever it was that made her freeze. "Grace, you need to tell me what's going on?" She shook her head and gulped in some air."

"Sorry...I just thought I saw M...Max's car." She stuttered looking up at me.

"What does he drive?" it was an honest question. I didn't even know what the fuck head looked like.

"Mercedes. I don't remember the exact model but that silver one looks exactly like his." I took her hand and made my way towards the car.

"This one?" She nodded and looked around the inside.

"I can't tell if it is his or not." She shook her head and leaned into me. I wrapped my arm around her and sighed. "Why don't we just get to the clubhouse were many people can keep you safe. You can steal one of my t-shirts and boxers to sleep in if you want." Another nod and I was throwing her on the back of my bike. Helmet in place we took off for the club. Leaving the car behind us.

The clubhouse was filling up when we arrived. Members and their girlfriends or wives showing up to be together. A party of the century, not like the club knew anything else. Parties around here, they were hell on a freight train and didn't stop until everyone was down and passed out. Booze and chicks were passed around like joints. But this party, this party was family only. No whores, sweet butts, or bar flies. It would be calmer than our freight train, just laying the tracks for the train. After the families go home, that's when the train comes out to play.

We parked the bike and I helped her off. She pulled the helmet off and let it rest on the bike seat. I watched as members stood around their families, talking, enjoying each other's company, and showing the love their families and brothers deserve. A smile crept onto my lips as I felt Grace's hand graze my own. "Thank you for tonight." I glanced down at her.

"All I did was be a guard dog." I watched as her lips quirked into a smile before she walked away. My eyes strayed down to her ass then around the lot to make it less obvious that I was checking the princess out. I had a feeling that I was going to be guard dog a lot over the next few weeks. Maybe even some more tonight. I walked into the party and smacked my hand on the prospects shoulder. "Twinkle. Until I tell you or Jack tells you otherwise, she's your responsibility. I'm going to go enjoy myself." He nodded at me and I made myself scarce. I needed to stay away from Grace right now. It was either that or bury my dick deep inside that sweet pussy in front of everyone, even my president, her father. Wouldn't that be a great plan…Yeah only if I wanted my dick served on a silver platter and a bullet in my head.

GRACE

I woke up in the clubhouse and the only reason I even knew where I was, was the huge spray-painted emblem on the ceiling of the room I was in. I stared up at it thinking about the events that took place last night. My head was pounding with fragments of the night flashing behind my eyes. There was a moment where I was dancing on a table. Another when I was all over a man, I couldn't identify who it was though. The last thing I saw was landing on my back on the bed and kissing the same man. I had slept with someone, but I didn't know who... SHIT!

The sound of the toilet flushing came from the bathroom and I froze. Closing my eyes except for a slight crack I waited for the man to appear in the doorway. Light spread across the room and I had to turn my head away to keep from going blind. "Sorry, I didn't realize you were awake." I knew that voice. I wasn't sure if I should have felt relief or not, but I wasn't on edge anymore and that had me relaxing into the bed.

"Did we...." I trailed off leaving the question open ended. I could tell he was smiling before he said anything.

"No, we didn't princess." Okay relief washed over me now. I opened my eyes and laid them upon Cody's naked chest. It was still delicious and I kind of wished I would have never ran away with Max. I probably would have stayed with Cody. He got caught up with the club though and we would have fallen apart anyways. Life is funny sometimes. "But we can." His voice was rough making me smile.

"Probably shouldn't." I said leaning up on my elbows. "Besides, I heard my dad was going to serve up the balls of anyone who touches me." He smiled and leaned over me placing a kiss on my lips.

"Yes, he did, however, he doesn't have to know. If I remember correct you do know how to be quiet." He had that right but what he didn't know, was that I didn't want to be quiet any longer. I wanted people to know I was getting my pussy destroyed. I smiled at him and sat up more.

"I should get back to my place." I swung my legs around and got up. "Man, it's cold in here." A grin came across his lips. "What?" his hand gestured to my bottom half and I looked down. "Oh my god." My eyes searched the room looking for my pants. "Where the hell are my clothes?" I heard him laugh and clothes popped into my field of vision. I stopped and took a deep breath before taking them from him. "Thank you."

"Bathroom's right there if you'd be more comfortable changing in there." Cody said gesturing towards the intended room. My legs made their way into the room and I leaned against the door. He'd already seen me naked before, but it didn't change the fact that it was my body and I chose who got to see me naked and when. And with everything that had happened before? I just couldn't bear the thought of being out of control of who saw my body. I could feel the emotions rushing up and over my skin. Goosebumps were rising. Panic not far behind. The lights were flickering in and out on me. My body leaned against the wall sliding down putting my head between my knees. My eyes stared at the floor and my crisp white panties. It then dawned on me that I wasn't wearing panties last night, Noah had cut them off when we had sex. And now I was wearing panties. Cody must have gotten me some. I sagged back against the wall. I really wish I could have just fallen in love with Cody and missed my chance on Max. Although, I'm sure with Cody we would have popped out a kid or two by now. I let out a sigh and righted myself on my feet before I got dressed and faced the day. My day of being followed by a prospect or Noah.

I made it back to my apartment after a long talk with

my parents about how I was to never get that disoriented ever again because it could have been Max taking me home instead of Cody offering up his bedroom for me. I parked in the lot and looked around. The Mercedes was gone. I was hoping I would have found out who owned it by now, but I guess that was going to be a mystery forever. I trudged to the apartment and looked around smiling at the familiarity of the place. It was home for now and I think it was exactly what I needed at this moment.

It felt like the walk down the hallway was going in slow motion. It wasn't working well for the hangover either. Shaking my head, I tried to clear the haze. The door to the apartment was unlocked as I walked in. Goosebumps rose as I stepped into the familiar setting of my apartment. Something didn't feel right. My eyes wandered around the kitchen and living room. Nothing was out of place there. I moved to my bedroom and peeked under the bed and in the closet. Nothing out of the ordinary. The bathroom was empty. I sighed and made my way back into the living room.

Plopping on the couch, I looked down at the Devil's Pride logo on the shirt I had slept in. I should have changed while I was in my bedroom. I leaned my head back closing my eyes. A floor board creaked behind me. Sitting, up I spun around and looked around the room. The room was as empty as before. I needed to relax, badly. I went back to leaning my head back with my eyes closed. I still had the feeling that something wasn't right but I'm sure it was just my imagination. At least I hoped it was. My stomach was beginning to get queasy. A faint, familiar smell settled in my nose. My eyes snapped open as a hand covered my nose and mouth. "Hello, darling." His voice sent chills of fear down my spine and my eyes met his. Maxwell Beckett. My normal was beginning to set. My eyes fluttered shut as the darkness took over my body.

I woke up on the couch hesitating to open my eyes. I was begging that it had been a bad dream. I couldn't do this again. My health depended on me being away from him. And if it was really happening then I didn't want to open my eyes. I could feel hot tears sliding down my cheeks as the pain of being with him crushed me like a tidal wave. Snot was flowing and I had to move to wipe it away. "You're awake." A new found hate for him was rearing its head. I opened my eyes and slowly moved to sit up. I didn't want to go through this shit again.

"What the fuck do you want?" I asked with more bite than normal. I knew better than to try and fight with him. It would just hurt more in the end. The sly smile was settling on his lips and I knew what was coming. The blackout was going to come on as fast as the pain his fist was going to. I needed to be strong though. I've never hit him back. I watched as he stood before me. I was scared and he knew it. My palms were getting sweaty and panic was rising in my throat. I stood up on shaky legs and looked him in the eyes.

"I just want you back. This isn't your life Grace and you know that." I tried not to flinch when his hands landed on my shoulders, I failed. The tiniest flinch escaped me showing him I didn't appreciate his touch and that no matter what I did I was scared. It confirmed what he already knew. What he fed off was my fear. It fueled his desire and only put my life in danger. I was a fool for not walking away when everything started. And I was a fool now for letting him touch me and not leaving on the spot.

"Max. No. I'm not going back to you. This is my life, this is exactly who I am. I was born in the club and I will be close to the club always. Even if you don't understand that. I always will. I need the club in my life and you don't want me to be a part of it. I can't be that girl you wanted me to be." He signed and turned around frustrated. He spun back around and pointed his finger in my face

"You were a better person than the fucking biker trash you associate with. You were better than your father and mother. You had a future going for you with me. Here you'll be nothing, nothing more than a whore for them to use and discard. Come on get your things you're coming with me." I scoffed.

"Why would you fight so hard over biker trash then? It's not like I'm any use to you except to be your sex toy. You only used and discarded me too. I should have never gone with you Max. I could have been married by now and happy. I wasn't happy with you. I never truly was." His face was turning a harsh shade of red. My mind blurred as my heart raced. My vision was pulsing with the rhythm of my heartbeats. Darkness making tunnels to see down. Max looked like he was so far away though I could reach out and touch him. His hand came crashing down across my cheek and my eyes shut. Not a second later my eyes flew open. Anger heated my chest the way his hand had warmed my cheek. Balling my fist, I reared back and flung it forwards into his nose. A crunch sounded as blood poured out. His white shirt was covered within seconds, staining red. "Oh my god." I ran for the kitchen and got a towel. "I'm sorry, I don't know what I was thinking." I said and held the towel to his nose for him. He lifted his eyes to me and I could tell he was smiling.

"I see you got a back bone again." The words sent a chill down my spine. I was going to pay for fighting back. I stepped back and watched him nurse his nose. "We can try this again. I'll get an apartment around here and just drive between here and the job. We really can work this out, Grace. I don't want to lose you, even though you probably broke my nose." I sat on the couch and looked up at him.

"I can't be with you, Max. It's just not logical or a good match. I think you need to move on and find someone else to use as your toy. I'm not doing it anymore." He let out a sigh and sat next to me.

"Think about it. I'm going to go get this checked out and then we should have dinner. No expectations. Just dinner and talking." My father was going to kill me if I got back with Max. I don't need Max though. Noah was a much better lover anyways. Behind the building, he just, he was able to speak to my body's needs. He knew what I needed before I did. Max could never do that. What was I doing comparing men when it was a literal life or death situation I was sitting in.

"I don't need to think about it. I'm not going to dinner with you. Max, we need to just end this once and for all. I'm not going to get back with you and you need to accept that. No matter how much you plea with me, I'm not coming back to you." He pulled the towel away from his face and it looked like the bleeding stopped.

"Alright. I'm going to get my nose checked and then I will call you later." He stood up and I watched him walk towards the door. "I love you Grace. We will get through this rough patch." Rough patch? What the hell was he talking about? We were done. I had just told him that. Fucking prick wasn't getting it through his thick skull. Maybe another punch to the nose would help him understand it. I rolled my eyes. "I can't wait to play with you again." He turned and walked out the door, leaving me to the peaceful silence he left behind. The only good thing he could have left behind.

NOAH

Cold air assaulted my body as I felt the blankets getting dragged off the bed. My eyes popped open and I watched as a club whore positioned herself over my morning wood. Okay, not that bad of a way to wake up. I smiled and as soon as my head was at her core I slammed up into her soaking body. Her eyes wandered up to mine as she clenched around me. "If you want to ride it, do it." I wasn't going to do any work. She had to get me off and herself off. I watched as her little body rode me and as she got off, twice. She pulled me out of her and her mouth went to work to finish me off. It was slow going as it definitely wasn't the woman I wanted to suck me off this morning. I closed my eyes and thought of blonde hair and red lips wrapping around my cock. I exploded in the whore's mouth and watched as she swallowed it. My dick was limp after knowing full well he didn't want to invite her to keep going.

I must have pulled the bitch into my room with me last night. I don't know what happened most of the night. Getting black out drunk when I was looking to run was my forte. I rubbed my face and sat up. The whore got dressed and looked at me expectantly. I raised my eyebrow. "What?" I snapped. She needed to fucking leave and do it now.

"Well I was wondering if you'd like to get some breakfast with me?" she asked looking at the floor. I shook my head, my hair falling everywhere. In whore tongue, she wanted me to take her on a date so she could say that I was going to claim her. That wasn't going to happen that was for fucking sure.

"I don't do breakfast. Go find breakfast with someone else." I got up going into the bathroom shutting the door. A shower sounded nice though. I got in and let cold water spray me in the face. My body ached from whatever I did last night. Rolling my shoulders, I finished the shower and wrapped a towel around my waist. The stereo was blasting from the main room and a small smile played with my lips. I pulled jeans on and boots and walked out into the main room.

"You couldn't put a fucking shirt on Noah?" I smirked and looked at Diesel. Diesel is the treasurer of the club. He's also bald and a single dad but hey he's a good asset. He's the only Diesel mechanic.

"You're just jealous." I said and grabbed a cup of coffee before leaning against the counter.

"What would I be jealous of? Your keg that is coming in?" He said laughing. I looked down flexing my stomach muscles.

"More like a six pack, but hey the dad bod is in style you can still get chicks, they just happen to drool more over my body." I smiled and took a sip of coffee. "Is there anything on the agenda for today?"

"Church at noon, but that's it. Jack has the prospect on his daughter." The door opened and I looked over seeing Twinkle come in. My eyes went over to Diesel.

"Doesn't look like he is. Twinkle, who's on Grace?" I asked. He looked at me.

"Beast said he had her last night and I haven't heard anything else." Great, he's probably been fucking her. The whole club knows they have a past. I could feel my fist clenching around the coffee cup. I needed to relax. She wasn't mine. There was so much running through my head. I wanted to bash it against the wall or counter, whichever hurt more. I opted for rubbing my eyes raw. I needed to just get a grip. And I was going to have to keep telling myself that. I was already fucking pussy whipped. Lord help me.

Beast came out of his bedroom and I waited for what felt like eternity for Grace to follow. She never did. "Where's Grace?" I asked. He raised an eyebrow at me.

"She left two hours ago. Why?" I looked over at Twinkle and went to my room grabbing a shirt and my jacket on the way out. "Noah, what the hell?" Beast was yelling at me.

"She's supposed to be watched at all times. Jack's orders." I said walking out to my car. Thank god the drive to her apartment was short.

Walking up to the apartment, I passed a man whose shirt was stained red with blood that had come from a newly broken nose. I'd hate to be in his shoes. Stopping at Grace's door, I knocked before letting myself in. "Grace?" I called out.

"Yes?" she said poking her head around the corner from the kitchen. I walked around and noticed the blood by the couch. Turning to look at her, I noticed she was scrubbing blood off her hands. It suddenly clicked what had happened and I grinned. She didn't need the club to look after her.

"So, that was your boyfriend I passed in the hall?" She nodded in reply. I leaned against the counter. "Do I want to know what happened?" I asked. She let out a sigh and turned the water off drying her hands on a towel.

"They guy with blood down the front of his shirt? That was Maxwell." She looked down at the floor for a bit and I watched her, hoping she'd continue. "He was in the apartment when I got here this morning. Wanted to get back together. He didn't take it too well when I said no. Told me that he'd take me out for dinner and we'd talk about it. I was scared the whole time he was here." Tears started to descend her cheeks. No woman should be scared of someone this badly. My feet were taking me away from her and out the door. I stopped once outside and watched as the bastard's car pulled out of the parking lot. I dialed Techy and waited for the connection to pull through, repeating the license plate over and over in my head. Techy was the guy that everyone went to, to hack or do whatever technology thing that we need.

"Tech...I need you to run a plate and do a background check for me." I demanded into the phone. I gave him the name and plate along with the connection to Grace.

"I'll get back to you with the information once I get out of bed asshole." I shook my head and disconnected going back up to Grace. The apartment was clean of blood when I re-entered the doorway. I closed the door and watched her throw away the last of the evidence that anything had even happened.

"Grace." She looked at me and ran her hand through her hair. "Are you comfortable with him knowing where you are?" She shot a smile and nodded.

"Yes, I'm okay with that. I can handle anything he throws at me."

"Do you feel safe with him around? Has he ever done anything to you to make you feel that you needed to run for your life?" I got a shake of her hair in response.

"I needed to get out of there but not because he was going to kill me or anything. I just needed to work on my health and be away from him. He's a toxic man and I didn't think it was a good idea for me to be around him." I nodded and leaned against the wall.

"Do you want me to stay here for awhile until someone else can come here or do you want me to leave you alone?" I wouldn't be able to leave her completely alone, but I could sit in the parking lot until Twinkle could get here. But I didn't want to do that either. I didn't know what the fuck was going on anymore. Grace was an entity that I was drawn to and she was one I didn't mind being drawn to. I just know that it was going to be hell to get through shit with her. The messed-up ex and her father being my boss. Yeah, that was perfect, just perfect.

"If you don't mind staying...I'd like it if you did. I don't know if he's going to come back and I don't think if I could go through another encounter alone." She looked tired.

"I'll stay. I don't have anything going on today except church at noon. I can take you with me to that though." I said and took my leather off draping it over the arm of the couch. I was probably an idiot for it, but I could manage sitting with her for the day. Twinkle could take over tonight. Her eyes came up to meet mine and I smiled at her. She returned with a small upturn at the corner of her lips and moved to sit on the couch. I sat next to her and grabbed the television remote. "Is there a certain show or movie you'd like to watch?" I asked and looked over at her. She shook her head.

"I don't usually watch TV." I raised my eyebrow at her.

"What do you do for entertainment then?" I asked.

"I like to read but I ran out of books to read. I'd have to go to the store to get more."

"Would you like to do that?"

"I wouldn't mind but I don't have money to get any right now either. I'm supposed to start work today and then I'll have spare money in the next two weeks, I hope. Speaking of work, I need to call my boss and explain what happened and to ask to start tomorrow." I smiled and got up putting my cut back on. "I thought you were staying with me today?"

"I am. We are going to get you some books and anything else you want. No sense in being cooped up here when you said there's a possibility he could come back. We could even get some lunch if you'd like." She gave me a genuine smile and got up.

"Give me just a few minutes to grab some new clothes." I chuckled.

"You look fine babe. Just throw on shoes and lets go. We can even run to the club and pick up my bike."

"Lord no, I'll stick with the car. It's too cold to have the bike out."

"It's not that bad." I said. She shook her head.

"It's too cold for me."

"I could always warm you up after." That one just slipped out... fuck I was flirting and didn't want to be. I shouldn't be.

"And how would you plan on doing that?"

"Blankets. Lots of blankets." Good cover bro...I was mentally slapping myself for even thinking dirty right now. She didn't need my horny ass in her life. Even though she did look upset for a little bit. I didn't need to give her my shit right now.

"Can we just stick to the car?" I nodded and pulled my keys out.

"Come on. I'll buy you all the books you want." I said opening the door to exit her apartment. She pulled on tennis shoes and walked out in front of me. The lot was pretty full and my car was parked right on the curb near the door. I smiled opening the passenger door for her letting her slide in. I carried myself around the car and got in starting the engine.

The mall was five minutes away and soon she had me nose deep in books she wanted to get. Maybe I shouldn't have said I'd buy her all the books she wanted. My arms were getting tired from carrying the stack she had loaded up in them. I looked like her bitch, but our club had a reputation to uphold and treating women with respect was one of the reputations we wanted shown at all times. Even though a lot of the time it wasn't held to the normal standards, but that was behind the closed doors of the club. A woman is a person not an object to have. Unfortunately, other men liked to think that they are objects and that they can just put their dick in them whenever they want. Someone needs to beat it into them that women are worth so much more than to be some toy for them to use and discard. From what Grace has told me about her ex, he's one of those boys. They will never grow into men either.

The checkout counter seemed to be miles away with the load of books she was having me carry. And of course, she didn't stop with what was in my arms. Nope, her arms were full too. It was going to take five heavy duty paper bags to get all these out of the store. We got shocked looks the whole way to the counter and I just smiled.

GRACE

I felt bad getting as many books as I did. But in my defense, he did say as many books as I want and I did tone it down from the whole store. Carrying the books out to the car was the next challenge that we needed to complete. There was a total of six bags and they were shoved full to the point of explosion. "I'm sorry…I probably should have toned it down more." I said hauling them out the door.

"More? You had toned it down?" Noah asked me. I smiled sheepishly and kept my head low.

"I wanted the whole store." I whispered and walked towards the car. He followed me and unlocked his car. I had no idea how he managed it with four of the bags in his hands.

"We could have bought the whole store." He replied. I stopped dead in my tracks and stared at him.

"What?" I asked. He turned to look at me after depositing the bags in the back seat of his car.

"We could have bought the whole store."

"Lord no, that would have been way too much money." A small smile crossed his lips.

"Money isn't an issue babe." It was simple and honest. And it made my heart do flips. No one knew how much of a book worm I really was but I think Noah was getting an idea. With Max, I wasn't allowed to read books and fill my head with nonsense as he had put it. With the load we had gotten from the store just now, I was going to need another room just for bookshelves. Unfortunately, I didn't have another room for them. I was going to have to pile them somewhere in my room and hope that sometime soon I would be able to afford my own place with two bedrooms and make a library out of one of the rooms.

"No. I'm fine with this. It's more than enough to keep me busy. Thank you so much for doing this for me." I said putting my own bags in the backseat. I was appreciative of him buying them for me and at the same time I felt selfish for getting as many as I did.

"You're welcome. Lunch?" I had to admit I was hungry, but I didn't know for what.

"Sure. I'd appreciate that." I knew what he was going to ask next.

"Where would you like to eat?" I didn't know the answer to that. I bit my lip and looked at him.

"I don't know what I want to eat. You choose a place and I'm sure I'll find something I want." I offered hoping he wouldn't make me choose.

"Alright. How about..." I watched him as he looked around the parking lot and thought about the possibilities. "How about Chinese?" Oh lord. That sounded amazing. Could I just marry this guy? It was like he was reading my mind. Books and Chinese food. How could a girl go wrong? I really needed to not think like that... I wasn't ready to get married and I didn't believe Noah was either. Noah wasn't the fuck boy type but I knew he wasn't the settle down type either.

"Chinese sounds amazing." I said with a smile. He returned the smile and opened my door for me. I slid inside and buckled the seatbelt.

Soon we were off towards a Chinese restaurant and getting out of the car. I could smell the food outside and it made my stomach roar with anticipation. I hoped he hadn't heard my stomach, that would be embarrassing.

My words were right. The food was amazing. I was full to the point of bursting when we walked out of the restaurant. Noah got the door for me and I smiled sliding in the seat. I watched as he walked around the car. Now if I could have him for dessert, I'd be happier. Oh god. I needed to start literally hitting myself or something. Noah and I couldn't possibly work. My father is his boss for crying out loud. I should do something to get Noah out of my head. He was like a fucking drug and I wanted the high. It was probably going to be tough, but I needed to do it. Not to mention him being around all the time? I was screwed. That man was sex on a motorcycle. He was delicious and I never would have dreamed being with someone like him. I still shouldn't dream about it. But I'll let myself have the fantasy.

Noah drove me back to my apartment. He let the car idle in front of the door and I looked in the backseat smiling. "It might take a couple trips to get all those books inside." He smiled and turned the car off.

"I didn't expect you to do it alone." He said. I watched a little as he got out of the car before I followed. I went to grab bags and he moved me out of the way. "I got it. If you could get the door, please?" I smiled and went to the front door holding it open for him. My eyes went to his arms as he carried all of the bags past me. His arms were bulging with muscle and I had to bite my lower lip from saying something that could land me in bed with him again. I followed behind him and tried to keep my eyes anywhere but his ass. Anywhere but his... My eyes were glued to his ass. And that's when darkness took over and the sound of a thud as I ran into the one damn pole in the building's lobby. My arms flayed out clipping Noah's arm and hanging on. My face was in his back and I took a step away to right myself. "Are you okay?" he dropped all of the bags and turned to me, holding my shoulders.

"Yes, I just wasn't paying attention to where I was going." I could feel a blush rising into my cheeks. My eyes glued to his chest unable to look at his face.

"What were you paying attention to?"

"Your ass." My hand flew over my mouth and I could feel my eyes growing wide shooting upwards to his. A smile was on his lips that reached his eyes. He found my honesty humorous or was it my reaction to my honesty?

"You were staring at my ass?" Ah fuck it. I didn't need to be embarrassed about it. I was staring at his ass. Big deal.

"Yes, I was. Problem?" I dropped my hands and bent over to pick up a couple bags.

"Nope. None here." He said and bent over picking up the bags I couldn't get. I opened the apartment door and carted the bags in before I collapsed from the weight. The thoughts running through my mind were making me dizzy. I stumbled over a bag and felt arms wrap around my waist. His fingers touched the bare skin along the top of my jeans setting it on fire. With my skin tingling, I was feeling even more light headed. My hands covered his as I regained my balance. I turned towards him and looked up into his eyes. The fire creeped its way between my legs.

"Noah..." His eyes had the same fire in them that I was feeling between my thighs. "I want you." He growled low in his throat. His lips were just a whisper away from mine. All I had to do was lift myself on my toes and close the distance between us. My feet rose putting all of my weight on my toes closing the distance. Pressing my lips against his, it was pure bliss. A second later I was on the kitchen counter with Noah between my legs. His thighs spread my legs wide as his hands threaded their way into my hair. His lips dominating my own. The soft caresses became urgent and persistent. His tongue invaded behind my lips and tangoed with mine.

A knock sounded on the door and Noah pulled away stepping completely from me. I sat there panting on the counter trying to regain composure. The knock was definitely the bucket of cold water that we needed. The knock came again sounding like a cannon on the door. I jumped off the counter walking towards the door. Noah's hand came out stopping me where I was. "Let me check it. You look a mess right now." He whispered and went to the door. I went in the bathroom and brushed out my hair before splashing cold water over my face.

When I walked back out by the front door, the door was closed and Noah was leaning against the arm of the couch. "Everything okay?" I asked. He looked up at me and nodded.

"We can't do this Grace. Your father would have my balls and I need to stay on his good side right now." And that my friends were the words of rejection. My chest tightened as I looked at the floor. My eyes moving around, not focusing on one thing. Thoughts and memories assaulted me and tears began to form. I had almost forgotten what it was like to be rejected. I was used and abused by Max but never rejected. I get why he was doing it but the normal unconfident teenager thoughts and response came through everything. 'You're ugly to him now.' 'You slept with him once already, why would he want you a second time?' 'Used and abused again.' 'You aren't good enough for him Grace.' 'You're just damaged goods and what can he do with that?' My mentality was going down by the second. The state of accomplishment I had achieved diminished into nothing. The memories persisted, feeling as if they were demons ripping the skin from my body, baring me to the world.

"I…" I choked up and nodded going over to the front door, grabbing the bags we had dropped there. I dragged them across the floor towards the bedroom. I saw Noah's hands reach for some of the bags but I was determined to do it on my own. I shook my head at him and looked up. "Just leave." I watched as he straightened. "Please leave." He rubbed the back of his head ruffling his hair.

"All right." He said pulling out his phone, walking out the front door. I sagged against the hallway's wall and looked at the bags. I should return them. But the book lover in me didn't want to. This was a horrible dilemma to be in. I felt terrible that I had him buy all those books for me. I should have toned it down even more. I didn't know what to do now. I wanted to keep them but the morally condemned person inside of me wanted to return them knowing that I shouldn't have let him purchase them in the first place. This was becoming a shit show.

My body was sore as I woke for work the next day. It was my first day and it needed to be perfect. I wanted to keep this job for as long as I could. I dressed simple as he never gave me requirements for a dress code. I had on black slacks and a nice button up making my outfit considered business casual.

Work was fast paced and by the end of the day, I had gotten the hang of being someone's assistant. I just hoped that he wasn't the type of boss that would have me picking up his dry cleaning. The clock was slowly ticking to five in the evening as I sat and watched it. There wasn't anything else for me to do and I watched as the second hand ticked around moving the minute hand slowly. Mr. Steel came out and I looked down at my desk. I had already organized it and there wasn't a thing on it. He smiled and came over leaning against my desk. I looked up at him. "It's close enough to five. You can leave if you'd like. You did great today." He said racking his knuckles against my desk. I smiled and looked up at him.

"Thank you very much. You sure you don't need me to do anything else today? I'm willing to stay if you need me to." I replied. He pushed himself off my desk.

"Go home Grace. You've done more than I expected today. I'll see you tomorrow." He walked back into his office. I gathered my purse and went to his door.

"Thank you for this job. You really are a life saver for taking a chance on me. I hope you have a good night." I said. He turned towards me with a heart stopping grin.

"You're welcome. Now get out of here before I find something for you to do." He joked. I smiled and waved good-bye walking towards the doors.

The cool air of the night was settling in and I was beginning to regret not bringing a jacket with me to work. I closed my eyes and leaned my head back taking a deep breath of the chill. I heard the rumble of a steel horse and my eyes fluttered open. Looking over my shoulder, I saw Noah watching me. I smiled and waved to him before heading to my car. There was a paper on my windshield and I slumped thinking it was a parking ticket at first glance. When I pulled it off my window I saw it was a regular note. Upon opening it a smile hit my lips again as I read it. I looked over at Noah and laughed as he pulled up next to me. I took a pen out of my bag and scribbled an answer to his question on the paper and handed it back to him. He looked down at it and a smirk spread across his own lips. I was now going to have dinner with one of the hottest men I knew.

I had rushed home and flew to my closet to change. No, it wasn't anything fancy but I didn't want to be in my work clothes when I went to dinner with him. I didn't know why he wanted to have dinner with me, but I got to spend time with him and that was enough right now. I hoped that we would grow into something. I'd even take friendship at this point. He was the only man besides my father and Cody that I felt comfortable around. I didn't know why but I wasn't about to fight being outside my comfort zone.

Minutes later I was in Noah's car and we were heading to dinner. The car smelled like him and leather, a delicious aroma that I wished I could get into a candle. I'd have that baby burning all the time and probably burn down the apartment building. I couldn't get enough of his scent. I closed my eyes and focused on not sleeping with him. Most of the club members didn't double dip unless it was a girlfriend or wife. I wasn't either of those and Noah probably wasn't interested. He refused me the last time. I needed to get drunk. That was one thing I was sure of today.

Dinner was amazing. He took me to Big Daddy's Burgers. One of the best burger places in Duluth and it was the most missed one since I had left. I leaned back from my plate and stretched. "That was the best burger I've ever had." I said with a smile and looked down at the plate that still had a shit ton of food on it. Guess I was going to need a box. I looked up at Noah and saw his plate empty. "Holy shit. Where did you put it all?" I was shocked and looked under the table. There wasn't a scrap anywhere. I heard him chuckle and I poked my head back up. "What?"

"I ate it babe." He said with a smirk. I stared at him.

"How the hell did you eat all of it?" I asked.

"Lots of work outs, need lots of food." He said and rubbed his stomach making his shirt rise. His abs showing as he did so. I felt my eyes hood over and I looked up at him. I wanted him and I wanted him bad. I needed to keep my head clear of inappropriate thoughts. I guess I should be happy that I trusted him with my body. I felt like I shouldn't trust anyone with it. But I can't think that all men are the same because they aren't. Noah proved that before I had even slept with him. Hell, Cody was even a great representation of that. I felt everything drain out of me and I looked down at the table. Depression was taking over and I had to hope that the nightmare memories wouldn't come next. I didn't need to faint in front of Noah.

"Thank you for dinner." I said still staring at the table. I knew he noticed a difference in me and I was glad he wasn't saying anything.

"Do you want to go home?" He asked in hushed tones. I nodded and sighed. He waved to the waitress and a box appeared in front of me. I watched Noah's hand take it and he loaded up the last of my food for me. I felt helpless and I knew it wouldn't be long until a blackout came. I got up and pulled my coat on. I needed to take time for myself. It was time for me to hole up and focus on me. No more men. Just work and focusing on me. I probably wouldn't be able to completely get rid of men, but I could stay home and do yoga or something. Maybe I would take up running. Seemed like a pretty good idea to me.

NOAH

I saw the moment she closed off from me. I don't really know what happened or what she was thinking but I felt like an ass. I hoped bringing her home was the best thing. As I sat in the car I watched her walk up to the building. I had to wait until Twinkle got here but that was fine. It seemed like she wanted to be alone. I looked around the parking lot and checked out all the cars looking for the douchebags Mercedes. I didn't see it from scanning the lot. I didn't know if he was even allowed around her. All I could do was hope that she was smart enough to get a restraining order or some kind of protection against him. I was going to have to ask her next time I saw her, even though I didn't know when that was going to be. I was glad I was going to be on one last run for the season next week and then it was back to the daily grind of working on cars.

Twinkle showed up in a beater of a car and I laughed. Bastard wouldn't be able to chase someone if he needed to in that piece of shit. I got out of my vehicle and lit up watching the smoke curl from the end after the first drag. Even though there wasn't much to update Twinkle on, I still sat there. I watched as he got out of his car and came towards me. "Hey Noah. Anything new for me?" He asked and I shook my head.

"Nope nothing new. Took her to lunch so she wasn't cooped up. Just make sure you watch for the silver Mercedes. You know the plate number." I said and looked at the building. It was quiet around here. I just hoped it stayed that way. She didn't need shit going on when she needed to heal. "Keep me updated on what's going on too. You may need back up."

"Yes sir." I looked at him with one eyebrow raised.

"Sir? Who the fuck do you think I am? The fucking pope?" His eyes went wide.

"No...No..sss....No." he stuttered. I shook my head.

"Just let me know if I need to come back. Don't follow her too close if she leaves." I saw his nod before I turned around. I flicked my cigarette on the ground and got back in my car. I wasn't going to stick around here any longer. I'd do something I'd probably regret later on.

I didn't want to go back to the clubhouse. I turned my brain off and let the open road take me. The next thing I knew I was outside of his place of operation. It had been about a month since I checked in with him and I knew I needed to do it. Letting out a sigh, I got out and went to the door knocking. I waited a moment before knocking again. The bastards never liked to answer the door. I tried the handle and finally lost patience after finding it locked. Taking a step back I reared my boot back and forcefully planted it next to the door knob ramming the door open splitting the lock.

Walking inside the place was like walking through a ghost town. Not one of the bastard's men popped out of anywhere. The deeper I went into the warehouse without seeing someone the more pissed off I became. "Where the fuck are you, ya bastard?!" I ended on a yell. The sounds echoing off the bare walls. The fucking Scottish took off again. Fucking asshole. He was always doing shit like this.

Slamming the door open, I went to the car. I was fuming mad and needed to release some of the fucking energy. Otherwise I would blow up on the club and blow my god damn fucking cover. That would be just fucking perfect right now. I sighed and roared my baby to life and let the open road take me as her prisoner once again. I watched the miles tick by wishing I had brought my bike instead of the car. The bike always gave me a sense of freedom, spiritual freedom. I won't have many more days to ride and I should be making the most of it. Thank god, I still had the run to look forward to. I'd go insane if I didn't get that one last ride in before the snow fall.

Winter was always a bitch around here for us. Business was always so fucking slow.

What I really wanted was across the city holed up in an apartment. I wanted to taste her again and the lust was something I needed to control. Maybe a club whore would be around when I got back. I could go balls deep in them and they wouldn't complain one bit. And to think it was all in hopes that one of the members would pick them up as their ol'lady. I was beginning to think I'd like to make Grace my ol'lady. I sighed and drove my ass back to the clubhouse. That was something that wasn't going to happen. Ever.

The club was empty when I arrived. There was a theme going on tonight and I was going to lose it. Moving inside the club it was like an explosion went off inside. Hollering and hooting and it was all towards me. "What the fuck?" Jack came over with a grin and I spotted Ralph across the room. Our eyes met and I turned back towards Jack.

"Brother!" he yelled getting close. My ears rang for a tad and I shook my head as if to shake out the sound.

"What the hell is going on?" He kept his grin plastered on his face.

"Well it's a party."

"No shit it's a party. But what for?"

"It's your anniversary as a brother." I looked at him.

"Since when do we have parties for that?" I was confused and didn't know how to react really.

"We've always done them." He said clapping his hand on my shoulder. "You're usually too busy with something else for these parties." I chuckled. I guess it was true. I was usually balls deep in a sweet butt or elbows deep in a mechanics special.

"Well then. Let's party!" I yelled raising my fist. A roar erupted from the brothers and music began blaring from the speakers. I smiled at Jack. He leaned in.

"We need to talk." He whispered in my ear and I nodded as soon as I saw his eyes. My heart was racing. There were two things I was afraid of him knowing about. The first being, I fucked his daughter. That was the biggest fear I've ever had. Second, I was two timing him. I followed him back to his office and closed the door behind the two of us. He sat behind the desk and gestured his hand to the chair across from the desk. I felt like a school boy about to get scolded for something I did wrong. I sat trying to keep a relaxed posture. Legs wide with my arm hanging over the back of the chair. I probably looked like I didn't care about what he had to say. I moved my posture and leaned forward resting my elbows on my knees. Now I just felt like an idiot and a thug. How the fuck was I supposed to sit? I had been in his office a million times and couldn't remember how I usually sat. I decided to say fuck it and stayed where I was.

"What did you want to talk about?" I asked, keeping my eyes trained on his face and movements.

"Ralph." My whole body relaxed. Yeah, I should still be afraid of the shit that could be going down soon but it wasn't going to be anything as bad as him finding out I fucked his princess, against a building in the open.

"What about him?" I asked.

"Has he been asking about information about the club? I know that you've been seeing him at least once a month." Eyebrows drawn together I tried to play off confusion as much as possible.

"Why would he ask about the club?" Jack shrugged and eyed me.

"He's not the best of company son. I just want to make sure you know where your loyalty lies. How's my daughter doing?" I smiled.

"Are you grilling me about everyone I talk to?"

"I'm genuinely curious about my daughter. I still don't see her as often as I'd like but knowing she is near has me at ease more than I used to be."

"She's fine. I took her to lunch and the bookstore the other night. She seemed like she didn't know what to do and mentioned that she didn't have any new books to read." He raised an eyebrow.

"She's always been an avid reader. Filled her head with stories." A smile came to his lips and he shook his head. "She tried to buy the whole store didn't she?" It was my turn to smile as a laugh escaped.

"She went home with 6 bags full." He let out a laugh.

"Sounds like my princess." He stood up. "Come on. We have a celebration to get to." I stood up and left before him. It was loud in the main room. Balls were cracking against each other as a couple brothers hustled each other. I scanned the room and that's when I saw her. Grace had come to the party. She looked like an angel the light above her making a halo. I was the devil and she was a saint. An elbow rammed into my ribs and I looked over at Diesel. He was a big brother and could take almost anyone in this room down with one arm tied behind his back. He's tried it on me before. He had to break loose of the rope to wrangle me down to the ground.

"You'd like to be balls deep in her wouldn't ya." He chided. A smile crossed my lips. Little did he know I'd already been there. "I don't blame ya. Personally, I'd sixty-nine the fuck out of her." My blood was starting to boil from the comment and I looked back over at her. Thinking about her kept me calm. Seeing her eased my blood into a smooth river. I kept the smile in place and looked at Diesel.

"Yeah except none of us will get the chance. Jack would have our balls on a platter." I said and went towards the bar. This was going to be a rough night and I needed to get hammered. Seeing Grace after I just dropped her off and knowing that every man in the club wants her. It was the icing on the cake that I didn't need.

The whole night I watched her. The whole night men were talking to her. And the whole night, I wanted her. When I blew out the candles on the cake the ol'ladies made me, my eyes never left hers. I was her self-assigned babysitter. My job was nothing more than to make sure she was safe and I was excelling at taking care of her other, more personal, needs. I rolled my neck around and took the three-finger drink of whiskey like a shot. A hand grazed my back and I turned to whoever it was. I came face to face with Peyton. She had her girls propped up for everyone to see and her hair was eighties big. Her makeup was caked on and looked like it needed to be sliced off. "Hey Noah." She was already slurring and we were barely through the party.

"Hey…Peyton." I said raising an eyebrow.

"You remembered my name." She said with a smile. "I wonder if you remember what sex was like with me." I had to physically keep myself from rolling my eyes at her. She was one of the whores that slept with the whole club and made rounds every night. Sometimes she made two rounds through anyone who will take her to bed.

"I remember. Mostly. But I'm not interested tonight doll." I said grabbing the bottle of jack off the counter and walking away. She looked hurt but whatever. I was on a mission to get drunk and I was going to do it alone, in my room.

The hallway seemed like it was a long fucking walk around a park. When I reached my room, the door was slightly ajar. I shook my head and went inside shutting the door behind me. Ralph stood by the dresser one elbow up on top. The rest of his body leaning against the drawers. "Boy, you haven't been checking in like you should." His thick Scottish accent making it almost impossible to know what he was saying. Years of being around him made it semi-understandable.

"I tried to check in today. But you were nowhere to be found." I said taking a swig off the bottle.

"Any news for me." It was more of a demand than a question. I shook my head.

"Nothing's been going on around here. No gun runs, no drug protection, literally nothing." I said. There were some things that were going on but I wasn't going to tell him that. Grace coming home was the most exciting thing to happen around here in a while. It got people talking and moving around. Getting with her right away probably wasn't the best idea I've had but I'm sure there are worse things I could be doing.

"Nothing. Really? What about Grace coming home?" Of course, he knew. I should have known.

"It's been exciting for everyone but that's not club business. That's Jack's business." Just thinking about her had my jeans uncomfortable. Ralph watched me and I looked around the room. I had nothing else for him.

"Alright. Check in next month and we can talk more. I know there's a run going on soon that you are going on. You'll tell me about that and what you guys picked up." I nodded and opened the door for him. Sometimes I felt like I should be ordering him around. He slapped my shoulder as he passed through the door. I shook my head and stood there for a moment making sure he was gone. Closing the door something stopped me from shutting it. I looked through the crack and found Grace. Her make-up was smudged under her eyes and she still looked like the most gorgeous thing I've ever seen.

"Are you sober?" she asked leaning against the door jamb.

"Yes." I hadn't drank enough to render myself unable to drive, or anything else she wanted.

"Will you take me home?" I grabbed a sweatshirt and keys, closing the door fully behind me. She leaned on me and I handed her the sweatshirt.

"It's probably cold outside." She smiled and took it from me pulling it on.

"Thank you." I smiled bringing her outside. It wasn't too bad outside and I didn't know how much she drank. The cold air made me want to shiver. Getting to my car was almost mission critical. The beast roared to life as soon as my ass hit the seat and my foot connected with the clutch. Grace was putting on her seatbelt as I left the club's lot. I watched as the lights on the street started to disappear as I sped by. I felt Grace before I knew what was going on.

My dick was free and her lips were wrapped around the head. My head was screaming 'get her off of you. You can't stay the night. Jack's going to have the balls she's playing with on a platter.' My cock however was loving every fucking moment of what she was doing. I found an alley and pulled into it, parking in the darkest spot I could find. Her head came up as I pushed the seat back. "Glove box baby." She looked at me before opening it. One lone condom was sitting inside. It was opened and rolled on me before I could get my pants off. Grace straddled my hips while pulling her panties to the side. It was quick but she was satisfied and that's all that mattered to me.

Grace laid her body against my chest. My hands caressing her back, holding her close. When she finally moved, I saw the tears in her eyes. I wanted to ignore them, but if I did, I'd be treating her like any other whore. And she was far from a whore. Besides I wasn't that much of a prick. My thumb wiped away a single tear that escaped and I watched her, noticing her down cast eyes. "Happy or sad tears babe?" I asked softly.

"Will you stay the night?" I knew I shouldn't, but I couldn't make up some kind of excuse not to. "I don't want to be alone tonight." Those words would haunt me until the devil took me.

GRACE

Taking a deep breath, he was all I could smell. The masculine scent of Noah filled me making me sigh. I could get used to waking up next to him. My lady parts were sore and complaining as I stretched. Even my back was doing a number, but I felt relaxed and sated. His arm snaked around my waist and pulled me closer. A smile graced my lips as my hand went over his. Thank god it was Sunday and I didn't have to get up just yet. This feeling of being in his arms, it was pure...bliss. My shoulder tingled as his lips grazed the skin there. "Good morning." Noah's whisper sent shivers down my\ spine. I rolled over facing him.

"Good morning." I said leaning close kissing his cheek. He smiled. His eyes were still low from waking and it was the best thing I could have ever seen this morning. There were so many things running through my mind while his eyes showed me the calm, soothing ocean blue waves around his pupil. This smile was never going to leave my lips today.

"I somehow have to make it back to the club without causing too much of a scene. I might have to say I went home with another woman." He chuckled and the thought of another woman being with him was enough to destroy the smile on my face, except I had to keep it in place to make it seem like I wasn't breaking inside. I couldn't start catching feelings for him. That wasn't in my plan. It was just supposed to be some casual sex here and there. And I was supposed to be working on myself now. But of course, I ended up back in his arms last night.

"Noah..." the smile disappeared. His eyes came to mine and I let out a soft sigh. "We can't keep doing this." My voice was barely a whisper. I knew this, whatever this was between Noah and I, it needed to stop. I wasn't going to be able to keep something like this quiet. Not for long, anyways. "We aren't going to be able to keep this a secret for long, we both know that. You're under my father's thumb all the time. I like you and I love the sex, but we shouldn't keep this up." I didn't want to leave him. He offered me comfort and helped me through things. I was feeling like a normal person with him.

He rolled onto his back and I watched as he got comfortable. "Whatever you want babe."

"Are you going back to sleep?"

"Unless you're kicking me out or going to fuck me, yes." He said as he flung his arm over his eyes. I rolled my eyes and laid back down. "Did you just roll your eyes at me?" How the fuck… The wind flew out of my lungs as his body rolled on top of mine. I stayed silent and stared up at him drawing in air. "I'll ask one more time darling. Did you just roll your eyes at me?" I nodded my head and watched him. I was beginning to take back what I had thought. I wasn't feeling so comfortable around him. A smile crossed his lips. "I don't like when females roll their eyes at me. It's a level of disrespect." My body was shutting down. This wasn't okay with me.

"Please get off me Noah." It felt like my throat was closing on me. Air barely able to get in and escape.

"I won't be getting off of you anytime soon. Darling I'm going to get you off and leave you wanting more before I leave. I need my fill of you if you want us to separate. Sadly, I don't think this one last time will be enough for me. But I'll make it work." His lips were on mine, feverishly devouring me. The comfort was coming back to me as I melted into the bed. His hips pressed into mine spreading my legs apart. His hand went between us. Fingertips against my inner thigh, they grazed the skin heading north. A soft sigh escaped my lips and I arched into him. Hoping his fingers would touch where I needed them most.

Denial rang through me as his fingers crossed over to

the other leg and repeated what he had done. My nerve endings were on high alert. I was sure that if he touched me at my core an orgasm would rip through me. This is what this man did to me. "Noah." I moaned. I felt his smile against my knee and looked down at him. I hadn't noticed he had even moved. A moaning scream ripped out of my lungs as his mouth came in contact with my core. I clutched the sheets and waited for the high to end. When he pulled away from me his face was glistening. What the hell?

"That was a good one baby. Squirted all over me." I was mortified. My hands covered my face as heat rose up into my neck and cheeks. I leaned my head back and pulled my hands down keeping my eyes closed, still trying to catch my breath. Pressure caught me off guard and soon my eyes were rolling back. I was never going to be the same after today.

I laid in bed watching Noah as his muscles rippled through his body underneath the skin. He was getting dressed and getting ready to leave my life for as long as we both could stand it. I was terrified of being without him already and I shouldn't be, we were just fucking. There were supposed to be no feelings involved. Feelings developed, at least on my end. As soon as he pulled his cut on, we wouldn't know each other's bodies or needs. We'd just know each other's names. It was the beginning to a new life for me and it was going to be a sad new, new start.

GRACE

*****One Year Later*****

Every morning for the past year I would have a cup of coffee before heading off to work. After work I would go home run, shower, have dinner and watch a movie or read a book before bed. The next day would be a total repeat. I used this whole year to work on myself and keep myself together. Max hadn't come around over the past year, which was a god send. I was stress free and had my routine. Life was good for me. Life was...safe. The word bounced around my head and never left. The word echoed around the walls that kept my brain in captivity all day.

I don't want a safe life. I've never really known a safe life. Comfort was found in the life that I have right now but there was a comfort in that life also. I needed some sort of excitement. A year of being without anything exciting was well, boring. I texted Beth from my desk, telling her that I want to get out of the apartment. It was time for a change.

Beth continued texting me throughout the day setting up plans. We were going to meet up at The Gopher and Beth had invited about fifteen people to come along. After work I would have three hours to get ready and be at the bar. I hadn't been out in over a year. What did people wear out these days? Do I wear pants and a shirt? Or do I put on a dress? There were so many decisions I had to make and I hadn't even thought about what to do with my hair. That was a tragedy all on its own. I was beginning to realize why I didn't go out anymore. It was too much work and all of this was to look presentable and fall in bed and do the shit all over again in the morning to go to work.

"Babe you do realize that The Gopher is a biker bar, right?" Beth said as she fixed her hair. I stopped and stared at her. A biker bar? Since when? The fear Max put into me over a year ago still kept me away from them as much as possible, except when I was with my father's club for family events. My dad still had someone on me at all times. I hadn't even taken my own out since I had gotten back to town. I had made it through two rides since I had come back to town and after everything, I still felt like I would knock them over. And if it was anything like the motorcycle owners I knew…I would be screwed. Or worse, never found after my death.

"Well it's too late now. Everyone is going there. Let's go party with some bikers." I said. I was more than nervous, I was trembling with terror. Beth's smile lit up her face and then she handed me the only pair of high heels I owned. They were an impulse buy, putting them on would almost be like I'm pursuing the change I wanted. I stared down at the spikey heels and I was sure that I'd have a broken foot by the end of the night. I still put them on.

Our cab pulled up at the bar and there were bikes lining the curb on both sides of the street. I froze staring at the bikes. Beth pushed me out the cab. "Fuck, Gracie go!" Beth was yelling at me as I all but fell onto the pavement. Steading myself my eyes wondered over towards the bikes and a couple of the men standing outside the bar. They were the big muscled type of men that could seriously do some damage to a girl's knees. What the hell was I doing at a place like this? Yeah, I looked like I belonged but internally I knew I didn't. It wasn't my life anymore. Beth grabbed my hand and dragged me towards the door. I'm sure I looked trashed to these men stumbling along behind her. My feet almost unable to cooperate with the pull on my arm.

The dim lighting in the bar was hard against my eyes. Everything seemed black to me. Once my eyes adjusted, I looked around and saw that every man in this place was wearing leather cuts. The vests decorated with patches. Showing wars they served or sarcastic comments or rockers displaying clubs. Looking around all you could see is clubs upon clubs mingling around the bar. It smelled of beer, leather, sex, and citrus. It was an intense place to be inside of. The walls were a dark red and everything was accented with black. The bar was stained black and it was everything male. The bar alone could bring a girl to her knees.

"Babe? You okay?" Beth was asking me. I nodded and walked towards the bar with her. We ordered two beers and found a table.

"I really don't fit in here Beth. Even though I kind of feel like with my background I should." She smiled and looked around the place.

"I'm pretty sure you're not supposed to fit in babe." Beth gave me a reassuring look and took a drink of her beer. The rock music vibrated through us as I brought my beer to my lips. "Besides if we did fit in here I'd be worried." She giggled as she said the words and I had to shake my head. Looking a little to my left I noticed a man staring at me. This man, oh did he do something to a woman's libido. Mine was on fire just by a look. Fantasies plagued my mind as our eyes stayed locked for more than a few seconds. Those fantasies happened to be memories. His scent and hard stare had me begging before and it was starting to happen all over again. I had almost forgotten about the way he looked at me, the way he touched me. I turned back to Beth and tried to calm myself. Beth looked over to where I had been staring and a smile graced her lips as she turned back to me. I took a swig of my beer hoping it would help me.

My eyes swung to from Beth to him. His black hair had gotten longer, just barely brushing his shoulder. And the piercing blue color of his eyes seemed to have gotten brighter and sharper than I remembered. I was captivated by him and I didn't think I was going to be getting away from him as easily as I had before. He was the man I had dreamed of for many nights over the past year.

"Hey Doll." His voice was deep and rough, vibrating to the deepest most secret part of me. My breath hitched as his hand touched mine. He smiled as if he heard the change in my breathing. The sounds of the heavy metal drowned out my ears only allowing them to pick up his or Beth's voices. Beth looked at him and smiled. She always was more outgoing than I was. I looked up at him and smiled.

"I'm not drunk enough for you right now." I said. Noah chuckled. I was memorizing everything about him from his elbow up to his eyes. His arms were picture perfection of sculpted muscles. His face had chiseled cheeks and the slight dusting of facial hair. Sharp lines contrasted with the facial hair. He was a work of art as if he was produced by the Greek gods. His smile was the best part and most gorgeous thing I had still ever seen. It contained straight teeth and warmth that could heat up the coldest heart.

"Wanna dance?" He asked me leaning close. I nodded and stood up. Beth took a drink of her beer and watched Noah take me out onto the dance floor. His hands were gentle and gripped my hips pulling my back against his front. A smile caressed my lips and I began dancing with him. His hand slid around landing on my belly, pulling me closer. It felt…nice. Our bodies moved to the beat as one. His lips close to my ear whispering sweet nothings into it. "I've missed you." Was the first thing he said. I leaned my head back on his shoulder and closed my eyes. I didn't think I would ever hear him say that. He really knew how to get a woman feeling things. His hips grinded against my ass and I could feel his growing length press against his jeans. His hand clasped mine spinning me out of his embrace. The intensity in his eyes pierced me, deeply. His hands pulled me back to him. Palms down on his hard chest, my eyes reached up to his. He leaned down. His breath cascading across my cheek. "Wanna get out of here?"

All I could do was nod and keep my eyes on his. He smiled grabbing my hand. I glanced over at Beth as we walked by. The table was surrounded with people that had been invited out. Most of them women that I knew from back in the day. Beth was talking to a guy. She smiled and winked as she saw us pass by. I lifted a hand and waved quickly going outside with Noah.

The fresh air assaulted my face just as Noah let go of my hand. I looked up and down the block and realized Noah had his motorcycle. I stared at him and watched his eyes as his hands brushed against my chin securing a helmet on me. My knees began to shake a little from the touch of his fingers. His eyes penetrated mine. His thumb pulled my lip from my teeth. My heart raced as my panties grew damp. Just the one touch from him and I wanted to combust on the sidewalk. Sucking in a sharp breath I watched as desire pooled in his eyes distorting them and making them a deep grey blue. I smiled and put my hands on his chest. His lips curled into a smirk and he left me standing there. His leg swung over the steel horse. He looked so masculine that I could feel my knees wanting to give. He looked over at me as I walked hesitantly towards him. I stood there and stared at the bike. How the hell was I supposed to get on the thing. I could barely spread my legs in these fucking pants.

"Come on babe." His rough voice jarred me from my thoughts. I looked at him.

"I can't get my legs that far apart in these pants." I said barely above a whisper. He smiled and got off. He pulled my back to his front and put his lips against my ear.

"I'm going to pick you up and put you on it. When your feet leave the ground spread your legs for me baby." I nodded and put my hands over his. I was a little surprised with how easily he lifted me up before setting me on the backseat. His leg slid over the machine again and he looked over his shoulder at me. "Wrap your arms around me babydoll. It's going to be a wild ride." I smiled and leaned forward wrapping my arms around his waist, hoping this wasn't going to be the only ride I'd be taking tonight. The bike roared to life and before too long we were leaving the bar in our dust.

The ride was amazing. The wind whipped through my hair and I felt safe with this man. He parked outside a warehouse building. "I just have to do something inside and I'll come back out to you." He smiled slightly taking my helmet off of me. "Please don't go anywhere." I nodded and watched him walk inside the building. I let my head hang forward and watched the ground as if something was going to happen.

Moments later Noah walked out of the building. I lifted my head to look at him. A smile creeped across my lips. He, however, looked pissed. Like the kind of pissed off where someone had pissed in his cheerios. I didn't know if I should be afraid of him. The smile fell away as he got closer turning into a lower lip bite. He came to a stop in front of me and gently place the helmet on my head fastening it. "Sorry, I didn't want you in there around the men I had to talk to." He almost whispered as if he didn't want to admit he was looking out for me. "That's okay." My smile rose again and I considered his eyes. "So, where are we going?" A smile tugged at the corner of his mouth. I wanted to stand on my toes and kiss his lips. His fingers brushed my chin as he pulled away from doing up the helmet. My stomach was doing flips as butterflies invaded my territory.

"Depends on where you want to go. We can go to my place or yours." He looked at me like he fully appreciated the woman I am, or pretending to be. The urge to kiss him was getting unbearable. I held strong for my sanity.

"We can go to my place." The words fell out of my mouth like it was no big deal. I hadn't had a man in my apartment since...no don't go there. I smiled up at him receiving a smile in return. Oh my, that smile was seriously something to swoon over. His arm came around my waist and he easily lifted me onto the seat of the bike. After he gracefully straddled the bike we took off towards my place.

Putting the bike in my guest parking spot he helped me climb off the bike. Disappointment flowed over me when he didn't wrap me in his arms pulling me against him and off the bike. My helmet came off of me and I couldn't wait to have him upstairs. His fingertips brushed my cheek my eyes grazing their way up to his. My cheek leaning into his hand. A smirk caressed his lips as he dropped his hand. A smile made its appearance on my lips. I turned going inside the building.

NOAH

The woman before me sashayed her hips while walking into the building. The smile was plastered on my lips unable to leave. Following her, I watched as she bent over to take her shoes off. Damn her ass was perfect, nice and round, that apple bottom kind of ass. My eyes staying firmly glued to her ass as I walked behind her. Her ass suddenly getting too close her ascension jerkily stopping.

"What the hell?" Looking up I placed my hand on her arm walking around her.

"Stay here." Pushing the door wide I looked inside. Her apartment a disaster. I stepped inside and pulled my gun out of my jeans. This night started out as just wanting to get laid and now I was searching her apartment for an intruder. Ever the knight and shining armor. What the fuck was going on with me? First the dancing and even just the approaching her and now this shit.

Checking every damn closet in her apartment, every fucking corner, I found no one. Stepping back out into the hallway I looked at the woman standing there. Her eyes jerking up to mine. "It's a disaster in there but it's empty." I said stepping out of the way to let her by. She walked into the apartment and looked around.

"Oh my god…" her voice traveled out to the hallway. I went in my eyes scanning over her. She looked upset and I could understand why. Leaning against the door jamb I watched her. Her eyes were misted as she looked around. Biting her lip, she returned her eyes to mine.

"I can go if you want." I said waiting for a full, blown out of portion, reaction.

"You don't have to it doesn't look like anything was taken... but I should probably let the police know about this." She said coming closer to me. I smiled brushing hair out of her face.

"Well I really need to take off then if you're going to call the cops." I pushed off the door jamb a grin spreading my lips. I knew she understood why but not the full extent of the why.

"Will you come back?" She asked. Her eyes fluttered a bit and she leaned into me more. Her hands came to my chest making my dick twitch. Fuck I wouldn't be able to get out of here fast enough. I should really just find some bar fly. Yes, that's all I needed was just some random pussy, even if it was some pussy I had already had. This woman was doing so much to me already. After a year of not seeing her. It was like she had disappeared into thin air. I smiled going towards the door.

"Maybe." I replied. Her sweet as sin voice traveled through the air to my ears.

"What if I call you after the police leave?" She simply wanted to know if I would come back and give her the good time I promised both of us when I decided to come home with her. She was almost begging me and it made a grin spread across my lips as I looked over my shoulder at her.

"If that's what you want baby. I'll stick around the area." She smiled and sucked her bottom lip in between her teeth and came towards me. Her hand grabbed me by my neck and our lips crashed together. She still tasted as good as I remembered. My tongue explored her mouth, every inch of her delectable mouth. She leaned into my side pressing her breasts against me. My hand sliding down her back, cupping her ass. Her moan vibrated through my mouth as my lips curled upward pressing against her lips.

"Well doll, you call me as soon as those pigs are gone and I'll be back." I pressed another kiss to her lips giving her ass a slap. Her body responded molding to my side. It was almost heaven. Stepping away from her I went to the door. I felt like that bad boy I was supposed to be but I only wanted to be this woman's badass biker. The shit I was thinking already was pissing me off. I needed to distance myself. She nodded sucking her bottom lip in again. I left her standing in the doorway, walking down the hall towards the outside where I left my bike and my balls.

Parking my bike about a block away I watched from the shadows. The pigs were pretty quick, must have been at the donut shop down the street. It only took them an hour to trickle their way out and make their way back to the where ever they came from. I watched the last cruiser pull away before pulling my phone out. Not a second later my phone went off with an unknown number on the caller I.D. I put the phone to my ear and heard her breathing through the line.

"Well hello doll, I've been waiting for you." I smiled as a swung my leg back over my bike.

"Noah. They're all gone." Her breathy voice urging me to commit sins with her.

"I'll be there in a second doll. I'm just down the block." I put my phone back in my pocket starting up my bike and putting my helmet on.

Pulling into the same spot I was in, I went to the door I had walked through an hour before. She was there waiting for me in high heels and a night dress that barely covered her. The lace at the top of the dress swooped down low between her breasts. Too bad I didn't know how busy her building was otherwise I'd take her right here in the front entrance. She opened the door grabbing my shirt before pulling me to her. My lips crashed into hers. My hands going to her ass. Her fingers tangling themselves in my hair. My erection pressing against my jeans as her hand slithered down my chest and over my abs. I grabbed her wrist before she could go any further. I smiled as her lips turned into a pout. My teeth nipped her lip pulling it away from her own. "If you touch my cock right now we won't make it to your apartment. I'll lay you out on that little ass table over there and fuck you into next week. If we get to your apartment first I'll fuck you until you're sore and unable to walk without thinking about me." I watched as goosebumps rose on her arms and across her chest. Biting her lip again, she looked up at me. Her eyes telling me exactly what she wanted.

"Lead the way baby." I whispered pulling her lip out from between her teeth. She smiled taking my hand turning to go to her apartment. Her bedroom was cleaner since I had last been in here. There were no clothes lying around and no drawers left open. Man, I'd fuck this woman daily just to clean my place. Cleaning is a bitch especially when your damn roommate can't make anything to the garbage can. Her nightgown pooled around her feet making my thoughts go from cleaning to where my cock was going. A black lace bra with a matching thong covering her body. My dick now throbbing to be inside her. I smiled taking my cut off setting it gently on a chair. Turning towards her, her body pressing against me. Her hands sliding up my shirt before going back down and grabbing the hem of it. As soon as I was free of my shirt, my arms went around her waist picking her up. Tossing her on the bed I caressed her cheek before planting a kiss on her neck. Her giggle sounding in my ear as I unhooked her bra. Her body leaned back allowing me to fling the garment across the room. Smiling I kissed the soft spot below her ear. Her moan vibrating through her chest as she arched into me. The grin she gave me as I watched her beneath me, lit up the room and I couldn't help but smile with her.

She reached up kissing me. Her hands went to my jeans unbuckling my belt. I lifted my hips up allowing her to push my pants down springing my cock free. Her eyes widened. Sucking her bottom lip between her teeth. Leaning down I pulled her nipple between my lips. Her shoulders digging into the mattress. Her hands skimming into my hair. I made my way across her chest sucking in her other nipple, showing it the same attention. Grace moaned wrapping her legs around my waist, her heels digging into my ass. She urged me towards her entrance and I pulled away from her breast.

"Baby, I'm not ready to be in you yet. I still have a lot I

want to do before I take your pussy." Her body trembling at my words. I grinned pulling her legs away from my waist. My fingers skimmed across her lower belly and Grace squirmed against me. I hooked a finger into her thong and pulled it down just above her knees. Pulling her legs up her thong used to keep them together. "Wrap your arms around your legs and keep them against you and together as much as you can." She did as I asked. Smiling, she peeked around her legs looking at me. My hand gripped my cock and stroked it while she watched. Her tongue slipped out wetting her bottom lip. This woman was a serious kind of beautiful. Grabbing a condom and rolling it on was easy. Keeping myself out of her was not. "Don't move." I said and smacked her ass. She moaned and I could see her moisten before me. I licked my lips and planted my face into her pussy. She was sweet like pineapple. A cry sounded from her lips and I had found heaven again. Making her come was just the base of the cake

    I stood, stroking my dick along her pussy. Her cunt lips convulsed anticipating my cock. "Someone's eager to have me inside them." Pulling back getting on my knees I ran my finger along her lips rubbing her clit. I was pretty sure that she was going to come before I even began what I was wanting to do to her. "I promise to give you multiple orgasms and make you scream my name." She smiled trying to maneuver her hips closer to me. Grabbing her legs, pinning her down, keeping her body where it was. "Oh no baby it's coming don't worry." Moving her up the bed more going straight for her core sucking and licking. Grace moving her hips against my tongue trying to ride my face. Using my tongue to fuck her into her release. My name echoing off the walls, the voices laced with satisfaction. Her hands digging into the comforter of her bed as she rode the waves of bliss back to earth. Looping my fingers into her thong I tugged it off her ankles, spreading her legs wide and free, before licking and sucking my way up her body. Her eyes glistening with ecstasy as she looked up at me. Her smile pure bliss. Pleasure radiated from her lips making me groan as my own met hers. Wrapping her arms around my shoulders Grace began deepening the kiss.

"That. Was. Amazing." Grace panted into my ear making me smiled.

"And I'm not even done with you." I smiled thrusting inside of her. Her body arched into me as her pussy clenched my dick like a vice. Her breath catching, legs wrapping around my waist. After a few thrusts I knew I was going to be done for shortly. Grace was climbing quickly towards another release. Pulling out I looked at her.

"What are you doing?!" Grace was almost hysterical and I couldn't help but chuckle.

"I'm making it last longer. Fortunately, I don't want to leave yet and I'm going to make you remember who I am. I'm going to make sure that whenever you move tomorrow, baby, you're going to think of me. And each time you do you will clench your legs together and think of how delicious our time was together." I leaned down and nipped her ear lobe. She moaned and dug her heels into my ass.

"Please, Noah." Grace moaned out and grabbed onto my biceps. I leaned closer to her ear.

"Beg for it." My breath caressed her. Grace pierced me with a smile before leaning up to my ear.

"Noah, I need your cock inside of me. I need that big, thick, cock of yours inside of me. Now." She was demanding, begging making my cock twitch against her pussy. I groaned thrusting back inside of her. "Oh fuck, Noah." I smiled and let her milk me.

"Oh yes baby." I was so done for. I came into the condom after slamming my cock into her one last time collapsing on top of her.

Grace wrapped her body around mine and I smiled pulling back to look at her. She had a lazy grin on her face and her eyes drooped.

"Sweetheart, why don't we get you in bed." She nodded and kissed me. I smiled and got up pulling the condom off, tying it. Grace leaned up on her elbows and watched me. I pulled my jeans on and picked up her thong sticking it into my back pocket. She smiled and got up.

"So, will I see you again?" Grace smiled and put her hands on my chest. I pulled her close against me.

"Oh sweetheart. I sure hope so." I leaned down and kissed her while grabbing her ass. She squealed rubbing against me. I smiled and cupped her ass lifting her up to bring her back on the bed.

"You know you should get some sleep. It's almost three in the morning." Grace looked over at the clock and gasped.

"Jesus Christ. I have to work in six hours." She sighed and leaned against her pillows.

"Call me anytime sweetheart. I'm always around and if I'm not I'll make sure to come to you as fast as possible." I grabbed my shirt and looked at her. She smiled at me and nodded. I left her apartment and got on my bike going to the clubhouse.

The club was just dying down from partying when I arrived back. Whores who didn't have a man to be with tonight were leaving and members going home to their wives and kids. I didn't want to drive all the way home and I had shit to do here tomorrow. There was a long list of cars to be fixed in the garage and the faster I could get to them the faster they would get done. Ever since Ralph's last fit when I checked in with him I wasn't about to sit around my house either. He was in full on prick mode. He wanted something on the club and knowing better I never asked why. That might have to change. I wasn't his bitch and didn't think I should have to act like it. I only did it because I owed him a favor. I'll never regret having him do it. I'll only regret agreeing to his terms of service. His terms of service was going to hurt every relationship I had ever made in the club if I continued to follow through with them. I needed to tell Jack what was going on and let him know I feel my loyalty lies with the club and not Ralph and see what type of action we should take. But telling him, it could be my death wish.

The bright sun shined into the window and right over my face. I shook my head as I sat up and rubbed my face. It was going to be a long fucking day and I wasn't going to have any time to bullshit with anyone. Things needed to get done and they need to be done yesterday. Pulling on a new tee shirt I walked out into the main area and ran right into Diesel. "Fuck man." He grabbed my arms and I looked at him.

"What?" I asked.

"You can't just run into people. Why the hell are you here anyways?"

"Well dumbass I happen to have a room here as Road Captain. All the officials have rooms here."

"I know smartass. Why aren't you at your house?"

"I have shit to get done." I said jerking away from him. I pulled my cut on and walked towards the door.

"Most of it's done Noah. Some of the guys got bored last night with the party and women hanging all over us that they went and did a lot of the work already."

"What hasn't been done?"

"Mostly Grace's tune up." He said.

"I'll do it. Need something to do for the day anyways."

"She's going to need a ride to work today." Fuck if I went near her I was going to be balls deep in her again. Even though that's where I wanted to be right now. God, she was something else. She had distracted me for over a year in my head and now she's back, in person. I needed to do something about her. But, what? I still needed to fucking talk to Jack.

"All right. I'll take her." I said and left going out to my car. As soon as I got back I was finding Jack and telling him everything. It had been three years and I needed to get it off my chest. I didn't feel right having not told him. I should have told him three years ago. It was official I was going to be signing my death certificate today. Maybe I could get in bed with Grace one last time…no I needed to just get this shit over with.

I let Grace know that I was waiting outside for her and lit a cigarette. A few moments later she came out the door and

I watched her. She looked as hot as she did the night before. The make-up was still set and she had a tight skirt and low-cut blouse on. My dick was already throbbing. I couldn't do anything about it though, this was probably the last time I was going to see her. Her legs bare and those delicious heels she wore last night on her feet again. This woman had legs for days and I didn't know how I was going to keep it in my pants. I guess it was either that or she was going to be late for work. I wasn't about to go talk to her father though after I fucked his daughter. This whole thing was fucked up and if I wasn't going to die from telling Jack about this shit with Ralph then I was going to have to tell him about Grace. "Fuck." I whispered and flicked the cigarette butt out the window.

Grace got in the car and I looked over at her. I wanted to tell her that if she saw me after today we couldn't continue this shit we've been doing. Yeah, we were just sleeping together but fuck me I shouldn't be wasting her time when I might not be around long enough to do anything besides fuck her. Her eyes met mine and I smiled at her. "Do you know where you are going?" I kept my smile in place. I remembered where she worked. I stalked it for a good month after she quit calling. I hoped she would have seen me but she never did. I was only there to make sure she was okay.

"Yeah. I do." I said putting the car in drive and pulling out of the parking lot.

The drive was short and silent. Neither one of us talked at all. It was almost as if she knew something bad was coming. Or maybe that was the paranoia in my mind fucking with me. I watched as she got out of the car. I felt terrible for sleeping with her. I knew she deserved better than someone like me. "Grace." She turned and looked at me. "You should probably find someone better than me to be with." She looked confused. I couldn't explain it. I just felt like it needed to be said.

"Noah. I feel like you're saying goodbye." She said her voice barely a whisper.

"That's because I am." I said and turned away from her. "You better get to work. I have something to do." She shut the door and stood on the sidewalk as I pulled away from the curb. Today was going to be rough and leaving her was probably the worst part of the day I was going to have.

Jack was outside the garage smoking when I arrived. I sighed and stared at the clubhouse sign for a moment before getting out of the car. He was going to kill me for this but he needed to know. Going over to him, I rubbed my hand through my hair. "Jack. I need to talk to you about something. Privately." His eyes pierced through me and right away I knew something was up. Now probably wasn't the best time but it needed to be done.

"What's up brother?" he asked.

"I need to tell you something, even if now is a bad time." I replied. He flicked his cigarette on the ground and stomped on it.

"How private?" He asked

"Anywhere you want, as long as it's you and me." He looked at me and waved me over towards the club. I followed him through the club and into his office shutting the door. Jack sat behind his desk and I paced. "Look this shit ain't easy to even talk about or even think about right now." I rubbed my hand through my hair and stopped pacing, avoiding looking at Jack. "I made a deal with Ralph when he introduced me to you. He gets me in I give him information." I looked at Jack in the eyes. I didn't like this shit one bit but I had to fucking do it. Jack rubbed his chin and leaned back in his chair.

"I know." He stated. I leaned against the desk my hands flat on the top.

"What?" I was confused as fuck but in shock.

"He told me. That's why you've been in the dark. You're a good kid and I didn't want to see you on the streets with that asshole. He does shit to people. Noah I'm glad you told me. Shows your loyalty to the club. And the club knows all about this double crossing."

"The whole club doesn't want to kill me? What the hell is

going on then?" I asked.

"We were having fun with it and besides, we voted they were alright with it cause we knew the whole situation. They had bets going with how long until you would break." Jack chuckled.

"Are you fucking kidding me? Who's got the bid right now?"

"Texan." I smiled and nodded.

"I get half." I laughed.

"You can take that up with him Noah." Jack said.

"Oh I will be." Jack smiled and stood up.

"Let's get the hell out of this office and get work done. They left the tune up for you. You hurt that car in anyway I'll kill you myself." I smiled.

"I'll run faster than you can fucking catch me." I retorted.

"I'll catch you. I'll catch you when you least expect it." By the balls was left unspoken

"Shit. Speaking of unexpected. I have something else to tell you." Jack stopped and looked at me.

"Now what?" He looked fed up already.

"Grace." I barely got her name out of my mouth and I was shoved against the wall Jacks arm and knife at my throat.

"Did you fucking touch her?" I couldn't lie I was scared shitless. But it had to come out.

"Yes. It just happened but I ended it before anything else could happen. Except that it happened a year ago and then last night. But I promise it's over. I'm not going near her again."

"You're a brave boy, son. Coming to me telling me you've touched my daughter in ways I don't even want to think about." I nodded.

"It's a day of confessing sins, I guess." Jack put his knife away.

"You broke it off?" He asked

"Well...I didn't tell her flat out it was over, but I'm going to do that if I live through today. She knew something was up when I dropped her off at work. I told her I was saying goodbye so I'm hoping she got the hint but when I pick her up from work I'm going to talk to her and tell her that you know what was going on and I have to end it. My loyalties lie with the club and that's where they have to stay. I can't split them between her and the club and I'm not the kind of man she needs. She deserves someone better." Jack smiled and pulled his arm away.

"Arm or leg? Choose or I'm doing both. And then you'll be fucked. Cause you really won't be able to ride until you heal." He said pulling his gun out of his back.

"Well it's better than being dead." I said.

"Yeah, when you pick her up bring her back here. I'm going to have a chat with my daughter." I nodded and moved towards the door. There was shit to be done and getting shot just got added to my to do list for the day. Lucky me. "I'll call the doc and have him on hand." Jack finished.

GRACE

Noah had picked me up at work and brought me back to the clubhouse. My car was still on the lift. "Noah. My car isn't done, why am I here?" I asked. He rubbed the back of his neck before opening his door. I got out and looked at him. "Noah. Why am I here?" He turned to me and sighed.

"Your father's request. I told him about us." He stated. I froze where I stood and watched him.

"He's going to kill you." He shook his head.

"Doc's waiting already. He's not going to kill me but I am getting shot." He informed. I closed my eyes and dropped my head.

"I'm sorry this is happening to you." I voiced fear riding my spine.

"It's a bullet. I've taken one before. I'll be fine Grace. I did tell him that we are ending this, whatever this is." He said waving a hand between us.

"I don't want it to end." I whispered looking up at him. I could feel hot tears pooling. I heard the club door slam shut and my dad was walking across the lot, arms by his sides, gun in hand. He wasn't fucking kidding. My dad was going to shoot him. "Did you tell him it was all me? That I pushed you into it or something?" I asked panicking. He shook his head.

"There's no getting out of this Grace. I put my dick where it didn't belong and now I have to pay for it." He got out of the car and walked over to my father and I watched as my dad raised the gun to meet Noah's arm.

"Well Noah. Leg or arm? Your choice here brother and if you don't choose in the next five seconds, I'm shooting both." My dad was calm and collected. I got out of the car staring across the lot at what was unfolding.

"Arm." Noah's voice rang out, then the shot was fired mere seconds later.

My dad turned to look at me as I covered my mouth realizing I was screaming. My dad came over to me and kissed my cheek wiping tears away that I didn't know I was shedding. I had never seen him shoot someone. I knew he had guns but I didn't…hadn't seen him use it before.

"Sweetheart, it's okay." My dad held my face in his hands.

"You just…." I couldn't even finish my sentence.

"I only did it because he told me he's been sleeping with you darling." My dad just shot someone because he was sleeping with me.

"What the hell Dad! You just shot Noah because I fucked him a couple times?! Jesus Christ!" I didn't even know what else to yell at him. My dad started laughing.

"You are just like your mother some days did you know that?" He questioned me while still chuckling.

"You've told me on multiple occasions, Dad." I said rolling my eyes.

"Look Grace, if he hurts you in anyway let me know. I don't mind if you date him he's a good one." My dad was talking quietly probably to make sure no one else heard him. I nodded at him and looked at Noah. He was holding onto his arm where my father shot him. Was I worth a bullet to this man? We had only fooled around a couple times. There was no way I could mean more than a barfly to him. I smiled and kissed my dad on the cheek.

"Thanks daddy, but I don't know if he wants that." I said low enough so only my father heard. He nodded.

"What are you doing today darling?" He asked as if we didn't just have a serious conversation about him shooting the man that was fucking me. I shrugged looking up at him.

"I don't know yet. Why?" I asked. My dad smiled.

"Would you mind going on a ride with your old man?" I smiled and looked at my sandals.

"Still have my old jeans and boots here?" I asked. He grabbed my hand and brought me inside the clubhouse.

"Sure do, Gracie." I smiled and went into the bathroom to change quickly. I came out face to face with Noah. He looked me over and smiled. I smiled walking around him. His heavy footsteps sounded off the walls behind me. I looked over my shoulder at him.

The ride was a short one like I had suspected but it was just the open road, my dad, and me. It was rejuvenating and freeing knowing there was nothing to hold me back anymore. Noah knew all about my past already and it was just a matter of time until he knew all about me. I needed to be up front with him and just tell him I don't want to be fuck buddies anymore, I want more. I didn't know if I could do it though.

It had been a week since my reunion with Noah. He was all I could think about but I couldn't find the courage to call or text him. The days went by slowly and work kept me about as busy as a bee, but I wanted more of Noah. I wanted Noah back with me and in my bed. I wanted him on top of me thrusting inside me, making me feel like the woman he saw in me. The woman I used to be and who he helped bring out of my corporate shell. I couldn't take it anymore. I had to text him. Seriously a week and I was still clenching my legs together with just the thought of this man and my heart skipping beats.

I can't take it anymore. I need you. I'm still clenching my legs together when I think of what you did to me. I want more. –Grace

I set my phone on my desk and waited. I hoped he would reply. I looked up and saw my boss standing next to my desk. My boss stood just a few inches over six feet tall, had the most luscious dark brown locks I had ever seen. His eyes screamed authority and grace all while his posture was relaxed as he leaned against my desk. I bit my lip and waved at him. He smiled and leaned down closer to me.

"Grace, I have to ask you something." His words were soft and I smiled realizing I wasn't in trouble.

"What's that?" I asked and relaxed.

"Well I know you do everything for me as my assistant but I kind of don't have a date for tonight for that charity ball." I looked up at him and waited. This was new. I've never been asked out by a boss before. A blush rose to my cheeks warming my skin. It was a miracle I could feel anything besides the emotions and explosions that Noah had been giving me for the past week. "I was wondering if you would accompany me since I don't exactly have the time to run out and find someone now." I smiled. "You can even take the company credit card to get yourself a dress and such even get your hair done if that's what you want. You'd be a life saver if you did this for me." He was going to allow me to take the company credit card to go shopping...I was so not going to be stingy with that one.

"I can do that. I don't have plans tonight anyways. What time is the charity ball at?" He smiled pulling his wallet out, handing the credit card to me. Nerves were assaulting me and making me feel as if was I was going for a job interview.

"It's starts at eight pm. So, I can have a car pick you up at seven. If that's alright." He smiled tucking his wallet away. "I'm guessing you know what to show up in though? I really hate shopping so I would prefer not to go." I smiled nodding.

"I have it under control Mr. Steel." I got up after shutting down my computer.

"I'll see you later then." He smiled backing up a little bit. "Seriously Grace. Thank you for doing this for me. You're awesome." Mr. Steel turned around and went to his office. I now had to figure out what the hell I was going to wear to some charity event when all I really wanted was to be wrapped around a steel horse. Or rather wrapped around Noah. Fuck me.

After a few hours of shopping and finding a dress and getting my hair done I was almost ready. I was putting on my make up when the doorbell rang. I looked at the clock and hit the buzzer to let whoever it was inside the building. A moment later someone was knocking on my door. I pulled my robe on and opened the door. Right outside my doorway was Noah. I bit my lip and thanked god I had finished my make up before opening the door. He smiled at me and I couldn't help but return the smile.

"Noah." My voice was barely audible. My breathing uneven and short. He came close to me and pulled me against him.

"Going somewhere?" His voice was rough and went straight to my groin. I nodded incapable of speech at the moment. "Where?" it was almost a growl and I looked up into his eyes.

"I have to go to a charity event with my boss." My hands went to his biceps holding on like nothing was holding me up.

"Well what time are you going?" I had to look over at the clock again. It was six forty-five. Shit I needed to be dressed in a few minutes in order to be downstairs on time.

"Seven. I need to get dressed." I pulled away from him and went into my bedroom taking my robe off. He must have followed me because I was in his arms again.

"Call me when it's over baby. I'd like to have you screaming again." He leaned down kissing my shoulder. I shuddered, leaning into him. His hands ran up my corset and then back down to my hips. I nodded and looked at him over my shoulder. His lips brushed mine and I felt like this man was meant to be mine. A smile tugged at his lips and before I knew it he was walking out my door. I pulled on my dress on before going downstairs to wait for the car I no longer wanted to get inside of.

My phone never left my hand during the charity ball. My heart was telling me to text Noah but my brain wouldn't let me send the text. My emotions were scrambled.

I walked up to my building and saw Noah waiting by the front door. He was leaning against his bike and I smiled. He stood up and I watched as his t-shirt stretched across his muscles, clearly showing off his abdomen. He was like sex on legs. I should really stop asking him over, it will make everything so much easier when he tires of me. Is he just fucking me though? I need to just stop…after tonight. I smiled and walked over to him.

"Well this is a nice surprise." I said. He wrapped his arm around my waist and smiled kissing me. My knees shook so badly, I would have collapsed if he wasn't holding me up.

"To let you know. No, I'm not fucking anyone else…and I hope you're not fucking anyone else because I don't share." I stared at him confused. "Your eyes gave away what you were thinking. Or maybe I just know you that well." His lips crashed back into mine. I wrapped my arms around his neck. I was extremely happy to hear him say I was the only woman he was with. I turned and unlocked the door and retreated inside my apartment with him.

NOAH

I awoke in Grace's bed the next morning. There was just something about this woman that made me think about her day and night and making me want nothing more than to be balls deep inside her. Maybe, just maybe, I could start dating her or something. I don't date though it's too much work for someone who has a life like mine. I should just leave her and not look back. There was just something about her, and she wasn't just attractive, she was familiar. I needed to figure my shit out and fast. I heard the water turn off and I pulled my jeans on hoping I wouldn't get a hard on when she came out of the bathroom. I finished getting dressed and walked around her apartment.

I had a run to do today and it was going to be the last one until winter was over. Unless we did runs with the cargo truck this winter. Who the hell knew what Jack had planned though. I didn't know anything anymore. I had my head so wrapped up in Grace that I wasn't even thinking anymore. My thoughts were all about her. How her day was going and all that shit that made a man whipped. I wanted to bang my head against the wall and hope it would knock some sense into me.

Grace emerged from the bathroom toweling off her hair. I smiled seeing the robe and knowing that she was naked underneath was the icing on the cake for me. Too bad I didn't have time to have a round two with her. "I have to get going." I told her. She nodded.

"I figured you wouldn't have waited for me to get out of the shower to tell me that." She replied.

"I'm not that rude." I replied.

"I didn't say that you were. I was just saying I understand

that you are a busy man." She said with a smile. I shook my head walking towards her.

"What are you doing to me woman?" I asked before placing a tender kiss on her lips. The shit I was feeling for her was going to both my heads. Her dad hadn't killed me yet but I'm positive that she was going to be the death of me. I left her apartment looking over my shoulder as the door shut behind me.

The run went as smooth as could be expected. No confrontation and better yet I was earlier than expected back to the clubhouse. I needed to talk to Jack and let him know the details about the run. I walked into the clubhouse and looked around. Stoner was sitting at the bar and he nodded at me. He used to be a pothead until Jack put his foot down and told him he wasn't going to stay with the club unless he eased up on the Mary Jane. She made him do twisted shit and it usually had us paying with bullet holes.

"Hey, Stoner do you know where Jack is?" Stoner took a gulp of his drink and pointed toward the office. I walked by him patting his back as I passed. Jack was having a heated discussion with someone and so I stood in the hall and waited.

Fifteen minutes later Delilah walked out of the office. I sighed and watched Grace's mother leave the hallway. Stepping into the office Jack looked up at me. "What the hell do you want?" Well this was going to be a lovely discussion.

"Just wanted to update you on the run that I did." I said.

"Right, right. Come in. Shut the door." I did as I was told.

"The run went smooth no problems. And no I didn't look at the cargo."

"Why not?"

"Why not what?"

"Why didn't you look at the cargo? I gave you this assignment to report back to Ralph. He's not going to keep quiet for long, you have to give him something." I stared at him, astonished that he was even thinking of doing this shit. He slid a folder over to me and smiled. "Take this to him. Make sure you read everything so in case he grills you on it at all, you'll know everything you delivered." I shook my head and leaned back. I stared at him for a moment longer before lunging forward and picking up the folder.

"You sure you want me to do this?" I asked.

"I wouldn't be giving you the information if I didn't want you to. Go give it to him and then you'll be keeping up your end of the bargain and we will feed him some bullshit. I want to know what he has planned." I nodded and agreed.

"It would be in our best to know what he has planned." I replied and got up flipping the folder open. "I'll see when I get to meet with his highness and then I'll let you know when it is." He nodded.

"Go study. I've got other shit to do now." I walked out the door shutting it behind me. I felt her before I knew she was there. Turning my head towards the entrance of the hallway I smiled. I didn't know if I believed in God, but at this moment, if there is one, I believed that, that heavenly father sent me one of his angels to try and keep me away from the devil. All I would end up doing was drawing her closer to the devil. Maybe this whole thing between her and I is a bad idea after all. We don't have Jack's approval and I don't know if I could be more than what we have now. She's not going to want this forever either. In that moment, I turned away from her and went down the hall to the room I kept at the club closing the door on her and how I felt. I had to get this shit with Ralph over with before I could think about my future. The whole time my brain was screaming at me. What the fuck was I doing not pursuing her? I took a bullet for that woman already. I sat on the bed flipping open the folder again. Grace and I were going to have to wait.

The run I did wasn't anything special. The cargo was just standard hand guns and some candles that the guns were hidden under. I got paid for the job and sent on my way. It was something to feed Ralph for now but I knew he was going to want to know about the bigger jobs. With me being Road Captain, there was no way he was going to believe that I wasn't in on the big runs and keeping them from him. I called the bastard to set a meeting

The meeting was set for the next afternoon at three. It was right when I got off work from the shop and Ralph knew I would have to leave early in order to get there on time. This would have made Jack suspicious had he not known what I was up to. Good thing he knew. I made my way back to his office. I knocked before turning the knob to go inside. "Jack it's all... Jesus fucking Christ!"

"Get the fuck out of here Asshat!" Jack yelled. I spun around and slammed the door behind me and walked towards my bedroom. That shit was going to be permanently scarred behind my eyes. Seeing your club president balls deep in his wife was not something I wanted to ever see again. God damn. I shook my head and looked around my room hoping to find a bottle or fuck that even a joint would probably help me. Nothing, I had nothing in my bedroom to help me forget what I had seen. A knock sounded on my door. I turned and stared at it. A second knock came shaking me out of my daze.

Grace was on the other side of the door. She looked delectable and had me raging a hard on like a fourteen-year-old boy going through puberty. I must not have gotten a good look at her earlier. She had those leather pants on that she wore to the bar and a shirt that hugged her breasts. I smiled and grabbed her arm pulling her in my room and closed the door. "You shouldn't come to a man's room dressed like that." I whispered walking her backwards until she hit the wall. She had a devilish smile that was making me think that the Devil had sent her instead of God. Her hooded eyes were calling to me and I want to take her against the wall. I couldn't right now. I had a never-ending list that needed to be accomplished. Not to mention I didn't even know what the fuck was going on between us.

Grace leaned forward and nipped my lip. I smiled and looked at her. "Sweetheart. As much as I want to do this and how bangable you look right now, I have to get work done." I said and kissed where her shoulder and neck met. "Later though I'll help you chase your wildest fantasies." I heard her let out a purr like sigh in my ear and a smile spread across my lips. Pushing away from the wall and her I went over to the bed grabbing the folder to leave the room. This folder wasn't leaving my sight until I handed it off.

"Noah?" her voice was fucking sweet as sin. I looked over at her. "Don't forget about me tonight. I have this feeling that we won't get much time together after tonight." I nodded. She was probably right about that but the life of a club member never went as planned. It was one hell of a ride that you had to suck up and just ride the shit out of until you were dead.

"I could never forget you, Grace. You were running through my mind everyday over the past year. I'm not about to forget you that easily." I said walking out the door. Only downfall about tonight was that there was another fucking party at the club and I had to be here for it. I didn't know how we were going to get around that. Life was probably going to be hell after tonight but if I had to take another bullet to spend one more night with her then I would. She wouldn't ever stop amazing me.

The walk down the hallway was short and full of relief as I could see Jack's door open. I peeked inside and looked around for him. He was over by his filing cabinet. I reached over and knocked on the door. "Hey Jack?" he turned and looked at me before waving me inside. "I just wanted to tell you about the meeting I set up with Ralph. It's at three tomorrow afternoon." He gave me a nod.

"Sounds good brother. Let me know what happens after your meeting with him. I need to know if he's planning on doing something with the information." He said his back still to me.

"Can do. What if he sends me off right away?"

"Try and stay. Or lurk around a corner and listen. Do whatever you have to, to get intel on the bastard." He said. "Go get your work done and don't lose that file." I stood up.

"Hey Jack." I didn't know why I was even asking this. "Do...

Would it be alright if I dated Grace?" I asked mentally kicking myself. He probably going to kill me at some point.

"Don't hurt her." He said sighing. I looked over at him.

"So, I have your permission?" He turned around.

"You do but only because you're the only fucker I know with balls big enough to ask me if it's alright and you're not a bad kid. She deserves happiness and you seem to bring it out in her."

"I'll do my best." I said hoping I could give her everything she deserved.

"You done now? There's shit to be done around here. Tell the prospect to clean my office too. I'm going out for a ride." I nodded leaving the room

"Oh Twinkle!" I hollered down the hallway. I smiled as he came rushing into the hall from the bathroom wrapped in a towel. "Prez is leaving he wants his office cleaned." I smiled knowing full well of what exactly he was going to be cleaning up. "Make sure you lick the desk clean."

"Lick it?" Twinkle questioned. My smile got wider.

"Yes, Lick it. And take a picture as proof. Need to be sure you did it." Jack walked by laughing as soon as I had told Twinkle to lick the desk clean. I'd probably puke as soon as I saw the picture but I guess we'd have to see if he actually did it. The smile never left my face as I walked through the main area and out the door. I was probably going to be labeled a sick fuck for this one but pranking the prospects was part of the job.

I saw Grace out in the lot leaning against her car. I smiled. She must have slipped out the back door. But now that I got permission to be with her there was only one thing I wanted to do and one thing that I was going to do. It just had to wait until Sunday and it was Thursday. Can't proclaim someone yours just randomly it has to be in church. I'm sure someone will fuck that announcement up.

My smile dropped away as I saw another car pull up and a man walked up to Grace. He handed over a vase of flowers. I stood back and watched before I finally leaned against the building lighting up. She wasn't mine yet so there was nothing I could do about another man giving her flowers. Soon though I'd take down every man that tried to do that same gesture. It pissed me off beyond belief that he had the balls to show up here and talk to my woman. I rolled my neck watching the other man talk to my woman. Thank fuck he wasn't here long, just long enough for me to finish my cigarette. I flicked my cigarette before making my way towards her. She looked up as I approached and a smile lit up her eyes. "Who was that?" I asked pointing to where the man's car had been.

"That was my boss. He needed me to give me something that came to the office."

"And what went to the office for you?" I looked in the back of her car spotting the bouquet. "Flowers? Who are they from?"

"I honestly don't know. Tanner gave me tomorrow off and he didn't want them sitting at the office over the weekend."

"There's no card?" she shook her head.

"No, no card. I asked who delivered them and he told me it was from Sam's Florist. I don't know if they keep records of the buyers and I doubt they would give that information over." She said shrugging. "I was just going to give them to my mother or throw them away. I don't think she's gotten flowers in years." I smiled.

"Give them to your dad to give to her. After the rough morning she had with him I'm sure she'd love them."

"Rough morning? What happened?" She asked worry lines crossed her skin. I smiled trapping her with my body against her car.

"The kind of rough morning I want to have with you every day I can." I whispered kissing her neck.

"Noah what are you doing? If my father sees this…"

"He's not going to do anything about it sweetheart. You're mine and I got permission. As of Sunday, you'll be mine in front of the whole club." Her eyes met mine and I continued to grin.

"We don't have to sneak around anymore?" she whispered. I shook my head and placed my lips against hers.

"No more sneaking. I'm yours and you're mine. Every night you will be in my bed or I'll be in yours."

"What the hell are you doing Noah?" I pulled away from Grace and looked over my shoulder. Fucking club whore.

"What the fuck do you want?" I yelled. Grace stepped away giving Peyton a full-on look of who I was touching.

"You know she's off limits." I looked over at Grace and smiled. Grace returned the smile.

"She's off limits to everyone else except me." I said loud. Yep I just randomly claimed her and I'd do it again and again. "Grace, be my ol'lady so I can get rid of her." It was more demanding then I wanted it to be but it just came out that way. Grace nodded and I turned towards Peyton. "Grace is my ol'lady now. You fuck with her you fuck with the club. Got it?" I said firmly. Peyton physically took a step back from the authority I held over her.

"Yes." She barely whispered it. I watched as tears began to stream down her cheeks.

"Oh, for Christ's sake." I said turned back to Grace.

"My father really gave you permission?" she asked. I nodded.

"You can ask him yourself if you want." I whispered kissing her.

"Noah, I gave you fucking permission to date her. Not make out with my daughter in front of me." Jack hollered walking by us. I smiled staring at Grace.

"I'm not just dating her, Jack. I claimed her." Grace's smile disappeared as she stared over at her father.

"You didn't tell him that part, did you?" She asked in a whisper.

"Nope." I'm in trouble. Next thing I knew I was being thrown across the lot.

"You didn't fucking ask permission to claim her!" Jack was bellowing.

"I just asked her if I could and Peyton wouldn't leave me the fuck alone." I yelled back. I was lying flat on the pavement. I've done a lot of stupid shit. But this was probably the stupidest.

"You don't have my permission for that." Jack's head was hanging forward. The strings of clarity and calm slowly snapping.

"I love her." It flew out of my mouth and I looked over at Grace at the sound of her gasp. She had her hand over her mouth and tears in her eyes. My own eyes left hers and went over to Jack. He had his hands on his hips and head hung shaking back and forth.

"Fuck, Noah. You better her treat her better than your cut." I barely heard him say it. It was then I knew it was safe to get off my back.

"And ride her as much as my Harley." I said with a smile.

"That shit I don't want to know about." He said with a chuckle.

GRACE

Most of the ol' ladies lived with their man. Noah wanted me to move in with him but I didn't want to move out on Beth so suddenly. I had to give her a little notice that I was moving out. Sudden nausea hit me like a freight train. I had to brace myself against the wall just to keep from falling over. My vision blurred, making the nausea worse than when it first hit. I needed my bed.

The feeling of being horizontal instead of vertical was one of bliss. The release of tension and pressure eased the nausea and kept me sane for a few moments. I was thankful that I didn't have to work today. I would have felt worse if I had to call in. It was almost making me feel worse. But I knew being up and down all day would result in a nice projectile vomit show for everyone at the office. With my phone on the pillow beside me I closed my eyes hoping my body would relax just enough that I could fall back asleep. I wanted to let the darkness take me as its mistress.

Half-awake I cracked my eyes seeing a shadow in the doorway. My heart began racing as recognition dawned on me. It had been so long since he had been around. I wanted to close my eyes and pray it was just a dream. That he wasn't actually here. Maybe I had a fever and was delusional. My wrist touched my forehead. I wasn't warm. I reached over and pinched my arm. Fuck! I'm awake. I groaned and rolled over. This wasn't happening. This couldn't be happening. I spent a whole year trying to forget him. To forget the fear that was still inside me. My back to the door I tried my damnedest to calm my heart rate. Rustling noises made me hold my breath. His arms came around me and I flinched. The familiar feeling of slime rolled across my skin. The pain and fear that surfaced made me feel as if I was suffocating. Max wasn't a figment of my imagination. He had me in his arms.

"Shhhh, baby, it'll be alright." Tears were coming on fast. I pulled my body forward and began the slow process of standing up while fighting the nausea.

"I have to go to work." I croaked grabbing my purse. He got up and came towards me.

"I'll drive you."

"No. I'm driving myself. You need to go away." I was firm. Anger was rising. He made me the pussy I was and still am. If it wasn't for him I'd have the life I should have and felt like I deserved. He made me feel useless just like a caged animal. This animal was breaking free. I wasn't playing his fucking games anymore. They were bullshit.

I left the room on wobbly legs and made my way to the kitchen beginning to make a sandwich. Hoping the food would calm me or I'd vomit all over him. Max joined me in the kitchen when I was cutting the sandwich in half. I looked up at him and felt something take over my body. I felt as if I was watching from afar. The thing my body did next was astonishing. It also relieved me at the same time.

It was a slow walk around the bar. The knife still in my hand. I watched as Max reached for it. My grip tightened as a battle cry ripped through my throat. The carving knife came slashing through the air piercing Max in the shoulder. He staggered back tripping when the linoleum floor turned to carpet. I watched as a smile crossed my lips. I grabbed his ankle pulling him back to the linoleum. He wasn't getting away from me. Straddling him I ripped the knife out of his shoulder. Blood painted my skin and I felt as if I was being reborn. The blood of my enemy was being shed and I wanted more of it spilt. His hands gripped my arm.

Quickly I pierced his chest, ripping my arm from his grasp. A cry spilt from his lips. The sound was like music to my ears. Pulling the knife out and piercing his chest over and over, blood sprayed the carpet, me, and the bar. A soft cry came out from his lips. I placed the tip of the knife in the floor by his ear leaning down. His fingers dug into my cheeks. Manicured fingernails attempting to claw their way to my own blood. I smiled smacking his hands away, watching his energy drain. "Now you won't be able to fuck with anyone anymore. I'm going to watch as the life drains from your eyes and wait until your heart stops beating. Your games end tonight." I whispered. Max's eyes grew wide as I straightened myself out.

"No…Grace don't. I'll leave you alone. I'll never touch another woman the way I did you. I promise." He was begging and if I had a dick I'd probably have a boner right now. Taking the knife out of the floor and going straight for his heart. The shocked look on his face was one that would probably help me sleep at night. Who knows how many girls he has tormented, how many women he's made his bitch until I ended it. He would keep the same shit going. Getting off him and leaning against the bar I finally felt like myself again. His life was still slowly draining as I watched his eyes glaze over. His blood soon stopped flowing and the panic rose in my throat. How the fuck was I going to get rid of this all?

A sob ripped through me. I backed up until I was far away from the mess. My eyes stayed on his feet. I didn't know if he was actually dead. Deep, gasping breaths entered my lungs leaving in a whoosh. I felt like I was getting the wind knocked out of me. What the hell was I supposed to do now? I didn't know what the fuck I was going to do. I looked around as tears ran down my cheeks and the questions burned in my mind. I noticed a vase with flowers shattered on the floor. The bouquet I was going to give my father to give to my mother. He must have taken them down with him when he fell. My eyes landed on the single white rose in the bouquet. Blood tainted it. I watched as the blood dripped down into the puddle beneath it. Little splashes and ripples making their way to the edge of the puddle. Max's tainted blood was spilt. I had spilt his blood.

A ringing sound had my eyes leaving the puddle to find the source of the noise. My phone in the bedroom where I left it. My brain needed a moment to process what was going on. It felt like the ringing went on forever and my body was in slow motion. Finally, the ringing ended.

Stepping into my bedroom, I reached for my phone waking it. I saw Noah's name flash across the screen. Realization dawned on me. The club had killed before but never talked about it. Noah had to know what to do. I dialed him back even though it felt like it was going in slow motion. My body sagged onto the floor as soon as I heard his voice. A sob ripped through me. "I need you. Noah, I need you. I did something terrible. Please come to me."

"Where are you?" he asked. His voice was soothing.

"Home." I whispered fear present as I clutched my phone even after the call disconnected. I had finally realized what I had done. Taking a deep breath, I dropped my head to my knees and cradled my body. The phone slid across the floor until it hit a wall and I sat, waiting.

NOAH

Grace had been so scared on the phone. Her voice was dripping with fear. My heart was pounding in my ears. What would have her so scared? I grabbed Cody while he was balls deep in a whore and threw clothes at him. "I may need back up." I yelled at him. He looked pissed that I was stopping him. "Beast you're the only other person besides Jack that Grace trusts. I need you. Something happened at her apartment." I watched as Beast's eyes went from lust to pure horror. He ripped himself off the bitch and threw his jeans on.

We rode to her apartment in silence. At a stop light simultaneously, we lit a cigarette and rode the rest of the way. I was stressing and had no fucking clue what we were walking into.

Flying into her parking lot, I threw the kick stand down and got off my bike. I scanned the lot like I had been for the past year. The difference being I spotted his fucking car. The cigarette dropped to the ground and my boots thundered down her hallway. The bastard was mine. The door opened and I stopped dead in my tracks. There was blood everywhere. Panic rose and my own blood ran cold. "Grace?" Beast collided with my back.

"Holy shit. That's a lot of blood." Beast stated. Well wasn't he captain fucking obvious.

"Shut the door." I said walking farther into the apartment. The door clicked shut and I scanned the room. "Grace?" rustling came from the bedroom and I walked towards it. Grace stood looking like Carrie from the Stephen King movie, in the middle of her floor. It was the time the students covered Carrie in the pig's blood. Okay maybe not that bad. Relief washed through me. Her eyes narrowed. She had blood matting her hair and streaked across her clothes and skin. Her hands looked as if she had played in it like it was finger painting.

"You're late." Her voice was hard. "You weren't here when I needed you. You should have been here." I saw the knife and walked towards the destruction. Glazed dead eyes stared up at me. I whistled low.

"Damn woman. Are you on your period? Do I need to be worried if you are?" I said. I didn't care if she was honestly. Knowing that she can take care of herself had me getting a hard on. I was going to marry this woman. Through hell or high water, nothing was going to stop that wedding. I turned back towards her. She looked freaked and I didn't like how it messed with her features.

"This isn't a joke, Noah. I don't know what the fuck to do!" her voice was rising to hysteria. Panic taking over, her body shaking.

"Babe. I'll take care of it. Go clean up and get changed. We are going to start moving you out of here tonight. I don't give a fuck if you are leaving Beth high and dry. I'll pay your rent for the month. Then you are going to call your boss and tell him you need a few days off of work and that you will for sure be back by next Monday. Life goes on and you are going to need to accept that right now. We will get through this and after you leave this apartment today you won't know what even happened to him." I said putting my hands on her shoulders and looking in her eyes. "I got you babe." I knew everything I said was rough and tough love, but it was honest. Having lost many people in my life I didn't feel a thing when it came to death. I couldn't even be compassionate. She wrapped her arms around me and I held her knowing full well I was going to have to take my shirt off to hide the blood. I sighed and relaxed once she made her way to her bedroom and then the bathroom.

I looked over at Beast and sighed. "This wasn't the kind of shit I was expecting." He said. I nodded in agreement and looked around me. Blood covered almost every inch between the bar and the linoleum. It wasn't very much but the red made it look like a huge mess. The lifeless body stared at the ceiling growing colder by the minute. I never knew how strong that woman was until today. If she could fight him and kill him, she wasn't going to have any problem being an ol'lady.

"Shit Cody. I don't even know where to begin cleaning this up." Beast laughed.

"Call in the prospect. The whole club is going to find out anyways. You're going to have to talk to Jack though. And that's going to be a shit show I don't want to be around for." He said. I rubbed the back of my neck. Yeah that was going to be one shit show I didn't even want to be there for. Taking out my phone I dialed Jack.

"What?" Great he sounded pissed as all hell.

"Something happened at Grace's." I said.

"What do you mean something happened at Grace's. Is she hurt?"

"Define...No she's not hurt." Being a smartass was not a good idea right now. "Max showed up."

"That bastard. I'll be right there."

"No hurry. He's dead." Total silence on the phone.

"What do you mean he's dead?"

"I mean he took a carving knife to the chest and shoulder. Multiple times. Eyes glazed over, not breathing, dead. Deader than dead. Still warm unfortunately."

"Fuck what did you do Noah?"

"I didn't do it sir." Respect to him a given but respect for Grace growing beyond what I expected.

"Grace killed him?" he asked. I let the silence do the talking for me. "You let Grace kill him?"

"No sir. She called me after he was dead. Beast is here with me. I didn't even know what I was walking into until I walked into it. Jack, she's okay. Just a little terrified and has no clue what to do about the body. Obviously, she doesn't want to tell the cops but she needs help getting rid of it. She's getting cleaned up right now."

"I'll be right over with the rest of the club. The devil knows that the club is going to find out about it anyways." He said hanging up the phone. Putting my own phone back in my pocket, I could feel the anger rising inside me. This was the sick fuck that did malicious things to Grace and made her live through it. He was the sick fuck that raped her over and over and sometimes had his friends join in. Probably fucking drugged her.

"Noah, what are you doing?" Beast asked. I looked over at him and his eyes were glued to my hand. Looking down my arm I saw I had taken my gun out trigger finger ready to pull. Taking a deep breath I put the gun away and went to the kitchen looking for a garbage bag. I was going to chop the fucker into little pieces and tie him up. Then we would be back to move Grace into my home and that's where she is going to stay for the rest of her damn life. I wanted to light up but knowing that Grace probably wouldn't approve of that in the apartment I'd have to opt out for going outside once I found the damn bags. My stress level was through the roof. Stopping where I stood, I looked over at Beast.

"Garbage bags. Will you find them? I need to go smoke." I mumbled making my way to the door. "If Grace asks for me I'm outside." It seemed like a long walk to the front door. As soon as the fresh air hit me it was like the stress melted away. I didn't know what to think right now. Wanting to be with her now was just one too many things on my overflowing plate. Not to mention more stress. I'd have to ask Jack for her hand and then planning a wedding? Fuck I'm way over my head in this. Lighting a cigarette, I watched the smoke curl around the end. The cherry burned bright red as ashes burned off. Engines roared off in the distance. The Devil's Pride rolling into the parking lot.

I leaned against the building and inhaled the toxins. Jack parked his bike next to mine and walked up to me. "How bad is it?" he asked. I sighed and put the cigarette out.

"I'll show you. Just have to make sure she's dressed." I said. Jack nodded and we made our way inside. Beast was leaning against the bar when we walked in. "Where's Grace?" I asked. Beast nodded his head towards the hallway and I made my way down it. "Grace?" I asked getting to her bedroom. Pushing open the door confirmed she was still in the bathroom.

I knocked on the bathroom door. "Baby?" I heard a click before the door was opened. She stood there still covered in his blood. Moving her backwards, I stepped inside closing the door. My vest went on the hook on the back of the door and I peeled my shirt off before going to work on her clothes. The water was ice like it had been running the entire time she had been in here. Pushing my jeans down and stepping out of them, I wrapped my arms around her and set her in the tub away from the water. Heating the water up again I grabbed soap and a cloth. Lathering the cloth in soap and water I started to caress her skin cleaning it of the sin and crime she committed.

"What are you singing?" She whispered. I hadn't realized I was singing but I knew the song.

"Every Breath You Take." I whispered pausing in my clean up. She turned towards me and I did all I could to keep still. It was like I was frozen watching her. She got on her toes, her lips meeting mine. I wrapped my arms around her and held her against me, letting her take what she wanted. What she needed.

"Do you really love me Noah?" she asked against my lips. My hand stroked her back.

"Yes. I love you Grace. More than I intended to." I replied. She seemed to melt into me. Her head resting against my shoulder.

"Show me how much you love me." I was instantly sporting a hard-on. I kissed the top of her head.

"Your father is in the other room baby. I have to show respect towards him. And what I want to do to you would take us hours to complete. We don't have that kind of time right now." I watched her as she took a deep breath and leaned her head back some. The spray from the shower hitting her face. She was the most beautiful creature ever created. I was angry that someone hurt her but thankful because it drove her to my arms.

She had lived through so much and still craved love. I would fight for this woman until the day I died. She was going to get everything she asked for and much, much more. I wasn't going to hurt her. She owned me. She owned my heart.

Getting dressed again was like being reborn. I knew exactly how I felt with clarity. I needed to get her patch on her and body inked with my name. The ink was always after a wedding. Members, once married, never divorced. It was exactly as the vows said, 'Until death do us part.' I had a feeling that this, between Grace and I, wasn't going to be sunshine and rainbows but what relationship was? Our relationship would probably get shit on by God and I didn't give one flying fuck. She's mine until the end of time. When the devil himself came for me I'd find a bench in the seven rings of hell and wait for her. I didn't care if this made me selfish. Grace was stuck with me.

I let Grace get dressed in peace and left the bathroom going into the kitchen where Jack was. "I'm going to bring Grace to my place and I'll stay with her for awhile until I'm needed at least." Jack looked over at me and nodded.

"Take care of my girl." Jack said as he looked down again.

GRACE

*****A few days later*****

I woke up in Noah's bed. His bedsheets were black satin with a black comforter. The curtains were black and even pulled back they darkened the room to look like it was night time. The walls were painted a shade of gray. It was a dark room but showed his life with the club, his loyalty to the club. The Devil's Pride Symbol painted on one wall, rockers included. I smiled and got up. Everyone knew we were together, but I didn't understand why I couldn't stay at my own place last night. I went out into the kitchen and looked around his place. It was a real bachelor pad and I felt like I was intruding. Sure, I felt like there was something growing with Noah but I didn't want to be a burden on him. He cradled me at night and wouldn't let me leave his sight. Nightmares of what happened assaulted me at night and during the day. I was always looking over my shoulder, not accepting that Max was actually dead. I roamed around a little more and found a room with its door shut. It opened easily and I stepped inside flicking on the lights.

My mouth fell open and my eyes scanned the room. It looked like something out of a horror movie. There were chains hanging from the ceiling, whips and cuffs hanging on the wall, and smack dab in the middle of the room was a large four poster bed. Was he seriously into all this? He liked to whip his women? Would I even like that? Christ, what was I getting myself into. I stepped further into the room and ran my hand along the mahogany footboard of the bed. I turned back to the door and stopped in my tracks. Noah was standing there with his hands in his sweat pants pocket watching me intently. I bit my lip and walked towards him. His arm came out and wrapped around my waist pulling me close to him. I stared up into his eyes and watched as the desire he has for me swirled around them. I was honestly scared shitless about what all this meant. I needed to talk to him but I couldn't bring myself to say it. I'm sure he could see the questions in my eyes. He gave me a nod and pulled me out of the room shutting the door.

"Look, Grace, yes I'm into all this but not strictly, if you couldn't tell by the way we have had sex." He said reading my thoughts. Awesome, he was totally into BDSM and I had no idea if I would be even okay with this. Is that why he choked me over a year ago?

"Noah...I need to think." I said.

"Grace, I won't mind if you never want to step foot in there. And if you do I won't make you do something that you don't want to. We will choose everything together. It's a team effort." He said.

"Noah...I need to think about this. I'm not sure if this something I can even begin to ask questions about." I said and walked past him to the bedroom. Noah followed me and I grabbed my jacket and purse.

"I would like to go to my parents, Noah. I can't think clearly around you." I said and looked at him. He looked like he had lost something important to him. His nod told me he knew that I needed space and that he would bring me to my parents. After all this time I could feel the tingling feeling associated with the blackouts creeping up my spine. I forced it away, keeping my mind clear.

Noah dropped me off at my parents a half hour later. He told me to call if I had questions or if I needed anything from him. I just needed to figure out if I could give him a chance. He was fucking sex on legs with a steel horse between them. It was a damn near dream come true for me that he came along. The

BDSM though, could I really be okay with that? He did say he didn't need to do it, that it wasn't something he did regularly. I suppose I could try it out and at least give him the chance he deserves before being a stuck-up bitch that wants nothing to do with that side of sex. What would be wrong with giving it a try?

I sent Noah a text that I would like to talk at some point. He replied telling me that he would be waiting for when I'm ready. I sat in silence on the couch and spent the whole day there. My phone rang multiple times and I didn't answer it. I just didn't know what to do. There was so much going through my mind with the BDSM shit that I didn't even know where to begin. I needed to form some sort of question so I could ask Noah about it. Nothing would form tough. I was at a complete loss for what the hell I should do, or what I should ask. I went to bed that night with an overloaded mind.

A message was waiting for me when I got out of the shower in the morning. It was Noah asking if we could have lunch and talk. I let him know that I had to go into work but that I would gladly go to dinner with him instead. I just booked myself a date with a biker. My thoughts started going to when we were in bed together. If I didn't clear up my head then I would never get anything done at work today.

Work went by quickly and I went home to change. Noah messaged me to meet him at the clubhouse at eight. I had an hour before I needed to meet up with him. Now I needed to figure out what I was going to wear…Do I hike a skirt up on the bike or do I wear pants? Fuck me. I was freaking out over a man who was into BDSM and shit that I didn't even know if I was going to be staying with the man… I even contemplated going to this thing naked but I'm sure we wouldn't get anything done then, well talking wouldn't get done. I decided on a dress on the casual side and got ready.

Noah was waiting for me inside the clubhouse. Jerk-off cat-called as I walked in and I watched Noah glare at him. "Jerk-Off if you even dare think about her when you get off tonight—"

"Noah and I will both have your balls and dick on a silver platter." My dad cut Noah off. I smiled and went over to my father kissing his cheek. Jerk off was one of the bald men. I didn't know if that was by choice or not. He got his name by masturbating when he's nervous or anxious. I guess it was a disorder. He was the newest member. After a few times of talking to him I learned that his favorite thing to do is to build bikes from the ground up. He's good at it too.

"Hi daddy." I said looking over at Noah. Heat filled his eyes as he watched me. Fear racked me along with nerves but I couldn't let that stop me. This man before me was something I wanted and needed in my life. He was different from past boyfriends and I needed something new.

"Hi baby girl. Have fun." My smile stayed put and I went over to Noah. Noah's eyes raking over me. A smile slowly spread across his lips.

"Ready?" Noah asked. I nodded my head and followed him outside. He walked towards my car and I stopped.

"We are taking my car?" I asked and looked at him.

"Well sweetheart, I didn't believe you'd like to get on a bike before we had this conversation. My lips spread into a grin as I walked over to him.

"I want to ride your bike. Noah…I want to try whatever this is. The BDSM and all, I just don't exactly understand what that whole side of sex is." I said. Noah's lips crashed into mine as I wrapped my arms around his neck.

"I was going to take you to dinner, but I think our conversation should probably be in private. I could get a private room at that one place you like." Noah said and rested his hands on my hips.

"I don't believe my favorite place has private rooms. We can just go back to your place. I'll cook dinner and we can talk or whatever we need to do." I said. He smiled opening my car door for me. "Follow me home." It was a simple request that was probably going to change my whole world. I nodded getting in my car and watching as he walked over to his bike and got on. That man was going to be the end of me and I knew it, but I didn't care.

Noah opened my door when we arrived at his apartment. I smiled taking his hand going with him inside. I was worrying about what I was going to cook and whether he was going to like it or not. It seemed like a normal worry but underneath it all I was worried about if I was going to be able to handle his kind of sex and what would happen if I couldn't handle it. I know he had said that it was fine if I didn't like it, but I still wanted to try for him. Besides relationships are about compromising, aren't they?

His apartment was the same as it was when I left. Nothing was even out of place, his shoes by the front door were lined up and he put his in their spot when they came off. Noah was the kind of man who was organized and focused on details. I hoped like hell I was enough for this man. I don't think I could see him with some club whore. I had heard of my dad fucking a few behind my mother's back and it was disturbing that my mother put up with it. Ol' lady or not I would be bitch slapping someone for it and leaving their asses. My mother was a different woman though, I thought she was one tough broad to stay and try and work things out with my father. I needed to make it clear to Noah before we started anything that if I caught wind that he was fucking a club whore it was done, I was done. Noah stopped in the kitchen and looked in the fridge.

"I don't have much around here…We could order a pizza or something though instead." He said shutting the fridge door and looking at me.

"That works for me." I said. Then we could just get down to business, talking about where the hell this was going and what the fuck we were going to do.

I walked around his living room, our living room, as he ordered pizza. I was so happy I didn't have to keep my shoes on all night. My eyes wander through his music collection and paused at my favorite band. A smile crept over my face as I pulled it from the shelf and placed it in his cd player. My finger hit play and Hinder's "Without You" started playing. I felt my hips start to sway as I nibbled on my finger and walked over to the window. A pair of arms wrapped around my waist from behind and I smiled knowing it was Noah. My body relaxed into him as my hips kept up a rhythm against him. His hands pulled back resting on my hips as my hands came down positioning themselves on top of his. His lips pressed against my neck just as a smile spread across my lips as I pulled away.

"Noah, we need to talk before we do anything." I said turning around. Noah smiled pulling me flush against him. His arousal was clear against my belly. I giggled and looked up at him. "Noah, I'm serious. I just need to get a few things out and after dinner we can take care of…um…that." I said. Noah let go of my waist taking my hand going over to the sofa. Well I guess this was the best time to just get it all out there.

"Okay, I'm just going to say everything I need to then we can go from there." I said. Noah nodded and waited for me to continue. I took a deep breath doing what was expected of me. "First, if we have any sort of relationship that involves us fucking and I catch you fucking or anything with a club whore or any skank I will leave, I've spent too many years watching my mom just stand by when my dad was out with club whores. Second, I know nothing about BDSM. I would like to try it but I want to go slow. I need to learn about it before I can just jump into it. Thirdly, how did you get into it all? I know it's not really something you just think hey maybe I can do this and she will like it." I finished with my heart racing not knowing if I really wanted to hear the answer to my only question. Noah sat still for a moment and then leaned back into the sofa looking into my eyes.

"For one, babe, I never planned on fucking anyone besides you. Your father made it clear that if I hurt you he had a bullet with my name on it and let's face it he's one scary son of a bitch, and I have also watched your mother sit on the sidelines while I have known your father has fucked around on her. Second, BDSM is taught and I will teach you at your own pace. I don't plan on taking you in there until you are fully ready for it all. Thirdly, I got into it in my teens. I met a woman who had shown me a way to blow off steam instead of committing the crimes I was. When she suddenly died in a crash, I went back to the crimes and your dad found me. I've only done so much with the BDSM that I'm no pro at it. She taught me a lot but there is more to it than I know. I don't want to know more than I do right now either. I don't get off on hitting someone it's more of them being at my mercy while tied up. It's a thrill that I plan on showing you over time, one that I crave occasionally. We don't have to go in there every time we have sex. In fact after pizza is done being consumed I plan on taking you on this couch, then maybe I'll take you over the kitchen table, and maybe I'll take it to the bedroom." Noah said. My pussy was already clenching at the imagery he had given me. How could this man be real? I leaned forward and kissed him. Noah's hands planted firmly on my ass and lifted me to straddle him. That's when the doorbell rang.

NOAH

The damn doorbell just had to ring at that moment. I was finally through to her and I wasn't going to fuck things up and lose her. Well I was going to fuck her but that was besides the point. I sighed and got up setting Grace on the sofa. The delivery boy was so not getting a tip for being so early. When I checked the peephole, it wasn't the delivery boy. I caught a glimpse of a cut that did not have my own colors on it. I chained the door as quietly as I could and shot a text to Jack to notify him of the trouble at my doorstep. The doorbell rang again and Grace looked over at me and opened her mouth to speak. I put a finger to my lips indicating her to stay silent. Grace stared at me and watched as I moved slowly over to her.

"Noah boy, I know you're in there!" The Scottish accent came through my door and I shook my head taking Grace's hand and headed towards the balcony. Grace paled as she realized I was going to make her climb off my balcony. She had bigger things to worry about, not that I would tell her that though. I dropped down the ladder I had installed when I moved in and climbed down waiting for Grace to get on the ground. I heard my door be kicked in and I pulled Grace under the balcony out of sight. I couldn't believe these assholes had the nerve to show up at my place. I only saw the one member through the peephole but there could have been more. I crashed my hand over Grace's lips to keep her silent keeping my eyes scanning around for movement. I heard his footsteps on my balcony and pulled away from Grace, pressing her against my back. I figured the brute would find the ladder and climb down. If he did I'd be ready for him. I pulled my gun out of the waistband of my jeans and waited.

His boot came into view but he stopped climbing down. Another male voice came from inside my apartment and pulled this one out of his pursuit. I almost sagged with relief as I listened to the man stalk across my balcony and inside the house. I looked over my shoulder at Grace turning slowly towards her. "Come on we're going to make our way to the street. Slowly though and stay hidden." I whispered and took her hand staying along the building.

We made it to the street and I saw Jack and a few other of our club members come hastily up the road from their bikes. Jack pulled his daughter into his arms and looked her over. I had to stop myself from rolling my eyes. Did he seriously think I would allow any danger to come to her? She looked scared to death and I kissed her forehead.

"Go over to the bikes down the road. The prospect is sitting down there he will keep you safe until this is over." I said and pushed on her back to get her moving. Jack looked at me.

"What the fuck happened? How do they know where you live?" He said trying not to yell. I shrugged.

"They could have followed me home tonight or tapped my phone I had ordered pizza for Grace and I." I said. I heard a car coming down the road and saw that it was the pizza I had ordered. I stopped him and handed him the money for the pizza.

"Get the fuck out of here." I said and left the pizza in his car. He took off scared shitless. I probably wouldn't be able to get pizza from there again.

We assessed the situation and figured that there were three men in my place. Jack wanted to send Bullet and Beast before anyone else since they have military experience. I shook my head though.

"No, Jack they were looking for me. Why don't I go in and then have Bullet and Beast follow me." I said. Jack sighed and nodded.

"Alright we will do it that way. Just don't get your fucking head blown off." Jack said and I started walking towards my apartment hiding my gun behind my back. Bullet and Beast followed at a short distance and I stepped inside my apartment. The Scottish was sitting on my sofa and I put my gun on the counter.

"Fancy seeing you here." I said and looked over at him.

"Fancy seeing me here. Boy, you have a debt to be paid. It's time to pay up." He said and I stopped in my tracks looking at him.

"What are you talking about? My debt to you has been more than paid." I said. "You got me out of juvie like 20 years ago. I don't owe you shit." I was getting angry with him.

"You owe me your life boy. And I know how you are going to pay up." He said getting off my sofa.

"Yeah, and what is it you'd like me to do?" I asked.

"I want you to hurt her, like you said you would. Prove your loyalty to me. She's pretty, but you need to stick to whores. Do what you're good at." He had the nerve to chuckle. My fists clenched and I started to walk towards him. A hand stopped me and I looked over at Bullet. I knew I was in deep shit when Jack walked in.

"You have some explaining to do Noah." Jack said and I looked at the Scottish man.

"You're a dead man." I said to him and pulled out of Bullets' hold. The Scottish left and I sighed turning to Jack.

"I'll explain everything Jack. I'm not going to turn on my brothers." I said. Jack looked around then back at me.

"You can explain in church." He said. I'm pretty sure my death certificate was just signed...again

I let them all leave first and grabbed Grace's keys and her bag. It was probably better that we didn't see each other again just in case I was going to be dead in a few hours. I really hoped I had nothing to worry about. The walk to where she stood was short and my brothers were getting on their bikes and Jack leaned against his. Grace ran up to me and wrapped her arms around my neck. I held her for a moment and pulled away.

"Grace...We should talk." I said. She nodded and walked with me back towards my building. Jack and the brothers took off as soon as we were by Grace's car. I sighed and looked at Grace.

"I can't talk about anything that just happened really... But I think you should find someone else to be with... I'm not good enough for you and I may not be around anymore after tonight." I said and handed her, her things. "Your dad will probably have a bullet in me for this but I think it's the right thing." I said and watched her. Confusion was written all over her face and I sighed. I leaned over and kissed her one last time like my life depended on it. I stepped back abruptly ending the kiss and opened her door. "I'll get all your things packed up and bring them to your parents. I'm sorry. I love you." I paused to chance a glance at her. "Bye Grace." I said and watched as she went through the motions of getting in her car and driving away.

GRACE

I drove to my parent's feeling concerned about what would happen to Noah. It was something that actually scared me. The deep concern I had for Noah made me feel things that I know I shouldn't. Especially because it's been such a short time I had been with him. Falling fast and hard in love with Noah was not part of my plan. I wanted to cry and I was sure he just cut things off with me. I needed to not feel anything about this, we were just starting to date, no big deal. I would just have to go find someone else to bother I guess. I looked around my parent's house and decided that I was going to make a huge change. I went to my computer and wrote a long letter to my boss.

The next morning I got ready and I thought I had looked fucking good. I was done with suits and everything else about my life that wasn't actually me. It was time to implicate the change and make it happen. I wasn't going to get fucked over anymore and I wasn't going to watch my world crumble. I am taking charge and making it mine. My leather pants were probably a little too tight but that was alright. My push up bra gave me the cleavage that went perfectly for the low v tank top and vest combo I had paired with my pants. Now I needed my boots. I found them at the back of my closet and pulled them on. It felt great to have them on again. Max…Nope I wasn't going there. I text my dad and asked if he still had the key to my Harley. The message I got back from him made me smile.

Twenty minutes later I was at the clubhouse. My beautiful custom Harley my father built for me with his own two hands sat outside the clubhouse. He had sent it off to be painted right before I was supposed to get it. He had it painted burnt orange. It was such a sight to see I almost cried. My dad came outside when he saw I was outside and handed me the keys to the bike. I smiled at him and threw my arms around him.

"Thank you, daddy." I said and kissed his cheek leaving a smudge of red lipstick on his cheek. I laughed and wiped it off as best I could. My dad smiled and looked at me.

"It's good to have my baby back." My dad said. I noticed movement over his shoulder and saw my sister Mac then Noah coming outside the door.

"Daddy...I know I'm not supposed to but I want to ask. What is going to happen with Noah?" I asked. My dad looked down at me and smiled.

"Sweetheart, he explained everything. It's going to be fine. I promise. I may have to put another bullet in his arm soon but it's going to be alright." He said and kissed my forehead. I couldn't help but smile.

I grabbed my purse from my car and put it in my saddlebag with my folder that was keeping my letter to my boss crisp and flat. Noah faced the clubhouse building and I shook my head pulling my hair back and putting my helmet on. My bike purred and rumbled between my legs. The vibrations were better than my vibrator making it feel fucking great to get back on my bike. I took off to work and felt everything falling back into place.

Once at work I walked straight up to my boss and handed him my letter. He almost dropped his coffee as he looked me over. I can look hot, at least when I want to be. I smiled as I left his office and went to my desk. Work was full of stares and went by fairly quickly. I was relieved when I left the building towards my bike. I pulled my hair back and got my helmet on. The vibrations were welcoming as I let myself get carried away with the open road.

I was so conflicted with my life and what had happened with it, my thoughts took me on their own journey as I rode. When I finally stopped, I was in front of a building that was located in a city about two hours from my current home. The sign in front of the building told me there were apartments for rent. I took a picture of the sign and address so I could call them tomorrow. I needed to uproot everything I had and get away. I didn't know how long I was going to be away but I figured it was time for that change. I could always find a club near by to check in with. As long as they were Devil's Pride associates.

On my way back to the clubhouse I ended up stopping in front of Noah's. It still looked the same and I was actually upset I wouldn't get to try his sex lifestyle. It would have been a great change in that area too. I sighed and continued to the clubhouse to get my car. My bike had a designated spot right inside the boy's garage. My dad was always careful with where it was put. I parked it and walked towards my car. Music was thumping from the clubhouse and I smiled.

A party was probably just getting to full swing by the sounds of it. I remember the first party I ever went to. It was for my twenty-first birthday. My dad made sure the club whores stayed away for most of the night so that I could enjoy it. It was a few of my friends and a bunch of professional drinkers known as family. I had gotten so drunk that night I didn't even remember most of it. My dad told me I had puked a few times and ended up fainting on him. He had put me in a room at the club and slept outside my door until morning to make sure any of the boys weren't out of their drunken minds to try and do something.

I jerked out of my memory when the clubhouse door flew open slamming against the building. I fished my keys out of my purse and stopped when I saw it was Noah. I wanted to talk to him until I saw the famous club whore hanging on his arm. He sat on the picnic table and lit a cigarette not noticing me. I silently thanked god and got in my car. His head jerked up when he heard my door shut. Peyton, the whore, looked right at me and smiled undoing Noah's pants pulling his dick out. I sighed and tried like hell not to get jealous...it wasn't working very well. It took everything I had to pull away once she started sucking him off. A single tear rolled down my cheek as I left the lot. I was right though. I needed to get away.

NOAH

Peyton was sucking on my dick and I barely felt it. I was empty inside knowing the woman I wanted to be with pulled away with my heart. She was my lifeline. Once I told her that we needed to end things I died inside. I was completely in love with someone I had spent a good few years of my life watching grow into a woman. The last time I had seen her when I was sober was when she had turned eighteen. Then I fucked her when she was twenty-two.

I pulled Peyton off my dick, standing up I zipped my jeans. Peyton leaned up kissing my cheek before going inside to suck some more dick. I knew Peyton was clean because Jack makes every barfly get checked regularly. Even after she sucked me off I couldn't get it up. I sighed walking back in the club grabbing my jacket.

"Taking off already Noah?" a familiar, fatherly voice sounded to the left of me. Looking that way I saw him. Scrap was a great brother and also Vice President of the club. He always showed his loyalty to each and every brother. I nodded to him and went back towards the door. Scrap's hand came down on my shoulder.

"Look, brother, I know you've been pounding them. Why don't you stay here for the night so you don't do something stupid." He said and I smiled.

"Nah, brother, you've been the one pounding mine." I laughed. "Do you want a ride home or are you going to crash here?" I asked him. He smiled and looked over at his o'lady.

"She's got me brother." He said and sauntered over to her. I couldn't help but smile. Scrap and Peaches were like something out of a motorcycle fairytale, one that every brother wanted but was too afraid to commit to.

As I pulled up at home I could feel the emptiness eating away at me from the inside out. I had almost wished the Scottish had shown up again so I could beat the fuck out of him. What I wanted to do most of all was get Grace back. I was madly in love with the woman and so was my dick. For once in my god forsaken life, my dick and heart were in sync. I turned on the stereo and listened to Eminem's "Superman", how fitting. The lyrics played over in my head. "I can't be your superman." I said to the empty room. My thoughts were swirling in my mind. All the what if's in my life were on repeat. What if I can't get Grace back? What if she doesn't want me back? What if….What if….What if? Most of my questions revolved around Grace. No matter what I did I couldn't get her out of my head. Maybe working out would help clear my thoughts for a while. I was running out of options to stay busy…especially at two in the morning. I doubt Grace would be….No I need to stop with Grace. She's out of the picture and I'm done. I don't need to try to reinstate anything that I have terminated with her. It was good while it lasted. I just wished I would have gotten her in the playroom for just a while, just shown her a peek of that side of me. With that thought fantasies plagued my mind while I worked out and my dick made a tent out of my sweats.

Nothing had changed with the fantasy and dick tent pole situation. After working out I sighed and pulled my cock out of my sweats. Palming it firmly I started to stroke it while I imagined it was Grace's fine little fingers stroking my dick instead of my own calloused hand. I bet it would feel great and then to feel her lips come around my cock, I moaned and felt my balls tighten and release. I leaned into the couch and grabbed some tissues to clean off my stomach. Fuck this, I needed Grace back . I had never stooped down to jerking myself off. I had an ultimatum, get Grace back or I'd be palming myself until I was fucking over her. I doubted that would be anytime soon. I took a shower and got on my bike.

I pulled up in front of Grace's parent's and looked at the

house. I shouldn't be here but I couldn't pull away. I made my way up to the door and leaned my forehead against it. This woman was seriously going to get me to do something insane. I knelt down and picked her lock getting in easily. I went in quietly and looked around. It was quiet except for Grace's moans coming from her bedroom. This was a bad idea. If she was already fucking someone after we broke it off, I was going to lose my shit. "Oh fuck, Noah." It was so quiet I barely heard it. Was she seriously moaning my name? I walked slowly to her bedroom and peeked inside. It was just Grace. I smiled and leaned against the door frame. Grace was touching herself while asleep. My name sounded like heaven on her lips. I don't know what came over me but next thing I knew, my clothes were off. I got in her bed and pulled her hand out from between her legs and sucked on her fingers. Grace's eyes fluttered open and I pulled her fingers out of my mouth and smiled at her.

"Noah?" her voice was gravelly with sleep and it only turned me on more than I already was.

I leaned down and kissed her and pulled her close to me. Grace moaned into my mouth and I smiled sliding my hand into her panties, rubbing my palm against her pussy lips. Grace's fingers dug into my shoulders and her tongue danced with mine. Inserting two fingers inside her I massaged her walls. Her hand slid down my torso and she palmed my cock making it twitch. A moan escaped my throat. She smiled against my lips making my heart swell. I leaned into her and kissed her with everything I had in me.

Waking the next morning with Grace tangled around me. I smiled and pried her off me and got up getting dressed. She looked peaceful and sated. I grabbed my keys leaving Grace in bed. The sun was just coming out of its slumber. I walked over to my bike and saw a piece of paper sticking out from under my seat. I pulled it out and slipped it in my pocket. I probably just started something with Grace I never should have but I hoped it would be worth it in the end. I got on my bike and made my way to the clubhouse.

GRACE

I awoke tangled in my bedsheets. My dream was amazing, three orgasms even from the Noah from my imagination was worth it. I smiled and stretched feeling sore in my nether regions. I froze mid-stretch and sat up. I had dreamed everything last night hadn't I? I got up and showered. Throwing on skinny jeans and a tee I went out to my car and stopped dead in my tracks. My beautiful black as my soul Chevelle had red paint thrown all over it, three of the four tires were slashed and I fell to my knees in front of it. The car was my baby, my father and I had built her from the ground up. He had given it to me when I was sixteen. I called my dad and turned over so I was sitting on my ass leaning against the grille of my car.

My dad pulled up with the whole club behind him, even the prospect who was driving the tow truck. I was devastated that something had happened to my car. Noah was the first off his bike and over to me.

"Are you okay?" He asked helping me off the ground. I nodded and looked over at my car. My dad came over and hugged me.

"Hey baby girl... We'll fix her don't worry." He said. I nodded and looked over at Noah.

"What time did you leave this morning?" I asked him. My dad went from loving and compassionate to cold hearted in about the two seconds before going over to Noah and cold cocking him. I heard a crunch and Noah's nose was gushing blood.

"Daddy!" I yelled going over to Noah. My dad went over to the prospect and helped load my car up.

"Are you okay Noah?" I asked. Noah pulled his shirt off and

held it against his nose.

"I'm fine. Why do you want to know when I left?" He asked.

"Was my car like that when you left asshole?" I asked. Noah smiled shaking his head.

"No Grace your car wasn't like that." He said.

"So what time did you leave Noah? There are surveillance cameras around the house." I said.

"Seven." It was all I needed and I went inside to the computer. Searching the footage was going to take time but I needed to know who did this to my car. I'd go crazy if I didn't find out.

At eight-thirty in the morning a car I had recognized came onto the screen. I watched as Peyton got out of her car and grabbed a bucket of paint pouring it all over my car. A man was with her and he was the one who slashed my tires. I watched as they got back in the car and drove away. I couldn't go to the police because that would just bring heat for my dad. I stood up and looked at Noah.

"I would like a ride please." I said grabbing my jacket. Noah took my hand going to his bike.

At the clubhouse, I could hear my dad throwing things in the garage and swearing. I sighed and got off Noah's bike. Beast came out and hugged me.

"Doll, don't go in there. You'll be going off just as much as your father." He said. I looked at him questioningly.

"What the fuck are you talking about?" I asked. Beast looked at Noah and then leaned his head back sighing.

"Your bike..." I took off running for the garage and saw my bike was on the ground and smashed into pieces. I grabbed the nearest thing, which happened to be a ratchet. Chucking it across the room putting a dent in the wall. I looked around the garage pissed off as all hell. One of the sludge hammers had red paint on the handle, the same shade of red that was all over my car. I smiled and walked over to the clubhouse. Noah was following me around as I blew off steam. But the heat kept on coming. If my life was a cartoon, I'd be red faced and steam coming out of my ears.

Inside the clubhouse, my smile grew even bigger as I saw Peyton coming into the main area from the hallway.

"Hey Peyton. I think Beast needs you for something." I said. Peyton looked at me raising her eyebrow. She walked out of the club house. I followed her. My mind calm knowing what I was going to do.

"Oh, hey Peyton." I yelled. My face went completely stoic. Peyton turned around and looked at me.

"What, Princess." She sneered. I stopped in front of her face to face, tit to tit and lashed my hand out grabbing her throat and pushing her against the six-foot wooden fence encasing the clubhouse lot. My fingers squeezed around her thin neck and my other hand reeled back punching her across her right cheek. Peyton screamed when I let go of her throat and let her drop in a crumpled heap to the ground.

"You crazy bitch!" Peyton yelled hoarsely and I knelt down in front of her getting very close to her ear.

"If I see you touch my shit again…you'll see crazy…and my shit includes Noah. All of him. You ever suck him off in front of me or if I even hear of you touching him, I will find you and I will kill you." I said standing up walking towards the clubhouse.

NOAH

Grace just fucking punched Peyton. I could already see her eye swelling and turning black. The bruising was coming on quickly telling everyone Grace had broken Peyton's cheek bone. It was fucking glorious though. It made me want to whip my dick out and palm it, all because I saw Grace being independent. I went inside the club after her. I walked down the hall a ways before her hand grabbed my arm and she pulled me into my room. Her lips smashed into mine and my hands went to her ass picking her up.

"Noah, fuck me. Please." She begged. My inner dominant was coming out and I wanted to please her as best I could but with something new.

"Do you have any idea how much you begging turns me on?" I asked sucking on her lip pressing her against the wall. Her hands were working on my zipper and I groaned. "Baby, I want to do something new with you." I nipped her ear and put her down. She looked up at me confused. I walked over to the dresser finding a makeshift blindfold. "Lay down baby. I'm going to take care of you." I said. She did as I asked and I grabbed a toy out of my dresser. Strutting over to her I pulled my shirt off to use to tie her hands to the headboard. After securing her hands I put the blindfold over her eyes and got off the bed.

"Noah?" she barely whispered. I could hear the fear seeping into her voice.

"Don't worry baby. I'll take care of you." I said and went to the kitchen grabbing a glass of ice. I smiled and set the anal beads in the ice. Going back in the room I locked the door and set the glass on the nightstand. Taking an ice cube from the glass I put it in my mouth and kissed her letting it slide between my lips and in between hers. She smiled and sucked on the ice as I undressed her. I grabbed another cube and spread her legs. I ran my finger along her core while I sucked on the cube to make it a little smaller. I blew cold air onto her crease and she squirmed. I stuck the ice cube out a bit from my lips and slid it against her inner thigh going towards her core. I stopped just before touching her pussy and repeated my actions to her other thigh. Grace moaned and started to twist against the hold on her wrists. I put a hand on her stomach keeping her still. My lips and the ice cube rubbed against her pussy making their way slowly to her clit. Her moan echoed in my ears and I started feeling as if I would combust if I didn't get inside her soon. I pulled away taking the cube out of my mouth.

"Babe do you still have ice in your mouth?" I asked. She pushed the ice out holding it with just her lips. I smiled and pulled it out of her mouth.

"I'm going to need to you suck on something." She smiled making me chuckle. "No, not my cock baby." I whispered pulling the beads from the melting ice.

"Open your mouth." I said. She complied, and I was getting slammed with fantasies of her being my submissive in my playroom. I inserted the beads into her mouth and watched as she started to suck on the silver balls. I sucked on my own fingers for a minute or so and grabbed another ice cube. With Grace so open and exposed to me I was going to have fun for a while. I pressed the ice cube against her clit and she jerked her hips off the bed. I smiled and swirled it around her clit. Using my fingers to play with her ass getting it ready for the beads. Grace's moan sounded like heaven to me.

Keeping up with fingering her ass, I spit out the ice cube hearing it hop across the wooden floor. I licked my lips and kissed her pussy, sucking her clit between my lips. The coldness of her clit to the heat of my mouth had to have felt amazing for her. Grace's hips bucked off the mattress and she tried to ride my face. She had to be getting close. I inserted my second finger into her ass and massaged her walls apart. While using my other hand to reach up and caress her breast, rolling her nipple between my thumb and forefinger. She pressed her breast into my hand and my tongue began its assault on her pussy. Her juices tasted sweet and I couldn't get enough of them in my mouth. I kept my fingers in her ass stretching her and reached up plucking the anal beads from her mouth.

"Bend your knees Grace." I said and kissed her stomach. I pulled my fingers from inside her and started to insert the beads. Grace's knees fell together and I had to separate them.

"Keep your knees apart sweetheart." I said and licked my tongue up her pussy lips. Pushing between her lips I lapped at her core, keeping her focus on my tongue and not on the beads going in her ass. Once the last ball was inserted I made a trail of kisses up her torso.

"Keep them inside you or I'll keep teasing you." I said finally reaching her lips and kissing her.

She pulled on her restraints and I smiled kissing her neck. My hands went to her hips and rubbed circles with my thumbs. She moaned and started to rub her pussy against the bulge in my jeans.

"Oh baby." I moaned "Does that feel good?" my voice barely a whisper. Grace whimpered as I stepped back grabbing her ankles and flipping her on her stomach. My hand made contact with her ass cheek and I watched as her toes curled. Her fingers curled around my comforter.

"Noah." She whimpered. I pulled my pants down.

"Get on your knees." I demanded and watched as her pussy was revealed to me once more. I tore open a condom and rolled it on. I kneaded her ass cheeks and pushed my cock forward just letting the tip rub against her lips. She quivered beneath me with anticipation. I smiled smacking her ass a little harder than before and impaled her with my hard cock.

"Oh, Fuck, Noah!" She screamed. I pulled out and ran my thumb down her pussy lips. She pushed her ass towards me lowering her chest on the bed.

"Noah, please take me." She was begging again and my cock twitched hardening more, if that was even possible. Pushing my cock inside her feeling her walls press against my dick. I moaned letting my head roll back. I pulled back repeating my actions while Grace screamed my name each time. I thrust into her to the hilt and reached up untying her hands from the bed and pulled her back against my chest. I kissed her shoulder and massaged her wrists. I slid my hands up her arms gently caressing her and loving her every curve. My hand went to her clit and I pressed my fingers against it. Her hands gripped my forearms as I lifted her. She ground her hips into mine and I pulled mine back pulling my cock completely out. The whimper that came out of her throat made me thrust my cock back inside her heat turning her moan into a guttural sound. Something animalistic. I took a step off the bed and pulled her back making my cock go deep inside her pussy. Her head fell against my shoulder and I wanted to keep her on my cock forever.

I pulled out of Grace and sat on the edge of the bed. I grabbed her hips and pulled her forward to me. Her perfect tits were in my face giving me access to her nipples. Pulling one into my mouth I spread her legs farther apart and sat her on my thighs.

"I want you to put me back inside you, without taking the blindfold off." She palmed my cock immediately and got my cock inside her on the first try.

"Ride me Grace." I said and wrapped my arms around her inserting a finger in the ring of the anal beads playing with them. She groaned leaning back starting to grind her hips on my cock. Her pussy felt damn good and I could feel my balls tighten. I pressed my thumb against her clit rubbing the nub in circles. Her walls started contracting around my dick and I lifted her and started pounding relentlessly into her. I dropped her down on my legs and cock as her orgasm exploded throughout her. My hand smacked her ass and I pulled the anal beads out putting them back in the glass. Her pussy milked my dick as I laid her on her back and pulled the blindfold up. "How was that for an orgasm?" I asked. She mewled at me as I pulled my dick from her pussy. Grace had a lazy grin on her face and I leaned down to kiss her. Her eyes searched mine for a moment afterwards.

"You didn't finish, did you?" She asked. I smiled and shook my head.

"I want to look in your eyes as I finish inside of you baby." I said. She leaned up kissing me and palmed my dick pulling me back to her pussy. I knew it wouldn't take me long with her. Thrusting a few times, I looked down at Grace. Her hands were pushing against my chest.

"I want to ride you until you get off baby." The words left her lips and I could have exploded right there. Laying on my back taking her with me, I watched as her tits bounced while she rode me.

"Oh, fuck, Grace I'm going to come soon and I can't fucking wait." I said, my voice was strained as my balls tightened. Grace surprised me by jumping off my cock and pulling the condom off. Her lips came around the tip of my dick and I couldn't hold it any longer. I thrust my dick deep in her mouth and emptied my seed down her throat. I moaned as she sat there playing with my balls and hallowing out her cheeks sucking on my cock. This broad was my dream come true and with her father's permission I was going to make her mine, legally. I had already claimed her to the club. That little break up we had was just a disagreement. There was no getting rid of an ol'lady once claimed in front of the club.

GRACE

I popped Noah's cock out of my mouth like a lollipop and licked my lips swallowing everything he emptied into my mouth. He was smiling at me. Straddling him once again, I leaned over and kissed him. He held me against him before turning us so we laid down on the bed together.

"I really needed that...Thank you." I said looking into his eyes. His eyes looked as if they were seeing my soul rather than the surface of myself. I felt bared to him and it felt right. There was nothing this man could do that would make me run from him. He was mine and sometimes men needed to be protected by their queen. Noah leaned over and kissed me pulling the blanket over us. I smiled getting close to him. Whoever I had heard 'naked cuddles are the best cuddles' from, knew the damn truth. We laid there in silence for a while and I traced circles around his nipple.

"Noah?" He looked down at me. "Why did my father hit you?" I asked. He rolled onto his side and moved down so we were eye to eye.

"He hit me because I told him we weren't together anymore." He said. I stared at him.

"Well you told me that too and you came to my bed. Which I still have no idea how you got inside my parent's house." I said. He smiled brushing his fingers over my hair, petting me.

"I picked the lock." He said.

"I should have known you would be capable of something like that." I said. He wrapped his arms around me and kissed my forehead.

A knock sounded on the door and Noah sighed. He got up pulling his pants on and opened the door.

"Oh, good you guys are quiet." I heard Bullet say. Noah smiled and looked back at me.

"I'll be back." he said and left the room. I got up getting dressed and opened the door. Stepping out into the hallway I looked both ways and made my way to the kitchen. I was starved after that excitement. Opening the fridge seeing a ton of food inside made my stomach growl. I pulled out a bowl that had fruit in it and set the bowl on the counter, digging in with a fork. Peaches came in with a grin.

"Hey sugar. Enjoying the fruit for that party?" She said chuckling. I looked down at the bowl and curled my lips into a smile.

"Whoops." I said. Peaches just laughed.

"It's alright sugar. You don't eat enough anyways." She sat by me. Her eyes scrutinizing me.

"I eat enough. I promise." I said putting the lid back on the bowl. Peaches smiled. Her eyes never leaving me as I put the bowl in the fridge. I turned back around.

"What?" I asked.

"You just look different." She commented resting her chin on the palm of her hand. I raised my eyebrow at her.

"Different how?" I asked.

"Just...different dear." She said and got off the chair. Noah came around the corner still shirtless. I almost drooled at the sight of him. Peaches laughed and patted my shoulder. "Well that explains everything." She said going to the fridge emptying it of the copious amounts of food. Noah came around the bar wrapping his arms around my waist.

"So, I just got yelled at for making you scream so loud everyone had to leave the clubhouse. But even outside they could hear you." He whispered in my ear. His lips curled up with a smile. I laughed turning bright cherry red. I hid my face in his chest and he laughed.

"Noah! It's not funny!" I yelled into his chest while pulling my hands up to cover my face.

"Grace, you are just so damn adorable." He pushed his fingers in my hair tugging on it, tilting my head up, I smiled. He leaned down and pressed his lips to mine, making the blush run cold. Would I ever get enough of this man? My hands slid up around his neck, pressing his body against mine.

"I'm going to go and get dressed and then I think we should go for a ride." He said. I nodded and looked down at my clothes.

"We should stop at my parent's so I can change." I said. He smiled and nodded.

"I'll be back sweetheart." He said and walked down the hall. Peaches came and put her arm around me.

"Oh babe, you have got it bad. He's got it bad too." I looked over at her.

"What do you mean?" I asked.

"Well maybe it's the honeymoon phase of your relationship but that boy's in love with you." She said and walked back towards the fridge. I smiled and nibbled on my nail.

Mac came into the clubhouse with Bullet trailing behind her. Mac was yelling something about him being an asshole. Bullet was defending himself against whatever she was accusing him of. Our father came storming in from the hallway. "Now what the fuck is going on?"

"Mac and Bullet are arguing." I said.

"I'm starting to feel like a damned referee with both my fucking daughters messing with my brothers." He hollered shaking his head before going back down towards the office. I blushed and grinned up at Noah.

Noah and I were at my parent's shortly after leaving the clubhouse. I went inside looking in my closet. I had no idea what I should change into. An arm wrapped around my waist and I smiled. Their other arm came around my neck and pressed in. My hands clawed at their arm and I screamed.

"Listen closely." It was that Scottish voice. The man got close to my ear and pulled me against him.

"You are going to help me get Noah." He said and his breath on my neck made me nauseous. His hand went under my waistband of my pants and I felt his calloused hands move my underwear to the side rubbing my clit. My hands went to his wrist trying to pull his hand out.

"Please stop!" I was screaming, tears were running down my face. I wouldn't let this happen to me. One of his fingers penetrated my core and I tried to pull away but he was too strong.

"You're going to help me or I will be back to taste you." He said pulling his finger out and releasing me. I leaned against my closet door and watched as he sucked on the finger that was inside of me. He winked at me and disappeared. I slid onto the floor and cried into my palms. That was the worst thing to happen to me. I heard the door open and close and footsteps coming towards my bedroom.

"Grace?" Noah yelled. I sobbed as I saw him come in my bedroom. I jumped up to him and buried myself into his chest. He held me stroking my hair.

"Baby, what's wrong?" he asked. I looked at him and tried to calm down. He sat me on the bed and pulled out his phone.

I grabbed his hand and stopped him from calling anyone. Finally calm enough, I told him what had happened. He pulled me close to him and held me.

"I have to call and tell your dad. But I promise you I will be personally putting a bullet in his head." He said and kissed me. I kissed him back with all I had. He brushed hair out of my face and dialed my dad. My dad was going to blow a gasket just for that man coming into his house, let alone violating me. I quickly changed into something that would be suitable to ride in. Noah walked out into the living room to talk to my father. I sat on my bed again wanting to cry. I needed to suck it up and try and forget it ever happened. Ignorance an o'lady's best friend.

My dad showed up not too long after Noah came back in my room. He came in frantically looking around for me. Noah stepped out of the way and let him see me. He came and wrapped his arms around me.

"Are you alright?" He asked and held me at arm's length.

"I'm okay, dad." I said. I stood up and rubbed my hands on my jeans.

"The man...he wants me to help bring him Noah. I don't know why...he said if I didn't help; he'd come back to taste me." I said. Noah looked at me and leaned against the wall.

"You never told me that." Noah said.

"I know I figured you would be hard on yourself for him even touching me, let alone fingering me." I said.

"HE WHAT!" My dad screamed and grabbed my arms.

"He fingered you and no one told me until now?!" He yelled at me. I was honestly scared and my eyes filled up with unshed tears.

My heart was racing. This was the first time I was ever scared of my father. The anger was radiating off him and my knees started trembling. My dad pulled me against him and rubbed my back. I could feel the familiar sensations coming for me. Between the fear of my dad and the fear of the man's threats I wasn't going to keep it at bay. "My baby. I'm so sorry." My dad hid his face in my neck and I wrapped my arms around him. He was shaking and noises were coming from him. I moved my hand to tell the guys to leave the room. They filed out and I held onto my dad.

"It's okay daddy, I'm okay." He pulled back and looked at me, tears were streaming down his face.

"I love you baby girl. If anything happened to you or your sister... I don't know what I would do. Your mother already hates me and I couldn't stand losing you too." He said. "

"Did momma leave you daddy?" I asked. He looked at me and I saw it all in his eyes. He lost my mom. How could she just leave the love of her life? I sighed and kissed his cheek.

"It's okay daddy." I said and wiped his tears away. I couldn't believe what was happening. He loved my mother and I know she loved him. He calmed down as well as he could and left to face the men in his living room.

"We are going to find this fucker and end him." My dad was saying. I stepped out into the hallway and leaned against the wall.

"Church ASAP. Once everyone is there we will convene." He said and went towards the door.

"Graciebell I'll see you later." He yelled down the hall.

"Bye daddy!" I yelled coming out into the hallway. Noah came over to me and kissed me lightly.

"After church, we will go on that ride and figure out what to do." He said. I smiled slightly and nodded.

"Can't wait. I need to tell you something I've been thinking about when you get back to me." I said and watched him leave my childhood home.

NOAH

Church was a mess. Everyone was talking over everyone else and you couldn't understand anything for most of the time. "Everyone shut up!" Jack bellowed. The silence that followed was almost more deafening than the chatter of twenty rowdy men drinking whiskey. "The Scottish is going to meet his maker. I'm done with this bullshit. It's one thing to attack a brother…" Jack looked at me. "It's a completely different thing to attack a family member, especially my daughter." He said. All members nodding their agreement. "This needs to be handled and we are going to handle it now. I think we should make him think that my daughter is helping him get Noah. That way she doesn't get hurt anymore and if he tries anything, I'll kill him." He continued. "So, what's our plan?" he said.

"I think we should do exactly as you said boss." Bullet said.

"Wait though. That's putting Grace in danger. I don't think we should do that." I said.

"Noah, if we don't use her as an asset we're fucked then and she gets hurt. You heard what he told her. If she doesn't get him you then he's going to taste her. He already fucking fingered her." Beast interjected. "Besides she'll be the most protected woman ever. Because if she gets hurt"

"You'll all meet our maker." Jack cut Beast off. He was serious. It was as if something had seriously taken over Jack. His hate and hunger for war fueling the devil inside him. If we didn't get this mess under control all hell would break loose. And that hell…was Jack.

"Why don't we just hand me over and leave her out of it?" I asked with a sigh. Bullet looked over at me with a look of frustration.

"Would he believe it if you just went and she didn't deliver you? I know I sure as hell wouldn't." He reasoned. I could see his point. And with knowing Ralph for years, I knew he wouldn't just accept me. Once he had a woman, he would have her fully and she would become his pet until he was done with her. He threw women away like trash with a nice long slice of the jugular then wrapped in big black garbage bags to be left on the side of the road outside of town. Rubbing my hands over my head. I knew I had to look crazed.

"No there's no fucking way he'd just take it. He's violated her and with his track record…He won't stop until he's had her fully." My back leaned into the chair before looking down at the table.

"So, we stick with Grace delivering you. And this is how it will happen. Noah, you will have to walk Grace through all of this. We don't want her messing this up. She's going to find out where she needs to meet with Ralph. Then she will drive with you to where he decides to meet. And after that someone will get her out of there." That was the stupidest, most vague, plan I had ever heard of. There were no details. No concrete ideas. How the hell were we getting her out of there? What the fuck were they going to do if something happened to her besides going in guns blazing? I leaned my head back looking towards the ceiling sending out a silent prayer. They may be my brothers and I knew they would have my back but I'll be damned if they could come up with a decent plan. They went into details as much as possible. The plan was to have Grace bring me to Ralph and they were thinking they would get her out. Then infiltrate the meeting spot taking Ralph's team out.

The gavel hit the table and Jack was the first one to get up leaving the room. I stayed back and sat in my chair thinking over the plan that we had discussed. Grace was going to tell the man that he could have me and then everyone would move in, mainly to get Grace out of the way, then come save my ass. I didn't like using Grace and of course they left me to tell her all about this shit ass plan. Bullet came back in the room and sat across from me.

"You okay there Noah?" he asked.

"I don't like using Grace as bait for this. It's reckless." I said getting more than upset. The anger reaping its way through my body.

"Noah, I think you are in love with the girl." He said. I rubbed my lip with my forefinger. I stood up and smacked my palm on the table. I had already proclaimed my love for her in front of everyone.

"I'm going to get my shit done. Later, brother." I said and left the room. I went to my bike and swung my leg over. I had to let Grace in on the plan and have her turn me over to the stupid ass Scottish, Ralph.

I arrived at Grace's and sighed. I really hated this idea of using her as bait…but I guess we weren't really using her as bait. We were using me as bait. I went up to her door and knocked on her door. She opened the door and was in a towel and I felt my dick twitch. I needed to stay calm and not get horny like some fourteen-year-old boy.

"Hey, I need to talk to you. But you should get dressed first." I said.

"Why?" she asked. I stepped inside her place, closing the door as she dropped her towel. The not getting horny like a fourteen-year-old boy…yeah It wasn't working. I was hard as rock before I even got inside the door. I closed her door before pulling her close and kissing her. She wrapped her arms around me pressing her breasts against my chest.

"Now you're dressed." I said. She laughed and pulled back walking towards her room. I watched her naked ass until she rounded the corner. I followed her and smiled as I saw her shirt get pulled down over her head.

"The club has a plan and it's not one that I enjoy. They all think you should turn me in to the Scottish, but I know he won't really let you go but they are planning on saving you and me." I said. Grace looked at me and sat down on her bed.

"Just like that? They want me to turn you in and just wait?"

she said. I nodded.

"Alright. When do I turn you in?" she asked.

"Well that I don't know entirely. They wanted me to get you on board with it first before we figured out all the details." I said. She got up and kissed me.

"I have faith in the club that we will be saved and then maybe we could actually have a relationship." She said. I looked at her.

"You actually want to have a relationship with me?" I asked. She nodded throwing her arms around me kissing me.

"Besides the anal beads were fun. And I'd really like more of that." Well just call me a fourteen-year-old boy.

With Grace on board with everything we could set the plan in motion. And maybe get some more details in the fucking plan. Then we would just have to hope that the plan could be executed smoothly. Grace and I went back to the clubhouse to talk things over with everyone and I had a big question to ask her father. I was a bucket of nerves and couldn't seem to calm down.

"Noah! My office now!" Jack yelled as soon as I walked in. Great, then I could just get the big question over with, maybe... I went into his office and he sat behind the desk.

"Everything okay with the plan? I heard you didn't really like the idea." He said.

"Yeah, I don't really like the idea but Grace and I both have faith in the club and my brothers." I said. His nod told me that he understood where I came from. Even though he wasn't going to agree with me. "He will try and kill her though. It won't be just me that he will try and off. He will go after Grace and I can't allow that and if he doesn't try and kill her he will probably make her his for the rest of her life." I said. Jack stood up.

"Well I expect you won't let that happen. Since you love her and made her your ol'lady. Yes I know you told me that it was over but you claimed her. You know for a fact that once you claim a woman she's yours until the day you die. You'll take care of her or I'll leave you to Ralph." He said. I sighed before nodding my acknowledgement.

"Yes." I stood up and looked him in the eye. "I want to make your daughter, not only my ol'lady but, my wife, if you'll let me." I said. My heart was pounding as I waited for an answer. He stared at me and I couldn't back down. My nerves were destroyed by the time he answered. When his smile came relief flooded through me and he held out his hand.

"Welcome to the family brother." He congratulated. I smiled physically showing my relief.

"You know for a while there I was really fucking nervous about asking you." I said.

"As you should be, she's one of my babies." Jack said leaving the room. I took a deep breath before going in the hallway. Grace stood a few feet from me. If I hadn't seen her when I came out the door, hell I hadn't even seen her I had sensed her, I would have collided with her.

"Everything okay?" she asked.

"Yeah everything's good." I said with a smile before pulling her into my arms.

"Let's go get the details down of what they want us to do exactly." I said. She nodded then kissed my cheek. Turning around she walked in front of me out into the main room. My eyes drifted down to her ass and I smiled. If she said yes, that ass was going to be mine, for as long as we both shall live.

"Noah!" Jack bellowed. My head jerked up and I looked at him. He narrowed his eyes at me and I smiled a little and looked at the wall. The smile plastered on my lips. I could see Jack shaking his head out of the corner of my eye. Grace turned and looked at me. I smiled at her and leaned to her ear. "Your father, uh, caught me staring at your perfectly curved ass." I said swiping my hand over her ass. She smiled up at me as we went and sat down at a table.

Everything was gone over in detail and decided on when and where we would send Grace and I in. That is if the jackass Scottish would let us pick where the fuck we would meet.

The club would barge in after the situation is assessed and I gave them the signal to let them know what they were up against. It was mission critical to get Grace out of there safely. As soon as the signal was given Grace had to run as far as possible, run until she couldn't run any longer. Hopefully she'd make it into the arms of someone waiting for her on the other side. We all stood up and everyone got ready for an epic barbeque and some cake. I hung back watching the club file out before either Grace or I stood up. Her hand was linked in mine, my eyes drifting down to where our hands intertwined. The only thought I could conjure up had me sweating in nerves. I wanted to make her mine, but I wasn't sure if this was the right time. I visualized a ring being on Grace's finger after her accepting and everything seeming to fade away except her and I. We had to make it out of this shit I had gotten us in and then I would be making the leap I was desperate to make. As soon as this was over, I'd ask her.

The food was fantastic and the cake was even better. It felt like a huge family get together. Now I just had to get my woman home and hopefully make her scream my name a hundred times. Grace walked over to me with a beer in each hand and I smiled all while my dick got hard. She handed me my beer and I pulled her into my lap.

"Hey baby." I said a little drunk and kissed her neck. She smiled and turned to me.

"I think we should get out of here so you can scream my name over, and over, and over again." I said smiling. Grace leaned over and kissed me. I kept kissing her and leaned forward putting our beers on the table and turning her more so she was straddling me. I felt her heat through her jeans and wanted to take her right there. I couldn't wait to get her home. Maybe we won't go home, maybe we will just go in my room at the clubhouse. Grace ran her fingers through my hair and I kept my hands on her hips grinding her down on my crotch. She moaned and I pulled her even closer to me. Bullet came up to us and tapped me on the shoulder.

"No offense but I'm pretty sure Jerk-off…is ya know…gonna jerk off to this pretty soon and Jack is getting kind of pissed about the show you guys are giving us all." He said. I smiled and got up taking Grace with me. Grace stood up and swayed a little bit.

"I think we both are a little drunk." I said holding her against me. "We should probably get the prospect to drive us home." I said. Grace smiled and nodded. "Unless you want to just stay here and we could get to everything sooner." I said and wiggled my eyebrows at her. She giggled and held onto my biceps.

"I think we should go home because I have to go to my last day of work tomorrow." She said. Last day? When did she quit and why? I smiled calling over the prospect.

"Hey Prospect!" I yelled. Twinkle came over to us leaving the girl he was talking to behind. The look of disappointment on his face was great but I had other plans than to gloat.

"What's up Noah?" he asked looking between Grace and myself.

"I need a ride, we need a ride. My woman and I. I need to get her naked but shh don't tell her daddy." I said slapping his shoulder. Grace laughed and went over to her dad. I watched her and smiled. I didn't care to get her naked anymore. I just wanted to keep her by my side, always and forever. Like the princess in a fairy tale.

GRACE

I pulled the blankets up to my chin and smiled as arms came around me. I looked over at Noah and ran my fingers up his chest. Noah groaned in his sleep and I giggled. His eyes opened his hand splayed out across my naked ass. I leaned my head against his chest and finally felt it pounding.

"Oh my god." I moaned.

"What baby?" Noah asked.

"My head hurts. What all did we drink?" I asked.

"You know, I'm not even sure." Noah chuckled.

"I have to go to work soon. I should probably get up." I said and rolled over to sit up. Noah's arms pulled me against him and back down on the bed. I giggled as he got on top of me kissing my lips.

"Quickie before work?" He asked. I laughed looking at the clock.

"I can't I have to get up like now to shower and get ready." I said and pushed him off me.

"How about in the shower?" He asked. Smiling I went into the bathroom starting the shower.

I came out and got dressed while Noah wasn't in the bedroom. He came and leaned on the door frame as I pulled my hair out of my towel. He had a smirk on his face and I looked over at him.

"What?" I asked.

"Nothing, just thinking." He said. I smiled and walked over to him.

"What about?" I asked. He leaned down and kissed me.

"Just everything sweetheart. I have to run to the clubhouse after I drop you off at work." He said. I nodded and went to finish getting ready.

The ride was over too quickly for my liking. Noah pulled his helmet off to give me a kiss goodbye and a few moments later I was facing my last day of work. My boss gave me a farewell present and told me that if I ever needed to come back I'd have a job. It was the nicest thing a boss had ever done for me and I was very grateful for the offer. He even handed me my bonus check that every employee gets at the end of the year. I went outside and waited for Noah to pick me up. I waited and waited and waited. Finally I called him. The phone rang but I got nothing on the other end. Maybe he was already on his way here. I went inside and sat on a bench that was facing the doors. I looked up after a while seeing Beast coming in the building. Where was Noah? I got up meeting him by the doors.

"Where's Noah?" I asked. Beast looked conflicted and sighed rubbing the back of his neck. Beast had been my best friend at the club for as long as I could remember. And I was the only one that could call him his real name, Cody.

"Shit Grace. He went into the plan without you. He doesn't want you involved in any way." He said. "Don't worry though I get to sit with you and hang out like old times. We can get a movie or play some video games. Besides Black ops three is coming out soon and I know you like the Seattle Seahawks, one of the players is going to be in the game." I smiled and shook my head.

"I'm going to be worried about Noah mostly. I won't have my A game." I said. Beast smiled.

"Come on we gotta get you some clothes from your place and we are going to the clubhouse. Peaches will be there too and she's making roast for dinner for us." Beast said and wrapped his arm around my shoulders guiding me to his car.

"Noah wouldn't let me take the bike, since he claimed your ass to us all." He said. I looked up at him. "He claimed me to all of you?" I asked. Beast nodded and opened the door of his car for me.

"You know I always thought you were a truck man." I said

and got in.

"I'll get a truck eventually. Just used to the car and don't want to let her go yet. She's my ol'lady until further notice." Beast said laughing. I shook my head and closed the door.

Beast stopped at my parent's and I went inside. He followed me in and rummaged through the fridge for some food. My bedroom was trashed when I went in. Underwear and clothing were strewn out over my bed and floor. Most of the items were ripped and torn.

"Cody!" I yelled. He came running in my room. I looked at my closet and saw I had nothing left for clothing besides what was on my back.

"Guess we can leave…I have no clothes." I said. Beast sighed letting my dad know what had happened through text and we took off for the clubhouse.

"I'll take you to get new clothes after I hear from Jack." Cody said. I nodded and sat out in the main room of the club.

All clothing shops besides Walmart had closed by the time we heard anything from my father. Beast apologized a thousand times but there was nothing he could do. He offered to give me his shirt but I knew Noah wouldn't like that one too much. I ended up in Noah's room where I found a shirt and some boxers of his. I pulled them on and went back out to the main area. Beast was still there and he had hooked up the PlayStation for us, just needed food before we began anything. Making a plate of roast and potatoes, Peaches left us. I sat and ate it halfway through I had to stop eating for fear of barfing everywhere. Beast had started playing the game on his own after scarfing down two plates of food. Sighing I leaned on Beast. He looked over at me which got him killed on the game.

"You don't look so good doll." He said and I nodded.

"I don't feel well either. I think I'm going to chill in the bathroom for a bit maybe some water on the face will help." I said getting up. I swayed on my feet. Beast stood up holding onto my hips keeping me steady. "I'm okay." I said and made my way to the bathroom.

For a few minutes my stomach just churned and rolled. I tried the sticking your fingers in your mouth trick that I was told worked but it didn't. I got off the floor and washed my face and hands patting them dry, going back out to sit on the couch.

"Hey, you alright?" Cody asked.

"Yeah I think it might just be stress of everything." I said nodding.

"Yeah wish I could just throw it all up sometimes too." He said laughing. I smiled and curled my knees up to my chest.

"Well I'm going to have to go shopping tomorrow." I said and looked at him. He groaned and fell back on the couch handing me a water bottle.

"Thanks." I said. "Maybe Noah will be home and he can take you. Like the good little boyfriend." Cody said. I laughed and hit his arm playfully. He smiled and rested his temple on his fist.

"It's good to have you back sweetheart. You know that guy you were with...Your dad didn't want to see it all but... just....fuck. Grace, we were all worried about you. You know you always have a family here and that the club has your back." He said. I nodded as the tears started to come. Memories of Max flooded my mind and Beast wrapped his arms around me pulling me to him. It was the memories of why I was scared of Max and his abuse, the pain I went through, all of it came back as a storm and I cried into Beast...and he just held me. His hand stroked my back until I calmed down.

"Sorry." I croaked. He shook his head wiping my tears.

"Don't ever be sorry. Embrace it be strong Grace." He said.

"It's hard sometimes. I can in front of people but it always breaks me down at night." I sighed and looked at him. "My dreams get to me, he gets to me in my dreams, that's where I fall apart." I said and slouched into the couch.

"Oh doll. It's okay. I'd offer to sleep with you but uh... Noah.." He said. I smiled sadly.

"I'm aware you can't technically touch me in anyway because Noah claimed me." I said. He nodded and grabbed my hand.

"But I'm still here for you babe." He said. I smiled.

The video games were great and reminded me of what exactly I'm missing from my life. I don't have any interaction with other people I used to. I need to find stability and also grow close to people I love, not just Noah. Cody and I kept talking throughout the night and I was grateful he was there to sit with me. It was after three in the morning when we heard from my father again. He looked upset when he hung up the phone and I wasn't sure if I wanted to find out why. I was scared out of my mind that something had happened to Noah. Cody looked at me and I had to look away I couldn't see Beast as one to get upset like he was. He leaned over and pulled me against him.

"I'm so sorry, Doll." He said. I was numb something had happened to Noah I was sure of it. He was dead. It was the only explanation for what was happening.

"Who?" was all I could get out. Beast held me tight.

"You're dad...he was shot." He said. I jerked away and looked at him.

"Was it fatal? Is my dad dead? Did they seriously call you to tell you that my father died? Oh my god, Daddy!" I was yelling and the flood gates were opening. I had never expected this. I always thought my dad was invincible and that nothing could ever hurt him. My poor dad, what about my mother? Oh sweet baby Jesus. This was going to crush her. She just left him too. I looked up at Beast, who hadn't said a word.

"Babe, he's not dead. Calm okay? He was shot in the side of the abdomen. It went straight through and didn't hit any major arteries, veins, or organs. He'll be okay. They just wanted me to prepare you to see a lot of blood. They are on their way here with him." He said. I felt so stupid.

"Sorry, I just assumed the worse. But he's okay?" I asked.

"Yes, he's fine...or will be." He chuckled.

I was glad Cody warned me. When they came in there was

blood everywhere. It was all over my dad and all over everyone else. I didn't know if they were all injured or if it was someone else's blood, not that I needed, or wanted, to know. Noah came in last and our eyes made contact. I jumped off the couch and ran over to him throwing myself at him.

"Noah!" I yelled and sobbed into his shoulder. His arms came around me and he held onto me.

"I thought I lost you." I said. Noah just held on tighter and picked me up. I was so happy he was with me. He sat on the couch and held me until I stopped crying. Pulling back I looked at him.

"Did it go alright? I mean besides my father being shot." I asked. He nodded and brushed hair out of my face and wiped my tears.

"It went mostly as planned." He said. I smiled weakly and laid my head on his shoulder.

"Someone broke into my parent's again." I said. Noah looked down at me and rubbed my back.

"Well I think those will stop too. Anything taken?" He asked. I shook my head.

"No, just every clothing item I owe was ruined besides what I was wearing." I said.

"I'll take you shopping later." He said.

"I tried to subject Beast to it but we didn't hear from anyone in time so we had to wait." I said and giggled. Noah smiled kissing me.

"It's good to have you in my arms again." He said.

"It's good to be back in them." I said wrapping my arms around his neck kissing him again. His tongue danced with mine and I pressed myself against him.

"Babe, let's go to bed." He said. I nodded and got up. He took my hand and led me to his bedroom inside the clubhouse.

NOAH

I couldn't sleep at night anymore. The same nightmare kept happening. It started right after I turned myself in to the Ralph. He kept telling me how he was going to get Grace and have his wicked way with her. Repeatedly, saying how beautiful she was and how delicious her juices tasted on his fingers, that she would have been perfect for his cock and that her tits would have been a sight to see bouncing around while he tied her up and fucked her. My heart couldn't take most of what he was saying. The fact that he even touched her, let alone fingered her had my body rigid and on fire for destruction. The whole situation played in my mind all night, every night.

Ralph egged me on with things about Grace. He wanted me to act out. When he didn't get a rise out of me when he talked about her, he cut to what he really wanted, info on the club. I told him a bunch of bullshit he seemed to drink in like it was fucking top shelf booze. The club stormed in just when they said they would and that's when everything went to hell. Jack was shot within moments of the infiltration. The whole club went after Ralph. He had five shots to his head and everyone else surrendered. All members lining up and put a bullet in Ralph's men at the same time. It looked like a fucking firing squad. The nightmare that she was getting raped by Ralph daily and that if I died I wouldn't be able to save her from that life, that I wouldn't be able to have her to myself. Yeah, it was selfish but I wasn't going to give her up for anything or anyone, not even Jack and he tried to make me.

Grace was sleeping peacefully on my chest and I stroked her back. She had on my tee shirt and boxer shorts I had left here as extras in case I ever needed them. I was so happy to see her when I got back that I needed to collapse in bed just to comprehend that she was still mine. That I was still alive to hold her and make love to her. I wrapped my arms around her and just held her. I was so content with this moment. My body gave me no indication of passing out until it happened.

I awoke to find Grace gone. Sitting up I became frantic. I ran out to the main area, when I didn't see her, I ran back to my room and found her coming out of the bathroom. Scooping her up in my arms I held her. My heart racing, I was so scared. She wrapped her arms around me gazing up at me.

"Are you okay, Noah?" she asked. I nodded leaning down to kiss her. She turned her head and I kissed her cheek.

"Are you okay?" I asked.

"I just threw up I don't want to kiss you until I can brush my teeth." She said.

"Are you not feeling well?" I asked. She shook her head.

"No. I'm sure I'll be okay though." She sighed.

"Why don't you lay down for a while then?" I asked cupping her cheek.

"I would like to go buy some clothes and a toothbrush though if you don't mind taking me." She

"Anything for you babe." I said.

Shopping, god I hated shopping. It took Grace hours to get one damn outfit, that didn't even include any of the good stuff that I wanted to take off of her, no that took another whole fucking hour. How can one person go shopping for so long?

"Babe, are you almost done? I'm getting pretty bored here." I said. Grace poked her head out of the changing room she was currently in and smiled at me.

"I promise I'm almost done here then we just have to run to one more store." She said. I groaned and flung myself back on the too pink bench. I heard her giggle and I couldn't help but smile. My Grace. I couldn't wait for that to be legally true. I just had to ask her.

"Hey babe. I have to run somewhere quick. Just go to the next store without me and I'll meet you there." I said standing up. Grace opened her door and stepped out in one of the sexiest things I had ever seen. My eyes scanned over her body and landed on her feet that were hugged by some killer high heels.

"You know that outfit really doesn't say wife." Grace looked at me with wide eyes. Shit I slipped. What the fuck did I just do?

"I mean ol'lady. It doesn't say ol'lady." I said hoping it was covered up. She smiled.

"Hold on we need to talk. Just let me get dressed." She said and went back in the dressing room. I gulped.

"Babe I'm just going to run to the bathroom." I said and took off to the jewelers. I had to get a ring. She knew I was going to ask her. Just better get it over with… in the middle of the mall. Not quite the setting I wanted, but I had to do my best with what I had.

The ring I got was perfect and it looked to be her size. It had a big black diamond with two white ones accenting the band. I hoped she liked rose gold though I've never seen her wear any jewelry. I was already getting nervous and I text Jack and told him I fucked up and it was more than likely going down in a few minutes. Jack told me good luck and I called Grace to find out where she was. She was still at Victoria's Secret. I was not proposing with underwear all around me. I sat on the bench and slipped the box in my pocket to wait. "Grace?" I asked. She came out of her stall dressed and I smiled at her.

"What store next?" I asked.

"We don't have to continue to go shopping." She said smiling slightly.

"I don't mind sweetheart." I said. Grace came over and kissed me.

"I love you Noah." She said brushing her fingers across my cheek and lips. I smiled pulling her close against me. She pulled away a little.

"I need to go to the bathroom quickly. Do you mind checking out my things? I'll be back in a few." She said left for the bathroom. I put her things on the counter paying for them. I waited outside the store with three more bags added to her collection. I called her to find out what bathroom she was in. I didn't get an answer. I was starting to panic a bit and went to the nearest bathroom.

"Grace!" I yelled in the open door.

"Noah?" I whipped around and looked at her.

"Jesus, I was scared something happened to you." I said pulling her against me.

"Noah, I think we should stop at the drugstore again." She said pulling away from me.

"Anywhere you want babe. You okay?" I asked. She nodded and grabbing a couple of the bags. I grabbed the rest of them and wrapped my arm around her waist.

She came out of the drugstore with a small bag and I looked at her. "Did you get what you needed?" She nodded staying quiet.

"Are you sure you're okay?" I asked. She looked up at me and pulled the single content out of the bag.

"I'll be better when I know for sure." She said and my eyes drifted over to what she was holding up. Holy fucking balls. She was holding a pregnancy test. I whipped my eyes back over to her and stared at her. My pulse quickened and sweat was pouring out of my skin. A baby, I wasn't prepared for a baby. What the fuck would I do if she was pregnant? I went back to the clubhouse and grabbed all the bags out of the trunk. She waited for me and I put the bags on the pavement quickly.

"I love you Grace." I said kissing her and pulling her close to me. I was scared out of my mind, sure we hadn't been together that long but I knew I wanted to be with her for the rest of my life but I wasn't sure I was ready for a baby. I guess I can just hope she's not pregnant for right now and if she is I'll have to deal with it. She held onto me for a little bit and I pulled out the ring box.

"This isn't because of the pregnancy, well if you are, I've been thinking about this for a while and I was going to ask you on my birthday in a couple weeks, but a baby is a big thing why not make it huge?" I said smiling at her. She looked up at me and then at the box. She showed no emotion and I opened the box and got on one knee.

"Grace, will you marry me?" I asked. Her eyes drifted to mine as tears were slowly slipping down her cheeks.

"No." It was one simple word and it crushed me. Fucking tore me apart. Two simple letters and I was a devastating pile of nothing.

"No?" I couldn't believe it. I rubbed the back of my neck before picking up the bags and tossing the ring box in my car. Grace just stood there and I went inside. Everyone in the club screamed

"Congratulations!" as soon as I walked in. It was like being hit with a truck. I walked by them all and set the bags in the bedroom. I couldn't believe this was happening. I wasn't even mad, I understood why she said no. All the shit happening around the club, with her dad healing from being shot. Of course, my head didn't want to believe that. I wanted to believe it was just the wrong time, but maybe there wouldn't ever be a right time. She probably didn't even want to be with me and felt obligated because of the things I did for her. I sat on the bed and she came in with tears streaming down her face. Looking up at her I sighed.

"Are you okay?" I asked. She smiled a little before sitting next to me.

"I came in here to see if you were alright and you're asking if I am." She stated. "Noah, I don't feel like it's the right time, that's all, I love you dearly and I would love to marry you some day, just...not right now. I need to figure out if we are actually going to be having a baby first and I want to get over that step before we add more to the chaos." She explained but I didn't want to listen to her.

"One thing at a time kind of deal?" I asked. She nodded leaning over kissing my cheek.

"Noah, I love you with my whole heart, body, and soul.

Don't ever forget that." She said standing up going in the bathroom. A knock sounded on the door. Getting up I stupidly answered it. Beast was standing outside it.

"Did you hurt her?" he asked me angrily. Having Beast mad at you was one thing that could have made anyone cringe or run for their lives. And the fact that he was accusing me of hurting Grace. It was almost more than I could bare at the moment.

"God no, I'm pretty sure I am the one hurt." I said stepping out into the hall closing the door behind me.

"What happened brother?" He asked.

"Well she surprised me with a fucking pregnancy test and when we got here I laid my heart out for her and she fucking told me no. We might be having a baby and she told me she wasn't fucking marrying me!" I was screaming towards the end and shaking. Beast slapped my back.

"Go get a drink brother. She'll come around." He said and I sighed.

"I'm going for a ride. Tell her to call me with the fucking results." I said leaving the hallway. I couldn't even bear to be around when she took the test. I was so fucking scared. How could I become a father? My own was a piece of shit.

GRACE

I stared at the ceiling as I waited for the pregnancy test to show me the result. I heard everything Noah said and screamed. I had hurt him deeply by rejecting him. I felt horrible, I love the man and I couldn't say yes to him. It was a pity really. The only thoughts that kept running through my head was what if I couldn't keep him around. My mother had lost my father and he was now really losing her, she had, had enough. I sat on the floor pulling my knees to my chest. I was going to find out the result of the test and then make some calls. I didn't have much left at my parents since all my clothes were gone. I really had a TV and a couch and a bed, along with some cooking supplies. I stood up and looked at the test after the three minutes were up. The test was negative. I could feel a huge weight being lifted off my shoulders. I wasn't ready for a baby. I came out of the bathroom to Cody sitting on the bed. He looked up at me and I smiled slightly.

"So, are we all expecting a huge ass belly to be coming soon?" he asked. I giggled a little and shook my head.

"No. I'm not pregnant." I said and sat next to him.

"Could you give me a ride home? I don't want to stay here anymore." I said. Beast nodded and got up grabbing a couple of the bags. I grabbed the rest and we went to his car. Everyone had disappeared. I'm sure they knew I had rejected Noah. I wanted to cry for him but I couldn't let myself.

My bedroom needed to be cleaned desperately. My ruined clothes were still everywhere. I sat on my bed collecting the clothes that were around me. I would worry about cleaning later. Hefting everything into a huge pile I climbed into bed falling asleep almost instantly. Dreams, plagued me with white. They were filled with a huge wedding and Noah was standing at the altar. The image dripped away as rain came pouring down. I stood in the middle of a rainstorm crying with nothing in sight then everything went black.

The next morning, I was alone in my bed. I should probably get used to this again. The feeling of waking up alone was horrid. Being used to someone being there was a wonderful feeling but when they weren't there when your eyes opened to the sun shining? It was a huge pail of cold water being dumped over your head, reminding you of the reality you weren't facing. I'm sure Noah wouldn't be around much longer. I looked at my phone and saw a missed call from Noah and a few text messages. I'm sure Beast told him that I was at my place. I got up and went into the kitchen to make some coffee and breakfast. There was a knock on my door and I checked the peephole before opening it.

"Delivery for Grace Sinner." The boy said.

"That's me." I said. He held a huge bouquet of flowers and handed me a card before handing over the flowers.

"Thank you." I said and he left without another word. I closed the door and set the flowers on the counter. I opened the card and sat at one of the barstools.

> Grace,
> I'm sorry for being such an ass and taking off.
> I hope to see you sometime today.
> Maybe we can have dinner tonight and talk?
> -Noah

I smiled a little as I put the card on the counter. We could talk but I wasn't sure about dinner. I grabbed my phone sending him a text.

The flowers are beautiful. No dinner. I will talk however. – Grace

My phone pinged almost instantly.

When? -Noah

Sighing I replied back to him.

Tonight, whenever I don't have a job or anything, so I'll be

home all day and probably all night. -Grace

I didn't get a reply. I put the flowers in a make shift vase and sat on the couch staring at the flowers. I remembered the picture I took of the sign with the apartments for rent. Pulling it up I wrote it down on a notepad on the coffee table. I was so confused with all my feelings maybe it would do me some good to get away for some time and just think through everything. I turned my phone off before turning some music on. It was time to start cleaning my bedroom.

A few hours into cleaning I had the ruined clothes all thrown out and the new ones laying on my bed. A pounding was sounding from my front door. Rushing to the door checked through the peep hole to see who it was. Noah was standing with his head against the door and his arm above his head. I opened the door looking at him.

"Hey." I said. He looked up at me. His eyes roaming over my body before pulling me to him, kissing me.

"Why weren't you answering your phone?" He asked.

"It's been off for the last few hours. I needed to clean." I said. He looked around sighing.

"Fuck I was scared. You never called me about the test." He said and I looked at the floor.

"I forgot." I said.

"Well? Are we having a baby?" He asked. I shook my head no. He pulled me into a hug. We stood there him just holding me. "I wasn't ready to have a baby. I was freaking out the whole time." He said. Pulling away, I walked to my room. My emotions were everywhere and I didn't know if he should really be here. He followed me into my bedroom. I started hanging up my clothes, focusing on the fact that I had things to do that didn't involve him. He sat on my bed watching me.

"Grace?" Stopping I looked at him. "Are we still together or do you want us to be done?" He asked looking directly into my eyes.

"Honestly, I don't know what I want. I was scared shitless when you asked me to marry you. I do love you but I'm not ready for that kind of commitment so soon and I was scared to have a baby. I wasn't ready for that either but everything else I feel is up in the air." My mind was racing with the speed of my heart. "Maybe it would do us some good to have time apart." I said. Standing up he put his hands in his pockets.

"If that's what you want." He said walking out of my bedroom. I wanted to cry and scream but instead I turned on my phone. I had to let it sit for a while to let every missed call and text message I missed come through. Sighing, I dialed the number for those apartments I found.

It was a short conversation and I had a viewing scheduled for this afternoon. I just had to get a vehicle to get there. I called Cody and asked if he could come and get me. He was there in fifteen minutes and brought me to the club house. Getting out of his car, I went to find my dad. He was sitting in his office talking to Noah, I waited out in the hall until they were done talking. A hour had to have gone by, by the time Noah stepped out. He glanced at me and then looked away, walking down the hallway. My heart was beginning the shattering process but I knew this would be best for me at this time. I poked my head around the doorframe to look at my dad.

"Hey daddy?" I asked. He looked up at me.

"Yes." He said standing up. I walked into the office.

"Could I borrow your car? I have to go upstate for something." I asked. He raised his eyebrow.

"What's upstate?" he asked. I nibbled on my lip, hesitating to tell him I might be moving. "Sweetheart you do that when you're about to lie. What is it really?" he said. I looked up at him.

"I think I'm going to move. I haven't fully decided on it but I found an apartment that looks promising. I have a showing this afternoon for it and it's two hours away.." I said. My dad sighed.

"Am I losing you too baby girl?" he asked, emotion seeping out of his voice. He seemed to be really upset over this.

"No, daddy. I'm only going to be a longer drive away. I might move back after a while." I said.

"Is this because of Noah?" he asked. I shrugged my shoulders.

"I guess it could be a little bit." I said looking at the floor. My heart wasn't fully breaking yet because there was still a chance we would be together.

"If you move away doll, he'll find someone else." My dad said the words I knew were true. I could feel everything crumbling around me. I knew I should stay and fight but I didn't know how much fight I had left in me.

"Dad, I…it was too soon for the proposal and I was freaking out because I thought I was pregnant. I don't know if I want to be caught up in all of that just yet." I said. My dad handed the keys to his truck over.

"Go see if you really like it." He said. I quickly hugged him.

"I'm sorry, Daddy." I whispered.

I walked out of the club and got in his truck. Everything hit me. The pain of knowing that if I leave Noah will find someone else and I'll just be another notch on his bed post. I didn't want to be one of those women that are used for a temporary time and thrown out. I have seen how the other men treat women. How they bounce around sometimes having two women in the same night, maybe even more than that. I was scared. I had to admit that. The feelings I have for Noah were deep ones, almost too deep for the amount of time we have been together. I love him but I couldn't have him. Putting the truck in drive I drove off the lot and towards the apartment showing. Hoping I wasn't making the biggest mistake of my life.

NOAH

I watched Grace pull out of the lot in her father's pickup. Her Chevelle was starting to look better now that we had grinded all of the paint off of it. It had new tires put on yesterday. She'd be able to drive it soon. Going into the bar inside the club I grabbed a beer. Jack came out and looked right at me.

"If you don't fucking man up and get her to stay around; I'll probably fucking kill you." He said. I looked at him as if he was crazy.

"What are you talking about?" I asked.

"She's probably going to be fucking moving two hours away because of you. You need to fix this shit storm of a mess before she makes up her mind. I'm already losing my wife. I'm not losing Grace too." He said and went outside. Sighing I took a pull off my beer. My life was a shit storm. If Grace moved then…I honestly didn't have a fucking clue what I would do. So quickly that woman had become my life that I wasn't sure how to do things without her. Her father was right though. If I didn't do something before she moved away I would never get another chance.

"Mind if I look around her stuff to see where she might have gone?" I asked Jack.

"No, go."

Going over to Jack's house, I let myself in and looked around and through her stuff for any clues of where she may have gone to view this apartment. The only thing I could find was a fucking phone number that wasn't from this area. I sat on the couch and tried to figure out what to do. I didn't want to force her to stay here but I didn't want her to go either. I was in love with her. A lightbulb went off inside my brain and I smiled getting off the couch leaving, locking the place up.

Two hours later, I had booked a vacation for Grace and me, leaving tomorrow. I wasn't sure if I could even get her to go but I had to try. I wanted her back and maybe some time alone and away from everyone would help her see that I need her, even if she wanted to go just her. I was scared that she would pick that option, but this was all I had. It was all I could do. A tropical island with lots of beach area was what she could look forward to. No sex, no distractions, nothing, just her and hopefully me.

Grace came back to the clubhouse just after eight that night. Coming inside, she handed her father the keys to his truck and went to look for, I could only assume was, Beast.

"Grace." I yelled over to her. She turned and looked at me.

"I'll give you a ride." I said and pulled out my car keys holding them up. She smiled slightly and came over to me. Maybe I wouldn't have to worry that she wouldn't come back to me. We walked outside and I opened the car door for her.

"Are you hungry?" I asked. Grace looked at me and smiled, nodding her head.

"I'm starved." She said.

"Take out and a movie at your place?" she beat me to asking her to dinner making me chuckle.

"I'm not sure my place is where you would want to be. It's pretty messy right now." I said. She shrugged her shoulders.

"You've seen my place a mess a few times." She reasoned. Smiling I shut her door and climbed into the driver's side.

"Where would you like to get take out?" I asked. Grace looked to be in deep thought over it. I smiled and watched her.

"Well, Chinese sounds good….but so does Mexican…You pick." She said as she looked over at me.

"How about both?" I said. She laughed shaking her head no at me.

"I can't eat Chinese food with Mexican food. That would just be wrong!" she was still laughing. The sound music to my ears. She was happy right now just as she should be.

"Well why don't we get one of them tonight and the other for lunch tomorrow." I offered.

"I'd like that." She said and we were off. Chinese takeout tonight and a movie, while I figured out how to drop the big old vacation bomb on her.

Take out and a movie, any couple's normal night in and for Grace and I. It was different and I liked it. I could afford a different life with her and I really wish I hadn't been rejected. We really needed to talk about everything that had happened. I looked over at her and put my arm around her shoulders pulling her closer.

"Grace." She looked up at me and I leaned down to kiss her. Her lips molded into mine and made me pull her closer. I smiled when we pulled apart and just watched her. "I think we should talk." I said keeping my eyes trained on hers.

"Well you sure know how to get my attention." She said sitting up a little straighter turning towards me.

"Are we an us or are we a no more?" I asked. Grace pulled her lip between her teeth casting her eyes up at me.

"I would like to be an us." She said never have I felt such great relief. "I just think we honestly haven't worked towards that as well as we should have." She looked at the couch as she spoke. I reached out and lifted her chin.

"Baby, I think we should move in together. I'll put off marrying you but just know someday you will be my wife." I said smiling. Her return smile made my heart swell to twice its size.

"I'm not taking the apartment two hours away, but I do need to downsize since I no longer have a job." Grace said and her eyes trailed back up to mine, leaving a trail of burning fire in their wake.

"Well I just have to kick my roommate out and we can live in my place." I said. She laughed and kissed my cheek.

"You don't have to kick Bullet out. He could still live there." I smiled at her and leaned over taking her lips into possession.

"I'll talk to Bullet and see what he says." I said and pulled her into my lap, where she stayed for the rest of the night with a smile plastered on her face.

At eight am I rolled out of bed to shower. I was in a great mood until I realized I had forgotten to tell Grace about the getaway vacation. I quickly text her to pack a bag because tonight I was taking her somewhere. She kept asking me where throughout the day and I had avoided it smoothly. I told her she needed a swimsuit and just a couple pairs of clothes and we would be on a plane to go somewhere special. She gave up asking by noon that day and it was a relief but at the same time I liked playing with her like that. I talked to Bullet and he was fine with Grace moving in, but he had one condition; We were to try to refrain from having sex while he was home, which wouldn't be hard because he was rarely ever there. Smiling I knocked on Grace's door. A crash sounded on the other side and I tried the handle.

"Grace!" I yelled frantic that something was happening. It was silent on the other side of the door. "Fuck, Grace are you in there?" I asked hoping for something. The door flew open wide. Grace stood in the doorway in some of the new lingerie I had bought her the other day. I gulped as my dick sprang to attention faster than a scorpion strike. Grace smiled as I looked her over. It was black and red lace that cupped her breasts perfectly. The black sheer fabric skimmed down over her abdomen and then a tiny red and black triangle thong covered her core with red strings hugging her voluptuous hips. I groaned feeling like my cock was going to tear my jeans off itself to get to her.

Grace's finger looped through my belt loop pulling me inside. I kicked the door shut. My hands cupping her ass. Her smile was the light I needed in our time of darkness. I was way too over dressed for this. My cut and shirt came off all at once as Grace unbuttoned my jeans. Sliding them down I stepped out of them as I lifted her up and she wrapped her legs around my hips. My erection pressed against my boxers rubbing against her. Carrying her to her bed I laid her out for me to see, fully. She is the most beautiful woman I had ever met and I didn't want to waste one more moment away from her. Leaning over her I kissed her. Her hand made its way down my abs and inside my boxers. I moaned as she gripped me. I was rock hard and oh so ready for her. I let her stroke me a few times before I pulled her hand away. Rolling her onto her stomach, her ass came into the air.

"Noah, I've been a very bad girl." She purred at me. Her cunt was glistening with moisture and I ran my finger along her thong. She moaned and looked over her shoulder at me.

"How bad have you been Grace?" I asked.

"Oh, so bad, Noah." I smiled looking at her.

"What did you do baby?" I asked and rubbed my hand against her ass cheek.

"I touched myself." Pulling my hand away I watched her.

"Have you?" she squirmed a little. My lips quirked on the side. Her nod giving everything away before she explained.

"In the shower, in bed, on the couch, I even did it on the kitchen counter." Smiling I flipped her on her back while smacking her ass. She groaned and clutched my shoulders once she was on her back. I nipped her nipple through the lace of her bralette.

"Show me." I said as she looked a little stunned. "Show me how you touched yourself today. I want to see you get yourself off and then maybe I'll take you there again." I nipped my way down to her waist line. Her hand followed my trail before slipping into her thong. I hooked my fingers under the strings pulling it off.

Stepping back I leaned against the far wall and watched as Grace touched herself. Her fingers circled her clit before she dipped one into her core. I stood there not moving letting her bring herself to climax. It was a glorious sight. Something I could have watched all day. Even though watching without touching my cock had been a challenge. A smile tugged at my lips and I walked over to her pulling on her foot forcing her to move to the edge of the bed. I grabbed her hand pulling her up to stand. She wrapped her arms around my shoulders and leaned on me panting. I smiled kissing her.

"I want you to punish me Noah. I want to try your world." It was mind blowing she even said it. The grin that was spreading just couldn't be helped.

"Alright baby. We will later." I stated cupping her ass again. "Where should we continue this?" I asked. Grace smiled and pushing me towards her bedroom door and out into the kitchen. I walked behind her watching her ass sway to her steps. She stopped by the counter. I framed her body with mine leaning down to kiss her neck before wrapping my arms around her waist lifting her onto the counter.

"Do it all over again baby." I said and stepping back leaning against the opposite counter. A pout made her bottom lip stick out making me want to nibble on it.

"Noah, I want you." She said, deepening her pout.

"You said you wanted to try my kind of sex. This is part of it baby. Touch yourself." I said crossing my arms. She bit her lip and went straight into her core. I smiled as she leaned her head back and moaned loudly so it echoed through the kitchen. I could only watch her for a little longer. I got on my knees blowing cold air over her pussy. She pulled her fingers out of her warmth. I grabbed her wrist sucking her fingers into my mouth. She gasped watching as I sucked the juices off her fingers sliding my tongue in between them. I could see her toes curling. Her thighs pressing together. A moaned escaped as I tasted her before popping her fingers out of my mouth.

Tossing her legs over my shoulders I pressed my mouth to her clit. She moaned laying back on the counter. My tongue thrust inside of her and her fingers went into my hair pulling. Smiling I inserted a finger into her pussy collecting her juices. Pulling back I ran my finger along her ass. She shuttered a flush taking to her skin.

"I think we might try here tonight." I said standing up a bit while inserting my digit inside her ass. She moaned arching her back off of the counter. I massaged the inner wall of her anus. Pulling her off the counter I turned her around bending her over the thing. I inserted my finger into her pussy again and a second one in with it. She moaned against the counter. Pressing my erection into her ass, she reached back stroking it. My hand made contact with her ass hard and she groaned. I fingered her a little more before going back to massaging her anus. Both fingers slipped in without a problem and I leaned over kissing her back. Kicking her legs together more she looked over her shoulder at me with a smile on her lips but fear in her eyes. My hand went into her hair pulling her off the counter to kiss her. She moaned into our kiss as I thrusted inside her. My fingers keeping with the massage. Her pussy clenched my dick and I pulled back out. Grace pressed her ass against me and my hand left her hair smacking her ass.

"Oh no, sweetheart. I'm just getting started." I said and thrust, hard, into her again and again. It was heaven to me and I never wanted to leave her. Her anus had stretched nicely and I pulled out completely. Picking her up I thrust my hand into her hair and my dick back inside her as she wrapped herself around me. My fingers found their way back to her ass slipping inside. Our lips clashed together and I brought her over the couch laying her down. I broke apart our kiss and pulled out of her again. She whimpered as I flipped her so her ass was in the air and her knees together. She leaned up on her elbows and watched me. I pressed the head of my cock at the entrance of her ass. She moaned as soon as it came in contact. My fingers gripped her ass spreading her apart for an easier entrance. My cock slipped inside, moaning at the tightness.

Fucking heaven. I stayed still for a bit letting her adjust. I could feel her juices flowing down over my balls. I looked at her watching as she bit onto her lip and watched me over her shoulder. My hips pulled back and then forward again making a slow rhythm. Her hands went to the back of the couch and clutched onto it. I thrust in a few more times and pulled out and sliding straight into her pussy. She moaned sitting up more taking me deeper. I leaned my head back closing my eyes enjoying the feeling of her.

"Noah." My eyes opened making contact with hers.

"I want to ride your cock." She purred making me almost combusted. Pulling out I stood up while helping her up.

"Where do you want to ride my cock?" I asked. A wicked smile crossed her lips as she pressed herself against me.

"First I want to ride your cock right here on my couch. Then I want you to fuck me on your bike." She said. I smiled and sat down on the couch and guided her down on my cock.

"You can ride my cock anytime you want baby. The bike might be harder to do right now though. It's at the club." I said and held her hips. She smiled leaning down to kiss me.

"Then we better go pick it up." She purred into my ear. I nearly lost it. This woman was incredible. The best thing to happen to me. She started to move, and I mean really move. Her hips ground into me then lifted and repeated, over and over and over again. Her pussy clenched me as her orgasm assaulted her. She stilled once it started. Flipping her onto her back I kept thrusting into her riding hers out and letting mine slide home.

I was spent and didn't know if I could even go and ride the bike right now. Never has a woman made me so happy and tired at the same time. I smiled kissing her belly sitting up more.

"So how was that for an introduction to my sex?" I asked. She smiled and sat up kissing me.

"It was…nice." She said bringing her lips back down to mine. I laid on my side looking over at her.

"Do you have a bag packed for tonight?" I asked. She smiled and nodded.

"Where are we going?" she asked.

"We are going on a vacation. We have to be at the airport in about two hours. Would you like to stay up more or would you like to try and get some rest?" I questioned. Grace leaned over kissing me softly. I smiled watching her.

"Might as well stay up. I'll never be able to nap." She said and sat up completely.

"Shower?" I asked and got up. I could feel Grace's eyes follow me to the bathroom. I looked over at her and jerked my head towards the bathroom. "Come on baby." I said going into the bathroom, hoping she would come and join me.

GRACE

After our shower we laid in bed not saying a word. We finally rolled out of bed an hour before we had to be at the airport. I still didn't know where we were going, and I was giddy and excited for this new adventure that we were starting. Noah grabbed our things and shoved them in the trunk of his car. Smiling, I got in the passenger seat and watched him fold into the driver's seat.

The drive was short, and we were at the gate in no time. "Noah, seriously, where are we going?" I asked in all seriousness. He smiled taking my hand.

"Sweetheart, we are going to a secluded island. Where it is just going to be the two of us. No one else." He said. I smiled wrapping my arms around him.

"Are you serious?" I asked, and Noah brushed hair out of my face kissing me.

"Yes, baby. We are going to an island, and we are going to be alone." He said kissing me again. Smiling, I ran my fingers over his jaw.

"Noah, I know things haven't been going great for us, and I know we haven't always made each other happy, but I love you." I said. He smiled wrapping his arms around my waist.

Our flight was called, and we pulled apart going to get on the plane. I was really excited for time away with him that I didn't even know what to do with myself. It was great that something was actually going smooth in my life and nothing could have made me happier than I was in this moment.

We got off the plane in California. Noah informed me that we had to stay one night here and in the morning we would be on our way to the island. I didn't want to sleep when we got to the hotel.

"Noah." I asked bouncing on the bed. He looked at me and smiled.

"Can we go out? I'm not ready for bed right now, and I've never been out of Minnesota and Wisconsin." I asked and he smiled.

"Alright, let's go." He gave in. I began jumping up and down kissing him. His hands smoothed down my back trying to calm me before cupping my ass. It was the best thing he could have done.

"Are you sure you want to go out?" He asked against my lips. Giggling, I nodded after pulling aways from him.

"Yes! Let's go!" I exclaimed. He laughed as we went out the door.

The night in California was amazing. It was so beautiful outside even at midnight. I had so many feelings running through me that I jumped Noah's bones at least five times before falling asleep finally. He calmed me, and it wasn't just the sex. Just being around him.

Noah woke me up at seven in the morning. After showering, I got dressed for our boat ride. Noah was waiting for me when I finally finished. He mumbled something along the lines of damn women, making me laugh. I thought I did pretty gould considering it was only an hour later. Grabbing my bag, Noah looked at me holding his hand out. I placed my hand in his. He shook his head reaching for my bag, taking it off my shoulder.

"I can carry it, Noah." I said crossing my arms.

"Babe. Let me." He said and leaned forward kissing me. Smiling, I let go of my bag, letting him have it.

"Well you sure know how to make a woman do what you want." I mumbled following him out of the room. He looked over his shoulder flashing a smile at me.

"Baby, I know how to make women beg for things." He said taking my hand. I blushed going with him out to the car. He put our bags in the car before pressing me against it. I smiled and looked up at him. His hips pressed into mine and pinned me to the car. I smiled as he leaned down bringing his lips to mine. I smiled and wrapped my arms around his neck. And that's when I felt it.

"Oh, son of a bitch...." I whispered under my breath. Noah pulled back looking at me.

"You should probably go and uh...check us out.." I said and looked around for any kind of store. Noah nodded looking confused as all hell going inside. I spotted a Walgreens not to far away and waited for Noah to come back. I looked up as Noah returned to the car.

"I need to stop at that Walgreens. If you don't mind." I said.

"Don't you have everything you need?" He asked and I shook my head no in response.

"I wasn't prepared for my period to come. It's the late one I was waiting for." I said. Noah whipped his head over to me.

"Oh, shit. Well there went my plans." Sighing he drove over to Walgreens.

"We can still...have sex you know." I commented. He nodded staying silent. I sighed getting out of the car going inside the store. It felt like the gates of hell had opened between my legs and Satan was just getting started with me. I quickly hurried purchasing what I needed and asked the boy at the counter if there was a bathroom I could use.

"We aren't supposed to let the public use it." He informed me.

"I understand that, but this is kind of a female emergency. I'm only going to use it for some privacy then I'll be gone." I said. The boy hesitated then nodded.

"Let me just ask my manager." He said calling his manager to the register. I stood there holding my legs together hoping that I would get a break and be able to use the restroom. His manager came up and thank god it was a woman.

"Is there a problem?" She asked.

"Well I was just asking if I could use the restroom. Just kind of a female emergency." I smiled at her. She returned a knowing smile.

"For that I'll let you this once." She said. I leaned back thanking god that something good was happening today. She led me to the restroom where I did what needed to be accomplished.

"Thank you so much. My boyfriend and I are heading on vacation and I wasn't prepared at all." I said.

"Not a problem." She stated with a smile. I came out not a minute later and she went in and checked the bathroom.

"Thank you again." I said and she nodded.

"Have a nice vacation." She said going back to work. I smiled and went out to the car and got in. Noah looked over at me.

"Better?" He asked.

"Oh, yes. The gates of hell are closed for now." I said smiling at him.

"The gates of hell?" He asked shaking his head. "Never mind, I don't want to know." He said driving to our destination, the docks.

NOAH

When Grace slammed me with her period thing I freaked out. I'll admit it I freaked out. I was flipping shit. I had planned this trip so that we could get together and make love and all that other shit. Fuck I was whipped. Helping Grace onto the boat after setting our bags down. She was the delicacy that I needed to take care of and was more than happy to do. I stayed quiet during the ride and thought everything over.

We pulled up to a dock and I threw our bags onto it before turning to Grace. She sat on the bench of the boat for a while just staring out over the water. She was so beautiful. The way the setting sun turned her blonde hair into a bright halo only emphasized her angelic nature. She was the most beautiful woman I had ever met and I had just treated her like shit because she's on her period. Going over to her, I anchored my ass next to hers.

"Baby." I whispered putting my arm around her shoulders. "I'm sorry I shouldn't have treated you like that. Just because you got something you can't control. I'm an ass. I'm really sorry for it." I pressed my lips against her temple. Grace leaned into me putting her hand over mine.

"It's okay Noah. I get it." She said looking up at me. I leaned down to kiss her.

"Let's bring things inside and then we can go ride around or something." I said. A small smile touched her lips as she nodded at me before getting up. My hand smacked her ass.

"You know I meant what I said earlier. I can still have sex. It's just a little…bloody." She commented getting me to laugh.

"Baby, blood doesn't scare me at all." I said.

"Plus the pleasure from sex… it makes it so much better

and a lot more bearable. Helps with the cramps mostly. But when a man still loves a woman, even when she's at her worst, when she's bleeding from places that are intimate, and you are willing to still love her, baby, that's what really keeps women alive. When she feels down and depressed because she's in pain, but when a man loves her" she straddled my lap wrapping her arms around me. "Women are able to get some relief and we feel secure about who we are with. They need to hear men say that they love them and that not even a little blood will take things away from them." She said. Smiling I ran my hands down her bare legs. My hands went up her back and pulled her down closer to me. I pressed my lips to hers and let our tongues tangle.

"If you still want to have sex…I'll have sex with you sweetheart." I made it known letting my hands slide down her sides. "And I'd yell it to the world if you wanted me to. I'll have bloody sex with you." She stood up and I followed suit. Lifting her up I put her on the dock before jumping up onto it.

Going up to the house we dropped our stuff off. Taking her hand I pulled her to the garage where our ride was stored for the duration of our vacation. The beautiful Harley that sat there was the second most glorious part of the vacation. The first was spending time with Grace. I heard Grace gasp and I looked over at her smiling.

"Would you care to go for a ride?" I asked. Grace smiled and nodding.

"Yes!" she squealed and I pulled the bike out. I smiled at her as she came over to me. Wrapping my arm around her waist I kissed her.

"Maybe when we get back Ill fuck you on this bike." I mused. She smiled kissing me again.

"I'd like that." She said and I released her. She swung her leg over the bike settling on the back before taking off.

The miles flew by as we drove around the island. It wasn't secluded as I thought but the house was far from the small town that was on the island. Grace's arms held on around my waist and I felt her lay her head against my back. Smiling I laced my fingers with hers against my stomach. Her hand rubbed against my abdomen descending lower. Her fingers touched my cock through my jeans and I felt it jump. I groaned and felt her palm cover my bulge completely. As her hand stroked the barrier. I had half a mind to pull over and fuck her on the side of the road, but she deserved better than that. I'd wait until we got to the house. Both her hands worked to unbutton my jeans and I leaned back slightly to give her access to it. Her hand slipped under my jeans and stroked my flesh. I moaned as she gripped my cock. Fuck, I needed to get her back to the house. Then again, I could just put her in front of me and she could ride me until we got home. I liked that idea. I ran my hand up her bare leg until I hit her shorts.

"Shit." I said and pulled over. Grace removed her hands from my jeans and held onto my waist again. I gave my head a jerk the side telling her to get off. I put the kickstand down standing up putting my dick away zipping up my pants. I looked over at Grace and pulled her to me crashing our lips together. I picked her up and set her on the gas tank and sunk back into the seat. Grace smiled wrapping her arms around my neck.

"I think we need to go buy you a skirt." I said and cupping her breasts. She bit her lip hugging me. I felt her teeth graze my earlobe, jerking away. Pulling her tank top down I exposed one of her breasts to me. My tongue flicked her nipple and she leaned back moaning. I smiled sucking her nipple into my mouth. Her fingers grasping onto my hair as I grazed my teeth against her breast. Her hips started to grind into me and I pulled back.

"Let's go get you a skirt. We aren't far from the town." I said and fixed her shirt. With a smile Grace smiled kissing me. Threading my fingers into her hair I held her against me. "Sweetheart. You wanted to be fucked on a bike. I'm going to fuck you on a bike. We just have to get you a skirt otherwise I'm going to bare you to the whole fucking island and make you scream my name." I said and leaned down kissing her collar. She giggled leaning against me.

"We should probably get me a skirt then." She said and I leaned back helping her off the bike. Standing up I allowed her to get on the back. Once she was settled we took off for the town.

Grace decided she wanted to walk around the town a bit and shop then get something to eat. I let her do everything her heart desired so that we could get on the bike and fuck once we got back. I was still hard from her rubbing her palm against my cock earlier. I watched as she looked around a shop and whenever she would pass me, she would rub against me or bend over and press her ass into my crotch. By the time she was done I could have come a few times. My balls were tight against me and my dick was throbbing. I looked out into the street and saw a drug store a few buildings down.

"Babe, we have to run to another store." I said looking over at her. She smiled nodding. Walking down to the drug store I went in grabbing some condoms. I put my arm around her shoulder as we walked back to the bike. I felt her hand dip into my back pocket and she squeezed my ass. I smiled and we got her items into the saddle bags except for a skirt that was probably way too short for my liking but I'd have us home in no time. She came strutting out of a store in the skirt that barely covered her and I smiled. She was trying to pull it down more as she walked over to me.

"I really think this is way too short for me." She said as I laughed.

"Baby, we will be home in no time and that skirt will be up around your hips with my dick deep inside you." I said and pulled her close to me. Her hand slid down my torso and she cupped my dick in my jeans. I grabbed her hands and put them on my shoulders.

"If you start that now I'll put you on your knees and make you suck me off in front of all these people. Showing them that you are mine and mine alone. Then I'll bend you over the bike right here and now and make you scream as an audience gathers to watch my dick plunge into your pussy relentlessly." I said against her ear. Moaning, she shivered against me. I smiled and picked her up setting her on the bike then climbed on myself, taking off for the house.

We pulled into the garage and Grace got of the bike. I climbed off and went into the saddle bag grabbing a condom. Grace smiled and rubbed her thigh against my dick and kissed my neck. Smiling I skimmed my fingertips against her legs pushing her skirt up around her waist. My hands gripped her ass and I liked the feeling that she had no panties on. I threaded my hand into her hair and pulled her away from my neck.

"On your knees Grace." I demanded watching as her tongue came out to lick her lips. I kissed her and sucked on her bottom lip pulling away. She lowered to her knees as I unzipped my jeans. One of her hands went between her legs and I could see her rubbing her clit. I licked my lips this time pulling my cock out. I took a step towards her. Her free hand gripped the base of my dick and her tongue came out licking a trail on the underside. Groaning, I felt heat and wetness wrap around my cock. Standing as still as I could I looked down at her.

"Oh, fuck baby." I said pulling my tee shirt off throwing it across the garage. Grace moaned as I used my hand as a make shift ponytail for her. Watching her I was fascinated as my dick went in and out of her mouth. She let her hand fall to the ground and she took my dick to the back of her throat I moaned as her nose touched just above the base of my cock. She stayed there for a few moments and looked up at me. Smiling, I pulled her back letting her breath. She stroked me and kept eye contact as she placed me back between her lips. Her tongue swirled around the tip and her hand kept working my base. She pulled her hand from the juncture of her thighs and cupped my balls. Pulling back I picked her up off the ground and kissed her letting our tongues mingle. The taste of me inside her mouth was intoxicating. My hand reached between her legs as one of her legs wrapped around my hip I rubbed her clit a little finding the string to her tampon.

Dropping the tampon on the floor, I grabbed the condom and pulling it on. Grace smiled as I stripped her shirt off of her and wrapped my arms around her waist. Her arms came around my neck and her lips met mine ferociously. We devoured each other as I swung my leg over the bike and set her back down on the tank. My thumb touched her nub as I positioned my cock at her entrance. Moaning she pushed herself closer to me. I smiled unhooking her bra and hung it over the handlebars. Her lips crashed to mine again and I thrust my hips forward entering her core. I felt her walls clutch onto me as she let out a moan. A smile spread across my lips. Stilling I let her adjust. Her breathing was heavy and she pressed her chest against mine. Her hand came to rest over my heart and I was sure she could feel it beating. Her eyes met mine as I brushed her hair back and kissed her like this would be the last time I saw her.

She rolled her hips. My hand settling around her neck tilting her chin up higher. My hips pulled back before thrusting back into her, hard. She gasped as I felt her hands on my torso feeling her nails digging into my chest. I pulled back thrusting into her again, and again, and again. I felt her orgasm on the brink as I slowly maneuvered off the bike. She laid her head against my shoulder as I laid her out on the hood of the car. I pulled out of her completely before thrusting into her. Her screams echoed off the walls of the garage. She grew taunt all over. Her core contracted around my cock as I thrust a few more times helping her ride out her orgasm. She leaned up kissing me and rocked her hips against me more. I sat down in a chair that was in the corner of the garage letting her ride me.

It felt like Grace was giving me a lap dance of sorts but the way she held onto my shoulder and leaned back as she rode me made it that much better. I felt my balls tighten and I picked her up setting her on the chair hammering my way to climax. I tightened all over and pressed my forehead to her shoulder. Her arms wrapped around me as I placed a kiss on her neck, making a trail to her lips. She smiled and I picked her up carrying her into the house and to the bed where we continued to make love for the rest of the night.

I awoke the next morning noticing Grace wasn't in bed. Smiling I got up pulling pajama pants on and went to the kitchen starting coffee. I looked in the fridge and saw a bunch of nothing sitting there.

"Guess we are going out for breakfast or at least to the store." I said to myself stepping back from the fridge. Grace was leaning against the counter next to the fridge and I smiled at her.

"Hey baby." I said. She smiled leaning over to kiss me. Pulling her against me I caressed her leaving her breathless from our kiss.. "Wanna go get some breakfast?" I asked. She nodded in reply.

"I'll just go get dressed." She said. Smiling I smacked her ass and went up to the room with her to get dressed.

We took the bike to a little diner in town that had the best pancakes I had ever had. I sat there once I finished and watched Grace. She was picking at her food and barely smiled. Something didn't feel right with her.

"You alright babe?" I asked. Grace looked up at me.

"Yeah I'm fine." She said taking a bite. I looked out the window quick then back at her. She set her fork down sighing.

"Have you ever felt like something was too good to be true?" She asked.

"Every damn day, sweetheart." I voiced. She locked eyes with me.

"I just feel like our relationship…it's something of fairytales. I know we fight every once in a while, but we just are never like in a horrible fight or anything like that. We just come together after anything and we mostly have sex. I don't even really know when we had a real conversation, besides you asking me to marry you. Noah we just—"

"We just don't fight enough is that it? You think we need to do things to sabotage what we have? Sweetheart. We could fight all the time, but we choose not to. Grace, we are meant for each other. We don't need to fight. It may feel too good to be true, but I think we should just live with it for now. Fuck everything else. I just want to be with you and that's it." I proclaimed taking her hands. Grace had tears in her eyes and I wanted to just hold her keeping her safe. That's what I would do too. I threw fifty bucks on the table pulling her from the seat. "Come on sweetheart. Let's go to the beach, or something. Do something to take your mind off the problems we are not having." I said as Grace's smile began to return. I pulled her to me and laying a slow kiss on her. She wrapped her arms around me. Smiling I pulled away from her.

"I still want you to be my wife at some point sweetheart. We don't have to get married right away. Just wear the ring and stay by my side. And in a few years we can get married and have a huge party. I'm practically begging you sweetheart." I said. I wanted to get down on one knee, but I didn't want her to feel pressured. I also didn't want to be rejected again. It just wasn't something I wanted to happen. Grace looked at me for a bit.

"Aren't you going to ask me the traditional way?" She asked. I laughed grabbing the ring out of my vest and getting down on one knee grinning.

"Grace, will you marry me?" I asked. She grinned nodding.

"Yes." Standing up I kissed her after slipping the ring on her finger. Applause sounding around us. I finally got her to wear the ring. Taking her hand, I pulled her from the diner. Going over to the bike she stood next to it and my heart just thundered in my chest. I was nervous but so fucking happy that she was going to be mine. Swinging my leg over the seat I handed her the helmet. She pulled it on before swinging her leg over the back of the bike and we took off to the house.

Grace went into the bathroom before I pulled on my swim trunks. The bathroom door opened, I turned to look at Grace. Stopping mid turn, I watched her. She had a towel around her body. A smile spread as my eyes wandered over her and I noticed there weren't any strings coming out of her towel. She dropped the towel making me feel stupid for not remembering about strapless bikinis. The bikini was leather and hugged her perfectly. She walked over to me. My hands taking her hips pulling her to me. She smiled as I leaned down to give her a chaste kiss. Her hands up my chest looping them around my neck. "Do you really want to go swimming?" I asked.

"Yes." She said and pulled away from me. I grabbed the towel she had dropped and followed her down to the beach.

Grace and I splashed and swam in the world's largest pool. It was cool compared to the hot air making my balls cower to my body. I didn't care though as long as Grace was happy. Too soon I realized I would do anything for that woman and it didn't matter to me what I had to do. Kill? Yeah, I'd done that, Run in circles chasing my own tail? I'd do that too. I would even hand her father my balls on a silver platter, only my balls and heart weren't mine to give anymore. They were all Grace's and I had to hope I wouldn't have to separate with either of them. I watched Grace wade through the water, her body was beginning to change to tan before going to a reddened state. Water droplets cascaded down her skin. Yup, I was hooked, so hooked in fact my dick was standing at attention for her making a tent out of my swim trunks.

She turned walking over to me. My eyes never leaving hers in fear that I would ruin this moment with her. She stood in front of me placing her hands on my chest. Taking her hips, I pulled her against me pushing my arousal into her belly. A wicked smile crossed her lips and her fore finger and thumb pinched my nipples. I sucked in a breath wrapping my arms around her grasping her ass in my palms.

"I think we have something to take care of." Grace's words were a caress to my ears. Bringing my hands up her back stopping on her shoulders keeping her close she tilted her head up towards mine. I captured her lips relishing in thoughts of our future, near and far.

"We should find something to do. You know, something to

do without sex for once. After all we are going to get married sometime and I know your body, but I think I should get to know more about the woman who is in here." I said laying my hand over her heart. Grace leaned back taking my hand. She pulled me towards the beach. Picking up her towel I wrapped it around her shoulders my arm anchoring it in place.

GRACE

Noah worked all day preparing a delicious meal that we ate by candlelight that night. It was nice, just the two of us and no drama. He told me everything about himself the whole deal. Opened his heart to me so to speak. He told me about the Scottish man named Ralph and everything that had to do with that whole deal. Ralph was someone who had saved his ass one day when he had been charged with grand theft auto in his younger years. Ralph set him up with my dad. When he showed up the last time, he wanted Noah to give him some intel about the club and he had responded with "It's club business." It was okay in my book and it was dealt with.

Noah had just poured his past out to me and I was grateful. I had already told him of what most of Max did to me, but I never really told him everything. He knew most of my life because he had seen me here and there and listen to tidbits of me grow up from eighteen and on. He just didn't know of the slavery Max put me through. I needed to tell him, but I was being held back and I didn't know how to get through the blockage.

"Look Noah, I need to tell you some shit...but I just don't know how to get it out." I cautioned looking up at him.

"Everything okay?" He asked. I nodded scooting closer.

"It's about...Max." his name could barely squeeze through my wind pipe. I looked at the bench we sat on and watched his hand cover mine.

"It's okay. He's not going to hurt you ever again." Noah coaxed lifting my chin. He placed a kiss on my lips and pulled me into his lap cradling me. Smiling I held his cheek in my hand.

"I know but I still have to tell you the rest of it. It's about your...playroom." I said and looked at his chest. His arms circled around me and he just held me, probably hoping I would continue.

"Tell me whenever you want. I'm not going anywhere sweetheart." Noah said kissing my temple. "And I won't pressure you to talk." I laid my head on his shoulder basking in his arms.

After a while I got up and started to clean up our dinner. Noah stepped outside with his phone and cigarettes. Watching him from the window was a sight to see. The darkness of the setting sun, it made him look fierce and godlike. Smoke billowed around him. A few moments later I had the kitchen and table clean and Noah was still outside. I sat down on the couch pulling out my phone and started to look for a new job. It wasn't a very good find, but I wrote some addresses down and looked up at the ceiling trying to relax. I heard Noah come in and I closed my eyes. Suddenly, Noah's hands were working over my feet and I let out a moan. There was nothing this man could do and not excel at.

His thumbs were pressing into the arches of my feet and it was the most unbelievable feeling. Leaning back, I rested my head on the back of the couch. His fingers started working their way up my calf and I thought I could have just fallen asleep right then and there. His lips brushed along my leg. Looking down at him I smiled. His return smile was genuine as he moved on to my other foot. All I could do was watch him. Noah leaned down kissing my calf as his hands stopped at my knee. I leaned my head to the side to get a better vantage point. He spread my legs and his lips went to the side of my knee making his way up my thigh. I bit my lip watching him. His hands caressing their way to my hips. His body kept moving upward covering mine with his own. His lips came down on mine and gave me slow caresses with his tongue. It was heaven on earth.

He lifted me up spinning us around without breaking the

kiss. My knees hit the couch and my hands went to the side of his neck where my fingers traced his jaw line. Pulling back I looked at him.

"I love you Noah." I said. Noah smiled, his hands holding my body close to his.

"I want you to know that I'm always here for you Grace, even if something horrible happens between us and we never work out. I'll always be here for you." He said bringing my lips down to his. I threaded my fingers into his hair kissing him with all I had. His lips went down my jaw towards my neck. Moaning I leaned my head to the side. I felt Noah smile against my skin and knowing he was happy was the greatest thing I could have ever hoped for. I was so happy that this man had strutted into my life. I giggled as his fingers slide gently down my sides. He pulled back looking at me. I bit my lip.

"Sorry." I said giggling.

"Are you ticklish there?" He asked and I nodded. His fingers put a little more pressure there and he started to tickle my sides. I was laughing and trying to get away when he flipped me on my back and pressed me into the couch pinning me with his hips. He continued his assault and I was laughing so hard I thought I'd piss myself if I didn't get away soon.

"Noah! I have to pee!" I yelled laughing. He laughed with me and kept going. "I'm serious! I have to pee Noah. Let me go!" I laughed more until he finally stopped. He leaned down and kissed me lightly and let me get up. I giggled and ran to the bathroom to relieve myself. I went in the bedroom to change into pajamas and Noah was laying on the bed. I smiled and went to my bag grabbing a change of clothes and changing. I could feel Noah watching me and I smiled looking over my shoulder at him. His eyes were roaming my body and I slipped the nightgown over my head. The silk felt amazing on my skin and I knew as soon as I turned around it wouldn't be on very long. The red silk hugged me slightly and the black lace barely skimmed the middle of my thighs. I tossed my clothes I was wearing into a pile and climbed on the bed. Noah pulled me against him and I smiled feeling his arms wrap around me. Maybe it was staying on longer than I thought.

I awoke the next morning with the sun beating in through the window. My back was cold so I knew Noah was gone. Come to think of it my whole body was cold. I glanced down my body and noticed my nightgown was gone. What the hell? I pulled the sheet up around my neck and looked around. I know we didn't have sex so where were my pajamas? My eyes searched the room for my nightgown and I got nothing it was nowhere to be found. I scooted out of bed holding the sheet to me and walked towards the doorway. There was soft music playing in the living room and rose petals were scattered in a row leading towards the living room. I smiled and followed them. What I found was the greatest thing to wake up to. Noah was standing in the middle of the room stark ass naked and his backside was to me. I bit my lip and walked slowly over to him. I could tell he was smiling and my eyes roamed his back memorizing the tattoos he had there. The MC's logo took up most of his back but there were little ones that curved his sides. The ones I saw daily on his arms were fully exposed and I watched as his muscles flexed when he moved his arms in front of his body. I smiled and walked closer to him and wrapped my arms around his waist. I could feel one of his arms moving back and forth as his hands caressed my own. I licked my lips and placed a kiss in the middle of his back. His hand came up taking one of mine and sliding it down his abs. The ripples in his abdomen made me drenched between my legs. He wrapped my fingers around his girth and I smiled stroking him.

Noah turned around and pulled me close to him. I looked up at him and he leaned forward cupping my ass and placing his lips on mine. I moaned into his mouth as I felt him at my entrance. My fingers pushed into his hair and held his mouth to mine.

"Noah..." I moaned and wiggled against him. He moaned and I felt his hands spread me. My fingers slipped down his neck and onto his shoulders where my nails started to dig in. Noah's body was impressive, and I wanted to keep looking it over, at least that was until he slammed himself into my body. I gasped as I adjusted to his size. It was always a surprise when he first entered me. I leaned back, pressing my body against him and started to grind my hips. His hands went to my hips and stilled me.

"Baby, slow down." He rasped kissing my throat. I moaned and stayed still. His lips traveled up my neck and nipped my ear lobe.

"I want to make slow passionate love to you baby. Make you scream my name as you come. Hold you close as it runs onto my cock." He whispered in my ear and I shuddered. I looked into his eyes as he pulled back. He slipped his arms under my thighs, making him pull out a little. He was going to drive me insane this way.

"Noah, please." I moaned.

"Please, what baby?" he asked looking down between us. I leaned my head back.

"You want this sweetheart?" he said and shifted his hips forward and then back out again. My legs gripped onto his waist and my nails dug deeper into his skin. His smile was the most beautiful thing in the world at that moment. He knew he was driving me insane and he was loving every god damned moment of it.

I leaned forward and kissed him like he was all I had left. His tongue thrusted in and out of my mouth just how I wanted him with my pussy. I held on to him and tried to move as slow as I could lifting my hips up and then easing my way back down, sliding him all the way to the hilt. He moaned and I leaned down placing a kiss to his throat. Noah backed up until his back smashed into the wall. It was a great sound and I smiled. He had his shoulders digging into the wall and his hips surged forward.

"Babe. You're going to hurt yourself." I said. He grinned and lifted my hips slamming me back down.

"Fucking ride me, baby." He said and I smiled.

"I thought you wanted it nice, slow, and passionate." I said and ground my hips in a circle. He licked his lips and stood up more. He shifted off the wall and sat on the couch.

"All I want now baby is for you to love me with your body." He said and took one of my nipples into his mouth. I moaned and closed my eyes. He pulled my legs apart and sat on the couch. I started to ride him clenching all my muscles around him. Soon I exploded and he flipped me on my back and pounded into me. He stilled and I felt him release inside me. He had my arms pinned above my head and I smiled up at him. My chest was heaving and he leaned down kissing me passionately.

He slowly pulled out of me and I throbbed where he once was. I could feel everything he emptied into me oozing out between my legs. Noah smiled and stood up. I watched him move around the room blowing out candles. I got up and went over to him beating him to the last candle. I pursed my lips and blew it out. He chuckled and slapped my ass. I jumped and looked up at him my lips still pursed. He grinned and met my lips kissing me. I smiled and then made my way down towards the bathroom. He came in not too long after I did and started the shower.

"Get in baby." He said and I smiled climbing in the shower. He climbed in with me and had me pinned against the bathroom wall seconds later.

"Round two?" I asked and giggled as he picked me up.

"I can't get enough of you baby. You're my drug." He said and I moaned as he thrust into me.

The day continued like that. The bathroom, the bedroom, the kitchen counter, floor, table, again on the couch, and then on the bike. It had been exhausting but amazing at the same time. We laid on the porch for a while and watched the sunset. It had been one of those days that I was happy to have been a part of. Noah's arms wrapped around me was the perfect ending to this vacation. I was sad it had to end tomorrow but he had to get back to work and I had to find a job. I really should just talk to my old boss.

Once the stars came out Noah got off our little blanket on the porch and picked me up along with the blanket. I giggled and wrapped my arms around his neck as he carried me inside. He went straight to the bedroom after locking the door and laid me down on the bed.

"We have to be up early so I'll try to keep my hands off you." He said with a smile. I laughed and kissed him before getting up to change. When I came back out Noah had his arms wrapped around a pillow and his eyes closed. I climbed into bed next to him and curled up against him. His arm came around me and I smiled falling into one of the best sleeps I had ever had.

Noah woke me up at five am to get ready and make sure I had everything together. I was still so tired that I was dragging ass around the house trying to find everything of mine. Noah had his stuff together in half the time it took me. He ended up finishing packing my stuff while I changed so we could leave. He was being very patient with me and I was grateful he wasn't one to throw a tantrum when I was being so slow. I sat on the bed after I changed and just took a moment. He came in the bedroom and stopped in the doorway.

"Everything okay there, babe?" He asked. I looked over at him and shook my head no. He came and sat next to me.

"What is it?" He asked and pulled me against him. I pulled my legs up and leaned into him cradling my knees to my chest.

"I think I totally skipped all the pain of being on my period yesterday due to how much sex we had and now it's hurting like hell. I seriously just want to curl up and not move for eternity." I said and tried not to cry. I was an emotional fucking wreck, which in a way was a great thing. It meant everything was about to blow over and be done with.

Noah packed up the car and by the time he had finished I had barely made it to the front porch. The cramps were making me move so slowly that I didn't know how I would even make it. Noah came back in the house and threw me over his shoulder. I screamed and held onto him.

"Don't you dare fart!" I yelled and he chuckled.

"Maybe I'll get one worked up for ya babe." He said.

"Oh god...please don't I'd probably barf all over your ass." I said. He bent down and put me on my feet by the passenger door.

"I wouldn't do that to you babe." He said and leaned down kissing me. It was amazing after everything I was feeling I could put my focus into him and not on the pain.

The plane ride home was shorter than I remembered going there. Noah said I slept the whole way which didn't surprise me. We stopped at both his apartment and my parents house to drop off our luggage then went to the clubhouse. My dad was there, and he welcomed us back like a big teddy bear, at least he did for me. When he pulled out of the hug he was giving me the look over.

"You look different doll." He said and I looked down at myself and shrugged.

"I got tanner but that's the only difference I know of." I said and looked back up at him. He smiled and hugged me again.

"Did you kids have fun?" He asked and I smiled.

"It was beautiful pops." I said and looked over at Noah. Noah had a smile plastered on his face as he watched me. I smiled back at him and then turned back to my dad.

"Hey is my car done yet?" I asked. The garage had had my baby for two weeks now and I wasn't very happy to be without a vehicle when I had to go search for a job.

"Doll there was a lot wrong with the car other than the tires and the paint. The engine was trashed too. I don't know if we can save her." My dad said and I felt my eyes start to fill up. That car had been my baby we built it together. The Chevelle couldn't be dead. My dad's hands cupped my face.

"Sweetheart, we will get you another car don't worry." He said. It felt like he didn't know how much the car meant to me.

"Daddy we built her together she can't be dead. Can't we

just completely overhaul her and rebuild her?" I asked. My dad looked over at Noah.

"Maybe Noah can take it on as a side job sweetheart. I unfortunately don't have the time to put into it that she needs. Then you can have that bond with Noah. He's gonna be around more now I think." He said.

"Babe, I'll take care of her." He said. I looked over at him and nodded that's all I could do. The tears were threatening to spill, and I just wanted to go home. I sighed.

"I'm going to go lay down until we leave again." I said and walked inside the clubhouse.

NOAH

Grace seemed pretty upset when she left her father and I standing in the forecourt. I sighed and looked at Jack.

"Did you two work everything out?" He asked me. I was scared to answer because I knew we hadn't, it was sex almost the whole vacation and I wasn't about to tell him that I spent our week long vacation banging his little girl until she screamed my name multiple times, but I couldn't lie to him.

"Nope." It left my mouth and I instantly regretted it. He shook his head as his face turned a little red.

"What did you do keep her in bed for a fucking week, fucking her brains out?" he asked. I couldn't help the smirk that came over my face as I shrugged my shoulders.

"Don't worry we'll work it out. I'll keep it in my pants until we do." I said and started for the clubhouse.

"You're lucky I don't cut the fucking thing off of you." He said.

"I'll even help you. Here." I said turning towards him and pulling my dick out in front of everyone in the lot. Everyone stopped what they were doing and looked at us, probably wondering what the fuck was going on. Jack shook his head.

"You got fucking balls there Noah." He said. I smiled and pulled them out too.

"Yeah, they're still there too." I said cupping them. Jack bent over and began bellowing with laughter. I chuckled and tucked myself back where I belonged.

"God, you are a fucking idiot, Noah." Jack said when he finally calmed down from laughing. I was grinning when I went inside to find Grace.

She was laying in my room and cuddled to a pillow. I laid

next to her and pulled her close.

"You alright, baby?" I asked. She nodded and looked up at me.

"I could hear my dad laughing. What happened?" she asked. I couldn't hold in my chuckle.

"I showed your dad what I use to pleasure his daughter more than once a day if I can." I said. Her hand covered her eyes and I could see a blush running down her cheeks and into her chest. It was great that she got embarrassed that I showed my cock to her father.

"You didn't…" she said and looked up at me.

"Oh, I did baby, but he told me to keep it in my pants until we talk about everything we need to." I said. She sat up a little and looked down at the bed. "We were supposed to talk on vacation, but we got distracted." I said. A smile crossed her lips and I sat up. "I want this to work between us baby. No secrets, except for club things that I'm sworn to never tell anyone about. We will talk everything out. I want to be coming home to you every single night. I want to have kids with you and only you. I need you in my life baby. I know we will fight and everything and that I can be an ass and I apologize for that in advance. I won't ever try to hurt you. It will always be you and me." I said. Grace leaned forward and kissed me.

"Alright. I think we should really get to know each other before we get too far ahead of ourselves." She said. I nodded and watched her fingers fidget with the comforter on the bed.

"I love you, Noah." Grace said and moved closer to me. I kissed her head and wrapped my arms around her. Grace fell asleep in my arms and I stayed awake most of the night just watching her knowing I'd have trouble for it later.

The next morning, I woke up and Grace was gone. I should have taken her home last night instead of staying at the clubhouse. I walked out into the main area and found Grace sitting at the bar having coffee and looking at a laptop. I grabbed a cup of coffee and sat next to her.

"What are ya doing, baby?" I asked. Grace didn't even look

away from the computer. "I'm looking for a job. Preferably something that I can walk to and that isn't a secretarial job." She said. I sat near her and just looked over her shoulder for a while.

"Are you sure you want a job again? You don't have to get one you know." I said sipping my coffee. She looked over at me.

"I didn't really want to depend on you for things I need and such." She said. I smiled and kissed her cheek.

"I don't mind. I make enough." I said and went to the sink rinsing out my cup and leaving it there.

"I like being independent though. I went to college to be independent. I just haven't found anything that would require that degree." Grace said and went back to looking for a job.

"What's your degree babe?" I asked and leaned and gains the counter. She looked at me again.

"Business with a minor in accounting." She said. I smiled and an idea came to me.

"Why don't you talk to your dad? Our book keeper just got fired and there are a few businesses you could manage if you'd like." I said and leaned over the counter on my elbows.

"May not be the best job in the world but we could all keep you close and then I could stop by and visit you at work… maybe Christian that office of yours." I said. Grace giggled and I leaned over kissing her.

I heard footsteps coming in the room and pulled away looking to the direction they were coming from. Jack walked in, in his boots and jeans turning on the stereo. Saving Abel's "The Sex is Good" came through the speakers and I smiled over at Grace wiggling my eyebrows at her. Jack came over and grabbed some coffee.

"Thank god you two were quiet last night." Jack said and looked over at us. I could see Grace's blush creep up her neck and smiled.

"We were talking like I said we would." I said and stood up straighter.

"Dad, Noah said you guys fired your bookkeeper…" Grace

said. Jack looked over at me.

"He trying to get you a job?" he asked. I smiled walking over to the hallway.

"Babe, I'm gonna go take a shower. I'll run ya home after so you can change and such." I said. Grace looked over at her shoulder at me and smiled.

"Okay." She said and I went down towards my room.

GRACE

My dad sat down next to me and I turned toward him. "You sure you want to work for the club?" he asked.

"Well I don't have many options out there for my degree. It would be something though I don't want to sit around doing nothing while Noah makes the money. I'm not a stay at home person, you know that." I said.

"I know baby. We just have so much that I don't want you apart of." He said.

"Then don't tell me. Dad, I don't need to be told everything that goes on. Just enough to keep it a job. That's all." I said. He nodded and took a drink of his coffee.

"I'll bring it to the table for a vote sweetheart. Then if it passes we will let you pick what job ya want. Lord knows we have enough of em." He said. I smiled and kissed his cheek.

"Thank you, daddy." I said and shut down the laptop.

"You're welcome princess." He said. I turned to him and smiled slightly.

"I haven't heard you call me that for a long time." I said and got up hugging him.

"I love you." He said and I could hear his Irish accent coming out. I smiled and pulled back looking at him.

"I love you too dad. Your accent came out." I said. My dad was a giant ass teddy bear when it came to me. His beard was growing down to his chest and his hair was long and turning gray. His body was huge and he still tried to work out even though he was getting older but he was always good to my mother and me and my sister.

The door to the clubhouse opened up and my mother walked in holding an envelope. I sighed knowing right away what was inside of it. My mom never wanted this life but when she married my father, she was stuck with it. He had been the president of the club for thirty years now.

"Grace. I didn't know you were going to be here today..." My mother said walking over to us. I smiled and hugged her.

"Noah and I ended up staying the night last night." I said. She nodded.

"I need to talk to your father." She said and walked towards his office. My mama was something else. She held her head high and left her hair down showing her level of confidence was through the roof. I wished they would work through all of this though. My dad kissed my temple and followed my mama into the office and closed the door. I didn't even walk down that hall. My ass sat in a barstool until Noah came out. I was sure I looked like I was going to cry. Noah came over and curled his arms around me and held me against his chest. I wasn't going to cry. I knew my mom was fed up with everything my dad had done but I also knew they were still in love. I couldn't imagine choosing to go without Noah. It was devastating that my parents didn't want to push through all the shit. I couldn't move from the barstool. Noah stood there and held me. I didn't even pull away when the other club members came into the room and neither did he. It was almost like he knew that I needed to be held right then and there until I felt like I could move. I pulled away when my father showed his face. He looked defeated and then my mom walked out of the hallway she didn't look like she was in a good position either. They both came over to Noah and me. Noah pulled away and I let him.

"We need to talk to Grace... alone, Noah." My dad said. Noah nodded and I stood up feeling like my world was crumbling and that the whole time my parents were married was a lie. We all crammed into my dad's small office and he sat behind the desk while I sat across. My mother went by my father's side and stood by him. I didn't know what they were going to tell me but I hoped it was something to do with how they were situated. My mother's eyes were shining with emotion and I sat there silently waiting. My dad looked up at my mother and smiled.

"We are going to work on things Grace. We don't want to give up on what we have." My dad said and took my mother's hand. I grinned.

"Oh god I was waiting for the worst." I said. My dad then looked at his desk and looked like he was going to break down.

"You know I would do anything for ye baby and this hurts to even have to mention this but…yer mudher and I feel the same way." His Irish accent thickened with each word and more emotions skimmed over his face. The worst was yet to come, I could feel it.

"We want you to get away from this life." My mother stepped in allowing my dad to calm himself.

"What do you mean?" I asked, terrified of the answer that I was sure was coming.

"We want you to move far away from Noah and the club. Find a nice job somewhere else. We will pay for an apartment somewhere until you can afford it on your own. Then we think you should cut all ties with us and the club." Each word that came from my mother felt like a stab to my heart. They wanted me to leave Noah. I was going to marry that man. He was good to me, better than I deserved and they wanted me to leave him. I felt like Max was asking me to do shit again.

"I can't leave him." I said quietly trying to hold the tears in.

"You need to. Grace, we don't want you to have to go through what I did. Noah will find another and so will you. You will find someone better than him." My mother was saying all the wrong things. I was twenty-two and they wanted to order me to leave someone I loved. It was like me telling them to get a divorce. What was this shit?

"I'm living with him." I said. My mother looked at my dad.

"Tell him you're coming to stay with me because we are getting the divorce." She said and turned back towards me. More stabbing pain to my chest. I couldn't believe what was happening to me. I was angry and upset. I heard the music being turned way up out in the main area. I stood up and strode out of the office. I wasn't dealing with this right now. My dad was being a pussy and not standing up to my mother because he'd do anything to keep her around.

When I came out into the main room I saw that some of the hang arounds had showed up even some of the club whores. I saw red when I saw Noah talking to one of them. She was wearing hardly anything. Fucking bikini top and shorts that had her ass hanging out of them. Slut. I stormed over there and barely noticed Noah.

"Hey baby." Noah said. I held my finger up to him and grabbed the slut by the hair slamming her head down on the table. Blood splashed all over the table and Noah jumped back. The whore looked at me and swung her fist hitting me in the cheek. My head whipped to the side and I reared my arm back bending it and slamming my elbow into her face. She stumbled back and fell onto the hardwood. My blood was boiling and I wedged my heel between the whore's chin and chest pressing down.

"You ever fucking speak to Noah again. You'll be lucky to live through that ass whooping that I'll give ya." I said a little bit of my dad's accent coming out. I turned to Noah and he was smiling at me. I stepped towards him, my blood was still heated and I slapped him across the face.

"I left to go deal with some shit was still in the fucking building and you were chatting with some slut." I was yelling and I didn't care. Noah's eyes heated and his shoulder came down into my stomach throwing me over his shoulder.

"Noah! Put me the fuck down!" I hollered. He set me down near the car and pinned me against it.

"Don't you fucking dare slap me inside that clubhouse ever again." He growled at me. "You do that again Grace you can pack your shit and leave." He said. I felt the color drain from my face and couldn't hold the sob back any longer. My emotions reared their ugly heads and everything flooded through me. I felt the tears coming on strong and I couldn't stop them. I looked down at my feet and let them flow. Noah moved to get closer to me and I pushed him back.

"Don't fucking touch me." I said and stepped away from him and the car.

"Grace, what the hell is going on?" Noah asked and I shook my head. Noah came towards me again and I stepped even farther away.

"Fuck Grace. What happened? We were fine before you came out of the office." He said.

"I'm done Noah.." I said. Noah froze where he was and I looked up at him.

"What do you mean you're done?" He asked.

"Like I said Noah…I'm done." I took the ring off my finger and laid it on the trunk of the car.

"I'm packing my shit." I said. I was breaking inside but I could see my parents point so much clearer now. I wasn't going to get a job with the club and I was going to respect their wishes and move away. As far as I could get, even if that meant moving to New York. I grabbed my bag from the back seat of the car and hauled it over to my parent's house. I'd get my shit later when my dad could make Noah stay at the clubhouse. I'm sure he'll drown himself in pussy or some shit. As soon as I got inside the house and sat on the couch everything hit me with such intensity. The sobs wracked my body and the pain made me tremble. I'd never been through such heartbreak in my life and I hated the feeling. The pain kept getting worse and worse until I finally blacked out.

I awoke to lights flashing by overhead. My head was pounding and I could feel air rushing into my nose. What the hell was going on? I looked around and saw men and women in scrubs pushing me on a bed. Great I was in the hospital. Why was in the hospital? I didn't see anyone familiar and so I tried to relax. My body refused to do so. I felt a sharp stabbing pain in my belly and screamed. The pain was almost unbearable and I felt something slick between my legs. What the fuck? I was wheeled into a room and a woman was the only one left in the room. She looked down at me and smiled slightly. I felt tears running down my temples.

"What's happening?" I asked.

"Right now we are going to undress you and figure out what is going on dear. You've lost a lot of blood. Were you attacked?" She asked. I shook my head no.

"Not that I am aware of." I said my voice raspy as another stabbing pain hit me. I clenched my teeth and squeezed the hand rails of the bed until my knuckles were white.

"The doctor is going to get you some pain medicine to help while we figure out what's going on." She said and I felt scissors against my leg. She was cutting my jeans off of me.

"How did I get here?" I asked.

"A man I'm assuming was your father called. Said you were laying on the couch passed out and there was blood everywhere on your lower body." I shivered and lifted my hips slightly to help her get my jeans out from under me.

"Are you able to sit up?" she asked politely. I pulled on the handrails and felt her hand go behind my back helping me sit up. Once up she clipped my shirt up the back and undid my bra. The instant the bra was gone I felt relief in my chest. I sighed and pulled the paper gown up over my shoulders and laid back down. She snipped the sides of my underwear and pulled those off too.

When she pulled them away I saw all the blood there. "Oh Jesus." I whispered and closed my eyes.

"Any chance you were or are pregnant?" She asked. I opened my eyes and looked at her.

"I had my period just last week so I don't believe so." I said. She nodded.

"We will do a test just to be sure." She said and went through the usual questions for a hospital visit. I laid in the bed and prayed that everything was okay. The nurse left and my dad came in the room. I looked over at him and he sat down by the bed. His hand clutched mine and I could see tears coming down his face and slipping into his beard.

"Daddy..." I said and screamed as more pain hit me. My dad's eyes widened in fear and he looked down at my legs. He stood up and went in the hall and started screaming for something I sat up and held my lower belly as I saw more blood coming out. I looked at the door as the nurse and a doctor came rushing in. The doctor gave me a shot and I felt like I was going to throw up. I laid against the pillow and closed my eyes just breathing through it all. I finally got relief from the pain and looked up at the doctor. He was handsome and smiled down at me.

"Better?" he asked. I nodded. "A lab assistant will be here soon to draw some blood so we can try and figure out what's going on. If we don't know after that then we will give you an ultrasound maybe we will find something." He said. I nodded at him and looked over at my father.

The tests went smoothly and my mother showed up shortly after my blood was drawn. I stayed silent as my father held my hand. I took comfort in it. I wanted Noah but I knew I had to do what I was told at least this once so I didn't ruin my life like my mother had ruined hers as she would put it. A nurse came in to check on my pain levels and such a few times before the doctor came back in. He looked sad and I tried to sit up more.

"This is the worst part of my job." He whispered and looked up at me. "I'm so sorry." He said and I became confused.

"What?" I asked, feeling fear creep up on me.

"You had a miscarriage." He said and sat in his stool. I stared at him.

"That's not possible. I took a pregnancy test a few weeks ago and it said negative and then I had my period last week." I said. He sighed.

"Sometimes, women experience bleeding like a period while pregnant. However, it was not a menstrual bleeding, it was vaginal which is okay. Something must have happened today whether it was physical or just stress caused you to lose the baby." He said. I shut down completely and stared at the door. I saw Noah down the hall and he just stood there watching. I looked over at my dad.

"I want him gone." I said and looked back at Noah. My dad looked down the hall and stood up walking towards Noah. I heard my mother sob and I didn't look away from Noah. He could have been the reason that I lost the baby. Everyone in the room close to me besides the doctor could have been the reason why I lost the baby. I looked at my mother.

"You and dad need to leave." I said. She looked up at me.

"Honey. I'm not going to—"

"Get out." I said more sternly than I should. My mother got up and walked towards my father. I watched as he whipped his head over to me and saw his heart break. I was moving. I was going to leave this world behind and find something else. I looked over at the doctor.

"Would you be so kind to close the curtains?" I asked. He nodded and stood up closing the curtains.

"Do you feel safe at home?" he asked. I shook my head gently.

"Not anymore." I said and laid back staring at the ceiling.

"I'll get security stationed by your door. No one will be coming to your room unless it's hospital personal." He said. I nodded and put my hand over my belly. The last straw was handed to me when I lost that baby. Life as I knew it was over. I wasn't going to go look for excitement anymore I was going to keep to myself and be the boring person I used to be. I was going to cut off all ties to The Devil's Pride MC. I was officially done.

NOAH

No one would tell me what happened. I had seen the ambulance go rushing through our gates towards Jack's house and knew that Jack and Grace were both there. I didn't stop myself and ran there. Something had to have happened. When I got there, they were carrying Grace on a stretcher and she was unconscious. I was starting to panic when Jack put his hand on my shoulder.

"Not now Noah." He said and climbed on his bike following the ambulance. I stood there and watched as Grace was taken away in the ambulance. I was scared out of my mind as I ran back to my bike throwing my helmet across the lot and squealing out of the gates, racing towards the hospital.

I saw Grace and her parents squeezed into a tiny room with a doctor. My heart was racing and I wanted to fall to my knees seeing Grace that way. I heard Grace's mother let out a sob as something bad was told to them. I wanted to go and be near Grace. Her eyes met mine and there was no life left in them. She looked over at her dad and said something then looked back at me. I was frozen to my spot. Jack came out of the room and walked towards me.

"Noah come on. She wants you gone." Jack said and I was defeated. I allowed Jack to push me out into the waiting room and into a chair. She really is done with me. Not moments later Jack's wife came out crying. He caught her in his arms and held her.

"She doesn't want anyone in there." She sobbed into Jack's chest. I looked at the floor.

"What happened?" I asked. Jack looked down at me.

"She had my grandbaby taken away from her." He said.

"Doctor said it was stress or something physical, but she lost it." He said. I slumped back into the chair. I could have killed our baby without knowing it. I closed my eyes and rested my elbows on my knees. This was possibly the worst day of my life.

"Let's go home lad." Jack said and pulled me up by my arm. I let him lead me out of the hospital and away from Grace. I went to my bike and threw my leg over it. Jack kissed his wife goodbye as she got in her car and drove away then he came by me.

"Let's go for a ride ya?" he said and got on his own bike. I nodded and waited for him to start up and go.

The ride wasn't long, but it was long enough for all my memories of Grace and I to rush through me. The day I first met her was a particular memory that kept floating through. Jack pulled off the road at some point and we stopped at a diner. I watched him as he got off his bike and walk towards the diner. I followed suit looking around as we got inside. Jack sat down at a table and I sat across from him. What the hell is going on? I looked at Jack and he was looking at me.

"I shouldn't have said you could have Grace." He said and I slumped back in my seat. Fuck me.

"Then why did you?" I asked.

"It looked like you would be keeping her close when she wanted to run. Now her mother wants her to run." He said and looked at the table. My back straightened and I looked at him.

"What do you mean her mother wants her to run?" I asked getting angry. I sure as shit knew what it meant but I wasn't about to let him know that.

"She told me to tell her that she needed to leave you and cut all ties from the club. I'd do anything for that woman and she wants Grace to go far away and have a life without the club." He said. I was seeing red and couldn't keep a handle on it for much longer. They were the reason that I no longer had Grace. The reason why I possibly didn't have a kid.

I stood up from the table and turned to the door. That's

when I saw our allies walk in. Shit.

"I'm extremely pissed off at you right now Jack." I growled and sat down next to him. Jack shook their hands and chatted with the president of the Tribes MC. He was talking about starting up a new deal when we heard a crash outside. I was out of my seat and running towards the scene before anyone could stop me. I saw a man standing above where my bike was currently on the ground.

"Hey, shithead!" I yelled. "What the fuck happened to my bike?" The guy was about the size of a fifteen-year-old boy who looked like he was thirty. He had a girl next to him and she hand her hands on her hips. She was smoking hot and looked nothing like Grace. Her blonde hair was curled down her back and her white tank top was showing off her tanned skin. She had hips that filled her jeans perfectly and I smiled at her. She smiled back and I noticed she had a split lip and yellowed bruising around her eye.

"Sorry, man, I just wanted a picture with it and I must have knocked it over." He was rambling and my arms shot out grabbing his throat. I turned towards him and pulled him close.

"You never touch another man's bike." I said and let go of him. He stumbled a bit and came back at me. His fist swung missing my face by an inch and I slammed my fist into his stomach making him double over in pain. He fell to the ground and watched as he cradled his stomach and looked up at me.

"Did you do that to her?" I asked pointing towards the girl. He tried to get up again and I pushed him back down with my foot.

"Did he do that to you sweetheart?" I asked. She gave me a slight nod and that's all I needed. My fist slammed into his eye socket feeling a crunch and the skin on my knuckles tear. I picked my bike up and made sure it was in good enough condition to ride back.

The girl just stood there watching me and I looked back over at her.

"What's your name darling?" I asked.

"Marie." She said. I smiled

"Well Marie. Would you like to go with me?" I asked. She nodded and I looked over at Jack.

"Alright. Are you hungry?" I asked.

"No." she said.

"I have to take care of something else first then we will take off. Sound good?" I asked.

"Yes." It was breathy and nothing what I was used to. I smiled and walked back towards Jack.

"You better son?" he asked. I nodded and went back in the diner to take a piss.

Jack finished up the discussion with the Tribes and I went back out to Marie. She was adorable holding her purse against her hip. I smiled going next to her.

"Do you really want to go back to my town with me?" I asked. She looked up at me. "Cause I could just do ya in front of your boyfriend here make ya scream a few times and let ya leave with him instead." The blush that crept up her face almost made up my mind then and there.

"I'd like you to fuck me on your bike." She said. I smiled and looked over at Jack and the Tribes. The made a wall between us and the diner so no one could see what we were about to do. She shimmed out of her jeans and threw them at her boyfriend. He watched in disbelief. I smiled at the fucker and rolled a condom on my dick. She threw her leg over and leaned against my bike's tank putting her ankles on my shoulder. I ran my finger from the back of her pussy to the front pinching her clit. She moaned and I smiled slamming inside her. She wasn't as tight as Grace was but I'd get her off just the same. I heard her boyfriend groaning on the ground and I smiled slapping her ass as I pumped into her. She was moaning and I could feel her clenching around me. I pulled out and pulled her ankles off my shoulders.

"Flip over baby." I said. She straddled the bike and pushed her ass into the air. I pulled my thumb through her juices and played with her ass.

"Has anyone ever done ya here baby?" I asked and she shook her head in response.

"Lean back." I said and pushed my dick towards her anus. She took me easily and I smiled.

"I'm gonna go fast and hard now that you've accepted me." I whispered and started slamming into her. She was so close I slipped out and slammed into her pussy as she screamed with her release. I smiled and kept pumping through it and finally got my own release. Her boyfriend was laying on the ground covering his eyes and I smiled pulling out of her.

"There ya go baby." I said letting her get up. I pulled the condom out and tossed it in a garbage can while tucking myself away again. I crouched by her boyfriend.

"That's how a real man gets his woman off. He doesn't fucking hit her shithead." I said and went back over to my bike getting on it. Jack and The tribes were on theirs. Jack took off for our town and The Tribes went their separate ways. I followed Jack to the clubhouse.

"I hope you move on as fast as you fucked that broad." Jack said after we parked. "I still need ya in this club." He said. I shook my head.

"My loyalty lies with the club. I'll never leave it." I said walking into the clubhouse. I didn't say another word to Jack that day.

    I awoke the next morning and ordered flowers for Grace and had them sent to her without a note. I was still pissed off that her father was making her leave me. I wasn't going to stress her out while she was in the hospital though. Beast had visited her last night and said she was doing better. I was glad she was okay and I felt stupid knowing I fucked that girl yesterday. I went out to the bar and got two fingers of jack. The plan was to get drunk until I couldn't stand anymore. Beast sat by me and nursed a beer. By the time I was almost done with the bottle of Jack Daniels, Jack walked into the room.

"Jesus Christ." He said and came over taking the bottle

away.

"Hey!" I yelled and slurred. Beast held me on the barstool and shook his head. I felt good. No I felt fucking great!

"Noah, let's get you in your room." Beast said and stood up.

"F-f-fuck off bud." I said and stood up. I had to grab the bar to steady myself. Beast threw my arm over his shoulders and walked me to my room throwing me on the bed. He shook his head and left the room. I passed out when my head hit the pillow.

GRACE

Cody said he'd be by today to help me get out of the hospital. They were just waiting for him to get there to sign the discharge papers. Cody was the only one I could trust right now and I knew that I had nowhere to go after leaving here. He told me that I could stay with him but I didn't want to intrude on him. I waited in that room for him to show up. It was almost noon and he had said he'd be there by eleven. I sighed and leaned back into the pillows closing my eyes.

I heard a commotion outside and opened my eyes looking at the clock. I must have fallen asleep because it was almost two in the afternoon. I could see Cody being pushed away from my door by hospital security and I got up going to the door.

"It's okay he's allowed in." I said to the security officer that was near my door. He nodded at me and let Cody through.

"Hey doll. How are you feeling?" He asked.

"I've been better." I said and looked up at him. Why couldn't I have just gone for Cody? He was handsome and his huge frame made this room even smaller. I could have just gone after Cody and been safe rather than be with someone who is probably off fucking the whole city right now. I sighed and sat down. Cody handed me a bag of clothes and I smiled pulling them on. He had turned his back when I had to take the gown off. He stopped the nurse from coming in to discharge me and waited until I was ready to let her in. When she came in she smiled at me.

"I just need you to sign this and we can get you on your way. The doctor wanted to let you know that there may be some bleeding and to just wear a pad it'll ease after a few days." She said holding a clipboard out for me. I signed it and then went over to Cody.

"Let's go." I said and stuffed the discharge papers in my pocket. He smiled at me and put his arm around my shoulders keeping me close.

"Your dad wants me to take you to his house. I told him no." Cody said and I looked up at him.

"I can go there. I just don't want to see Noah." I said.

"Yeah well Noah isn't up for seeing anyone right now either. Can barely keep his damn eyes open." He said.

"What's that mean?" I asked. Cody looked down at me and stopped walking.

"Sweetheart, he's drunk. So, drunk he can't get out of bed even to puke. One of the bar whores has been cleaning him up every time he does." He said putting both hands on my shoulders.

"Your dad told me everything that they don't want you two together and he's making you move far away. I offered to switch charters so that you would have a familiar face nearby if you need it." He said. Cody was like the older brother I never had. I loved him unconditionally for everything he does for me.

"You don't have to do that. You'd just have to come visit me and never give my information out to anyone inside the club. Even my father." I said. He smiled and hugged me.

"Sugar. The request is already been made. He's letting me go." He said. I smiled up at him and buried my face into his chest. He pushed me back a little and smiled.

"What would I do without you, Cody?" I asked. He put his hand on my back and walked out of the hospital with me.

He helped me get situated at his apartment before he left for the clubhouse again. I couldn't believe he was going to give up his life here to go be with me. Would Noah have done something like that? I would never know. He didn't even know I was moving away for all I knew. Cody told me he'd be back later and went to the clubhouse leaving me all alone in his apartment. I wandered around it most of the time just to get up and moving. I rummaged through his fridge and found that he had everything to make lasagna. I made lasagna that night for Cody and me. He walked in right after I had pulled dinner out of the oven. He smiled and came over taking the hot pads and lasagna out of my hands setting it on the table.

"We should have moved in together a long time ago, especially If I was going to be coming home to food." He laughed. I smiled and grabbed plates and sat down.

"I was bored." I said and cut the lasagna into squares before taking a piece for myself. Cody smiled at me and sat down digging into the food.

"Mmmm. Yup if I would have known your cooking was this good, I would have claimed you myself." He said and grinned at me. I smiled and ate a little bit then stopped.

"You okay?" he asked. I nodded.

"Just been thinking is all." I said.

"What about?" he asked popping more lasagna into his mouth. I looked up at him and set my fork down.

"About how life could have gone so much differently, if I would have fallen in love with you instead." I said. Cody cleared his throat and grabbed my hand from across the table.

"You didn't know you had the option. It's alright." He said. I looked into his eyes and for the first time I saw it there. He didn't just love me, he was in love with me. I sighed and got up going to him.

"I'm sorry I didn't know." I said and sat on his lap.

"It's okay Grace. Not like I could really touch you or anything. I just loved you from a far." He said.

"Will you wait for me?" I asked. He nodded and wrapped his arms around me.

"Of course, Grace I'll wait for you. I'm not going to be able to do anything except wait for you baby. We're gonna be living together up north." He said tucking his head underneath my chin. I smiled and wrapped my arms around his neck. We stayed like that for a while.

I woke up the next morning with Cody's arm slung over my waist and holding me close. I could feel his length digging into my ass as he spooned me. I didn't want him to be a rebound if I was going to be with him. I was still in love with Noah but that had to sail away. I was moving away with Cody at my side. My chest swelled at the thought of having to move on from everything so quickly. I was angry that Noah and my parents could have been the reason I lost the baby. Cody hadn't known why I was in the hospital at all and I felt like I should tell him before we left. I rolled over to face him and saw that he was still sleeping. I smiled and snuggled deeper into his chest closing my eyes again. Maybe I could sleep some more before I had to tell him.

Cody woke me up a hour later with a kiss to my temple. I smiled and stretched rolling over to face him. "Good morning." He said.

"Morning." I rasped. He smiled and pushed some hair out of my face. Had he always been this intimate with me?

"I just have to go get the final vote to cut ties and I'll be back after that and then we can sit down and search for an apartment around that area and take off by tonight." He said. I smiled and sat up.

"That would be great." I said and scrunched my shoulders together stretching my arms out. Cody's gaze dropped to my breasts and I suddenly felt naked. He tore his eyes away and I bit my lip. Well wasn't this awkward.

"Sorry…" Cody said getting up.

"It's okay. They're just boobs." I said. He gave me a deep belly laugh and looked at me.

"Yeah, just boobs." He said and leaned over me.

"Do you know how many of the men at the club talk about your tits? No one else's just your tits alone sweetheart. Every single guy in that club has talked about them. They've said that they are the best ones they have seen with clothes on. Some of the men say they are better than their ol'ladies tits. They have talked about what they would do with your magnificent tits if they had you for even a minute. Most grazes you feel at the club aren't accidental sweetheart and the only time I didn't hear about them was when your father or Noah were around." He was almost growling when he finished. I was turned on. I don't know how but Cody talking about my tits made my nipples pebble and a fire to be set to my groin. I could already feel the moisture coming out of me. Well, fuck me.

I was sure my chest was heaving and my hand came up grazing his cheek and feeling his beard. I wasn't sure how far this would go but I didn't care either. My hand went behind his neck and pulled him to me our lips barely touching. His hands were planted on either side of me and I wrapped my arms around him trying to get closer. He laid me down on the bed and wrapped one of his arms under my back. His lips caressed mine and his tongue slid against my bottom lip. I opened myself up for him and ran my hands through his hair. He pressed his hips between my legs and I groaned into his mouth. I pulled away from him and looked into his eyes. He leaned back down and kissed me more sliding his hand down my body and under the band of my panties his finger touched the bundle of nerves and I moaned arching my back. Cody pulled back, drawing his hand away from me and looked at it. Most of his hand was covered in blood and I almost died. I jumped up and ran to the bathroom, mortified. Now I really had to tell him.

After cleaning up I went and found Cody. He was sitting at the kitchen table. He looked as if he was praying. I sat down next to him and didn't say a word for a while, not until I had his attention. He sat there for what felt like eternity before he brought his eyes up to mine. I smiled a little and he reached over taking my hand. I found comfort in him and was extremely thankful for everything he did and was doing for me.

"Hey gorgeous. You alright?" He asked. I sighed and leaned my temple against my fist.

"No not really. I should have a feeling of loss right now, but I haven't. I never knew what was going on until they told me I no longer had it. I wish I would have known and I would have been more careful with everything." I said and looked down at the table pulling my hand away from his. He reached over and lifted my face to his.

"What happened baby?" As soon as the words left, I felt what I should have been feeling. Remorse and loss over my unborn child that I would never get to hold and never get to see run through a yard playing with their dad. I felt the tears rolling down my cheeks and Cody's arms came around me and he just held me.

"I was pregnant." I sobbed into his chest. He pulled me to him tighter and rubbed my back. When he pulled away, I could see that he was upset too. "It's okay. I'll be okay. I can't change it now, but I didn't even know I was pregnant. I thought I had gotten my period when Noah and I went on vacation or whatever it was, but it turns out it was just vaginal bleeding which the doctor said is completely normal. He told me that it was either stress or something physical that made me lose the baby. I hadn't been hit in the stomach when I stomped the bitch for talking to Noah and afterwards Noah had threw me over his shoulder. It could have been that or it was due to my parents almost getting a divorce or them telling me to leave and cut all ties. I just don't know what to make of any of it anymore." I ended on a whisper and looked into his eyes.

"Oh, sweetheart. I'll take care of you." He said. I smiled knowing it would be true. Cody always amazed me in the simplest ways. I stood up and wrapped myself around him.

"I love you, Cody." I said and felt his arms wrap around my back.

"I love you too Grace." He said and placed a kiss on my temple.

NOAH

I heard a bottle hit the wall above my head and shatter. The pieces scattered over the bed and myself. I opened my eyes after I didn't feel anymore pieces falling and sat up to look at who threw the bottle. Jack was standing just inside my doorway.

"What the fuck was that about?!" I hollered. Jack looked furious and I didn't care.

"I fucking need you to sober your ass up and help out. I don't think you've showered in weeks and I let you not show up for church because I knew you were going through some shit. Noah it's been three goddamn months since she left and you need to get your shit together. You told me after she left you that you were loyal to the club. Now man the fuck up and show your president some respect and fucking loyalty!" He was red in the face after yelling and huffing. I let my head roll forward and ran my hand through my hair. He was right I hadn't showered in a while and I felt like shit, but I did need to man up. I stood up and walked into the bathroom turning the shower on.

We had new shit going on with the club I remembered hearing about it but couldn't do anything because I was always so drunk. Fucking three months had gone by and I had no idea where Grace was. I missed her like hell and was a stupid fuck for not trying to find her instead of getting drunk. I should have gone after her. The grief that hit me was insane and strong. It felt like someone was stabbing me and I leaned my forearms against the wall and tried to take a deep breath. I slammed my fist against the wall and cleaned up then went to church, for once. Jack sat in his spot after everyone had sat down. I looked around the table and saw a few people staring. Beast was gone and I had no idea what was going on. Where was Beast? I sighed and looked down at the table.

"As you all can tell Noah is out of his fucking room for once and will from now on be attending every single session of church plus doing fucking prospect duties until I say." Jack said and my head snapped up to him. He was fucking me over. It was his and his wife's fault that I was depressed like this and I felt the rage creeping up I wanted to slice his throat open from ear to ear and watch his blood drain. It wouldn't have done anything at all, it would be taken as disrespect for the club.

"Now on to business. Everything with Beast was finalized. We also have a run coming up. Noah, you and Grease man are going to head up there first make sure everything is secure." Well fuck me I was actually getting some slack. That is until he cooks up some shit.

"You will meet up with the northern charter and pay your respects. Let them know I'll be up there the next day. Beast will be there so be nice boys. We need to make sure this run goes smoothly and absolutely no pussy or alcohol for Noah there." Jack said I sighed and leaned back. Fuck. Me.

The gavel hit the table and we all stood up. I'm sure Grease man will make damn well sure that I won't have any pussy and the fact that the northern chapter has pussy crawling around at all hours and I was going to be fucking hard as a rock the whole fucking time. Alcohol would help and jacking off will. Grease and I packed a bag and took off for the northern chapter.

The ride was long but scenic. I was glad to get off my ass finally and enjoy some time walking around. Grease immediately found some club whore to hang onto and I had to stay back. We walked inside the club and President Tommy greeted us.

"Welcome brothers!" he said grabbing Grease's hand and pulling him in slapping him on the back. He pulled me in doing the same and I smiled at him.

"Noah, here is gonna have blue balls forever. He's on Jack's shit list for some reason and he's not allowed to have pussy or alcohol." Grease automatically said and I inwardly groaned. I was so fucked on this trip.

The door opened and Beast walked in. He stopped dead when our eyes locked. "Noah." He said and came towards me pulling me into a hug.

"Beast, How the hell are ya?" I asked and hugged him back. Looking over his shoulder I was blinded by sunlight and my balls twisted. Her hair was longer then before it was almost to her ass now and she was radiant. I froze where I was and felt Beast pulling away. He looked over at her and I wanted to run to her. Knowing I couldn't kept me where I was. She stopped just inside the door and stared at me. I sighed and backed away from Beast. I couldn't go to her and I couldn't figure out what the hell to do. My head was fuzzy and I couldn't see anyone but her.

Beast went over to Grace and took her hand. What the fuck was going on? She followed him out of the club and she only kept her eyes on him. Didn't even look back at me or Grease. She was over me already. It felt like my chest was going to explode. I wanted to go after them and figure out what the fuck was going on but I couldn't bring myself to do that. I turned towards the rest of the club and noticed that they were all looking at me. Fuck, they knew too. I was so screwed and I didn't even know how to handle this shit.

"Alright I need a beer." I said and went over to the bar.

"No can do, Noah." Grease said. "You know Jack's rules."

The night consisted of talking to Tommy and Grease going in a back room at least eight times before I finally called it a night and went to a room. Beast had come back but Grace didn't. She probably didn't want to see me. It had been three damn months and it still fucking hurt knowing I could have caused her to lose our baby and to run away from me, following her parents orders. I was a fool for thinking that maybe I could get her back. She was attached to Beast like a child to their mother. She was frightened with everything around her. I sat on the edge of the bed and rested my elbows on my knees. I felt helpless. I couldn't ease her pain and fears. I was no longer with her. My body seemed to be on high alert for some shit to go down. I wanted to brawl or do something with my fists. I made the woman I loved someone who was fearful and threw her into someone else's arms. That night I didn't sleep well. Tossing and turning until the sun rose again.

When I went out into the main room there were naked women and bikers with their pants around their ankles strewn across the whole clubhouse. It was only a matter of time until Jack showed up and I'm sure Grace would be around for that as well. It was going to be a hell of a day and I needed lots of coffee to get through it. Just wish I could get some fucking pussy to get rid of the hard on I'd been sporting since yesterday. My thoughts have circled around Grace, all night. It has been nothing but her, driving me up a wall and through the roof.

The coffee was hot and I was grateful of that as it hit my tongue. I looked around and saw a woman I had never met before.

"Good morning." I said to her. She jumped and looked over at me.

"Sorry, I wasn't expecting anyone to be awake yet." She said. She had brunette hair that skimmed her shoulders and a small waist. Her mouth looked especially fuckable and I was told no pussy. Jack didn't say anything about blowing my load off in some whore's mouth. I smiled at her.

"Attached to anyone?" I asked. She looked up at me and smiled, a devilish smile that told me that even if she was attached she'd make me a happy man.

"No, I'm not attached to anyone. Tommy just pays me to clean up every time there's a party. Which seems to be quite often." She said. I smiled.

"Well would you like to take a break, maybe show me some loving?" I asked. She smiled and came over to me. I watched as she slipped onto her knees in front of me.

"I should warn you sweetheart. I can't take any pussy." I said.

"That's alright handsome. You can pay me back later." She said and undid my jeans.

I smiled and leaned against the bar drinking my coffee as she worked my dick with her hand. She came forward and her hands clutched my thighs. Her lips parted and went around my cock. Just once of her mouth taking me to the back of her throat, had me thinking of trying to sneak somewhere to fuck her brains out, quietly. Her tongue paid attention to the flesh underneath the head making me shudder. I fisted her hair and pulled my dick out of her mouth.

"I'm thinking that maybe we should break some rules and have some wild, but quiet, fuck session." I said. Her lips curled up into a grin and she stood up stroking my cock with her hand as she led me down the hallway to a bedroom. I'd probably get shit for this.

"Have you ever done anal sweetheart?" I asked. She nodded and pulled me into a room.

I came out of the room and went back to my coffee. I didn't fuck her, I couldn't, not with Grace fucking popping in my head. My coffee was cold and I dumped it out. The door to the clubhouse swung open and Beast walked in. I nodded my head at him and got more coffee.

"When do you guys leave on the run?" he asked. I looked over at him and took a sip of my coffee.

"Tomorrow morning. Jack is coming today to talk to Tommy and then we are leaving." I said. He came over and grabbed some of his own coffee. I looked into my mug.

"How's Grace?" I asked. Beast put the coffee pot down and sighed.

"She's doing better. She's the one who made me ask about when you leave." He said.

"Ouch." I said and took another drink.

"Yeah she's something else." He turned and leaned against

the counter.

"Look she is still in love with you but she's actually listening for once. She only comes here if it's a huge party and even then, she won't leave my side. She goes to yoga every day and she found a job and goes there every day and she recently got asked out by some suit. I was surprised that she even said yes with everything she went through with Max. Fucking suits, though think they are better than everyone. He told her right away that he didn't like her living with me and it was straight up the most hilarious thing ever." Beast laughed and I had to smile.

Beast and I bullshitted for a while until the clubhouse door swung open again. Both of us looked and saw Jack come inside. He looked at us and smiled nodding his head.

"He's here pretty early." I said and went over to Jack.

"Noah. Where is Tommy?" he asked.

"I'm not sure. He partied pretty late last night with his ol'lady." I said and he nodded.

"Well I guess I'll come back in a bit. Need to go do something quickly anyways." Jack said and looked over at Beast then back at me. "I'll be back soon." He said and walked towards the door again.

"Jack…will you tell Grace I would like to talk to her at some point. Just talk…I'm not going to try and get her back. I just want to talk." I said. Jack turned and looked at me and nodded.

"I'll tell her." He said and left.

GRACE

My father called and said he was in town and he would like to see me. I was going to let him but any mention of Noah then he'd be gone. I didn't want to hear anything of Noah, ever again. I knew that eventually he would pop into my life again but for now I was going to control it. He wouldn't be a part of it. My father showed up not too long after I got off the phone with him. I still loved him like my father, but I was still slightly angry with him for everything he said and commanded of me.

It was quiet when he came in Beast's and my tiny apartment. It was awkward at first and then he wrapped me in his arms. It wasn't bad at first that was until all the anger rushed forward and I hit him. My fist flew forward and hit him square in the chest. I was so mad at him that I couldn't' stop it at all. He looked at me and took it. There were tears in his eyes as I smacked his cut and beat his chest. He wrapped his arms around me and just held me as tears ran down my face. I finally stopped and just cried into his chest, all anger vanishing. His hand rubbed my back like he used to when I was little. It calmed me down now like it did back then. My tears resolved to sniffles and I pulled away wiping my face.

"I'm sorry, baby girl. You'll see this will all work out." He said. I just nodded and sat on the couch. "Are you sleeping with Beast?" He asked out of the blue. My head jerked up to this.

"Dad, no!" I said shocked. "I've been seeing someone else for now." I said. He nodded and sat next to me.

"Your mom and I miss you already. It's weird that you're not living close to us anymore." He said and looked at me.

"You guys can always come visit. And I'll come visit too." I said. He shook his head.

"You should stay here. We will come to you." He said and took my hand. I smiled at him and sat there. Something must have been going on with the club for him to not let me come down there.

We chatted for about another hour and then he left to go back to the clubhouse in town. Cody came home not long after. I smiled at him and got off the couch.

"Hey." I said.

"Hey. So, I have to tell you something." He said and looked at me. His eyes were saddened, and he watched me intensely.

"Cody... what is it?" I asked. He sighed sat down at the table. I sat across from him and watched him.

"I have to leave." He said.

"Why?" I asked.

"They want me to go on a run." He said. I couldn't help it but the word fell out.

"Where?" Cody looked up at me.

"I have to go to prison." He said.

"I'll most likely be in there for a few years." He sighed again and watched me.

"Oh, fuck." I said and leaned back. I knew I couldn't ask any more questions.

"They also want you to get close to this cop..." he trailed off. My eyes snapped to his.

"The club is going to use me?" I asked. He nodded.

"Your dad actually was the one who mentioned you do it. He feels you can get close and be unattached." He said and wiped his lips with his fingers.

"I don't like it, but it's really up to you." He said and folded his hands in front of him watching me. I sighed and looked at the table. Cody was going to jail for the club and I was going to have to get close to the cop.

"What's special about the cop?" I asked.

"I honestly don't know what we need with the cop. I think it's more so that someone can keep an eye on him while some shit goes down." He said. I nodded and stood up.

"Let's go to the club and talk this over." I said. Cody stood up and grabbed my shoulders.

"I don't think you understand, Grace. If you agree to this I have to beat the living hell out of you after you start getting close to him and you're going to have to turn me in." He said. My blood ran cold. I would be signing up to get my ass kicked by Cody. My eyes searched his for some hope that it wasn't true, but his eyes were all serious and sad. I got up on my toes and kissed him.

"It'll be okay." I said. Cody sadly smiled and led the way out to his bike.

We arrived at the clubhouse in a short ride and I wasn't excited for what was going to happen. I loved Cody more than I should have and I loved the club, but I wasn't sure if I could go through with my best friend beating the shit out of me to go to jail. We were going to have to set something up and I wasn't excited for that at all. My stomach was in my toes the whole time.

The plan was set in stone. After we walked around town a few times together, show up some places together and then he would start giving me some bruises and I would have to act afraid and when men approached me, particularly when I was in a department store. I would have to be jumpy and watching my surroundings kind of like a junkie but with a black eye, hoping that a sales clerk will call the police and the one cop that I need to seduce to come "rescue" me.

It was going to start today. Cody had to take me shopping in town. Act all lovey and jealous setting everything up before the next step. The next step was the execution. After a few visits he would switch the way he did things. Hatred and jealous rearing up their ugly heads. The things he had to do, I had already been put through with one man and now again with someone I had known almost my whole life, someone I could have fallen in love with but didn't, not fully anyways, someone I trusted. I was already scared to death of this plan and now I had to throw that fear towards Cody. My heart ached knowing that my father offered me for this. He knew what I would have had to go through to make this real. My anger that had vanished before came rushing back and stronger than ever. I didn't care if I ever saw him again. My throat was constricted with unshed tears and unexposed emotion. Cody took me in his arms after the meeting was over and he just held me. He was always good to me and I was very thankful for that. I wouldn't hold this bullshit against him either. He was a good man and a good friend. I stood up taking his hand.

"Let's go get this over with, please. I'm probably going to have to sleep with a cop before this shit is over." I said. He nodded and went over to his bike. I followed and Cody handed me my helmet.

"Let's get you something sexy." Cody said and smiled. I got on the back and we went to a little department store that sold almost everything. There was children stuff and then a little section that was roped off and had a sign that read adults only. Bear poked his head inside the closed off area and laughed.

"Babe. You should see this." He said and pulled me close. I smiled and peeked inside.

"Oh my god." I said. "Hey, there's a pocket pussy." I smiled up at him and whispered, "Think you could sneak it in?" I laughed as he broke a huge smile and dragged me along the store. He grabbed my hand and pulled me towards the women's clothing. Cody picked something up that would have covered me from right below my chin to beyond my toes and fingers. He gave it a questioning look and then looked over at me. I laughed and took it from his hands.

"Should I go try it on?" I asked. His lips flattened and he took it back and put it on the rack.

"Definitely not." He said and I smiled and pulled him towards the younger women's clothing. He smiled and pulled something off the rack that I would never ever wear in my entire life, at least for him.

"I'm getting this for you. What size are you baby?" he asked.

I looked up at him.

"Cody...I don't think I'd ever wear that." I said. He smiled and pulled me close to him.

"Sweetheart. I would like to see you in this before everything goes down." Cody said and I smiled.

"Alright. I'll wear it once. But then that's it." I said and got on my toes kissing him. Cody wrapped his arms around me and deepened the kiss. I heard someone clear their throat behind me and I turned and looked. The suit I had been seeing occasionally was standing in front of me. I blushed and chewed on my lip.

"I figured you would be breaking it off soon enough. Considering you are living with him." He said. I looked up at him then back at Cody.

"You're right... I'm sorry I was just trying to get over my ex. I'm sure you've done it before, and well Cody he's always been there for me I just never realized I've been in love with him this whole time." I said almost trying to explain. He nodded.

"Well, have a good day and enjoy yourselves. She'd never wear that you know." He said pointing to the clothing that Cody was holding. I smiled and looked at him.

"I told you." I said. The suit smiled.

"Grace, if you need anything let me know. I'll be more than happy to help you." He said. I smiled and looked at him.

"You are one of the kindest men I've met and I'm sorry it had to end this way." I said. He leaned down and placed a kiss on my cheek.

"Thank you for that dear. I'll hopefully see you around sometime." He said and turned away leaving. I turned back towards Cody. He was watching the suit retreat.

"He's one of the better ones." Cody said and looked down at me. I smiled.

"Yes. I did feel like that too." I said. He put the clothing back and then looked around. I watched him for a moment and then grabbed his arm. "Cody?" I asked and he turned towards me. "I don't know if I can do this." He said and didn't look at me. He kept his eyes on his feet and kicked the carpet with his boot. I wrapped my arms around him and laid my head against him. His arms came around me almost reluctantly.

"Baby, we have to do this. It'll be okay." I said. He rubbed his hand gently down my back and up again before pulling away. I sighed and looked around some more. Cody kind of stood off to the side and watched the place. I turned to him and held up a really skimpy piece, a really see-through skimpy piece.

"Baby, what do you think of this?" I asked and held it against me. Cody looked over me and I never got any reaction. Nothing. I wasn't happy about it, at all. I decided to say fuck it and went into the adult only section. I looked around and all I saw was a bunch of sex toys and more skimpy clothing. I wasn't sure on what I was going to do to provoke him, until I saw a group of guys probably college age looking over at me. I smiled and grabbed something off the rack and walked over to them.

"Hey, boys. Do you think this would look good on me? My boyfriend won't give me an opinion." I said and held it against me. A blonde boy smiled and looked me up and down.

"Baby, it'd look better off you." He said. I smiled and watched as the boy's faces dropped from extremely excited to horror. I knew Cody was behind me. I turned and looked at him.

"There you are baby. I was just asking these boys what they thought of this outfit." I said smiling up at Cody. I could tell he wasn't happy, but it was a reaction. Just with one look into his eyes you could tell Cody's blood was boiling. Murder was written in his eyes. He was seriously on my nerves for this one. The boys scattered before Cody even said anything. He turned me around and kissed me.

"You're mine." He growled and his hands gripped my ass. "Mine. All mine." He said and released me. I smiled and put the clothing back.

"Should we get you a pocket pussy for when you get locked up?" I asked and his face broke into a smile and he put his arm around me.

"Baby, I don't plan on being locked up for long enough to need one." He said and pulled me out of the store.

"I think we will finish shopping another day." He whispered kissing me on the temple. I grinned as we got on his bike going home.

NOAH

I couldn't fucking believe what was going to happen. Beast was going to have to beat the shit out of a woman he loved and that I was still in love with. I didn't want to even think about it but it wouldn't leave my mind. Everything I did when I found out was harsher than it needed to be. Grace was going to have her gorgeous flesh marred for the fucking club and she was going to willingly do it. It was going to be a disaster that I wanted to pull her from. I wanted to save her from the club. My bike needed work and I couldn't focus on it. The tools I used were strewn across the garage. I finally stopped when I threw a ratchet across the garage almost hitting the prospect above the ear. I picked myself off the floor and stormed outside. I pulled the crushed pack of cigarettes out of my pocket and lit one. Inhaling deeply on the toxin and slowly releasing it. It helped for the few moments I had it but that was it. The anger was still there. I wanted to do everything I could to make sure that Grace was never harmed. I wanted her back and felt like the damned lost puppy I had come to be. I wished that I could have made it all better and we could have ran away or fucking something.

    I wanted to be everything for Grace and yet I couldn't fucking go near her. It was the worst fucking situation I had ever been in. I had to watch her be with others while I couldn't have her. It was enough to chop my own fucking balls off. Adding the beating she was going to receive alone from Beast…it took the fucking cake. I felt like I was a hopeless case. Nothing in the world would ever fix this feeling except if none of this had ever happened. It was the second worst feeling in the world. Losing Grace was the first. I couldn't go to bed without thinking about her. I couldn't get her out of my head. The sex between her and I was earth shattering and now I was mostly stuck with my hand and that was hardly working. I couldn't even touch another woman without thinking of Grace. She had been everything to me and still was. I needed to find a new way around to get her back, otherwise I was going to be hurting for a long while. I watched as the end of the cigarette burn and blew the smoke towards it. I was fucked up in the head and wasn't looking forward to fixing it.

"Hey, jackass. Think you could pick up Grease without fucking up? He dumped his fucking bike on Highway 210." Jack yelled over to me. I stuck the cigarette in my mouth and grabbed the keys for the tow truck.

"Yeah I can do that." I said and got in the tow truck, driving to get the stupid fuck named Grease.

It was a fucking mess on the highway. Bike parts were thrown everywhere and all that was fucking left of his bike was the goddamn gas tank and frame. The tires were in the ditch and I had to fucking clean the shit up. We got the frame on the flatbed and then picked up whatever pieces we could that wouldn't harm someone else's car. I brought him and the frame back to the club.

"Think we could fix the fucker up?" Grease asked. I laughed.

"You're going to be building yourself a brand new fucking bike, man. The only thing that's fucking good that's left is the frame." I said and got out of the truck. I lit up a new cigarette and helped the fucker lift the frame off the flatbed. Jack came out and looked at Grease.

"Are you fucking serious right now? How the hell did you just walk away from that?" Jack yelled. I hadn't even asked yet how it fucking happened.

"A guy came running up off the side and shoved me while I was pulled over. Then he signaled someone and a fucking truck ran my bike over. I had to stand and watch it and they took off. I got the plate and a picture of the truck and the fucker driving. I plan on getting them back." He said. I smiled and blew out a puff of smoke.

"Well I'll be damned." Jack said as Grease showed him the pictures.

My phone dinged right when we finished getting all of Grease's shit cleaned up off the flatbed. I pulled it out and looked at it. The screen flashed unknown number and I opened it. It started downloading a multimedia message and I waited for it to finish. As soon as it popped up there was a fucking picture of Grace fucking another man. It wasn't even Beast either. It was some guy with perfect fucking hair, probably her suit. I wasn't happy that she had found something after me, someone who could touch her like this. I wanted to crush my phone but I couldn't, I needed the picture and the fucking number. I was mixed between taking my phone in the bathroom and jacking off to it until I felt relief and taking the phone to Techy. I decided to give it to Techy. Techy is the guy that does all the work for the hacking and tracking.

"Run the fucking number. If you do anything with the picture." I leaned over his desk at the shop and stared him in the eyes. That was until my eyes went to his damn shirt. I burst out laughing. "the fuck is with your shirt man. 'Come to the dark side we have motorcycles?' Oh, dear god that was probably the best thing I read today."

"Yeah well I'm a nerd so..." Techy replied.

"Anything with the fucking picture besides deleting the fucker when you have the number written down. I'll find you and saw your balls off with a fucking butter knife." I said. Techy looked scared shitless and I stood up.

"Besides, if you look and Jack finds out that fucking thing is on that phone he'll probably fucking kill you himself for looking." I walked over towards the door and saw Jack coming this way.

"Jack's coming." I threw over my shoulder.

"Holy shit." Techy said and I looked at him. His face was down at the phone and I could see the bulge in his pants growing.

"Shithead!" Jack yelled I sighed and looked at Jack.

"Not you for once. Where the fuck is Techy?" he asked, and I stepped away. I watched as Jack walked over and pulled the phone out of his hand.

"What the fuck are you doing? We need you on the car like now." He stopped and looked at the picture on the phone. He looked over at me.

"Is this your fucking phone?" He asked. I nodded and closed the door.

"Someone just sent that photo to me. I was asking dipshit here to trace the number." I said and watched Jack's face receive recognition over the photo.

"Delete the fucking photo and track that fucking number." Jack yelled and waited. I crossed my arms and leaned against the wall.

Techy scrambled to write the number down and delete the photo. I wasn't happy that he even got to see that photo. It wasn't a great experience to have to let someone see the woman you love naked and being fucked by another man. It could drive a man fucking nuts, that's for sure. I watched as Techy worked his magic and came up with a name and address from the number. I looked it over and mentally mapped out the address until the name clicked. George Mathis.

"Son of a bitch..." I grabbed the phone and chucked it at the wall watching it shatter. It gave me no relief. I walked out of the building and threw my leg over my bike taking off. I could hear Jack yelling as the distance grew between us.

I went to the address and snuck around a bit before barging in. There was a truck parked in the driveway and it looked like something George would drive. I looked in the house through a couple windows. There was only movement in the front of the house which looked like the living room. There he was sitting on the couch and staring at a TV. How the fuck did he get that photo? By the time I got to the front door to barge in Jack and Techy were both there. Jack grabbed onto me and dragged me away from the door. I was trying to be quiet and didn't want to hit Jack. When we were around the corner almost back to my bike he let me go.

"What the fuck was that?" I asked. Jack shook his head.

"You don't need to go barging in there with your head cut off like a fucking chicken." He said.

"Then would you care to explain why my old man has a picture of your daughter fucking another man?" I asked my voice rising a little. Jack stood there for a moment and Techy looked like he'd seen a ghost.

"We will find out soon enough. Get on your bike and let's all go back to the club have a beer and call church." He said. I wasn't happy. I was hardly ever happy anymore. The luminous light inside of me was diminishing every day and I felt like I did not have a purpose anymore. I got on my bike and went to the clubhouse. I wasn't panning on just having a beer though.

Jack called church for five and I had planned to be thoroughly shitfaced by that time. The depression over losing Grace had come back with a vengeance and seeing another man balls deep inside her made my heart break all over again. I felt like this shit was never ending. It was going on five fucking months now and I saw no end, whatsoever. I grabbed a bottle of jack and sat down on a bar stool. I wanted to be numb quickly. I wasn't going to take this one slowly. I took a swig off the bottle and then looked around for a straw. I finally found one and put it in the bottle, bending it over the lip and I tilted my head back letting the amber liquid burn down my throat and into my stomach. I felt a pair of eyes watching me and once I had finished the bottle I looked over and met the eyes. Grace was standing there and I felt like someone had taken the floor out from under me. My knees started to buckle and I had to grab onto the counter to keep from falling. I watched as she came around and helped me into a damned chair. Her hand came up and caressed my cheek. I looked at her and couldn't pull my eyes from hers. She looked like an angel. Did I die?

"Are you alright?" she asked me and I had to fight the urge to pull her to me and kiss her.

"I miss you." I said and she nodded.

"I know. I've missed you too." She leaned forward and placed a kiss on my cheek. My arms wrapped around her and I felt content for once. Although, it could have been the alcohol taking effect. I stayed like that for a while just holding her. I could feel myself getting hard and I groaned. She giggled slightly and pulled back looking at me.

"Sweetheart, you should take care of that." She said. I sighed and looked at my crotch.

"Damn thing hasn't cooperated with me since you left." I said. She smiled at me and took both my hands and pulled me to my feet.

"Let's go take care of that." and everything went from clear to black then I felt myself fall and darkness encased me. Grace screamed a little and then I couldn't remember anything.

I awoke in my bed what felt like years later. Grace was sitting beside me and I sat up. "What happened?" I asked. She giggled and covered her mouth.

"I'm guessing blue balls. But honestly I don't know." She said and looked over by the door. Beast was standing there and I nodded to him. He nodded back.

"What are you two doing here?" I asked.

"I decided to come down and see you guys since I'm going to jail soon." Beast said. I smiled and nodded.

"I feel ya brother." I said and swung my legs over the edge of the bed. "Take it easy Noah." Grace said. I looked over at her and smiled.

"I'm fine." I said and stood up. I swayed a bit on my feet but stayed standing. "I'm sure it's all the whiskey I just drank." I said. "I'm just really drunk." I walked towards the door and stumbled into the door frame. Beast reached out and grabbed me. I smiled at him and continued to walk out into the hallway. They followed me out into the main room. It was still empty except for a few girls still laid out mostly naked for the whole world to see. I felt Grace come up behind me and I looked over my shoulder at her and smiled slightly.

"I'm pretty sure I'm still super drunk." I slurred and swayed towards her. She put her hands up against my chest and I smiled fully. "Oh sweetheart. I think we need to reconnect." She smiled and pushed me back up straight.

"Yeah Noah I don't think that's going to happen. I have to be with Beast." She said. I nodded and went back over to the bar grabbing a bottle from the rack. I didn't care what bottle I grabbed, I just wanted more alcohol.

"Hey buddy I think that bottle of Jack did it for ya. Why don't you go lay down?" Beast said putting his hand on my arm. I looked at him.

"You know what I think you're right. I'm going to go crash now. It sounds like a good idea." I said and pushed myself off the bar and then went back down the hall towards my room. I slammed the door shut and fell on my bed.

GRACE

I looked at Cody after Noah retreated back to his room. Cody smiled slightly at me and I was torn. The man I loved more than anything in the world was hurting and it was because of me. I watched as he had downed an entire bottle of Jack and then had passed out probably from alcohol poisoning. He was a complete mess and I felt for him, I truly did, but I had a duty to do for the next few months before I could even attempt to fix this shit storm that was my life. Cody kissed my temple and went over towards some other members of the club. Against my better judgement I went into Noah's room. I knocked on the door and after hearing him mumble something like a "come in" I opened the door and slipped inside. He didn't move from where he was laying, his head did not shift towards me, even when I sat on the edge of his bed.

"Noah, I'm really sorry about everything that has happened between us and with my parents...I really want to work this out at some point. I've never wanted to let you go and I'm still fighting to come back to you. There are just somethings I have to do. I'm not going to sleep with Cody or anything like that. I found out I may have to sleep with the cop, but I don't plan on it. My heart won't let me fall in love again. It still is yours....and I hope that you will let me come back when I can figure out how to convince everyone else that we should be together." I said and waited for a moment. He let out a soft snore letting me know he was completely asleep. Everything I just said, he never heard. I wasn't sure how I was going to be able to get through this, but I knew I wanted to be with him. There was going to be a lot of pain in the next few months and I was scared as hell what was going to happen to me later on and then to Cody while locked up. I could only leave Beast while he was still here, but I had to be with the cop for a long time...probably long enough for a proposal to happen so there was no doubt I would have to sleep with him at some point. My life was a confusing fuck fest and I had volunteered for it all. Maybe I could get out of it before Cody got out? I just had to let him know I was going to move back here at some point. I could always tell the cop that I was leaving town to get away from Cody before he gets out.

I left his room just as quietly as I entered and went into Cody's room where we were staying. I sat on the bed and for the first time in a few months I wanted to cry. I tried to hold them back and keep them bottled but the pressure to cry was undeniable. A few tears leaked their way out and I closed my eyes. I felt weak and unable to help the situation at all. I heard the door open and close and my hands went to my face trying to hide that I was crying. I felt arms wrap around me and I peeked up at who was holding me. I should have known it was Cody. I flung my arms around him and held onto him. The tears came more freely, and I let the sobs consume me for a while. I looked up at Cody and wiped my tears away.

"I'm sorry." I said and his hand came up to cradle my cheek. I smiled slightly and he pulled me into his lap.

"Don't be sorry. I know it's hard being here, it's just part of our cover story." He said and I nodded.

"I'm still in love with him, Cody." I said and looked deeply into his eyes. They were kind and gentle and shining with love.

"I know you are. It'll take time to get over him if you want to leave him in your past." He said. I nodded and laid my head on his shoulder.

"I don't want him in my past. Everything was right with him. I felt like I was walking through the clouds when I was with him and I felt fireworks every time I kissed him. I want him in my life Cody." I said. Cody's arms came around me once more and he just held me.

"I'm sorry if talking about this is hurting you." I whispered. His hand rubbed my back a few strokes and then his head came down resting his chin against my temple.

"I'll find someone soon enough, Grace. I do love you but part of loving someone is letting them choose who to be with. If you want Noah...I'll help you get Noah." He said.

Cody was the greatest person I had ever met. He was willing to wait for someone else to love so I could be happy. I didn't know if he really was in love with me or not, but I wasn't about to ask. He sat down with me and we began talking about how to get my father on my side. Obviously, I needed to go through with the situation with Cody and the cop before I could get back with Noah and even then, I wasn't sure what I would be able to do to get a relationship back with Noah. I hoped we could kindle everything we had and could have.

Later that day we had to say goodbye to everyone. Noah never showed up which I was okay with, he needed to sleep off the alcohol he had consumed. The ride seemed to take even longer this time around and my ass was vibrating and hurting before we even made it a half hour into the drive. Cody refused to pull over and so I had to suffer. "Mean bastard." I grumbled and put my cheek against his back. His back rumbled with his laughter. He must have heard what I said. Oh well it's just the same I would have told him that eventually. I'll probably yell it at him once we get back, just to make a scene. It was a pretty long ride but eventually my butt went numb and my mind started to wander to Noah. I so desperately wanted to be on the back of his bike rather than Cody's and hear the rumble of his bike. I wanted to feel his back against my chest, and for a moment I let myself fantasize.

I felt prickles on the back of my neck and rubbed it. I had a bad feeling sink into the pit of my stomach and I bit my lip. Turning my head to the side I saw a car behind us. They were too close. I wrapped myself tighter around Cody and buried my face into his back. His leather smelt like wind and motor oil. It was a comforting smell.

"Are you alright?" He asked and I nodded.

"I think we are being followed." I said. Cody checked his mirrors and remained calmer then I could have been.

"I know." That was all I got from him. I noticed the sign to our town fly by and he turned a different direction then we should have to go to the clubhouse. I turned my head again and saw the car still on our tail. Cody pulled my hands tighter around him and twisted the throttle. His front wheel went up and I let out a blood curdling scream. I never expected the bike to go up and from Cody's expression after it went down, neither did he.

He had to have been going at least seventy-five when we flew by a cop. I watched as the cop came between us and the car and Cody pulled over. I released the breath I didn't realize I was holding and leaned my head against Cody's back. "You don't have any warrants, do you?" I asked before the cop came up. Cody shook his head. The car pulled up behind the cop and I watched in Cody's mirrors as the cop got out of the car. I turned around and watched three men climb out of the car behind the police cruiser.

"Oh, sweet Jesus." I murmured. Cody twisted around to look and watched the cop take his final steps. "WATCH OUT!" I screamed but it was too late. Cody started the bike up as bullets and blood flew through the cop's chest. I wrapped my arms around Cody again and we took off. I watched as the men scrambled into the car and tried to follow us. Cody pulled into a sheriff's station not too far from where we saw the cop gunned down. I thought my butt being numb was the worst problem of the day until I had seen that happen.

We went inside a little more than calm and I saw the police officer I needed to get close to. He was handsome in a way, but I couldn't focus on him. Tears were starting and it was going to be a miracle if I could stop them. Shock had ridden me like a bitch all the way to the station. I let go of Cody's hand and went to sit down with some tissues. The police officer that I needed to be close to came over to me and sat down.

"Are you alright?" he asked. I looked up at him with my tear-stricken face and shook my head no.

"We..." hiccup. "We just saw..." hiccup. "an officer..." I couldn't get the word out. More tears slid down my cheeks and I hiccupped. "killed." I finally said it. He stood up and I watched him as he grabbed more tissues. This was going to be a long interview.

I got pulled into an interview office while Cody got pulled into a separate one. After an hour or so of being asked to replay the horrific scene of the cop being shot, they asked Cody to go with them to the site. I sat at the police station holding a cup of coffee, waiting. By the time they came back I had the phone number of the police officer I needed to be close with. He had cheered me up and I learned some things about him. His name was Jared Hannibal and probably one of the nicer guys I met. I told him a little back story about myself and only let him know a couple things about my family and relationship with Cody. When they returned, I jumped when Cody touched my shoulder. I smiled tentatively at him and stood up.

"Thank you, guys for reporting this to us. We will look into it more." A sheriff said and Cody nodded. Jared leaned close to me.

"Call if you need anything." He whispered in my ear and then leaned against the counter. I smiled at him and nodded.

"Will do. Thank you." I said and took Cody's hand. We went outside towards his bike and he stopped.

"I'm sorry but I have to make a scene a little. He's watching." I nodded. "What the fuck was that?! You just let cops lean close to you and whisper shit in your ear?!" He was screaming at me and it took nothing for tears to come out. His yelling always scared me, which is probably why they were having him do this to me instead of someone else. I hated it though. The door opened right as Cody lifted his hand to me. That scared me even more. Jared yelled over to us.

"Hey!" Cody looked over at him and I looked at the ground

not wanted to show my tears.

"Are you alright Grace?" Jared asked. I still couldn't turn. I just nodded though. Cody got on the bike and turned it around knowing that I didn't want anyone to see my face. I had deliberately used my hair as a curtain and climbed on the bike. My cheek pressed against Cody's back keeping my face from view. We rode home and as soon as we were both off the bike, he rubbed his hand down my back. I jumped away and looked at him.

"I'm sorry Grace. I had to though." I nodded.

"It's okay, I just... you're yelling upsets me. I don't know why." I said. He wrapped his arms around me.

"Come on. He followed us. We gotta make our way inside." He whispered in my ear and I nodded. Cody led me towards the clubhouse his arm around my shoulders. We went inside together and I sat at the bar.

"It's beginning." I said. Cody nodded.

"I'm going to go update the club and Tommy." He said and left me by the bar. I watched as he retreated towards Tommy's office. It took a whole two hours for the club to get there have their church and come out. It was such a bore to sit there alone. I was very happy to see Cody come out of those doors. When he got to me he wrapped his arms around my waist and held me close.

"Cody?" I asked stroking his hair. He pulled me up and we started towards his club bedroom.

"I love you, Grace." He whispered and covered my lips with his. I kissed him back and we tumbled onto the bed. "I need you Grace." He said and his lips slipped down to my collar. I moaned and wrapped my fingers into his hair. He pulled my shirt up over my head and kissed his way down my torso. I watched as his head retreated down my body. I heard my zipper come undone and then my pants were sliding down my legs. "I need you just once. Please." He was begging.

His head disappeared between them and I felt his tongue caress my lower lips. I moaned and threaded my fingers into his hair holding on as if my life was dependent on it. His tongue used a slow assault against my clit and it had me drenched with my desire. I pulled him close to my core as his assault become more fervent. I felt my climb coming to an end and wrapped my legs around his shoulders, keeping my legs open so he could continue. The crash came suddenly upon me and I tried not to scream. Cody licked me one last time and laid feather light kisses up my legs and stomach. I reveled in the feeling of him paying such close attention to me.

His eyes met mine and I leaned forward kissing him. Shit must be hitting the fan soon because I would have never let this happen otherwise. He needed me and I wasn't tied down, exactly. My mind started racing and I tried desperately to hold on. I could feel myself going dry already and I sighed. It wasn't going to happen after all.

"Cody... stop." I said at almost a whisper. He looked at me holding himself up with his elbows. "I... can't do this." I said wanting to just sob. I felt mortified that my body wouldn't respond to his anymore. He leaned down and kissed my neck lightly.

"It's okay. I'm not Noah. I didn't really expect anything from you." He said and got up. I sat up and looked at my fingers.

"I'm sorry. I just don't respond to anyone like I do Noah." I said. Cody nodded and handed me my clothing.

"I'm going to help you get Noah back as soon as I can. I honestly don't want to hurt you like they want me to, but I have to. I'm sorry for everything that I'm going to do and the pain I'm going to cause you. This may hurt our friendship and if it does I'm sorry for that too. I want you to know that I'm only crossing this line to get intel. I hate everything about this and especially the cop. I've been trying to think of a fucking way around everything without hurting you, but I just can't think of anything. Make-up wouldn't work because it wouldn't hold up. I need to be locked up to get to someone inside and the club needs you to get close. I'm going to make sure that you are the happiest damn woman alive when I'm through with all this shit." He said and knelt in front of me.

"If you never want to work again, I'll support you. If you want to get away from Noah, my house is yours. If you want to be as close to Noah as you can, I'll get you two back together. No sense in two people who could be happy being miserable without each other. I love you enough to let you know that I will help you in anyway. Grace, I need you to know that most of all I need you safe and happy. That's all I ask in return." He said. It was a big thing and fuck, did I know it. I leaned forward and pressed my lips against his.

"How soon do you need to hit me?" I asked. I watched as he closed his eyes and stood up.

"Sometime between now and tomorrow morning. It has to happen tonight and then you will have to ask the cop to meet you at noon tomorrow. You'll discuss things and hopefully he will try and protect you. Then I'll find you and drag you away from him and we will come back here.... Where I have to give you some more bruises. I know you can make this real since you've been in a domestic abuse situation. We need it to be real." He said and I nodded. I didn't want to let him hit me, but the club needed it to be real. I was going to make sure I got a pretty penny out of this fucking deal.

"Get it done." I whispered

I sighed in defeat after the first blow. It was all coming back to me. Max and his abuse. I wanted to curl up in a ball and hopefully pass out. Maybe, it would get easier. I felt like a zombie when he finally finished. He had put all his anger and despair into the blows. I laid on the bed and tucked my knees to my chest. He sat down and I saw tears rolling down his cheeks. I felt the swelling coming on and my head was beginning to throb.

"Cody..." I croaked. He looked over at me and I noticed his eyes became deeper in color when he cried. "I need some time. Please." I said not asking for the time to be alone but demanding it. He nodded wiped his face and walked out of the door. I rolled to my back and stretched my body out. I hurt especially my right eye. It was going to be pretty gruesome in the morning. I didn't even want to leave the room looking how I knew I had to have looked. I pulled the blankets over me and faced the wall. The tears rolled down my cheeks and onto the bed. I had promised myself that I wouldn't let anyone do this sort of thing again. I broke that promise.

NOAH

I heard the thunderous noise of flesh on flesh. I heard her cry out in pain as Cody's fist slammed against her cheek. I wish I could help, I was helpless. I was not going to sit through that ever again though. I was ordered to do this, but I wouldn't follow orders anymore not when it comes to Grace. It was killing me that someone was laying a hand on her. Cody came out and I could see the anguish on his face that he was struggling to hold in. Now Grace had to get close to the cop. I'm glad she wouldn't have to go through weeks of torture for this. Just one incident and it was over. I was going to take her back. Cody left the clubhouse and I followed him. We invited Tommy's charter down to do a charity run for St. Jude's hospital.

He stopped by his bike and slumped to his knees in front of it. I wanted to kill him for what happened to Grace, but I couldn't, seeing him defeated in front of his bike was enough to chase the anger I held away. I could only relate to his self-hate. I walked over to him and placed my hand on his shoulder and got down on my knees next to him. He looked over at me and his eyes were the ones of a tortured soul. Something he never showed anyone. His eyes said everything about him. His love for Grace was shining in them and it was in the tears that fell. He knew she would probably never forgive him for this, and I knew she would try. It was just in her nature to forgive people. We sat there kneeling for god knows how long. I heard the door open and turned towards the man next to Beast. Tommy knelt by him and put his hand on Beast's back. One by one, the club came and knelt beside Beast, surrounding him with support. It was what the club was for and we dealt with the shit hand we were all given. All the men were outside and we all turned when the door opened again. My eyes didn't need to tell me it was Grace. My heart had started thudding against my ribcage before I even saw her. She was a complete mess. My Grace. I looked over at Beast, his shoulders were slumped, and he dropped his chest towards the ground and pressed his forehead against the asphalt. I stood up breaking the support I held for Beast and went over to Grace. She stopped walking when she saw me, and I wrapped my arms around her.

"I'm so sorry." I whispered against her hair and held her. I felt her arms come around me and she held onto me.

She said nothing when she let go and walked closer to Beast at the top of the pyramid. She took my place on the ground and knelt by him. Her whole body looked frail. I watched as her arms wrapped around his shoulders and held onto him. It was almost like I was intruding. Maybe she wasn't mine to take back anymore. I felt my heart rip in two again after just mending it. I leaned my head back and looked up at the sky. I prayed that day. I prayed with my whole soul that something would take me away from this misery. I didn't care how it happened just that God would show me mercy and take my life before I struggled too long with this pain again. I felt arms come around my waist and I looked down at who it was. Grace. She snuck up and held me together. She was the only thing keeping me here on earth and it was almost like she knew it. I wrapped my arms around her and held her close to me.

"I love you." It was so soft I almost missed it. My lips came in contact with hers and I felt everything coming back together. My emotions were like whiplash and I wasn't enjoying them at all. She made me feel things I never wanted to feel in a million years. When she pulled back she was white as a ghost and her lips were losing color. Panic hit me and I pressed my fingers to her throat looking for a pulse. Her eyelids were fluttering shut like she was fighting to keep them open.

"Grace!" I yelled holding onto her, panic rising. "Fuck!" I

couldn't find a pulse on her and Cody turned towards us. "Someone fucking call 911!" I yelled and laid her on the ground. Tommy was calling before anyone else could even say fuck. I listened for breathing but heard none. I started in on chest compressions and then breathing into her. She couldn't be dying from this. I kept going alternating between chest compressions and breaths. I heard sirens before seeing them and I kept up with the compressions. I wasn't going to lose her, not with her final words being I love you.

"Come on baby." I whispered. A paramedic came up and took over and that's when the feeling of helplessness started sinking in. I could do nothing more to help her. Her life was in the hands of the paramedics.

"I have a pulse!" one of them yelled and I could have fallen to my knees. I rode with them in the ambulance and was in shock from the whole situation. I watched as they took care of my ol' lady. She was fighting for her life and here I was watching, perfectly fucking healthy. I wished it could be me that was struggling to hang onto life rather than her. She didn't deserve this kind of treatment. She doesn't deserve to die, not like this. Not out of fear of being beaten. I was angry at the club for suggesting this. It was almost like she would do anything for the club, just like I would. She seemed to be holding on. Her eyes opened and they darted over to me. I watched her and didn't let my eyes leave hers. Her eyes fluttered shut and I felt my heart ripping in two. Nothing could compare to the possibility of her not living.

The paramedics were frantically working to keep her alive while they drove to the hospital. I felt as if time was standing still, everything was in slow motion and crippling my hope. I honestly didn't believe she was going to make it. Her heart was weak and her breath was shallow and far apart. By the time we got to the hospital Grace had coded twice and was barely hanging on. I felt numb and as if the world was passing me by while I died, while she died.

The doctors came in and out of the lobby and I stared at the wall across the room. I sat there with my elbows on my knees for what seemed like forever. The waiting room was as empty as I felt, when a doctor came in. The doctor was a woman who looked to have just gotten out of med school. She sat next to me and pushed her shoulder into mine. I looked over at her.

"She's going to make it." Everything from that day was crashing down. I felt relief and anger come flooding through me. I was going to make sure she survived and made it through all of this to marry me. Grace was going to be my wife and I wasn't going to let her out of my sights after this. I sighed and stood.

"When can I see her?" I asked and looked over at her.

"We don't want anyone in her room yet." She said quietly. "We are still monitoring her. I would like to suggest that you go home and get some rest. You can visit her in the morning." She said adding more strength to her voice and I sighed and nodded.

"Okay doc." I said and grabbed my jacket. She smiled at me a little and let me pass. When I arrived at the clubhouse Jack came outside and met me. With his new patch under his shirt he couldn't make it to the hospital. He still moved slow and wasn't keeping much down. His weight loss was apparent and I watched as he leaned against a pillar. These stupid attacks were driving our own charter insane. We had no idea where they were coming from or who was doing it.

"How is she?" he asked. I nodded.

"She's going to make it." I said and watched as he sagged with relief.

"They are not allowing visitors right now though. The doctor told me to go home and get rest and go back in the morning." I said. Jack nodded and pulled out his phone.

"I'm going to let her mother know. Thank you for watching over my baby, Noah." He said and gripped my shoulder before he slowly made his way back inside. I needed something to do and sleep was the furthest thing from my mind. My eyes wandered over to Grace's Chevelle that still needed to be finished. It looked like Jack might have been working on it while she had been away. Grace was understanding that it would be awhile with the car to be finished. I walked over towards the car and looked it over. The paint was all gone, and the tires were new. I opened the driver door and grabbed the keys. My body sank in the seat and I turned the key. The engine clicked and I leaned back. I was going to need something to do tonight and her car seemed like my best option.

Her car was a disaster on the inside. Paint had dripped under the hood and her engine was sticking and the alternator was shot due to the paint being on the posts. It had sat for so long that the paint had become something like cement. I wanted to do something big for her and replacing the entire engine would be happening for her. By the time I had my plan all laid out to rebuild the engine dawn was approaching. A smile crossed my lips and I walked over to my bike going back to the hospital. Grace was awake when I arrived back at the hospital. I pulled up a chair next to her bed and held her hand. She had a blank stare on her face and her eyes moved around the room. She seemed almost panicked.

"Grace, darling, it's alright." Her eyes focused on me and a tear slipped down her cheek. I kissed her knuckles and she pulled her hand away. A knock sounded on the door. My body tensed and coiled ready for anything. I stood up. A tall man in a sheriff's uniform entered and took off his hat. Grace's eyes looked over at him and I saw something click in her eyes. He came close to her and nodded his head at me.

"Do you mind giving us a few moments?" He asked me. I looked over at Grace and she nodded.

"I'll be alright, Noah." She said. I sighed and walked towards the door. I wasn't going far. My duty was to be by her side for as long as she'd allow me to be.

GRACE

Jared sat across from me and set his hat on my bedside table. I knew he'd be coming as soon as I woke up. I called him and told him I needed help. I felt like I was ratting out the club. He took my hand and his thumb rubbed across my knuckles. It was a soothing gesture and actually kept me calm enough to pull myself together.

"I need to ask you some things." He said. My eyes met his and I nodded. "Why were you…Why did this happen?" He asked. I looked down.

"He overheard me telling another woman at the club that I thought you were good looking. He lost his temper and dragged me into a bedroom." I almost whispered the lie.

"So you were….this happened because of your opinion of me?" He asked. I could only nod. I didn't want to lie anymore. "That's insane." He whispered and his hands rubbed through his hair.

"The men of the club…they are allowed to play with other women like club whores but if women even speak of another man…things happen." I said.

"So, you aren't the first woman to be beaten?" He asked.

"No, but I am the first that almost died." I said.

"Do you want to press charges against him?" this was the hardest question that I would ever face, and I knew it. No, I didn't want to press charges, but the club was expecting me to.

"I know this can be a hard decision for you, but if you don't he could come after you again." Jared said and I nodded.

"Yes…I'll do it." I whispered sealing Cody's fate. Jared nodded and he leaned over the bed kissing my forehead.

"It's going to be okay. I'll have an officer stand duty at your door. He will converse with you about everyone who tries to enter your room." He said. I nodded.

"Thank you." I whispered and could feel tears coming on. He smiled slightly.

"Everything will be okay." He whispered and went towards the door, putting his hat back on.

"Call if you need anything." He said and went outside leaving me alone for all of a minute. Noah came back into the room and I smiled at him.

"So, Beast getting charged?" he asked. My smile disappeared and I nodded.

"I didn't want to though." I said. Noah sat on the edge of the bed.

"When this all blows over…Will you finally marry me?" he still wanted me after months of being apart.

"Noah, I'm going to need time to heal from all the damage I kept hidden. I do want to be with you, I'm just asking for some time." I said. He nodded.

"That isn't a no." he smiled and kissed my knuckles. "You did well." He was smiling and I wasn't sure how to feel anymore. I felt as if everything was unraveling and I didn't want to dwell on anything. Noah was kind and all but all my insecurities and nightmares I had firmly locked away were flooding to the surface. I wanted to be stronger than I was but my emotional wellbeing was shutting down. I just had to hope that it wouldn't be as bad as the last time.

NOAH

Everything was in motion now, it all depended on waiting and Grace had to get closer to the cop. I hated every moment she had to be with him. I prayed that she wouldn't have to sleep with him either. My woman wasn't the kind to sleep around. There were so many what if's running through my mind that had me almost running scared. I couldn't lose her; ever. I sat down near her bed and watched her as she was dozing off. I watched her thinking about all the possibilities that could be if she made it through all of this crap. I felt my phone vibrating in my pocket and got up leaving to room to answer it. My caller i.d. told me it was unknown. Didn't help much it could have been anyone who was in the club. I put the phone up to my ear and listened.

"Noah." His voice was hard and rough.

"Jack." I said.

"We have an issue at the club. I need you here like yesterday." His voice was getting urgent.

"I'm on my way." I said hanging up putting the phone back in my pocket. I entered the room quietly and grabbed my jacket. Grace was still sleeping, and I smiled leaning down and kissing her head.

"I'll be back as soon as I can be sweetheart." I whispered leaving to find her nurse.

"Excuse me, Ma'am. I'm looking for the nurse taking care of Grace Sinner. Oh, hello, Nancy." I said smiling at her.

"Jesus, Noah." She said looking startled. I chuckled and leaned on the counter.

"Will you please let me know when Grace wakes up again? I have to go take care of something." I said. Nancy smiled and nodded.

"I'm not supposed to, but you know I've always had a weak spot for you." She said and stood up.

"Thanks doll. Just leave a message if I don't answer." I said leaving my number with her. By the time I got to the club the place was swarmed with the local PD. Jack came up to me and stood watching.

"We got everything cleaned but would have been a lot easier with you here." He said. I nodded and watched the club become a mess while the PD destroyed almost everything. "I have a job for you Noah." Jack almost whispered while we watched the mess become a disaster. I nodded at him.

"Details later?" I asked. Jack nodded and I felt my phone vibrate. I looked and saw it was Nancy.

"Hey Nance, is she awake?" I asked.

"Oh, yes she is Noah." She said with a sinister laugh.

"But I don't think you will be seeing much of her anymore." She said and hung up. I looked over at Jack. I ran to my bike.

"Noah, what the fuck is going on!" Jack yelled.

"Grace." It was all I could get out before tearing out of the yard. Jack flew side by side to the hospital.

Arriving at Grace's room I saw my worst fear coming to life. Nancy was preparing to administer a medicine into her I.V. before I could do anything Jack jumped forward and pulled the syringe from Grace's I.V. Nancy stumbled backwards and I caught her putting her in a chair.

"Fucking stay there." I said putting my finger in her face. Anger rolled off me. Jack came over and stood by her.

"I got her brother." He said and patted my shoulder. I walked over to the syringe and picked it off the floor where it had fallen. Reading the label of the vial she drew from. I was relieved noticing she didn't get any in Grace's system.

"Fucking Morphine. And three times the normal dose...I could kill you Nancy." I said and walked out the door going to the desk. The kid working the desk looked like he was gonna piss his pants when I walked up.

"Call security and the police. Now." I said sternly but as politely as I could. The kid fumbled with the phone and I nodded at him and walked back to the room.

I looked over at Nancy. "How much did you get in her?" I asked. Nancy had tears spilling out of her eyes.

"None of it..." she said trailing off at the end. Her eyes went to the floor, her arms pressed into the arms of the chair. I looked over at Grace and watched as she slept. I felt Nancy look at me.

"She slept through all of this?" I asked. Nancy looked over at Grace as soon as my eyes met hers.

"She just had a dose of morphine before my shift. She had woken up with pain, so they gave her some medicine for it." Nancy stated.

"I don't remember her getting any morphine while I was here." I said looking over at Jack. The Security came in the room and I stood up. "I want her investigated. I was here most of the morning and that nurse said this patient got morphine before she came on shift. She hadn't gotten morphine at all while I was here. I received a phone call from Nancy here saying I wasn't going to see Grace ever again. We... I motioned my finger between Jack and myself. "rushed here and Jack pulled the nurse away from the patient where she let go of a syringe full of Morphine that was three times the normal dosage. That's when I left the room asking the boy at the desk to call you guys and the police. Jack, here, stayed with the nurse." I said.

"Alright sir, we will get to the bottom of this." The security officer said to me. He looked over at Nancy.

"Ma'am will you come with us so we can get the details of both sides of the story?" He asked her and she nodded. Jack stared at her and slowly moved out of her way. The guard took her out of the room and his partner stayed by Jack and I. An officer came in and I recognized him right away. It was the bastard that Grace had to fucking get close to. He nodded to the guard in the room and he left.

"Noah, right?" the bastard asked.

"Yeah, and you are?" I asked. He reached taking his hat off and then held out his hand. He was a handsome bastard, if anyone heard that I'd get called gay for the rest of my fucking life, but I could tell how easy it would be for Grace to fall for him and it makes me hate him already. Not that I didn't beforehand.

"Jared." He clipped. I watched as he took a seat across the room. He stretched his legs out and crossed his arms over his chest. It was almost like he didn't want me knowing his name.

"Pressing charges?" He asked after getting comfortable.

"Wouldn't have it any other way." I said and leaned forward resting my elbows on my knees. My fingers were curling and uncurling, my palms were aching with adrenaline. I wanted to take it out on something, but I had nothing. Grace started to move and I turned my head looking over at her. Her eyes fluttered open and I stood up going over to her.

"Baby." I whispered and brushed her hair back. She looked over at me and smiled slightly.

"Hi, Noah." She said and then looked over at the bastard. "Jared." She said his name in such a breathy way I knew it was over before I even had another chance. Fuck! Jared went over to her and I watched as he took her hand in his palm. I was seeing red. He was seriously going to be the only cop I ever had thought of strangling in public. Unhappy wasn't even the tip of the iceberg. I had so much anger swelling inside of me that I had to leave the room. I needed to calm the fuck down otherwise I was going to jeopardize the fucking plan.

GRACE

I watched as Noah left the room. The anger rolling off him were like a tsunami's. It hit me with strong force and I knew he was angry with the situation versus with anyone else. I watched as his powerful legs stretched as he walked along the room and out the room. I turned my attention to Jared and smiled at him.

"How are you feeling?" Jared asked me. I nodded and sighed.

"As good as I can be I guess." I said and looked around the room. "What are you doing here?" I asked.

"Well there was an attempt on your life while you were sleeping. Noah had the desk nurse call it in." he said. There was an attempt on my life? What the fuck was that supposed to mean? Someone tried to kill me? My head was spinning and I didn't even know where to start asking questions. I sat up a little in the bed and adjusted the bed.

"What happened?" I asked. I wasn't sure if I did actually want to know but I already asked. I just hoped it would be a short tale and I would be rid of Jared soon. I did believe him to be handsome and would be someone I would date but I just couldn't handle him right now. I wanted my Noah. Mmmm, my Noah. Jared quickly told me what happened with my Nurse. I was in so much shock that I wasn't aware that Noah came back to my room. "Thank you Jared. I think I'm going to rest some more...." I said letting my words drift off. Jared nodded and stood up placing his sheriff's hat on top of his head. I watched as Jared left and I looked over at Noah. "I...." I couldn't say anything. My throat was closing up with emotion. Someone who I trusted to take care of me. I felt violated and defiled. "I want to go home. Now." I said finding my voice. Noah walked over to me and sat down on the bed next to my legs. I leaned forward and wrapped myself around him. "Why is this shit happening to me?" I asked and felt my eyes start to sting. Noah wrapped his arms around me and I let out a heavy sigh. The comfort he was giving me was my home. I wouldn't....I couldn't go through with this stupid plan.

"Noah." I whispered and laid my head on his shoulder facing his neck. His hand stroked my back and he held me.

"What baby?" He asked and rested his cheek on top of my hair.

"I can't do the plan…I can't go through with it. I've already done so much, I almost died. Twice now, apparently. Noah, I promised myself another man would never touch me like that. I wasn't going to be beaten again. I allowed it to happen for the club. I can't force myself to sleep with him too. Noah, I love you. I don't want to be with anyone else, not Cody, not Jared, just you. And only you." I said pulling back. Noah slid his hand up my back and into my hair, caressing my neck on the way. His torso leaned towards me and I met him in the middle. Our lips smashed together clinking teeth. The kiss started out fierce and slowly melted into all of our hidden emotions. Love, hate, depression, fear, and desperation flooded my tongue while his invaded my soul. He continued to lean forward and my shoulders pressed into the hospital bed. Noah pulled away and I was already craving him again.

"Well, I'll be damned… You two just can't stay away from each other. Now can you?" I heard my dad and looked over at him. I couldn't gauge if he was angry or not. He came over and pushed Noah out of the way wrapping his arms around me. I hugged him back and sighed into him.

"I'm okay daddy." I said and held onto him until he pulled away. His eyes were shining with unshed tears. His head dipped and came back up in a nodding motion and smiled kissing my forehead. My thoughts were running wild and I wasn't sure how to express anything.

"You are getting away from my club baby...from me. No more of any of it. The plan is terminated. You executed it to the best of your ability doll. Unfortunately, you need to stay away from family in case shit goes down. We will take care of the cop and let him know you skipped town and were afraid of the shit that had happened and you needed time away. Noah is going with you to keep you safe. I'm not going to let you go anywhere alone." He said and I looked over at Noah. He was smiling at me and a huge weight was lifted off me. I could still have Noah. That's all I cared about at this moment. I needed him like I needed air to breathe. But was this going to be a consequence to him? Would he have to leave the club to stay with me? More stress came down on my shoulders and I slumped back.

"Where am I going?" I asked.

"Noah knows everything sweetheart. He will take care of it." Dad said. That was all I got. "Noah's got it doll." I'm not a child and every turn I took in my life it felt as if Dad was trying to get me to do something else that I didn't want to do. I didn't want to be dependent on Noah, but I knew I needed him in my life otherwise I wouldn't be complete. I sighed and leaned back. My life was a complete fuck up. Dad rubbed his thumb across the back of my hand.

"I'm sorry, doll." Dad said and got up. He pressed his lips to my forehead. "We will always have someone at your door. Whether it's a cop or a member. Everyone will be checked before they come in. Nothing is getting to my baby again. Not on my watch." He said and pulled away. He released my hand and turned towards Noah. "When another member comes, you need to come back to the club to finish details." He said and Noah nodded. "I'll send a prospect and Bullet first." My dad said and left the room. Noah took over where my dad sat. I watched him as I slipped into numbness. I was as blank as the bare hospital walls. Noah was talking and I couldn't focus on him. I just stared at the wall across from my bed. There was a single mirror hanging on the wall and I could see the deep bruises and black eyes Cody had given me... I gave up the most precious thing for the club and it was going to be a long time before that ever returned to me.

My dad was right. No one got in my room unless it was okayed by a member of the club. My best friend stopped by and she didn't want to leave my side. She refused to let any males into the room. I loved her for it but she wouldn't even allow Noah in. I laughed when she denied Noah. It was great to actually laugh at something for once. In all the tragedy laughter was the greatest medicine I could have asked for. It wasn't long for Beth to allow Noah to come in. Beth wouldn't even let my father in the room even with all of my protesting against her. She wasn't scared of my dad and never had been.

It was only about a week longer and I was free of the hospital. Noah was keeping me updated with Cody and everything in the situation. It was not exactly easy hearing about Cody in jail but it did give the club an insider to relay messages to other club inmates. Things were happening around us and I was ready for it all to be over. The doctor didn't want me to travel after leaving the hospital, told me it would be best to wait about another week before going anywhere besides home. I couldn't stay in this town any longer. Noah had a bag waiting and was in the process of packing mine the day we got home. I didn't want to leave just yet though.

"Noah, I'm going to go lay down for a while." I said and walked towards the couch.

"Grace. We need to leave though." He said and I sighed.

"I know but I'm not feeling well enough to travel. I just need like an hour or so." I said and laid down on the couch.

NOAH

Grace was doing great at home, but we needed to get on the road. She wanted to relax for a while before we left but if we didn't get going soon there was a huge possibility of being ambushed, especially because of my colors and where we were going. I was getting anxious and not the good kind. My bag was packed, and I was taking my time packing hers since she wanted to lay on the couch for a while.

A hour had passed and I was sure we'd be here all night. I finally gave up and went to wake her. She looked peaceful sleeping on the couch. I sighed and grabbed my phone to call Jack. He was not going to be very happy.

"Noah. What the hell are you doing calling me? Shouldn't you be on the road, dragging my daughter with you?" Jack hollered into the phone.

"We are staying in town for the night. We would get ambushed at this time of night and Grace is sleeping." I said leaving the living room. Jack sighed and yelled something at the prospect.

"Noah get her moving right away in the morning." He said.

"I will, Jack." I said and heard Jack's phone click shut. I set my phone on the counter and went to the living room. Grace had lost a lot of weight from being in the hospital. She looked so fragile laying on my couch. I lifted her from the couch and moved her to the bedroom and laid down next to her. Instantly, she curled around me and I held her close.

Six a.m. came all too soon. Grace was still asleep against me and I didn't want to wake her. She looked as if she needed more sleep. I was concerned about how much sleep she was getting, but she must have needed it all. I left Grace to sleep a while longer and made my way to the kitchen.

Half hour went by and I had made coffee and was about to make breakfast when I noticed the time. I sighed and went into the bedroom. Grace was sitting up in bed and I leaned against the doorframe. She looked over at me and I smiled.

"Morning, sweetheart." I said. Grace smiled.

"Good morning." She said and swung her legs over the edge of the bed.

"Did you just wake up?" I asked. She nodded and stood up walking over to me. Grace wrapped her arms around my torso and laid her head against my chest. She felt so small and fragile against me. I wrapped my arms around her and kissed her forehead. "We need to get going sweetheart." I whispered and stroked her hair. I felt her nod against my chest but I didn't want to let her go. Every time I looked at her I felt as if I was being gutted and dying. She had hardly any strength left and I was going to make her ride on the back of a motorcycle for four hours. "Are you going to be okay on the back of the bike today? We can take a car if needed." I asked and stroked her back.

"No, I'll be okay on the bike." She said and let go of me. I smiled at her and grabbed my bag going outside tying it to the back of the bike. I went back inside and watched as Grace packed some clothes and personal items inside a backpack stuffing the thing full. I watched as she moved about still in her night shirt. My shoulder hit the doorframe and couldn't begin to comprehend how this beautiful woman before me agreed to be mine. My brain started running with the wind on what the hell we were going to do with everything else. Were the attacks against Grace something to do with the club? I ran my hand through my hair. The stress of not knowing what the hell was going on was getting to me. Leaving Grace to finish I went through the rest of the house to double check everything was secure and that nothing left behind would be something I would miss if we couldn't come back. The most important things in my life would be on my back and the back of my bike. As long as we were safe and the other members, I didn't give a fuck what the club did.

Grace found me in the hallway facing the one room I have only opened once since I first started dating her. Her fingers touched my hand and I looked over at her. She had a lift to her lips that made me smile and my heart to swell. She was the light to my darkness guiding me out of my personal hell since she came to my bed. We had a long road ahead of us and I wasn't sure where it was going to take us. I could only hope to move forward.

"Let's go inside." She whispered and caressed my cheek. I let out a deep breath and grasped her hand pulling her closer to me and shook my head. I didn't want to go in there. I didn't feel the need to go in that very room that had scared the shit out of Grace.

"I don't need to go in there. I'm going to get rid of it all and we can turn it into a bedroom. Or we can find a new place to live. Grace....I want you to move in with me and stay." I ended in a whisper my forehead pressed against hers. Grace's face was lit up by her smile. I wanted a life forever with this woman and I was going to have it one way or another.

"Can we try it just once? I want to know what it's like. Besides if I like it then we can keep it." She said and pressed her lips to mine. The kiss started out slow and sensual but as her arms came up and around my shoulder, she deepened the kiss and gave off urgency that she felt only I could tame. My hands cupped her ass and lifted her up, her legs folding around my waist. "Noah...I want you, all of you." Her words against my lips were my undoing. I opened the door that could change our lives forever and brought her inside kicking the door closed behind us.

GRACE

The introduction that Noah gave me blew my mind. It was unfortunate that we had to rush everything though. He told me that when we could actually take our time, he'd give me a proper introduction to his kind of sex, his world outside of everything else. We needed to get on the road before we royally pissed off my father.

It was chilly when we left and I just wanted to crawl back into bed never leaving it again. I had so many layers on that I was probably waddling to get anywhere. Noah had to help me on to the bike so we could leave. It was actually kind of embarrassing, but the winds can be brutal around this time of year and I needed to be prepared for it.

The ride was awfully long. It didn't help that I had to make Noah pull over to so I could strip some of the layers off because I was getting too warm for the ride to be any sort of comforting. A prospect had pulled up next to us at a gas station. Looking over at him I realized it was Twinkle. My father must have sent him incase anything happened to us. I checked my phone while Noah fueled the bike and saw a text from Mac.

Hope all is well. Dad's going bat shit crazy that you guys left so late. Apparently there was a deadline on when you were supposed to meet up with the other chapter. He's been throwing things and swearing up a storm here. -M

My father was a dramatic one at times but if there was a deadline for something that's when all hell broke loose at the club. I didn't know much about what they did but it wasn't entertaining at all when my father lost it. He had a temper that ran wild and usually ended with him throwing something. I quickly typed out a reply.

Sorry. We are doing good just stopped to fuel should be there soon. Hopefully no later than the deadline but who knows. Noah's been trying to fly there but his bike doesn't have wings. -G

Hopefully my reply would get at least a giggle since I left her there with my father. I had no choice though it was either leave or stay around and keep getting attacked. My father was strict that he didn't want that to happen even though I knew they could protect me. My sister and I haven't had a close relationship really at all during our lives and it was simple communication between us that made us connect and that was all we had. I started thinking that it was about time that we changed all of that. Unfortunately, that would have to wait until all this shit was over. Then hopefully we could do something about it all. When I moved in with Max it was hard to have communication with anyone. He was always watching what I did and it was a scary situation that I didn't want to relive even in my thoughts. Leaning my head back I watched the clouds roll by. It was peaceful looking up at the sky and just enjoying the sunshine and blue expanse.

Noah poked my shoulder and my head came forward my eyes meeting his. His smile spread across his lips becoming contagious. I could see Twinkle out of the corner of my eye being impatient. "What are you thinking about?" Noah asked. Grabbing my helmet, I slipped it on and stepped away from the bike.

"I was thinking about how I don't have a real relationship with my sister and my mind drifted to the situation I was in with Max and then I just stared at the sky to clear my head." I said watching his hands work at fastening his own helmet.

"You don't ever have to think about Max, Grace. He's in the past. Try and live in the now with me. Stay with me always. We will get through everything and we will do it together." He said caressing my cheek before swinging his leg over the steel horse. We took off as soon as I was comfortable again. My cheek pressed against the back of Noah's cut and the smile glued to my lips never left until we reached our destination…late.

The chapter's president, Tommy, welcomed us even after he got off the phone with my irate father. He had come over right after getting off the phone with my father and he wrapped his arms around me. "I'm so glad you are okay and safe." Tommy said pulling back from me. I smiled knowing that I still had some bruises showing from Cody. I forgave him. We all knew we would do anything for the club and this was one of the things we had to do. The job wasn't complete but right now we had to run and I didn't know all the details unfortunately. Cody was in prison, I had talked to him once or twice since he had been locked away. Noah was amazing with keeping me updated as much as he could. I couldn't know much about what the club does or did just that it's not my problem to worry about. The codes of an outlaw were strict for everyone, even the ol'ladies. Noah's arm came around my waist pulling me against him.

"I have to go into church with them. A prospect is going to sit with you to keep things calm. Hopefully some ol'ladies will be here soon and they can keep you company. Shouldn't take too long in there." He said pressing his lips to mine quickly. I nodded and pushed him towards the club.

"I'll be here when you get out." I smiled running my hand through my hair trying to smooth it from the helmet. A prospect from the chapter came over to me. His cut told me his name is Jace. He was handsome and looked like someone my sister would dig. I looked around some then looked at Jace. He wasn't very talkative and he had an arrogant air about him. His hair was blonde it went perfectly with his steel blue eyes and his height towering over me. I spotted a bench going over I plopped my ass down and leaned back. Jace looked like he didn't know what to do and just looked around hopeless. He must have been about twenty-four. I wonder if I could get him talking about anything. I smiled at him and leaned forward a little.

"So...Jace. What made you want to join the club?" My lips were moving before I could stop them. He gave me the same answers all prospects gave me when I asked. Brotherhood, a life worth living and pussy.

NOAH

Grace was with the prospect I had assigned to her when I returned. He was a good guy. I just hoped he didn't try anything with my ol'lady. Her laugh rang out around me. It was the most angelic sound I've ever heard. The smile spread across my lips before I could stop it. Walking over to Grace and the prospect I sat on the bench next to my woman. She rested her hand on my thigh silently telling me that this princess was enjoying herself. Placing my hand over hers I laced our fingers. "What are you two talking about?" I asked. Grace's eyes found mine as the smile on her lips grew.

"The usual. I asked why he wanted to join the MC." Grace filled with delight.

"And that is?" I asked looking at the prospect.

"Loyalty, brotherhood, and a reason to keep living and of course pussy." The prospect offered up. It was the reason why every brother joined. Reasons that made us a fucking brotherhood, in the first place.

"Where did you grow up?" I asked. Jace, as his patch read, looked around sighing.

"The streets. My mother was a prostitute and my father was her pimp until they started dabbing in drugs. They tolerated me until I could walk. Then they had me running the streets by the time I was ten. Mom was an addict after that and the sperm donor was the dealer. I was their donkey. Typical happy family. Until I was fifteen anyways. I got emancipated and of course no one wanted anyone without an education, so I had to study my ass off for my G.E.D. which I got at sixteen." He said. I saw Grace cover her lips with her hand, her eyes wide. This was the shitty part. We all come from different areas, most of them the streets. Drugs and women keep us together and off the streets, even though that was what had us on the streets.

"Well, kid looks like you came to the right place. After all most of the brothers are from the street. Some of us were raised in the club. I'm sure as long as you keep pushing and unfortunately take the shit from the brothers you'll be fine and get in unanimously." I said standing up. "Grace, the ol'ladies are here if you want to meet them." Grace smiled and stood up.

"I'll see you around Jace." She stated taking my hand.

"Well, I've been assigned to protect you miss. At least when Noah isn't around." Jace said smiling and going towards the garage. Grace leaned against me as we walked into the clubhouse.

"Noah." Grace whispered looking up at me. I smiled and kissed her cheek.

"What?" I asked.

"Well, I want to know more about everything that's going on...you know about me and the things that are happening with the club." She asked me.

"Grace...You know I can't tell you anything about that. I'm sorry babe. But club business..."

"Has to stay club business. I know." Grace said sighing. I nodded turning to look at her. Taking her hands I kissed each one.

"I'm sorry baby." I whispered. Grace nodded releasing my hands and going over to the kitchen area where the other ol'ladies were gathering. I knew she understood the circumstances and what not of the club. She grew up within the club being shadowed and protected, along with her sister Mac.

Rubbing the back of my neck I went more into the main part of the club getting a drink from one of the bartenders. I watched Grace like a hawk and waved away any woman that came near me. Most of the night Grace was upset with me but she knew the ways of our world. We couldn't tell the women anything. The less they knew the safer they were. Especially if we got caught with something. They couldn't be convicted with us. The club would be the only ones that were taken down. Razor came over to me sitting on the stool next to me. "Watching your ol'lady kind of strongly there aren't ya?" He said his British accent coming out strong along with the smell of alcohol on his breath. A party was in full swing in the club house and Grace was helping behind the bar.

"Well, it's my job right now. Keep the princess safe from all harm. Not that I have much to worry about here." I said smiling. "She just…she's pissed because I can't tell her shit about what we think is going on and it's all about her."

"What is going on with her?" he asked. My eyes strayed from Grace over to Razor. It would be safe to tell him he lives by the same codes that I do.

"Well, there was some shit that went down with me it was personal so she knows all about it and Jack wanted to use her as bait to take my personal shit down which we did but then she miscarried our baby and being beaten almost to death by Beast, so he'd go to jail, she ended up in the hospital after losing blood and one of the nurses there tried to make her over dose on morphine. Jack wanted me to take her away from everything to recover and sent us here since there usually isn't much action. But Jack thinks there is more going on than we know but we just haven't figured out yet." I said letting my eyes go back to Grace. She was fucking beautiful even with the fading bruises on her. Her ribs were healing great and I knew she would make it through everything. She was one tough broad and one day we would be together forever.

"Damn, Mate. That's a tough ride to go through. I hope the club figures out what the bloody hell is going on then." Razor said smacking my back and walking over to the bar. My fingers ran over my lips and I decided I was done with this party. Going over to Grace I kissed her cheek.

"I'm going to the bedroom sweetheart. Follow me?" I asked caressing her arm with my fingers and sliding my hand in hers. She looked up at me and smiled nodding in agreement that she too was done with this party.

      Bringing her into the bedroom, I stripped my cut and the clothing underneath. Grace sat on the bed unlacing her boots tossing them near our bags. Crawling behind her I stretched out laying on the bed. Soon after she was in pajamas and laying next to me. Her phone on the nightstand playing some music. She rolled into me and rested her hand on my chest. "A Thousand Years" by Christina Perri was soft compared to the heavy sounds of "Back in Black" By ACDC. The angel in the darkness was against me and it was my duty to keep her safe from my darkness and the clouds of the club. Her wings dipped in black was the edge she kept with her at all times to remind her of the things she had been through. The music continued to play softly as Grace's eyes fluttered shut and darkness enveloped myself.

GRACE

Waking up in a tangled mess with Noah my limbs were numb, my body warm from being pressed between the wall and Noah. Wiggling my body around I was able to free one of my legs from Noah's hold on it. The tingling sensation shot up my leg and into my hip. I curled my toes and released them hoping to get some feeling back. The next leg was up by Noah's waist and he was on top of my thigh. There was no way I was getting out of that one without waking him up. I pressed my hands against his chest pushing him over, hoping he would just roll on his back and I could possibly slip out from underneath him. I smiled as he started to roll over and feeling was a rush into my leg that had been crushed most of the night by him. Closing my eyes, I relished in the relief. A thud sounded in the room forcing my eyes to pop open. Noah was no longer on the bed. Crawling on my hands and knees to the edge of the bed I peeked over the side to see Noah staring up at me. His beautiful eyes captivated me but couldn't hold my laughter in. He sat up, his face an inch away from mine. "Was that really necessary?" He clipped. I raised my lips to his cheek giving him a peck.

"I'm sorry. I just needed to move my leg and you were on top of it." I whispered. Noah shook his head standing up. His lean body was something I'd never get tired of looking at. His ass came into view before he sat on the edge of the bed rubbing his hand through his hair. His hair tangled around his fingers creating quite the mess. A giggle escaped my lips making me curl my lips into one another. The corner of Noah's lips lifted. Swinging my legs over the edge of the bed I sat up next to him and kissed his cheek. "We need to get going don't we?" I asked.

His eyes swept over to mine and he shook his head.

"No, we are staying here for awhile to give you some time to rest and continue healing." Noah said. He leaned into my shoulder and cupped my cheek. "Besides. Riding as long as we need to it's going to make you sore and I don't want to push your body any further than the club has." I smiled as I leaned in pressing my lips to his.

"I love you." I whispered against his lips feeling his beard. My fingers skimmed through his hair avoiding the mess at the top. The silky strands slipping through my fingers. Noah pulled away standing up.

"I need to shower and then we should probably go visit everyone in the main room. I also have to call Jack so he knows we are here. I'll have to run into town and get a new burner phone though. You're welcome to come with me there or you can stay here and I'll stick Jace on you again." His voice was rough with sleep. I couldn't focus on what he was saying. "Grace." He clipped. My eyes left his chest meeting his eyes. Desire was burning deep inside of me and I wanted to chase it. But I was being held back. The bruises left behind from Cody were gruesome and I didn't want Noah seeing all of them.

"I'm sorry…I.. Your voice turned me on. But I don't want you to see me naked right now." I whispered ashamed of what I looked like because of the club. I should be angry, but I couldn't bring myself to be that way. The club was everything I knew and everything I was going to know by marrying Noah. It was all my children would know. And I wasn't prepared for any of it. My dad's sperm should have had a warning label. My hair came down creating a curtain around my face. I saw Noah's hands come around threading themselves into my hair and lifting my face up to his.

"Baby. It's going to be alright. You'll heal and if you don't want me to see you until then that's fine. I've lasted months without having you I can last another week. We will make it through all of this. I can see the doubt in your eyes right now. But baby you're stuck with me. And soon you'll be stuck with me until death do us part." I felt like I was being trapped. I gave up so much for the club already. Pride and dignity were hard to gain back when you give them up. You don't pride yourself when you willingly give up a promise you made yourself. You don't have dignity when you willingly allow a man to lay a hand on you when you said that you'd never let a man do that to you ever again. I had a chance of having a baby with Noah and I miscarried. I felt like I was failing myself and unable to pick myself up. Life itself was making me it's bitch and the challenge to keep on living was getting harder and harder every day. Why didn't Noah just let me go? I could have died and not suffered anymore. I wouldn't be assaulted with the healing process anymore. My eyes were beginning to mist the moisture threatening to spill over the edge.

    My mouth began to move but the words wouldn't come out. I wanted to end everything right here and now. The pain unbearable. Flash backs persisted showing the memories I kept buried for so long that reliving them was earth shattering. Reality became white noise, my eyes glazing over as the emotions and feelings replay in my mind.

    Work was long. My boss was on my ass more than usual and I was late getting home. Max was going to be so mad at me. He always thought these late nights were times I was cheating on him with my boss. It never mattered what I told him, he wouldn't listen. Standing outside the apartment door I prepared myself for the argument that was about to ensue. The last time I was late... I shuddered at the thought and opened the door to my beautiful apartment that I now shared with Max. "Max?" I yelled. My mind was thinking just love on him and maybe you can avoid an argument. I knew that wouldn't be what would happen though. The TV was on in the living room. I stupidly followed the noise and set my things on the counter in the kitchen before proceeding into the living room. Max was on the couch a bottle next to him almost drained of its contents. I could already tell it was going to be a bad night.

    "You're late darling." Max sneered. I closed my eyes trying to keep calm.

"I know I'm sorry. Mr. Wilson kept me late again. I told him that I needed to get home. He pretty much told me that if I didn't stay, I wouldn't have a job. Unfortunately, I need this job." I said hoping the lie of losing my job would be hidden. William would never do something like that to me. I was the only one that could keep up with the man. Max stood up my eyes staying focused on him.

"You know how much I hate you coming home late. Dinner's not done when I get here and we have less time together." He stated cupping my cheek. This is what he normally does, Grace stay calm. The worst is yet to come. My breathing was beginning to pick up and I couldn't control it. It was like I was watching the situation unfolding. I watched as the talking escalated into yelling. Yelling escalating into screaming and that's when it happened. Max's anger spiked like an out of control fever. His face flushing then turning bright red. His hand raising in the air striking out. The sound of his hand hitting my flesh echoing off the apartment walls. The assault never ending. His fist repeatedly hitting my body. I listened as I heard my cries, my pleas for everything to stop. I could see the tears streaming down my cheeks. My body fell to the ground as his polished shoe slammed into my ribs. The sounds of bones breaking riveting off the walls. One after another ribs broke. I counted six broken ribs. My body gasped for breath. My mouth forming words pleading for Max to stop.

When Max finally stopped blood was dripping from my lips, my legs were curled into my chest. My nose was crooked, the left eye swollen shut. He crouched down in front of my body. The whispered words, the whiskey on his breath, it all made me want to vomit. "Now you're going to see what happens when you make me unhappy. When you work late fucking another man. When you disobey my orders." Max stood walking towards the door. My one eye followed him out the door. A sigh of relief escaped my lips as my body struggled to get off the floor. Uncurling my legs, I flinched from the pain. Breathing was a chore at this point.

Finally making it off the floor I dragged myself to the bathroom. The process of cleaning myself up started I heard the main *door open and close indicating that Max was back. A drunken giggle sounded. I hung my head in defeat. What happened next was a breaking point. The woman that came home with Max was jumping on my bed. A few moments later Max was balls deep inside of her, her moans ricocheting off the walls getting louder with each slam of the headboard. I needed to leave but the only way out was through the bedroom. Taking a calming breath, I opened the way into the bedroom. Max's naked body was glistening with sweat already. The woman was on her stomach bent over the edge. Max's cock assaulting her ass. Blood ran between her legs onto my white comforter. Max's head turned towards me his eyes glazed over from the alcohol and ecstasy he was feeling. I turned away from him going for my purse in the kitchen and out the front door slamming it behind me.*

"Grace!" my hands were covering my face as tears were streaming down my face as I came back to reality. Noah's arms were wrapped around me. I was shaking in his arms feeling like I was suffocating. Pulling my hands away from my face, I beat my hands on Noah's chest pushing him away. Noah let me go as I stood up rushing to the bathroom emptying my stomach of its contents. Leaning against the tub the tears kept coming with no end in sight. Noah was standing in the doorway of the bathroom. His eyes looked helpless. He knew there was nothing he could really do except support me through this hardship. My hands went into my hair holding onto the strands. Sobs wracked my body and I felt Noah sit next to me his arms going around me pulling me to his chest. My fingers left my hair wrapping around him holding on like he could be a mirage. I thanked god that Noah was real and not just a memory as I traveled down the path to heal.

"I'm so sorry." I whispered into his neck. His hand stroked my back just being there for me. His comfort was everything at this moment. Exactly everything I needed.

NOAH

Grace's breakdown was a crushing point in my life. I wasn't sure how to handle it. Seemed like holding her was the right choice. She leaned into me seeking the comfort I could give her. The only thing I could offer. My hand stroking her back as sobs wracked her body. I just had to keep telling myself it was all a part of the healing process.

When the sobs calmed Grace pulled away keeping her hand on my chest. My hand covered hers keeping it over my heart. "Grace." Her eyes lifted to mine. "We should probably get off the floor." I whispered leaning over to kiss her forehead. Her responding nod was all I needed as I got up and helped Grace off the floor. She looked in the mirror beginning the process of washing her face off of all the tears. Even though she was vulnerable, she had never looked so beautiful to me. The way her eyes frosted putting her wall in place defending her soul against the outside world. Burying the pain deep inside of herself. The way Grace was holding herself together was tragically beautiful. Her strength could only grow from here, from this experience. Pulling her hair back I continued to watch her armor slide back in place. The dreadful scene was ending for her and I didn't know of anything that I could do to help her. Fighting this internal banter of hers, the chaos unleashing inside of her, Grace was on her own. Here and now, there was nothing I could do except support her. My heart hurt for her wishing I could do more for her than just be a support. Leaving the bathroom and Grace, I had to let her have space.

An hour or so went by before Grace came out of the bathroom. Her hair wet from a recent shower, eyes red and swollen from more crying. Standing up, I went over to her and wrapped my arms around her. "Grace, darling, I love you so much. You're not alone. I promise you. I'll always be here for you." I whispered the words in her hair. Feeling her hands slide up from my hips underneath my shirt. They stopped on my chest. Her nails dug into my skin. Her blonde hair tied up exposed her neck. My lips pressed against the sensitive skin just below her ear. Her body shuddered leaning against me. "Sweetheart. Are you all right?" The words exploded out of my lips.

"I will be." She breathlessly whispered. Her eyes found mine. Her armor was in full defensive mode. The things this woman had been through made my respect and love for her grow, along with my determination. I was determined to show Grace the best life I could, the life she deserved. "Noah." My name on her lips broke my thoughts. "Please take me. Make me forget everything." Her lips pressed against mine. Leading her to the bed we toppled over, I did exactly what she asked. Even if it was only temporary.

GRACE

A storm came in the next morning. Getting up I looked at my reflection. The bruises were almost gone. I could actually wear make-up without it making the bruises look darker. Searching my bags, I found an outfit and my make-up. Taking another step towards healing, I made an effort to look decent. Even if it is a lie, you pretend everything is okay until you forget. And one day you are healed. And one day, the lie becomes your life. Every day, you become someone else. You change, become a survivor It may take forever through. This was the healing I went through with Max. Looking over at Noah through the doorway I knew this time had to be different. I couldn't just pretend with him. Noah knew me, he could read me like a book. He stirred on the bed while I pulled on my boots and went over to Noah kissing his cheek leaving lipstick behind. The rain beat against the windows making me realize what I was going to do next. Rain was my favorite thing and I couldn't stay away from it. My sweatshirt stayed behind while I left the room.

An awning protected me from the wetness. Lifting my face towards the sky I smiled as the smell of fresh rain hit my nostrils. The sky lit up as lightning crashed through the clouds. The sound and sight reminding me I'm alive. Reminding me I'm a survivor of domestic abuse. Lightning struck the middle of the lot obscuring vision for a moment. A figure stood near the strike being blacked out from the bright light. I watched him. Leather squeaked as his arms swung by his side.

NOAH

Going in the bathroom, I saw Grace's things thrown everywhere. She had made an effort making me swell with pride. My girl was making progress. I knew she would beat everything she was going through. The internal battle would be one she'd win. Seeing my reflection, I smiled. The lipstick on my cheek was the second-best thing to wake up to.

The main room was empty. No club whores sleeping naked, no one cleaning. Inhaling I smiled as Grace's perfume made my nostrils flare. Walking towards the door, I lit a cigarette. The sounds of tires squealing against the wet asphalt made my skin crawl. Running outside I looked around my eyes landed on a black SUV turning out of the lot on two tires. Walking forward I kicked something as it skidded across the pavement. Grace's ring skidded to a halt in the pouring rain. Grasping it in my palm, I ran towards the road my bare feet splashing through the puddles. The SUV was gone.

Pounding on Tommy's door, I was panicking. We just got through one thing and now she took off. "What the fuck do you want!" Tommy hollered opening the door. My fist stopping before it hit him in the face.

"Security feeds. I need them and I need them right fucking now." I fumed. Tommy raised his eyebrow. He was stalling looking for more information. "Grace is gone. All I have is her ring and she took off in a black SUV. I need the fucking plate." I was tense. No tense wasn't even the word for it. I was taunt and stressed beyond belief.

Tommy got his ass in gear opening a heavily locked door. The extensive technology he had behind the door was exactly what I needed. Every video being recorded from every camera around the club was on screens around the desk. And it was all live. Sitting at the desk I started scanning backwards through the streams. It didn't take me long to get the footage I needed to. The video showed me exactly what I wanted and what had happened. I looked up at Tommy. "We need to call church." I insisted. Burning a copy of the video, I called Techy back home. Putting him on the job of finding the fucking plate for the SUV. I watched the footage over and over again before church. Each time making me more pissed off than the last. She didn't take off like I thought. She was rendered unconscious before being thrown over a man's shoulder. My heart hadn't stopped racing since I saw her ring on the ground. Getting up before I broke something, I went outside lighting a cigarette.

GRACE

Darkness surrounded me. My hands were tied behind my back. My head hurt like hell and I was beginning to feel nauseous. The movement of my body was rolling around and I couldn't tell where the hell I was. Moving my head around I realized there was a bag over me. One tiny hole was cut into it. Could I get it so I could see out of the hole? Only one way to find out. Rubbing the bag against whatever I was laying on I maneuvered it so I could see out the hole. It didn't move much but I could make out the back of the backseat of a vehicle. With how I was laying there was no way I'd be able to turn to see the driver unless I crushed my hands or fell off the seat. Now there was an idea. I could roll onto the floor and maybe catch something. Or whoever was driving would have to come and pick me up off the floor and I could probably catch a glimpse of them then. It was worth a shot.

Swaying with the vehicle I tried to roll off the seat having no such luck. I took a deep breath and nudged my knees close to the back of the seat using them to push off hopefully landing on the floor. A sudden jerk had me flying off the seat my legs sticking straight in the air boots against the window. "What the fuck are you doing back there ya?" The Scottish accent was pronounced and thick. The car came to a stop as I moved the bag, so my eye was close to the hole again. The door opened and slammed shut. I was enclosed in this tiny space all alone for now.

The door opened against my legs as they fell out of the air. My ankles smacking the running board on the vehicle. Keeping as silent as I could I watched through the hole. All I could see in front of me was the expanse of the grey sky and woods. Figuring this was the last scenery I was going to see I took it all in. At this moment I would have given anything to go back to my boring life.

After being flipped over the man's shoulder, he took me inside somewhere. Doors were opened and kicked shut. And lots of walking happened. My heart was racing. Survival was pumping through my veins. I wished this guy would have just knocked me out again so that I wouldn't have to feel like a dead mule. Maybe the phrase was like a sack of potatoes. I could only see the man's ass through the tiny hole and I was getting pissed off.

A set of stairs and another door slammed behind us I was finally on my back. The bag came off my head the light blinding my eyes. Trying to shield my eyes from the light my hands stopped just above my head. My eyes snapped up to my hands seeing handcuffs around my wrists. The cuffs wrapped around a pole on the headboard. A laugh echoed off the walls making me look in the direction of the man. He looked kind of like a James Bond look alike. Except his nose is crooked, his teeth weren't straight and he has salt and pepper hair on the sides. "Well darling, let's get this whole thing going." He bellowed. Get what thing started? What the hell did he want with me? I was a nobody and he had to fucking take me as I was finally fucking recovering? "Now, your little boyfriend killed my father." It all clicked into place. The Scottish man that was after Noah. It seemed like forever ago but that's why the man was after me. Noah and my dad killed his father. "And if they don't respond to what I tell them to do. I'm going to kill you." He announced. My life was hell it was fucking hell and I was going to die not fully living. At least it was a hell I could fight my way through. I hoped.

NOAH

Just minutes before church Techy called me back. The information he gave me sent me over the moon with relief and at the same time made me panic. The room was packed with every member of the club that could be there on short notice when I walked in. Eyes turned to me indicating I was the topic of conversation. We were supposed to be hiding here not getting fucking kidnapped. Leaning against the wall I hung my head forward closing my eyes. Techy told me that the plate on the SUV was stolen which was good news and bad news. The good part was that it wasn't the club's vehicle and she hadn't taken off. The bad news? Well it was a never-ending shit storm that just happened to be Grace and I against the world.

Filling everyone in with what was going on, mouths started firing. Everyone had the same questions I did. Who the fuck could have taken her? Who is really that stupid to take a president's daughter? Not to mention a member's fiancé? We all knew that there were plenty of people who would do such a thing but now it was up to us to figure out who did it and why? All while keeping the cops out of our shit. This was going to be a hard blow to the club. Was it a one-man job? Or were there multiple people. I knew I should have jumped on my bike and followed them. But in doing so I would have had no idea what I was walking into. I could have probably followed back far enough that I would have known where they were going and been able to check everything out. Only thing was if they suspected they were being followed what's to say they wouldn't kill Grace on the spot and be done with everything. Fuck my life. No, that didn't even cover it. My life was a shit storm of incidents.

GRACE

Barely any light was shining through the blinds just above the bed. Darkness was filling the already dim and cloudy sky. My body exhausted from pulling on my restraints, wishing the darkness would pull me into it to end the pain. The adrenaline calm in my veins. The mattress hard against my back and shoulders. My bladder crying out to be relieved. Laying there for hours without food and drink was excruciating. My stomach growled in agreement. "Hey asshole!" I hollered towards the door.

"What the fuck do ya want?" he bellowed muffled by the door. I crossed my legs hoping I didn't piss myself. I doubt he had any clothes I could change into in case that happened.

"I need to use the restroom!" I yelled squeezing my legs together. A soft "sum of a bitch" came through the door. The handle turned before slamming back into the exact same position it was in. My eyes focused on the handle hoping that wasn't all he was going to do. The bastard was going to pay for doing this to me. I just had to get loose. The handle turned again before the door slammed against the wall. The man came in the room dropping a bucket on the floor.

"You've got one minute." He said walking over to me releasing my hands. The cramps in my shoulders slowly faded as I began moving my arms around. Pain radiated through my back as I sat up. Staring at the bucket I was horrified.

"I can't use an actual restroom?" I muttered.

"No running water 'ere princess." He replied. Rolling my neck around I stood up. "Your one minute starts right now." He left the room closing the door behind him. My eyes watched the door as I dropped my pants squatting over the bucket.

Shit. There was no toilet paper.

"Can I please get some toilet paper?" I asked.

"Thirty seconds." He sneered. His footsteps fell away from the door and my bladder couldn't wait another second to relieve itself.

The door slammed back open allowing the man to come back in the room. I stayed where I was squatting trying to cover myself while my bladder continued its way to empty on the gas tank. Toilet paper landed in my lap. He turned his back towards me giving me some privacy. And in that turn, I had learned a lot. He was underestimating me which is exactly what I needed. Cleaning myself up and reassembling my clothes I sat back down on the bed. "Anyway, I could get some food? I'm starving." I asked trying to seem brittle and scared, trying to make it seem like he had all the power. The man stared down at me and I looked away. He seemed to get excited over the power he thought I was giving him. The vulnerability I was showing. If I didn't know better this guy got off on dominance. Maybe he did but this is just revenge. I had to tell myself over and over again that this wasn't about me. There's a bigger picture being painted. He didn't really want me he wanted either Noah or my father. Taking a deep breath, I watched his feet.

"I'll get you some food." He jeered fisting my hair pulling it tight. My scalp tingled and made me cringe. My neck bending to place the pain somewhere else on my body. A gasp escaped my mouth as tingles shot down my spine. I couldn't keep this up for long. I just wanted to go home. His arm snapped back giving my hair one last tug before releasing it and leaving the room. Tears threatened to spill from my eyes. More than anything, I wanted Noah.

NOAH

This shit was getting unreal. We had no idea where the fucking car went and Grace wasn't back in my fucking arms yet. It had been a whole fucking twelve hours since I had watched the videos. Twelve fucking hours. I felt like we were just sitting on our asses playing with our dicks with no explosion. Grace was out there alone. I needed to find her. Bringing her back to the club would be the only thing that could keep me together. My seams were already fraying and images flashed through my mind. Most of them the kind I didn't want to dwell on. Grace's dead body lying in the middle of nowhere waiting to be found. The echoes of flesh on flesh resonating though my ears as the memory of Beast beating Grace for the club slaughtered my mind's eye. I was terrified something had happened to her. The scent of her perfume was branded into my nose but missing in the real world. My fingers ached to hold her.

"Where the fuck is Noah?" The voice of my president carried up the ladder towards where I sat on the roof. The cigarette hanging from my fingers. As far as I knew they were still looking for some sign of Grace on the streets. Any clues to where she could be. Techy had been working on it since she had been taken from right under my nose. My legs stood my body up leading me to the ladder. Jack's eyes met mine as I stared down at him. Bringing the cigarette to my lips I held it there taking a slow drag off of it before swinging my leg over the edge descending the ladder. Turning towards Jack at the bottom I could see it all in his eyes. "We found her."

GRACE

Somehow, I convinced the man to leave me untethered from the bed. The mattress was still hard against my back but my arms being free had me making the best of the situation. The ceiling was old and looked to be caving in on itself. The prospect that the ceiling could end everything for me in my sleep was a moment I wished would come. My eyes wandered to the window next to me. The darkness on the other side of the blinds drew me to look out the window. Sitting up propping my body weight on my elbow, I lifted the blinds. Looking around outside it looked familiar but I couldn't place why.

The buildings were close together on the deserted street. The house I was in was close enough to the one next door that I could have reached out and touched it without leaning forward. Laying back down I closed my eyes hoping that I wouldn't wake up from this hell that keeps punishing me. Two beatings and a kidnapping was enough excitement in my life. Give me the boring back. People were never happy, were they? They get what they want but then decide that they want what they had. A sigh escaped my lips as I rolled to my side using my arms as a pillow. Hoping, dreaming that something would end all of this. My heart hoped it was Noah to come in and save me but my brain, my brain knew there was a better chance of that ceiling caving in on me and knocking me to my death. I felt chaotic as the darkness of sleep overtook me.

NOAH

Techy fucking did it. I couldn't believe it. I wanted to jump on my bike and rush to her. Jack had his hands on me before I could take a step. "Son, you can't just go barging in there. We don't know what we are dealing with, or who we are dealing with." Jack was one inch away from getting throat punched. Telling me I couldn't go get my girl, fuck that shit. I wanted her so I was going to go get her. I didn't care if it got me killed. She needed to be home with me and safe from the hell she was most currently living. As soon as I had her back she wasn't leaving my side either. If she wanted to go stand in the rain she definitely wasn't going to be doing it alone ever again. I'd be there right along with her getting drenched from the sky's tears. I'm sure my own tears would be shedding as I watched her smile again. Closing my eyes, I could see that gorgeous woman I called mine smile behind my lids.

"I need her back, Jack." I whispered. I felt defeated as I looked around. The club came filing out of the club house. All eyes were on me and that's when it hit me. They were waiting for me to make a move. To throw the brotherhood to the wind and go get my ol'lady. Taking a deep breath, I looked at Jack square in the eyes. "What do we do now?" The words whispered past my lips. Hope blooming in my belly gave me purpose and a goal. If whoever had taken her touched one hair on her...I hoped he liked staring at the barrel of a gun. Thunder rolled in as lightning lit up the sky. The clouds black as the monster being freed from its shell buried deep inside me. Hell was coming to take another soul to the devil.

We all sat down at the table with our eyes trained on Jack. He rubbed a finger over his lips his own eyes trained on the wooden table. The silence was deafening. Steeping my hands in front of me I leaned my forehead against them. The monster inside of me wanting to escape was beginning to be uncontrollable. We needed to figure out what the fuck we were going to do and we needed to do it soon. He was thirsty for blood. My mouth couldn't handle the silence anymore. "What the fuck are we going to do Jack? We can't possibly sit here with our dicks in our hands jacking off any longer." I said hammering my fist onto the table, emphasizing each word. Eyes turned to me. Judging my anger. Fuckers didn't understand the torture my body had been through. The worthless hours I had spent away on the streets. When I found something, I wanted to keep…an obsession came over me. It tore into my veins until it was all I thought about. Grace became that obsession. She is that obsession. It was only a matter of time until the beast rose out of me to take back what's mine.

"We are going to figure that out Noah." He looked at each member in the eye around the table. "Anybody have a ample idea of what we should do?"

"We could run in guns blazing." Razor said. I shook my head.

"I already tried to go that route. Jack stopped me." I retorted. The sarcasm dripping from my lips. "Obviously we need to investigate what the fuck or rather who the fuck we are dealing with and if there is a team or just one person. We can't risk men going down over this. Even though we are willing." They knew it was true, especially because she's the president's daughter.

"We will send out two members to survey the area and the house she's being held at then I suggest we reconvene tomorrow morning. Any volunteers?" Jack offered. "No Noah. Not you. You're a grounded solider tonight."

GRACE

Light shattered through the hazy darkness blinding my tired eyes. Squinting I could see around the room. It was as bare as my ass. No curtains on the windows or blinds. The mattress my ass sat on was just as bare. No sheets or blankets just the bars on the headboard and footboard. I didn't know what to do. Did I dare try and escape? Scooting off the bed my legs carried me to the door. I figured I might as well explore a little bit and maybe, just maybe, my captor would be gone and I could escape. He seemed to be doing this job alone. I hoped that Noah was looking for me and not drinking thinking I had left him. Tears stung my eyes. Batting my lashes, I vanquished them. Opening the door slowly I peeked out into the hallway. There were stairs to the left and a hallway that led to two more doors straight ahead. Moving forward I headed down the hall. Floorboards groaned beneath my feet. I flinched praying the next step didn't groan. The door on the left was the bathroom. It had a slanted ceiling and was dirty as all hell. The club house was cleaner than the fucking bathroom and those men are pigs. I stepped inside and spotted the toilet. My captor had said that there wasn't running water. I wonder if he lied to me. Going to the sink I turned the faucet on. Water came pouring out making me giddy. Closing the door, I quickly locked it and sat myself on the toilet feeling relieved that I could actually use a restroom and not a bucket. Washing my hands was probably going to feel like heaven.

After my bathroom adventure, I peeked back out in the hallway. With the coast still clear I crept into the next room. It was dusty as fuck and I turned right back around. The stairs would be my next adventure. Hesitation crept up my legs making me stop and listen. My heart was beating so loud I couldn't hear myself think. Hoping that I hadn't missed a sound or warning I crept my way down the stairs. The front door was right there at the bottom. I wanted so badly to beat feet out of here but I didn't know where the asshole was or what would happen. Looking through the railing I could see into the living room. A TV was on the light skipping across the darkened room. His feet came into view as I crept down the stairs further. Creeping to the bottom I could see he was sleeping and if he hadn't woken up yet I was in a good position. The stairway opened up into a hallway. Across from the front door was the kitchen. My stomach growled and I froze. If he woke up while I was down here…I couldn't imagine what he would do to me. A loud snore came from the living room and my body started to relax.

My feet continued forward going into the kitchen. It was bare no furniture in sight besides the counter, fridge, and stove. Moving to the fridge I opened it up as quietly as I could. There was sandwich meat and bread and that was good enough for me. Quickly throwing a sandwich together I scarfed it down as fast as my mouth would chew and swallow. The sandwich made my mouth feel like a desert. Sticking my head under the sink I poured water into my dry mouth before beating feet back up the stairs and into the room I was stuck in.

Time crept by before my captor came in the room. It felt like it had been fifteen minutes when in reality it had been 3 hours. He didn't know it but by waiting that long and being able to hear him snore in the living room gave me the knowledge that he was a heavy sleeper. I looked up at him as he entered the room. I felt his eyes roam over me before I saw them. His tongue came out wetting his lips. A feeling of disgust waved its way through my veins. A shiver running down my spine making my body twitch. Looking down at the bed I fought the urge to throw up.

His body made the bed dip. My eyes shooting up to his. I'd

be lying if I said I wasn't scared. This could be the end for me. It was very possible that I wouldn't see Noah, my parents, or my sister ever again. I could hope all I wanted that it wouldn't be true but reality was settling in and it was doing so very quickly. Defeat was weighing heavy on my heart. The detachment starting. Staring at the man before me, I started to let the emotions run through me. Tears dropped from my eyes landing on my thighs. "Shhhh. It's going to be okay. I won't hurt you as long as you don't do anything stupid." He whispered reaching over to me. I flinched pulling my face away from his hand as far as I could. His arm dropped down to the bed and a sigh left his lips. "I don't want to hurt you. I just want to hurt your little boyfriend. And by taking you, I'm doing just that. He said.

My head hit the wall behind me as I stared up at the ceiling. I knew my life was over and all I could think about was my memories of Noah and a stupid song that made me think of Noah even more. Tears rolled down my cheeks and neck. I didn't care either. There was nothing more I could do. Anger rippled through me. I needed to come up with a plan to get the fuck out of here. It was either that or I was going to get myself killed.

Pain radiated though my arm as the asshole twisted it behind my back almost bending it the wrong way. Shutting my eyes, I tried to focus away from the pain. The clink of metal on metal got my attention quickly. Spinning around as much as I could I tried to look behind me. The handcuffs were back in place. He slapped them back on my wrist. The relief was instant when he released my arm. My shoulder was throbbing and it made me happy. The pain indicated that this wasn't a dream. I was alive and I needed to stay hopeful. My vision blurred from tears collecting. I refused to let them fall again. His footsteps sounded on the hard wood floor. Silence echoed around me before the click of the door shutting reached my ears. A pad-lock was set in place on the door, sealing me inside this tiny room. I let my tears fall then. Nothing was going to

JENNIFER TURNER

get better. Nothing.

NOAH

Everything was made to seem like Grace was trying to leave me. Techy reported that he had seen her in an upstairs bedroom. Also, that she had been able to roam free as she had gone downstairs without him releasing her before going back to the bedroom. The only thing that was suspicious was that she ran back to the bedroom, like she was scared. I felt like I didn't know shit anymore. Was she leaving or was she actually kidnapped? My thoughts raced as I contemplated what the fuck was going on. Blindly, I stood up not knowing what I was doing.

Next thing I knew I was sitting next to Techy. I didn't remember the drive over or how I got there all I knew was that I was there. I could feel Techy staring at me. My eyes stayed trained on the house in front of us. "Brother. What are you doing here?" Techy had concern in his voice.

"I couldn't sit there anymore. Figured I'd come give you a piss break." I mumbled zoning in on the house. "What window is she?" His sigh was highly audible, but his hand raised anyways and pointed.

"Second story. Right most window." He said standing up. "Don't do anything stupid Noah. I'll be right back."

"My ass won't move until you get back." My body was rigid, ready to leap up. But knowing that if I went blindly in there, I'd die. And then who would save her. My ass was parked and it was staying parked until it had to move.

It was a long wait for Techy to come back. And when he returned, he had a shit ton of food in his arms. Cocking my eyebrow, I watched as he settled in next to me. "I'm under strict orders to piss in the woods from now on. Almost got a bullet placed in my dick for returning to the club to piss and get food and leaving you here." He grunted out before tossing me a bag of food. "Told me I was fucking stupid because you're a fucking loose cannon." He rattled on and on about what Jack had said about me. I quit listening. Grace was a half a block in front of me and all I could do was watch. I'll bring you home baby. If it's the last thing I do.

GRACE

I had to be losing my mind. I just had to be. A familiar feeling had washed over me. The feeling that Noah was close was enough to make my heart race and for my body to become buck wild. A smile crossed my lips as I lived in the moment. Before I knew what I was doing, My hand clutched my other hand. A deep breath later a loud crunch sounded. I wanted to scream but I couldn't let him know what I was doing. Letting the pain fade a bit and taking deep breaths to calm myself, I gripped the handcuff and pulled my hand and broken thumb out of it. Cradling my hand, I looked around for something, anything I could use as a sign. Opening the drawer of the nightstand up I found an old marker. I just hoped it still worked. Slowly I eased off the bed. Tiptoeing over to the window I moved the curtains. Uncapping the marker, I tried it out. Ink didn't come out. Wetting my finger, I put spit on it hoping that it would help. Still nothing. Leaning my head against the window I put the marker down and felt all emotion drain from my body.

A flash came across my face blinding me for a moment. Shielding my eyes, I looked across the street where it was coming from. Bushes moved and Noah popped out of them. Relief washed over me as did the urge to jump up and down cheering that I had been found. My hand pressed against the glass, watching him was something I would never forget. His finger went to his lips telling me to remain quiet. It was hard especially when I wanted to scream and jump out the window to run to him. All I could hope for was that this would all soon be over.

A noise came from over my shoulder. The padlock was

being taken off the door. I didn't have time to run back to the bed and put the handcuff back on. Horror crossed my face as I looked out at Noah one more time. I backed away from the window and as quickly as I could went back to the bed. He opened the door right as my hand slipped back into the handcuff. I had something to rejoice about and keep hope on my side. But until then I was back in his arms, I wasn't going to be cheering for anything.

NOAH

Grace was in the window. I had seen her with my own two eyes. I watched her struggle to write on the window. I had to let her know I was here waiting to get her out, at least if she wanted to get out. Excitement flowed out of me as I hoped and prayed that she would be wanting to come home with me. Tearing a mirror off Techy's bike I used it to make light flash across the window. It was starting to feel as if life was standing still. This beautiful woman was trapped or maybe willingly trapped inside this damned place. I wouldn't know until I got her out of there. I wanted so badly to just jump out of hiding and run in there, guns blazing. Unfortunately, Jack would have my fucking balls on a silver platter and I wouldn't be dead by his hand. Crouching just out of the hiding spot I stared up at the window. Her smile lit up my world. I could have sat there and stared all day. I needed to help her get the fuck out of there first. I watched as a scared look came across her beautiful features and she ran away from the window.

Sighing, I went back to Techy and handed him his mirror before leaning against a tree to watch the house. I felt that all this waiting was getting ridiculous. She was stuck in there possibly without food, I didn't know if he was giving her water. He probably wasn't so she didn't have to piss. Anger passed through my veins like an angry sea. I just wanted her in my arms and I wanted it to happen now.

My eyes scanned the area hoping for some sign that I could move in and handle the bastard. I swear if he touched her... "Hey, dipshit. Sit the fuck down." Techy was whisper yelling at me. My head fell forward making myself acknowledge that I was moving forward. If he hadn't said something to me, I would have blown our cover. Plopping my ass down with a thump I took a deep breath to calm myself. Terror was ripping through me now. If she was hurt in any way, I didn't know if I could live with myself.

The sun started to set behind the house portraying the horror that could be held inside. What if there was a band of them in there? He could have friends nearby watching us or inside the house standing security. He could even have more people trapped there besides Grace. We knew nothing at this point. "Have you figured anything out? Is he alone? Is she the only one trapped? Or in that house with him?" I asked Techy angling my face towards him. A sigh escaped him. I knew he probably had mentioned everything to me, but I didn't pay attention. I couldn't when she was mere yards away from me.

"She's the only one captive. He's the only one I've seen in the house besides her. So he's working alone." Techy answered putting binoculars up to his eyes. Looking at the ground by my feet I picked up a rock. It wasn't heavy. I could make it fly across the road and to the window maybe. Standing on the edge of our hideout, I eyed the house and the exact window where Grace was held. Pitching my arm back, I swung it forward hurling the rock across the street and hit just below the window. "What the fuck are you doing Asshat!" Techy had my shirt in his fists and I gently laid my hands on his wrists.

"I'm doing what I know best. Luring prey out." The front door of the house swung open as Techy dropped me. My hand fell on my gun and I sighed realizing I only had a hand gun with me. Watching him I tried to identify him. His hat was too low to see his face. Looking over at Techy, a wicked smile crossed my lips. "Run across the street and ask for random directions to somewhere. Try and get a good look at him. You still wear that stupid camera on your vest?" I asked. He returned a nod to me as was the realization that I was sending him in instead of myself. "Take the camera off and put it on your shirt. I'll hold onto your colors. I need to see this man's face." I said pulling his vest off for him, stripping him of his colors for the time being. Techy shook his head and took off across the road. I watched, waiting.

GRACE

A knock landed on the door downstairs. Looking at the handcuffs I tried to decide if I should get up or just stay put. Maybe I could hear what was going on if I stayed still. A man's voice was muffled through the floor. My ears strained to hear the conversation. I got nothing. I could only hear that they were talking but the words weren't forming in my brain. Comprehension was not my strongest trait at the moment. Sighing, I slipped out of the cuffs tiptoeing over to the door and trying the handle. He had locked it again. Looking over at the window I wondered if it would open. Heavy footfalls sounded coming up the stairs and I knew I was going to be in trouble if caught. Quickly, I pushed my hand through the cuff again and laid on the bed. My hand stung from the cuff, but I didn't have time to investigate it. The padlock came off the door and he stepped inside the room.

Shivers involuntary ran down my back. The vibes I got from this man made me want to scream and kick and cry. Pure insanity rolled off him in waves. His eyes blazed with evil thoughts. His eyes looked like rings of fire. The fear settled within as I stared into the pits of hell that were his eyes. "You notified someone that you're here, didn't you?" he asked his knuckles turning white from strain holding the edge of the door. My eyes grew wide thinking about the notification from Noah just minutes before. He was just across the street what if the man at the door was someone from the club. Fear iced my blood as my captor stepped towards me. "How did you do it?" He asked. I shook my head. I wasn't sure what was going on and I didn't want him to know that Noah was right there across the street. My mind was racing at the possibilities of what could happen. He raised his fist to me, that was the last thing I could remember.

The sun was beginning to rise from its slumber when my eyes opened back up. The bright light streamed in the window showing the room to me fully. The walls bare nothing in sight except a small table next to the bed and an empty closet. It felt like my brain. My brain however I was happy was quiet. It meant that I didn't have be fearful of emotions bombarding me. Stretching, I stood up creeping to the door trying the handle before opening it slightly. The hallway was silent. Pushing the door wider I stepped out of the room. A television was on down the stairs on the left of me. My foot found the first stair silently. Putting pressure on the stair I tested it for creaks. If the man was still in the house, I didn't want to alert him. Silently I moved down the staircase keeping an eye on my surroundings. The man sat on the couch in the living room. His head leaning over the back of the couch. His eyes were closed and a soft snore escaped his lips. Looking down the hallway at the bottom of the stairs I had two options. Door or kitchen. Moving towards the left I picked the door.

The door groaned as I opened it. I didn't dare look back before taking off running outside. Gravel bit into my bare feet. I only had to make it to the line of the woods across the street and I'd be in Noah's arms again. Running as fast as my legs would carry me. I collapsed. Everything going black.

My arms tingled waking me. Everything was black around me. My eyes blurry. Ass hurting from the hard-cold floor. Leaning my head back it rested against the wall as I took a deep inhale. Metal clinked together as my arms tried to relax behind me. I was captive again. A musty scent made my nose crinkle. Shaking my head, I tried to rid the smell from my nostrils. Pulling my knees up to my chest I rubbed my nose against one just willing the smell to go away. Metallic taste filled my mouth. Deep breathing was needed to push through the nausea. Blood never sat well with my stomach. It reminded me of sterile places like the doctor's office. Another wave of nausea hit and I had to rest my forehead against my knees. I needed to get the taste out of my mouth and fast if I didn't want to throw up.

A door groaned letting bright light shine through the darkness that is my prison. Squinting I watched as a shadowy figure descended the stairs. He got close enough and I saw the man who was slowly becoming my worst nightmare. I closed my eyes letting my head hang forward. My hair creating a curtain of discreetness. Emotions played across my mind as he crouched in front of me pushing my hair back. His hand gripped it thrusting my head backwards. My body was finally calming down from the adrenaline high. That's when I noticed something was off. My thighs were sore. My jeans were torn. Shivers ran down my spine as a gasp left my lips. My mouth wasn't the only place that was covered in blood. Dried blood covered the inside of my thighs. Scrunching my eyes shut I tried not to cry. I tried not to panic as another wave of nausea hit harder than before.

Opening my eyes, his face was too close to me. His musk filled my nose before I could hold my breath. Tears threatened to spill from my eyes. Emotions piercing through my mask as the fear and knowledge of what happened sunk in. I pulled my head as far away from him as I could. Even though it was giving into what he wanted. His smile showed everything. He feeds on fear and hopelessness. "I brought you food." His words slithered across my skin making me feel slimy. I stared at him and shook my head.

"I don't want any food from you." I said my voice hoarse. His smile grew to a grin as he watched me struggle to stay calm. "I don't want anything from you." My voice had gained some firmness as I regained control of my emotions. There was something about this man that rubbed me the wrong way. He slid a finger down my arm as I did the best to not flinch away. The touch made me feel like slime was sliding down my skin rather than a finger. My back tensed as a shiver started down my spine. Holding it together was tough, but I knew I could do it. I just had to be tougher. He leaned towards me, My head went to the side facing away from him.

"Well then I guess I'll have to starve you." His voice was soft. His breath hot against my ear. I closed my eyes and held my breath. I was already losing control. I wanted to scream while punching and kicking. I wanted to bite him and make his days with me a living hell. I knew that would just take up all my energy. Energy, I needed to save.

NOAH

My ass was starting to hurt along with my stomach from growling. Techy was getting annoyed from it too. Every time my stomach growled he inched away from me and got fidgety. A loud rumble echoed from my stomach and Techy stopped what he was doing to stare at me. "Will you fucking go eat already? He has her again there's fucking nothing we can do at this moment. Then you can fucking strap on some heat and when we get the okay you can finally fucking run in there, guns blazing." His voice rose from a whisper to normal range just to indicate that he was pissed off. Sighing I lifted my body off the ground.

"Anything you want from the club house?" I asked trying to be polite since I had pissed him off. He shook his head signaling that he wanted nothing but for me to go fix my problem. I turned away from him walking towards my bike. The armory was going to get robbed of its 'Man's Wet Dream' title today and I couldn't say that I wasn't happy about it. Every piece of heat that was in the armory was going to be strapped to me whether the club liked it or not. Or at least I'd try to strap it all to me.

The club house was empty when I got there except for Bullet. And he was just the guy I wanted to see. Without him I wasn't getting into the armory. "Bullet my man!" I hollered. His head whipped over to me. The oh shit look on his face told me everything. I wasn't supposed to be here and he wasn't supposed to do anything I asked of him. "I need fire power." I said. His head flung back as did his eyes.

"I can't brother." He said straightening himself meeting my eyes. "Prez orders." Fuck now what was I going to do.

"I only need a couple guns. Nothing huge. Techy told me to be prepared for anything and he sent me away because I got on his nerves for being hungry. Which reminds me I need food." My mind was racing a mile a minute. Moving forward towards the fridge, I grabbed all the food my arms would allow me to carry. The food scattered across the counter as I made enough to last me at least the rest of the day. Bullet watched me intently. "Did you want some food there puddy cat?" Doing my best to imitate Tweedy Bird. I got a raised eyebrow in response to my impersonation.

"No, I don't want any fucking food Noah. Why are you fucking around when your girlfriend is being held captive?" he asked his tone indicating his level of anger. It was getting pretty high. Stress was not something Bullet handled lightly.

"Why are you refusing to let me have fire power when my fiancée is being held captive?" I retorted correcting my ol'ladies title.

"I'm doing you a fucking favor, so you don't get your fucking head blown off." Bullet said. I sensed that he was going to be the one blowing someone's head off soon and it wouldn't be mine.

"How the hell does a hot head like you get to man the key to the armory?" I asked.

"Fuck you, Noah."

"About that, I'll be the one doing the fucking thank you very much. And if you don't let me in that armory, I'll break the door down and shove a honey badger so far up your ass you'll taste the gun powder." The threat spewed from my lips as anger erupted throughout my body. "I don't want to hit you brother, but my fiancée needs help and I'm not going to sit around and wait for a fucking signal. She almost made it out of there, I should go in. She could die if we don't do something but of course we aren't taking action, instead we are sitting on our fucking hands or playing with our cocks. We need to do something to rectify this situation."

My mind was buzzing while watching Bullet get off the

stool. Leading me down the hallway he produced a key out of his cut. "I'm going to get my balls chopped off for this...Just don't do anything stupid." It was more of an order than it was anything else. I was surprised he didn't notice that stupid is my middle name. A smile crossed my lips as the lock on the armory clicked open. Moving into the room I pulled the string in the middle of the room. Light flooded all of the shelves, spotlighting each and every gun we had inside. To a new member or man, it could make them cum in a matter of seconds of seeing it. Members and men a like dreamed of the armory we have set up. The most beautiful piece we had no one could touch. The Winchester 1400 20-gauge shotgun sat in a glass display case. Jack's great, great, great grandfather passed the gun down from the civil war. It was Jack's most prized possession until his girls came around.

Each member of the club had their own cubby of sorts. Mine had the most ammunition and guns packed into it. It was so full it spilled into the spare cubby. I had half a mind to load everything onto my back but seeing as I had the bike here I'd have to stick to smaller guns, guns I could hide. Putting a safety vest on, I finished strapping everything onto me or loaded into a bag.

Upon finishing I watched Bullet lock the armory up. He followed me down the hallway and I strode out to my bike. Strapping the bag down was a little hard and I had to think of the easiest way to get back to the hideout and not get pulled over and caught with unregistered guns. A hand came down on my shoulder. Jumping I pulled my gun out of the holster pushing whoever put their hand on me down locking their arm in mine. The gun pointed at the aggressor's temple. My heart rate sped up as I put the gun away and released my hold. Jack stood and rotated his arm a few times. "Sorry." I mumbled and turned back towards my bike strapping everything down.

"I get it son. You're jumpy from everything going on. You've hardly slept in the last two days. This should be over soon. Have you seen anything that would give us opportunity to strike?" He asked. Shaking my head, realizing there wasn't going to be an easy way to do this.

"From what I can tell he's alone. He never leaves and Techy went to the door to see if the man was alone. It's not going to be easy that's for sure. She's locked in the upstairs, what I'm guessing is a bedroom. We saw her roam freely, but she beat feet up the stairs before getting caught so there's no question that he kidnapped her and she's trying to be smart about all of it. She also knows that we are camped right across the street. She was in the window staring then tried to write something on the glass. When that didn't work, I broke the mirror of Techy's bike and flashed her with light. She saw me but that was it. She hurried away." I rolled my shoulders to release tension from my back and neck. I was sore from sitting and being unoccupied. Jack smiled.

"You'll have my word soon enough brother." It was the last thing he said to me before nodding his head and walking towards the club. I smiled swinging my leg over my bike burning rubber on the pavement. This asshole was mine.

GRACE

I could hear the roar of a bike going down the road. It sounded like Noah's bike. My mind went to memories of being on the back of that bike. I couldn't move anymore. My energy was depleted and everything seemed to be slowly leaving my body. My will to live was probably the strongest thing inside of me but even that was weak. The only thing that kept me going was knowing that the club knew where I was. I wanted Noah and even though I knew he was right across the street, my highest hope was, I'm going to die here.

Brilliant sunlight cascaded around me from a small window. The morning light too bright for my sensitive eyes. A migraine was coming on. Closing my eyes, I turned towards the wall trying to shield my face from the light. The throbbing made me want to puke. I relaxed as much as I could, but it wasn't helping. I was dehydrated and angry. The urge to kill someone was weighing down on me. I just kept on wishing I'd have the opportunity. There was no way I was going to be able to hold down my own for much longer.

Time crept by before my captor was opening the door. Squinting over at him was all I could do. "Morning sunshine." He whispered. The gravel of his voice was like someone playing bass in my ear drums. Flinching to the sound of his voice I used my arms to cover my ears.

"Oh my god…" I mumbled trying my best to shield everything. Light hurt, sounds hurt, my body just ached. I wanted to curl up under a rock and give the world the finger until this went away.

"Do you need to use the bathroom?" Chewing on my lip I nodded slightly trying not to jar my thoughts. He came over releasing the cuffs on my hands, relief filled my arms as they dropped against the floor. His hand landed on my ass surprising me. Turning as fast as I could without doing harm to my head I glared at him.

"What the fuck do you think you're doing?" I asked my voice not rising above a whisper. My hand flew to my head and the other to my stomach. I was for sure going to vomit today. The smile that was crossing his lips didn't make anything better. It made it worse. Thoughts of suicide corroded my mind. Tears began to fall. The hell I was feeling was making fighting to stay alive not worth it. He grabbed my hand pulling me towards the restroom. After accomplishing my business and washing my hands he had me return to the basement. My head was still pounding and my eyes had been shut the whole time I had gone to the bathroom. "Is there any way to dim the light in here?" I asked praying that he would fix it for me. A laugh sounded and my hands shot up to my ears. The pain radiating through my body. Taking deep calming breathes I waited for the nausea to pass. It was going to be a long day. Another prayer was sent up, asking for the strength to sleep all day long. With my head between my knees he cuffed me again. All I could do was breathe laying back down covering my ears and eyes as best I could. I passed out.

My migraine was easing back when I awoke. It was dark out. Laying on the bed staring at the wall I listened for something, anything upstairs. My ears weren't picking up anything but the slight throb in my head. Sighing, I moved a little before closing my eyes again letting the blackness devour my sight.

NOAH

As if it wasn't bad enough, when I arrived back where Techy was stationed, a cop was there also. My heart hammered in my chest. Sweat dripped down my back. There was no way I was making it past him carrying what I had strapped onto the bike and my person. Cracking my neck, I pulled into a driveway and turned around before the pig could see me. Getting clear of the block I sent a text to Techy.

Can't get through. Cop in front. -N

My phone vibrated in my palm. Techy's name flashing once before the screen darkened.

I see that. -T

I rolled my eyes. Thank you Captain Fucking Obvious. My phone vibrated again before I could put it in my pocket.

There's a road behind me by maybe 4 blocks. You should be able to hide the bike and head this way. -T

As if that would be easy enough. I shook my head and went to what I thought would be the spot and hid my bike. The walk felt further than four blocks. It felt like four miles. By the time I met up with Techy I was hungry again and glad I packed extra food. I threw some at Techy and sat next to him digging into my food. Techy didn't move. I glanced over at him and watched him. A muscle didn't even twitch. Reaching over towards him, my finger barely brushed his shoulder. His body slumped onto its side and his head turned towards the sky. Our cover had been blown. The bullet hole between his eyes was proof of that.

A red light flashed in my eye before quickly disappearing. Ducking down A shot landed just past my shoulder. Peeking over a mound of dirt and roots, the laser sight shined across my eyes. From the direction the sight was coming from, the gun was positioned in the living room window. I army crawled my way out the area, the duffle bag on my back. Shifting away from the gun fire I looked around the fucker was leaving the house. Pulling myself up my hand resting on my holster looking around to see if the fucker was going to come near. The woods were quiet. Pulling out my phone I hit my speed dial for Jack.

GRACE

    The silence and darkness deafened the air around me. Dense fog slowly lifting from my lids clearing to the dark room beyond where my body sat. The air cold yet suffocating. It was as if all my fears were the molecules in the air that I was breathing. Rolling my head forward my neck protesting from the movement. The cuffs groaned against the pipe I was hooked to. Reality sinking into my bones as quickly as the cold. Goosebumps were scattered across my bare legs and arms. Rumbling coming from down the road the only sound I could hear. Excitement choked me. Hope inflating my lungs. Pulling against the cuffs, I used all the strength I had in me. The scrapping of metal on metal met my ears making my body cringe. The goosebumps growing across my skin. A shiver running down my spine. Sagging against the concrete listening. The rumbling got louder. My hopes shattered as the single roar passed the house. Noah wouldn't be stupid enough to come alone. He would have called for backup when it was time.

    The roar of the motorcycle faded off into the distance away from the way it came. My heart thundered in my chest as tears pricked my eyes beginning to fall. My body was beginning to lose faith and strength. All dignity left my soul shredding it inside of me. A scream ripped out of my throat before I could stop it. The anger and despair making themselves known. I wasn't going to be saved.

    The door flew open with a heavy kick. Wood splintering and cascading across the floor. A heavy thunk sounded from the frame. The remains of the door slid down the stairs. Peeking up the lock was still locked and attached to its keeper. My eyes landing on the leather boots and lightly shredded jeans.

The sculpted arms were next until I landed on the beard and piercing eyes. Noah was here after all. "Noah."

Anger washed over his face and he rushed towards me his fist landing across my jaw. "If you don't quit your fucking screaming someone will hear you and I'll cut your tongue out." Choking back the fear and tears I had let run I blinked. My vision cleared of its mirage. My captor stood over me a knife against my throat. Gulping I looked into his eyes. Despair was hidden in the depths. He'd lost someone too. "My father said you tasted sweet. And I never actually believed him until the recent events that had me claiming you. Maybe I should do so again that way you stay quiet. Hmmm? Does that sound like a good idea love?" His breath brushed against my ear lobe. The heat making the vomit build up in my throat. I couldn't let that happen again to myself. I'd be in worse shape than I am. I let my head roll to the side looking away from him. His hand slipped down to my breast kneading the flesh, hard. If he kept this up, I wouldn't be able to keep the vomit down.

His breath skimmed my neck before continuing south. Taking a deep shaky breath, I closed my eyes preparing for the worst that could happen and probably would. A tear slipped passed my guard. Rage took over my body. Pulling on the cuffs, scrapping wasn't the sound that rang through my ears. My fists came down cracking against his skull. The cuffs indenting the skin. Thrashing my fists again and again on top his head, the cuffs biting into my wrists and the flesh around his skull. Blood running red across his scalp. The metal of the cuffs stained by his and my own blood.

His body crashed against my own. His weight bearing down, crushing my ribs. My hands pushing against his shoulders. The heavy thump of his weight bearing down onto the floor. My body was aching and protesting. It was finally my chance to get out of this place unfortunately my body was moving slowly and making its pain known. Getting my hand out of the cuffs hurt like hell. Skin tore and stayed with the cuff. Pushing through the pain and despair of my body's aches

I made it to the bottom of the stairs. My legs growing weaker with each step I take. Courage to keep myself going was draining slowly. The stairs looked dangerous and stupid, but I wasn't going to make it anywhere unless I took the stairs or climbed out the window. The stairs were probably the safest of the two.

Fumbling my way up the stairs my body slammed against the wall across from them. The front door opened easily and my feet landed bare on the straw like grass. The pricks from the blades making my feet feel as if I was walking on needles. The crunch awakening my ears as well as the fresh air awakening my smell. Color filled my sight. I stared rotating my neck to take it all in. My feet carrying me across the grass. It wasn't too long until the gravel of the broken road biting into my heels. Strength powering through my legs to keep me going. Where I had seen Noah wasn't far from me. I could make it there if I kept pushing.

Lights flashed before my eyes. Spots of color raging before completely taking over my vision. Hard pokes and thudding jogged my brain into recognition. I had made it to where I had spotted Noah. My cheek resting against the cold dirt ground. My eyes searching for movement of any kind. Lifting my head up my eyes landed on the black and red hole between a man's eyes. His glossed over eyes were haunting. He didn't stand a chance against that bullet. My eyes traveled across his chest to his name badge. It read Techy. My heart sank as recognition hit me. Pulling myself closer to him, a tear slipped down my cheek. He was a loved member of my father's club. Techy must have been watching the house with Noah and had gotten spotted. Moving my head around I looked for any sign of Noah. Relief flooded through me at the realization that Noah wasn't here, but also dread.

NOAH

Jack kept quiet as I explained everything to him. With Techy having been shot by the bastard who held Grace we were fucked. It was grounds for retaliation. No one kills a brother without consequences. I'd find out who this fucker was and what the fuck he wanted with my ol'lady. Jack still hadn't said anything. I could only hear his breathing. "Jack... I need to know what to do." I implored. A sigh released from Jack before he mentioned anything.

"Stay put. The club and I will be there shortly." He commanded before hanging up. Releasing the breath, I didn't know I was holding I put my phone away. I'd be lying if I didn't say I wasn't scared out of my mind. I was strapped to the nines with ammunition and guns but if I went in there half-cocked I could potentially get Grace hurt. We still didn't know what waited for us inside. For all we knew it was booby trapped. Techy was the only one who had seen inside. Sitting sideways on my bike, my feet touching the ground crossed at the ankles. I didn't know what was going to happen or what to even expect. All I have done lately is wait around. I could have been getting Grace back but being put on the back burner in a mission like this really busts your balls. I looked around realizing he hadn't chased me. I had hoped he had followed me.

Pulling a cigarette out of my pack, I watched the flame of the lighter burn for a moment before burning the end of the tobacco filled tube. The smoke filling my lungs was the feeling I needed. It calmed me as panic set in from not being able to do shit besides sit where I was and wait. Fuck waiting. I stuck my cigarette between my lips leaving it there, throwing my leg over the seat I straddled the machine. The roar of engines had me pausing before continuing to do what I intended.

The club pulled up alongside the curb next to where I was parked. Watching each individual member park their bike and shut their engines off, I could feel the support of the club around me. Getting back off my bike, I watched everyone do the same. Ashes fluttered with the wind. Turning the cigarette towards me I watched the ashes disappear and the tobacco burn. I had no idea why I ever started smoking. Just woke up one day and decided to do it, I guess. Maybe it was to relieve stress. Looking up I met Jack's eyes. His eyes were cold and calculated. We were on the verge of war and he was going to make the most of it. I drew in a drag from the smoke and let it out slowly. "Let's get this shit over with, shall we?" He suggested. I nodded flinging the cigarette into the street before heading towards my bike. Grabbing the extra things, I had packed in my saddle bags, we headed out.

"Let's bag this fucker and get everything over with. I want Grace in my arms again." I stated starting off towards the house that she was being held inside. This son of a bitch was going to meet his maker by my hand. And I didn't care what it took.

Getting to the house was a long ass walk. We avoided the middle of the woods and went around the outskirt. Although determined to avoid attention we stayed just inside the line of trees. The whole club walked with stealth to the house. I'm sure to the normal person's eye we could have looked like people out of the army. People who would know order and discipline rather than chaos and gore or motorcycles and grease.

The house seemed empty but that didn't stop us. Sneaking up to the door half of the men ran around to the back while the half with myself stayed at the front door. How Jack stayed so calm I didn't know. My nerves were shot from sitting around for so long, almost being shot, and being so close to getting Grace back. My heart was pounding along with the shallow breathing I had become accustomed to in the last few minutes. I could die in here if our intel was wrong. However, I would surely do it for Grace. There was no other thing or person on this world who I would risk my life for. And I wouldn't stop here.

The back door slammed in splintering against the wall behind it. Taking it as a signal I slammed my boot into the door making the door fly open banging against the wall. Storming inside the house, men flew by me checking the first floor. "Clear" was heard throughout. Looking at the stairs I moved toward them. He had to be upstairs we would have known if he wasn't here. Quietly I lifted my feet one by one up the stairs. Bullets followed me staying just as quietly. Lightning struck and thunder roared, rain poured.

Reaching the top of the stairs I saw the door to my right wide open. Bloody hand prints on the edge of the door and the door frame. My stomach dropped and my breathing quickened. I wanted to drop to my knees thinking the worst already. With Bullets behind me he had to push me forward a bit, forcing me to move towards the door. Peeking around the frame, the bedroom was empty. I was relieved but at the same time fearful. Where the fuck was Grace? I looked at Bullet. "She's not here. This was the room. She was held in this room."

"Someone's in the basement!" Someone yelled from downstairs. We ran down the stairs and found the man. Blood dripped from a wound in his head.

"Go upstairs find the keys to this bastard's van. We need to show him a lesson. Then call a prospect in to drive the van back to the club." I ordered. The plan that was forming in my head had me giddy and horny. The house had been ransacked and Grace wasn't there. Which made it look like this man wasn't alone.

The prospect took about a half hour to get here and we had the man, who was still breathing, inside the back and ready for him to roll away with him. His ankles and hands were tied BDSM style and the only one who could get him out without a knife was me. The plan couldn't be completed until he got back to the club and I would be there waiting on him. "Prospect. I need a word before you take off." I hollered. He came towards me and I pulled my keys out taking one off the ring.

"Yeah boss?" I chuckled. The authority he was giving me was great, but he was going to wish that I hadn't gotten it.

"This key is to one certain lock in the basement of the club. Take the asshole there and leave him. Lock the door behind you and do not let anyone else have the key except for me." I informed handing him the key.

"You got it." He said and went to the van where the bastard was held. After he left, I looked over at Bullet. He was the only man that I trusted to help the prospect get the job done and hold the man where I wanted him until I could get there.

The club decided to congregate back by the bikes in case someone were to come back to the house, someone we weren't expecting. Generating a circle in the middle of the street, the discussion began. "Where do you think she is?" Scrap came up to me. I shook my head. I didn't have a fucking clue. I felt as if part of me was fucking missing and I needed to find it. The urge was getting stronger and stronger. Desperation had me almost frantic, almost fried. I wanted nothing more than to fuck someone's day up. My muscles were taut. My day was getting worse by the second of not finding her. Where the fuck could she be. Everything was turning into a shit show. My vision was turning red as the anger I felt began pumping through my body faster than before. I had the bastard who had taken her, but I didn't have her.

Hopping on bikes every member geared up to go. Engines flaring and roaring to life. Looking up we noticed that Jack hadn't been with us. His hand slashed through the air telling us to kill everything and regroup. Doing as we were told we all stood near Jack. "We can't just go to the club and act like she isn't out there." He remarked. Agreement was known in our silence. We knew she was still alive. We just didn't know where.

GRACE

Leaning against the log that Techy's dead body was propped against I sat in silence with my thoughts. A vibration sounded over by Techy. I listened awhile before realization almost knocked me over. Techy had a phone! Scrambling I searched through his pockets before the call ended. My fingers brushed the ceramic of his phone. Gripping it tightly I pulled the thing free. Caller ID read unknown in big blocky letters. I let it keep ringing until voicemail picked it up. With Techy's cell phone in hand, I ran. I needed to get somewhere safe.

Blood pumped through me propelling me forward. Motorcycles sounded in the distance in front of me. A lot of motorcycles. Motivation burst through my veins, my legs running at maximum effort. A clearing appeared a few blocks ahead of me. The engines sounded much closer than before. That is until everything went silent. With the engines off I wasn't sure if I'd be able to find the nearest road. The good news is I hadn't heard them fade, just abruptly shut off. My heart pounded as blood roared through my ears. The trees thinned out until finally I poured out of the woods.

On my hands and knees near the line I saw the whole club right before my eyes. I wanted to cry tears of happiness. I had gotten out alive. Noah had his back to me. Shock numbed my tears before they could start. The Vice President Scraps looked over at me a grin spreading across his face. He slammed his hand into Noah's shoulder. "What the fuck was that for?" Noah growled. Scraps' smile widened if that was possible. His lips moved but I couldn't hear what he had said. He kept his hand on Noah's shoulder pointing him in my general direction. Every other member stopped what they were doing and turned towards me. Everyone except my dad. Taking a deep breath, I tried to calm my nerves. He was beautiful to me and it was the most beautiful thing I could have seen as soon as I got out of that hell. Smiles lit up every member's face.

My father finally spun to see what was going on. Tears rolled down his cheeks as he ran over and scooped me up in his arms. My arms went around him. Clutching him against me I buried my head in his neck. My father's arms were the greatest shelter I could have taken at this moment.

I felt him come near, hearing his knees hit the ground made me peek over my father's shoulder at him. His face was the look of utter disbelief. His hand lifted as if he wanted to make sure I was real. Pulling back from my father I looked over at the man I would never, ever be able to leave. Flinging myself forward I landed in his arms, right where I should have been this whole time. Right into the arms of safety.

ABOUT THE AUTHOR

Jennifer is a young aspiring author who lives in Superior, WI with her boyfriend and two dogs. She spends her days working full-time, playing with her dogs, along with playing video games, and reading. She also loves to ride her Harley and being with her family.

Made in the USA
Monee, IL
23 February 2020